The Free Woman

Blanche

Carol Walt

10/17/2

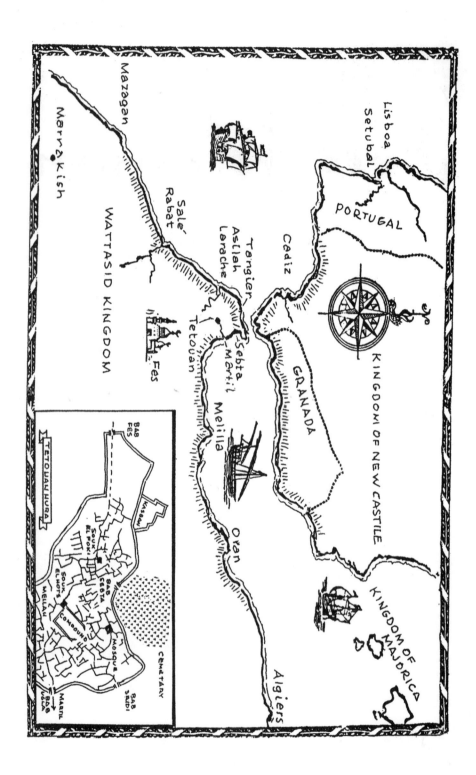

The Free Woman

CAROL MALT

ETHOS Publishing

Cover design, art and map by Harold Malt

ISBN: 0-9714692-0-2
LCCN: 2001 129215

ETHOS Publishing
2300 E. Mallory Street, Suite 303
Pensacola, FL 32503 USA

AUTHOR'S NOTE

This book began with the chance reading of a sidebar in a travel guide to Morocco. Mention was made of a folk tale about the exploits of a 16th century Pirate Queen.

Curiosity aroused, I had to know more about this young, heroic Berber woman.

Available sources were sketchy and confusing. The identity and deeds of the heroine often were attributed to a first wife. Spellings of historical names, tribes and places differed between English, Arabic and Spanish. For Arabic names that are unfamiliar or similar in spelling, a Glossary and a List of Characters can be found at the end.

My frustration was relieved on meeting Dr. Mohammed Benaboud of the University of Tetouan in the Moroccan city where many of Hura's exploits occurred. He provided the heroine's correct name, gave me copies of pertinent manuscripts and referred me to a Holy Man living in Chaouen, the village of her birth, high in the Rif Mountains. Sherif Moulay Ali Raisuni is not only a spiritual leader, cordial, and a fountain of information, he and his ancestors for more than four hundred years have occupied the very house in which the heroine spent her childhood. Her tomb is nearby.

Much of Hura's legend is true. In this biographical novel any errors or omissions of fact are my responsibility.

I dedicate this book with love to my dear husband and collaborator, Harold Lewis Malt. Together we did much of the critique and edit over Sunday brunch at a corner table in the Seville Quarter, Pensacola, Florida.

ALSO BY CAROL MALT

The Flicker
West African Art and Artifacts
Museums of Jordan: A Directory
Identity and Equality: Women and Museums in the Middle East

When the brave swear by their swords
One day and count them as something to
Win them glory and nobility, be satisfied
With the calligrapher's pen for might and
Rank, since for all time, God has sworn by
The pen.

The Poet
Abu Al-Fath Al-Busti

ONE

"Go with Allah."

Hura folded her long body and backed into the red and yellow box. The circlet of silver coins crowning her russet hair struck the eight-sided dome and tinkled. She eased herself onto the carpeted shelf and muttered, "This box was made for a child, not a fourteen year old woman."

The small hatch closed and its iron lock clicked shut as her older brother twisted the key. A trapped fly circled, refused to disappear and buzzed on her small nose.

Hura puckered her lips and blew it away. Pressing her ear to an air hole in the box, she listened to the raucous laughter of her male cousins as they pushed and shoved for places of honor in the procession.

The howda tilted as four of them grasped the long handles underneath the box and hoisted it onto their shoulders. She squirmed and tried to smooth the crushed folds of her wedding skirt, remembering the dismay of her brothers when she demanded it be red. Red, she insisted, just like the gown of the Prophet's virgin bride. Her starched blouse, dotted with ribbons, blue charms and coins that protected her against the evil eye and jinn, gleamed white. Silver bracelets and earrings felt heavy and ropes of pearls almost choked her.

She twisted her head to peer through one of the four air holes. She caught a glimpse of her brother Ibrahim in the early morning light as he mounted his horse and raised his arm. Riding short, his knees well forward, he pressed his heels to the sides of his horse. Everyone moved at his signal and the wailing and percussion increased to a crescendo. He rubbed his short black beard and Hura heard him say "*Bismillah.*" The box and its noisy entourage followed him out the citadel gateway to the shrill clamor of ululating tongues and the beat of drums bouncing off the fortress walls.

The long trek to her new home had begun.

Hura's half-brother Mohammed rode alongside the box, the shortness of his left leg not obvious in the stirrup. His saddlebag bulged and Hura wondered if he had brought his pet snakes with him. Also in the wedding party were six horsemen, holding loosely the cedar shafts of their iron-tipped spears, followed by a dozen foot soldiers armed with sickle-shaped scimitars. The number of soldiers alarmed her. Earlier that morning, she had asked him why so many soldiers were going with them.

"To honor you, of course." Mohammed had mumbled back with a sour look. Then his mouth had curled in a grin. "You are right. We don't need so many. I'll tell Ibrahim."

Who would dare challenge the wedding of the Emir's daughter? She could imagine the procession with her gray Barbary stallion prancing behind – festooned with a martingale of flowers and laden with woven bags containing most of her dowry jewelry. And bringing up the rear would be the four donkeys and two mules that carried sacks of coins, her clothes and the rest of her dowry.

She had argued then pleaded with Ibrahim for permission to ride her horse – she hated small spaces, or being confined. He finally compromised: "You can ride most of the way, but you must leave our village in the marriage box and arrive in it at Tetouan."

Hura now eyed Ibrahim through a peephole as they rounded a bend in the path. He sat regally in his painted saddle, forced to sit erect by its high cantle. In black pants and shirt, his legs capped with red leather boots, a red cape draped the hindquarters of his horse and molded the shape of his scimitar and dagger hilts. With his dark hair and brown eyes, he bore no resemblance to fair Hura.

Inside the wooden box, swaying to the gait of the bearers, Hura tried to relax. The tight space was stifling but aromatic with the perfumes of her Castilian mother and countless other brides. Impatient to be free, she could not move her legs, and her feet became numb. Soon giddiness took over the rest of her body. She could do nothing as they marched along but think. Her full lips parted as she sighed and recalled the months of preparation, the negotiations and the feasts leading to this dark confinement. She smiled in the darkness, half out of nervousness – half out of anticipation.

Hands groping, Hura sought the sugar-coated almonds she had saved, tucked in the front of her sash. The smooth, hard coverings slid easily between her fingers. They were all that remained of the marriage feast. Five tables had overflowed with roasted chickens, tender lamb haunches, tajines of mutton and vegetables, eggs, fruits, sweets and pastries. Her head still swam from the steam of the huge pots of stew.

She recalled the first day of the week-long celebration when one of her cousins presided over the ritual of limon o'sucar. Never before had she removed the hair from her body or under her arms as some women in the village did. That was for married women. And it was private – usually done after menstruation. She hiked her skirt to her ankles; her hand reached between her bent knees and stroked her smooth legs.

Hura winced, remembering that pre-marriage ritual. She saw herself in the middle of their reception room, on the large dining room table, laid out nude for all the women to see. Wide eyed, she watched as sugar was heated in a shallow pan on a brazier next to her and lemon juice squeezed into the bubbling mixture. It slowly turned brown and a sweet aroma filled the room. The older women tittering in the background pushed each other to get a closer view of the event. When the taffy began to stiffen, a small handful was gathered and formed into a pancake.

"Ouch! That's hot."

"Stay still! Don't move," her eldest cousin ordered. "It will cool."

Two other women hastened to press her back down on the table.

"What are you doing?" Hura jerked up, wincing at the burning pain from the hot pancake patted snugly over her pubic hair. "Do you have to?"

Again, the women pushed her down on the table. "You're the brave one, remember? You ride and throw your spear fearlessly, like a man. Can't you take a woman's pain?" Her cousin laughed.

Determined to be stoic, Hura lay still, eyes tightly closed. But she could not control the flinch when the taffy was ripped away from her skin pulling hair out with it. More batches of the searing limon o'sucar were prepared and applied to her arms and legs. Her skin puffed up red, swollen and tender.

Her cousin admired her work when she had finished. "*Behat Allah*, everyone come. Feel how smooth! Her husband will revel in this mound."

It seemed preparations for her wedding night would never end. Aunt Henati spent days decorating her hands and feet. That wasn't her real name, of course, but one affectionately given to her, acknowledging she was the best henna artist in the village. With a thin reed, Henati drew delicate interconnecting lines of sepia on her palms, fingers, up her arms and on her elbows.

In the darkness of the box, Hura stroked the raised, sinuous arabesque patterns created on her hands. She remembered Henati's unique specialty of hiding the name of the husband in the intricate design work, the flowing Arabic script almost impossible to detect or decipher. Her own name was enclosed in a cartouche – to remember in case she became lost in this change of her life. She knew wherever she went she could find herself there.

Aunt Henati did not neglect her toes and ankles, covering them with

3

reddish brown triangles, whorls, circles, diamonds and tendrils of design which led from each toe tip, chain-like to the ankle and formed a delicate shackle of thick braid and imitation metal pierce work. She painted the sole a solid slipper of color.

Hura bolted upright out of reverie, bumping her head again on the dome of the box. Someone was talking about her. With her ear against an air hole she heard Ibrahim's voice: ". . . hope Mandari will help me rid our mountains of the bandits and renegade tribesmen . . . wish our father had made it part of the marriage contract . . ." She lost his voice in the clack of horses' hooves on loose stones.

Soon Hura heard Mohammed: ". . . his problem . . . can't you see him when he finds he can't keep our mountain cat locked up . . . finds out what a rebel she is . . ."

"Don't tell him." Ibrahim shouted over the clatter.

Liar. Both of them. Hura ground her teeth. They said I would be happy in Tetouan. I will not be locked up. I will have freedom. Her thoughts went to her husband-to-be. What should I call him? What will he look like? Will he be one of those old, fat men? No. Surely, God has been wise. Ibrahim says I will be happy. Will I like his new city? Will he be good to me? Yes, I will be submissive as my brothers' demand. But children? That's what he wants, this war hero. He wants sons. She began to fantasize how her husband would be a lover who transported her in ways –

Suddenly the box jiggled unevenly, tilted, dipped and dropped.

"Let me out!"

She heard muffled curses from the bearers and scowled as she rubbed her bruised elbow. They can't see where they are going either. And they are leading *me*.

The lock clicked. The sun blinded her as the door creaked open.

"Mount up, we're out of town," Ibrahim said. "This is as far as most of our family will go." Once again, there were hugs and good-byes, smiles and tears.

Riding next to Ibrahim now, taking deep breaths, Hura raised her head and smelled the scented wind as they passed through a valley of kif. Young boys ran alongside offering handfuls of the feathery weed for sale to the wedding party. It reminded her of the time Mohammed caught her smoking the drug with one of her cousins and reported it to their father. Her father had only laughed. He had taught her many things – to ride and hunt with greyhounds and to use a spear. She smiled recalling Mohammed's rage that time she had disguised herself in boy's clothing, a scarf covering all but her eyes, and entered the spring festival, the Fantasia. She bested him at horsemanship. He said he would kill her for the deception, but her father had slapped his side in mirth.

4

How sad father couldn't see her now, as a bride. She cried for days when Ibrahim told her of his capture. Already a year had passed and he still suffered in a Tangier prison. Tears welled in her eyes. Would he ever be free? Would she ever see him again? Her new husband had been with her father in battle, and for his valor, the Sultan in Fes had appointed him Governor of Tetouan. How did he escape capture or prison? She must ask. And for his comradeship, he was promised Hura in marriage.

By the second day, the journey over the Rif mountains became tedious. Down-up, up-down, the clatter of horses' hooves on stones, picking up speed across valleys, slowing down on hills. Too much time for thinking. What would her life be like? Would she be lonely? She had always thought of herself as practical, but now she wondered if her husband would think she was pretty. What good were spears and greyhounds in a city? Uncertain, confused, scared – but honored to be marrying the Captain of the defense of Granada in Spain and excited to be going to his new city of Tetouan.

At last, that afternoon, as they rode into a narrow stony valley, Ibrahim stopped the procession and called for the box.

Hura eyed it in disgust. "Do I have to?"

Ibrahim gave her a wry grin and pointed a long finger. With a sigh, she squeezed in and once again, the lock clicked shut.

"Comfortable?" Ibrahim inquired with a rare hint of humor.

All Hura saw of him through the air hole was his sword and scarlet cummerbund moving alongside her. She forced a smile he couldn't see but the edge in her voice answered his question. "How much longer?"

"Before sunset. I'll quicken the pace through this valley."

Hura's mood changed again. No more dreams of being snatched by a dark and dashing Berber, thrown over his saddle and carried away to his mountain fortress. Now I go from one kasbah to another, from my Berber family to a Spanish Arab.

"Bandits!" Mohammed yelled and pointed to a cloud of dust flying down the hill and obscuring the intense afternoon sun. He wheeled his mount and jumped down to the shelter of nearby rocks.

Hura leaned forward, eye to an air hole. Could this be the hero of Granada come to carry her off?

"Tribesmen!" Ibrahim drew his scimitar. "Surround the box!" He turned his horse to meet the oncoming horde.

The box careened and overturned on its side.

Hura pushed back the band of coins that half covered her eyes. Her head ached again where it had smacked the dome. She struggled to tilt the box upright but it wouldn't move. Through one air hole she saw dirt,

5

twisted herself to look out the opposite hole and saw only a cloudless blue sky. Now she heard the thunder of many horses, and the whoop of battle cries. Soon, all around her men cursed, grunted and shouted as sword blades clashed. A man cried out in agony, then a thud as something heavy fell on top of the box blotting out the light. Something wet dripped on her cheek. She tasted warm blood, shivered, unsure what to do.

Fear and frustration became a cry of rage. She drew a sharp breath, screamed. "Let me out. Let me out!" But the box muffled her voice. In a frenzy, Hura crouched, took another deep breath and sprang upward, crashing her head into the tin dome, which shot off the wooden box. Shaking, she felt the top of her head where her headdress had mashed down her hair. Turning to look around she gagged. The arms of a headless corpse clasped her box.

Hura swallowed her rising panic. She managed to reach out and push the body away. It rolled off the box and almost reunited itself with its head on the ground. Its blood-matted hair shrouded half-opened eyes.

She placed her palm flat on the door and pushed. It creaked. She backed off, then struck it with both hands. The thin panel splintered apart. Hura wrenched out the pieces, gashing her palm, and squirmed through the small opening.

Scrambling erect, she grasped the spear of the fallen bandit and sought a target. None remained. Fast as they had passed through the entourage, wielding swords and spears, the raiders wheeled and dispersed. Again, a thick cloud of dust followed them, blotting out the sun. A few soldiers chased after them in vain pursuit. Her procession, once orderly, now seemed blown apart by a violent storm. The donkeys and mules had bolted. She turned and shuddered. Nearby a bloody body was twitching. Her cousin.

Ibrahim hurried to his sister. Blood stained his cape. His soldiers regrouped around her.

"Your shoulder! You're wounded."

"No. I sunk my blade in a bandit neck. Are you all right?"

She stared at her palm, now bright red. A sob of relief betrayed her. "Yes."

"Thanks be to Allah you weren't carried away. Those Beni Hassan tribesmen," his teeth gritted, "they chose your marriage to insult the house of our father."

Mohammed suddenly appeared and informed Ibrahim: "Three horsemen dead, two bearers near death, one guard beheaded and four foot soldiers wounded." His clothes were neither soiled nor sweat-stained. Hura noticed that detail in passing but in her anguish said nothing.

The half brother cast a glance at Hura, narrowed his eyes and smirked:

"Look, our sister in a bloody bridal dress holding a spear . . . al-Mandari will think he married a warrior, not a woman."

Hura flushed, jammed the spear point into the stony soil.

"That's enough!" Ibrahim said. "What else to report."

"The dowry donkey is missing."

Why the fleeting smirk? Hura pushed it from her mind. The shock of dead cousins and wounded clansmen pierced her heart. Tears of grief trickled down her cheek. She made a futile effort to wipe them away and appear brave.

"And . . . my horse, Sacony?"

"Gone."

Hura slumped on the side of the box. They had even taken her favorite horse. She plucked at a rip in her wedding skirt and saw it was splattered with dirt and blood.

Ibrahim put his hand on her shoulder, "We'll return to Chaouen if you wish. We will set out another day. With a much larger force."

Hura's trembling chin firmed. Like her brother, she knew what she must do. Her voice was firm. "No. Father would not retreat. We go on."

Mandari's white shirt smelled of soap and bluing. Restless, he rose from the wooden bench just inside the mosque, his knees stiff from midday prayer. At the open door where his troops stood idly he asked, "Any sign yet?"

"No, Sidi. But late afternoon shadows have not yet darkened the mountain."

Three times his aides had checked the cinch belts of their horses at his order. Now, leaning on their lances, peñons drooping, they glanced at one another then looked away. They knew their leader well. He was more accustomed to battle than waiting.

Mandari's face darkened. His lips curled as he formed the words: "Women like to dally, I know, but if that mountain girl is keeping me waiting on purpose . . ." The gold thread of his family crest shimmered in the waning light as he swung his embroidered cape over his shoulders. "Mount up! We ride out to meet them."

Atop his gold-embossed parade saddle his mood lightened. All day he had thought of his loyal friend Emir Ali Rachid, father of his new bride. Two years ago, before the bloody battle to retake Tangier, Ali had signed the engagement contract with him for Hura. Ali Rachid had also warned his daughter was not yet ready for marriage.

"She better be ready now," he mumbled to himself. His brow rose as he thought how honorable it was to marry the seed of such a respected marabout, a descendent of the Prophet. Now what he wanted most were

7

sons. Inshallah, sons.

His horse was still fresh when he sighted rising dust coming from the mountain pass ahead. Mandari stood in his stirrups. "I make out horsemen and a pack train." He adjusted his white turban, turned to his men: "Gallop!"

Hura's spirits lifted when she saw the soldiers racing toward them waving their colorful peñoned lances, reining in their mounts mere moments before overrunning her party. She admired the virile way the leader dismounted and hurried to her brothers, but when he stood next to Ibrahim, disappointment made her smile vanish.

He was short.

Maybe he's not my husband. Hura kicked her mule forward. Then she checked herself. He must be my new husband. I cannot ride up to him on a mule. Dismounting, she remained where she was and strained to hear what the men were saying.

The leader in the white turban strode over to her and took her bloodied hand. "Are you hurt?"

Ibrahim, at his side, made the introduction: "Your betrothed, Ali Abed Allah Muhamad al-Mandari."

It was so sudden, so matter of fact. She tried to regain some composure. "Oh, my lord, I'm so ashamed to have you see me like this. My nose is red and runny, kohl streaks my cheeks, my wedding dress is a disgrace . . . I am no prize."

He stared at her large, gray eyes, then the dots of the tribal tattoo that coursed her lip to her chin. His tan, lined face softened and he bowed to her. "It is the will of God that you live to make this union."

Smarting from the recent battle, Ibrahim interrupted. "Tribesmen ambushed us. A quick surprise attack. Caught us in a valley, killed, then fled with booty. Those dogs came from the south, from the Beni Hassan. I recognized their dress."

"Never mind all that now." Mandari waved his hand before him. "We must return to Tetouan before sunset. We'll get your sister cleaned up and have the wedding before dark." Hura watched Mandari assess the rest of the party with a battle-practiced eye – the soldiers, donkeys, dowry. "Where is your horse?" he asked her.

Hura quelled a sob. "Stolen." This was not the happy introduction she had envisioned.

Grim faced, Mandari mounted and spurred his horse to the head of the procession. Everyone fell in line. Remounting her mule, Hura saw Ibrahim riding in the front and Mohammed at the rear. Mandari had secured her in the middle of the line behind his warriors and ahead of the Rachid horsemen and pack train.

Purple shadows cloaked the mountain as they descended the last foothill. Poised atop the rocky Jbel Dersa, the city sloped down the mountain and spread over the large valley below. The lights of cooking fires dotted the landscape before her; hundreds of flickering torches illuminated the mountainside path. Were they a welcome sign?

Hura rode up beside Ibrahim. Her spirits again high, she leaned over: "I can't wait to see it in daylight. It must be a hundred times bigger than our village. I know I'll be happy here, just like you said."

As Hura's bedraggled wedding party approached the city, the trail became a wide dirt lane surrounded by goat-hair tents. She wondered why so many people were living outside the city walls. Now she could smell meat roasting on the campfires she'd seen from afar. That reminded her she hadn't eaten since morning.

Drawing closer to the upper walled city, the street became paved and houses replaced the woolen tents. She returned to her position in line as they filed through a breach in the city wall. Huge timbers for a future gate lay in the dirt nearby. Mandari threaded them through a maze of streets toward the center of the medina. Some areas appeared to be only rubble but others contained large houses. From the guards torchlights, she could make out elaborate recessed doorways and ornate balconies jutting out above them. Passing through a tree lined square they proceeded to a horseshoe-shaped gateway where notched decoration inside the arch appeared like teeth in an open mouth waiting to close upon them. The street narrowed. Everyone dismounted and entered the Mandari compound of multi-storied brick and stone houses abutting his massive fortress. A tower, its top in darkness, loomed in the torchlight.

"It's magnificent," Hura leaned over and whispered to Ibrahim in the courtyard. "More than you promised."

Mandari's Captain of the Guard, Abdul, grabbed the bridle of Hura's mule and handed it to a subordinate. "Walk it."

"Walk it where?" Hura asked. "We've been walking."

"My lord Mandari believes in custom," the Captain answered. Joining them, Mandari added: "A wise custom. The mule will be taken to the mosque, walked around it right to left, seven times so the jinn won't curse our marriage. Come. The imam is waiting for us."

Poised on a wooden chair in Mandari's reception room, Hura tried to focus on the holy man's words, spoken by rote so fast and in a strange dialect. But her head and every bone ached, she was exhausted, and she couldn't push the ambush out of her mind. Was that a bad omen?

The white-bearded imam stared at her . . . repeated his words again,

9

louder: "Do you agree to this marriage of your own free will? Will you dedicate yourself to be a good and pious wife? Will you agree to have children?"

"Yes. Yes. Yes," Hura said. She didn't understand much of his classical Arabic. She thought she would feel elated or ecstatic, overwhelmed with excitement at this important event in her life, certainly romantic. But somehow only felt relieved when at last Mandari took her left hand and slipped a thin silver band on her ring finger.

Then he removed an ornate gold pin from the front of his cape. "This was my mother's. It is my gift to you." He moved her pearls aside and pinned it on her blouse amidst the ribbons and charms. Candlelight dazzled the gold disk.

The vows were sealed quickly. The formalities over, Ibrahim's blessing was cut short by Mohammed's grumble: "Now that's done with, where are my quarters?"

Ibrahim scowled, then as representative of the family, turned to Mandari and said, "Remember *Hadith 53* tells us that *"The rights of a woman are sacred; ensure that women are maintained in the rights assigned to them."*

The new ring pinched when Mandari grasped her hand and led her to the patio where they climbed stairs to the balcony on the second level. She followed him along the open hallway to a dark wooden door. He stopped, knocked several times and entered.

"Wait here," he told her.

She peeked inside and listened as he walked directly to a light-skinned, shrunken woman lying on a divan.

The woman, wearing an elegant black lace mantilla, pursed her wrinkled face. "She is here?"

"Yes. We are married."

"You're so late I threw away the food!" the woman snapped as if she hadn't heard his news.

"I sent a messenger back at full speed."

"I received no message."

"No matter. The festivities are canceled."

Hura heard him call: "Come, meet Fatima, my first wife."

She stood open-mouthed behind her husband. Could she believe what she just heard? *A First Wife?* She'd not been told. Aunt Henati had mentioned that city Arabs, the rich and even the not so poor, had more than one wife in the harem. It never occurred to her that she would be one of those wives.

With a wave of a bejeweled hand, the aristocratic Spanish woman dismissed her husband from the room. Then she beckoned Hura closer, lifted her head for the new wife to kiss her brow, as was the custom.

Hura hesitated, approached the divan, bent down, and eyed the slick coal-dyed hair bound in a coil by a tall, jeweled comb that jutted from the back. Their eyes locked in silence.

"*Mabruk*. Congratulations," Fatima said at last. "So you are the new wife."

A lump rose in Hura's throat. The new wife. "I am Hura, daughter of the Sherif, Emir Bin Rachid of Chaouen – and now your husband's wife. I hope I bring this house happiness." Her voice cracked on the last word.

"I have no need of your happiness. Your marriage is an arrangement. You know your place and your duties in this harem." Fatima's gold bracelets clanked as she raised a glittering hand in front of her face, signaling the conversation over. Her fingernails danced like talons, long and pointed.

Hura retraced her steps on the torchlit balcony. From the dark patio below, she heard the sound of water splashing. She wondered where to go. An impassive guard stood in front of a door near the stairwell. When he motioned and opened the door for her, she entered and glanced around the room. Flickering candles revealed a sparsely furnished chamber smaller than Fatima's. The dominant feature was a high padded bed.

Her large leather trunk was at its foot and a small table on the far side of the room held a blue and white glazed water pitcher and washbowl. Her saddlebags already lined the entrance wall near a massive cedar wardrobe. High in the wall near the ceiling were two small windows.

The door closed behind her and Hura sat on the edge of the bed. She clasped her hands – nervous, confused, not knowing what to expect next. Aunt Henati had filled her ears with tales of the harem as a place where young girls enjoy rich food, beautiful clothes, jewels, games and pets. The cool room smelled of fresh rosemary and coriander.

Loneliness enveloped her; her shoulders drooped and a small sound came from her throat. She remained motionless for a short time, then collected herself and leaned over to wash in the ceramic washbowl. Traces of dried blood rimmed her nails. As she stared into the reddened water, thoughts of the raid returned. She shook her head to free herself from the memories. Drops of water from her face splattered the tiled floor. She began to search the room for her travel bag then remembered it had been stolen.

Undressing, she pondered: What will I wear? I have no nightgown. She paused. Nothing! I'll wear nothing to bed. She blushed with erotic thoughts and anxiety of the unknown, then slid between the sheets.

The compound remained silent for a long time. She waited, fighting off fatigue.

At last, she heard the sound of heavy boots on the tile steps. She pulled her sheet higher. The door opened. Mandari glanced at the sheet outlining her flat body, tossed his formal jacket on her saddlebags, sat at the foot of the bed and began taking off his boots.

"I saw to your brothers' comfort," he said, "on the first floor."

Hura had never before seen a grown man naked. When he came to her and pulled off the sheet, her eyes focused between his legs. In the middle of the great gray forest of hair his pink, limp . . . thing . . . seemed to have a life of its own. Suddenly it stuck straight out.

TWO

The foreign noise of a busy city – the high pitch of the muezzin calling for prayer, masons chipping stone, roosters crowing, animals braying, vendors hawking, tinsmiths hammering, woke Hura with a start.

Sleep came late and fitful. Over and over she had relived the horror and shame of her bedraggled arrival and hasty wedding. What must the Lord of Tetouan have thought of a country girl who shamed him so.

Hura knuckled her swollen eyes. No more guilt, enough of that. All would be better today. She was sure of it.

She rolled over. Her husband was gone. Sometime during the night, he must have returned to his own chamber. Just as well. Alone, she began washing herself, inspecting her swollen mound. She stared in dismay. There was no blood.

Hura threw back the coverlet. No blood on the marriage sheets either!

She knew she was a virgin, but her husband, what would he think? Last night in the darkness he had mounted her twice. It must have been dark when he left.

Mohammed's accusation came back to her. She could still hear the rasp in her brother's voice: "You disgrace our family with your manly behavior! Father is wrong to give you a horse. You ride a saddle like a man. If you don't make a virgin's show on your marriage night, Ibrahim and I will have to kill you for our honor and that of our father in prison."

Hura tentatively pressed the tender flesh between her legs. The lips stung to the touch, but there was no blood. She got on her knees beside the bed and searched the sheets again. They were still bloodless.

She heard a shuffling sound outside her door and the clinking of cups. A woman's voice called to her: "*Ya Aroose*, young bride. I have your breakfast."

Hura jumped back into bed and pulled the coverlet to her neck. "Come in."

The door opened and a woman brought in a large brass tray. "Ola! I am Isabel." The woman was short and shapeless with thick, braided gray hair. Wrinkles cascaded from her eyes to her cheeks to her neck, giving her a look of sadness.

"Thank you. Put it on the bed."

When the woman shuffled out, Hura tossed off the coverlet and looked down at the tray. There were the familiar olives and white cheese, small bread rounds, golden apricot jam, and a brown-shelled boiled egg. But there were other things she didn't recognize: a plate of brown powder studded with sesame seeds which had a pool of olive oil in the middle, ropes of shiny silver fish coiled in a bowl which smelled of salting and a dish of red honey combs like that of the bees. Famished, she reached over, grabbed the shallow edge of the tray and pulled it next to her. Like a child she stuck her finger in each delicacy and tasted. "What's this?" she wondered aloud, licking her finger.

Fatima pushed open the door and entered. "It is pomegranate."

Hura froze with sticky fingers in the air then quickly reached for the sheet.

In an accented voice, she heard, "I had my servant bring you breakfast and came to bid you good morning." She stared at the sheets.

"Good morning, Lalla Fatima," Hura said with the dreadful knowledge that she had come to check the sheets for bloodstains. "Would you like some?" With that, she jerked the tray, overturning the dish of pomegranate in front of her, spilling the red juice in her lap and over the bedclothes.

"You clumsy Berber!" Fatima backed away. "Look what you've done. I should have expected this from the *Imazigen*."

"Yes, what a clumsy Berber I am!" Hura lowered her eyes and began to pat the wet cotton bedding.

"Clean yourself," Fatima hissed and clomped out on thick sandals.

Hura clapped her hand over her mouth to restrain herself until Fatima slammed the door, then exploded in a loud chortle. Her giggling subsided when she thought of her husband's displeasure and the price she might pay for this 'accident'. She pushed the tray away thinking she must lock her door in the future, then threw the coverlet off and again surveyed her body.

Last night her husband had confirmed everything she expected. Her body was not attractive to him, probably not to any man. She didn't need a looking glass. Last year she had studied herself after the arrival of her womanhood, half expecting, half hoping. But she hadn't changed much. There was so little difference. She resumed her quiet observation: her breasts were too small, the tiny mounds capped by large pink-coned nipples. She ran her hands over her breasts and sighed. She knew men wanted breasts to grasp, to squeeze. Like Aunt Henati's. Even in the shapeless kaftan her aunt always wore, every man could see her pendulous breasts bobble beneath the cloth.

I'm too tall; my legs are too thin and my feet the size of a man's. She pulled the coverlet back up to her chin to hide her disappointment. There was nothing she could do about it.

The voice of Isabel intruded again. "Ola. Lalla Hura, are you there? Lalla Hura?"

"Come in. Come in. I've made a mess."

As Hura slid from under the covers to put on her kaftan, Isabel saw that her white body was stained with patches of crimson.

"Mistress Fatima is worried about you."

"Oh, what did she say?" Hura snapped. Her plan to be submissive and docile in her new home seemed to have vanished. She immediately regretted her rudeness.

Isabel gave her a stern look but hesitated to chide the young bride. As she gathered up the sheets for the laundry she merely said, "The holy book says to respect your elders."

Alone again, Hura poured water into the bowl on her nightstand and thoughtfully sponged the sticky juice from her body. Her mood changed from repentance to anticipation. She put on an embroidered kaftan then searched through her trunk for matching leather slippers. Today will be a day of discovery. I'll explore my new world and see this exciting city.

After pulling open the heavy door and seeing no one, she began walking the long balcony to the stairway. This wasn't a house, she marveled, but a palace. Hura passed by the room next to hers. Although dim inside, she could make out several sturdy leather-slung chairs, a desk and a long bench against the wall. Above the bench ran a long vertical slit in the masonry just wide enough for a band of daylight to seep through.

At the stairwell, she admired the wrought iron gate in front of her. She wrapped her fingers around the arabesque designs and pulled it sharply; it didn't budge. She pushed. It was securely locked. Angry, she kicked it, forgetting she wore only slippers. She limped back around the U-shaped balcony to the stairs at the other end. Another locked gate barred her exit. This time she shook it, then banged her fists on it, looked around and saw no one. Below in the stone paved courtyard a fountain spouted a small arc of water into its basin. Pots of yellow flowers surrounded it.

She yelled, "Hello! Hello? Is anyone there?"

A man appeared below; the toothless man she saw at the front door the night before. Her husband's manservant.

"Why is the gate locked?" She shouted down to him.

He stared blankly at her on the balcony. Soon Isabel's sad-looking face came into view beside him.

"Lalla Hura, this is my husband, Miguel. What is the matter?"

"The gate is locked. I can't open it."

"Lalla Hura, you cannot leave. You must stay behind the gate in the harem."

Hura's stricken look of shock brought the two of them up the stairs. Miguel unlocked the gate.

"Come with me." Isabel took Hura's arm and led her to the sitting room. "Sit down and let me speak. I know it's different in the Berber mountains. But in Tetouan, women of importance don't go outside alone. Maybe, if they have special permission it is possible, but no men who aren't their husbands or relatives can see them. Please believe me. It's very important that you learn about your *hudud*. It's your border . . . the boundary that keeps you safe."

Hura stiffened on the bench, eyed her in disbelief.

Isabel continued patiently, "My husband says that when God created the earth, he separated women from men. You must know that. There's peace and harmony only when one respects the boundaries of the other."

Hura fumed. "Do you think I'm a child? Do you mean I can not walk freely around my own house?"

"Well, you must talk to Sidi Mandari about that. He told us to keep you in the harem."

"But you can't lock me up here. Give me the key. I'm your Mistress, you must obey me."

"I'm sorry, Lalla Hura." A bone creaked somewhere in her back as she slowly rose. "I don't have a key. Miguel will unlock the gate when I'm ready to leave. And he's not subject to your orders."

Hura jumped up, balled her fists. "What am I to do here, all alone?"

"You're not alone. First wife Lalla Fatima is with you. Her chambers are just across the balcony."

"I can't ever go downstairs or outside?" Frustrated, Hura's voice choked.

"With your husband; to dinner parties and festivals, here in the house. And once a week to the hammam, for bathing."

Hura felt like a bird in a cage, she whirled around, fluttering and slapping her slippers noisily back to her room and slammed her door. Before it closed, she heard the distinctive jingle of jewelry in the hallway. Someone had been listening. "*Hudud*!" She grumbled. "I'm trapped."

THREE

Many leagues from Tetouan, the battered and bloody youth who sprawled on his back sought to regain his confused senses. Jabbering voices mingled with the sounds of roiling surf. His eyes focused and he struggled to sit up. A girl leaned over him, her slender fingers holding a dagger.

Her free hand gently pushed on his chest. "Lie still," she said. Then, scowling at the chattering women who pressed closer, she yelled, "Leave him be!"

He closed his eyes, reached up and felt the right side of his head where it hurt most. It was wet. Alarmed, he opened his eyes again to stare at his blood-covered palm. His eyes shifted back to the slender dagger. The double-edged weapon was clean.

Catching his glance, she smiled: "All of us carry them." She cocked a critical eye as she bent over him again. "You have a gash above your ear. I'm going to cut away your long hair."

"Don't," he murmured, "It's a sin," and he made a feeble attempt to grasp her wrist.

She raised her hand out of his reach. "What is?"

"Forelocks. Cutting forelocks."

"You're delirious."

Her hand lowered. "My, it's thick. Curly too." Her small hand grasped a lock, pulled at it gently, and sawed away. He winced at the sound of her pruning. That dagger was made for stabbing, not for cutting.

He struggled to lift his throbbing head.

"Don't move."

In the quick glance, he saw a cluster of some six or seven older women hovering around him. Most were half nude. The others wore low-cut blouses. He blinked hard. Never before had he seen a naked woman, not even Miriam. His boyhood memory of Cristóbal Colón floated across his closed eyelids. He saw the Admiral standing on the deck of the *Nina* returning from the Indies with a shipload of naked savages. How many times in his boyhood had he relieved his need while fantasizing himself a love-slave to a band of naked, wild looking women.

His tongue slid over salt-caked lips. His eyes opened again and he croaked, "Water. Please, water."

The girl turned to retrieve a cup. A big-bosomed woman, dark as lampblack, leaned over and playfully began to fondle him.

The young man rolled on his left side, swung his right hand to swat the woman away. A sharp pain in his right leg forced a groan, made him roll back.

"I said leave him alone. He's mine. Saint Brigid brought him to me." Then the girl's rosy-cheeked face turned to his and her voice softened, "Your ankle's puffed up. Broken, I think."

"And my head?"

"Big gash." She pointed to his temple. "From a sharp rock. Don't worry, saltwater cleaned it." The girl smiled, "You look . . ." she groped for the word to describe him, couldn't think of it, grasped the forelock on the other side and sliced the strands.

He shut his eyes again and tried to think. Her Arabic was so strange. Salt water . . . ah, the sea. Remembrance flooded his mind. His father, Miriam . . . so many others, all fleeing Fernando and Isabella's Inquisition.

How he hated the sea . . . the dark sky, howling wind . . . that overloaded boat . . . the shrieks of passengers when it rolled over . . . rocks. My God, that other boat . . . what happened to my father? To Miriam? His eyes shot open. Fingers were stroking, pulling at him. He jerked halfway up, fell back. His torn shirt hung over a leather belt lacking trousers.

"Getting bigger." One of the women chortled.

The girl whirled, fury in her eyes, the dagger ready to thrust.

A new, deeper voice some distance away swore: "*Dio Mio*. Out, you *putas*. Out!"

The laughing women straggled out with backward glances. He looked around.

To the sides and overhead, he could see nothing but blackness. He felt as though he was in a vast pit but when he lifted his head and squinted down between his feet, he saw dazzling sunlight. Confused, he gave up, focused on the girl who still leaned over him, saw a frown of concern. Blond hair framed her small face. His gaze shifted from her blue eyes and focused on her bare breasts. They were within easy grasp.

The sound of ripping cloth startled him. She tore away a strip of her white skirt. He made no protest when she lifted his head and wound the long strip around it.

"Now you look like a proper Arab."

His eyes closed once more and he slipped away into a deep sleep.

It was dusk when he woke. That rhythmic, periodic pounding was not in his head after all. At intervals, he heard a rising roar. He sat up and

18

grimaced as his right leg moved. His hand cupped his ear. He raised the thick black eyebrows that ran straight across his face.

The same young woman, sitting cross-legged beside him pointed. "Breakers, you'll get used to it." As she spoke, a huge spume of water erupted out of a crevice in the nearby jumble of rocks and soared upward. He now realized he was on a pallet in a cave. The floor was limestone and the sea pounded on rocks not far away.

She gestured again. "That big boulder. The one out there half-buried in sand. That's where I saw you. On your back. God watched over you. You could have been swept into the big hole."

He liked her strange accent, her breasts too. Small and well shaped. She must be very young. "What's your name?"

"Bridget. I'm named for Saint Brigid. I was born same as she. February first. Nobody here can pronounce the rest of my name."

He experimented moving his leg while looking quizzical.

"You couldn't pronounce it either, it's Gaelic. How do you feel?"

He touched his head. The bandage had a wet spot. "Much better. It's a good bandage. What did this Saint do?"

"Bridget? All I know is she was a virgin. Didn't want to marry anyone. So she prayed to God for help."

"That's all?"

"God caused her eye to melt. So no man wanted to marry her."

"I don't think you have that problem."

Her quick smile was lovely. He grinned in return, then his gaze roved as he tried to penetrate the darkness above and on either side.

"What is this place?"

She hesitated. "Do you want some tea?"

"No. Where are we?"

"The Pillars of Hercules."

That had no meaning. Shutters began to close over his tired eyes.

"Don't you know Hercules? He was the strong giant who pushed the land apart. Separated Africa from Europe. These grottos at the water's edge, they've been here for eternity. He lived in this same cave."

"I mean where is this?"

"Oh. West of Tangier. Near Tangier."

"West! Not on the Mediterranean?"

She shrugged. Her breasts rose. "Atlantic."

He put his hand out, touched the floor beside the pallet. The stone was dry, cool, uneven, and eroded into rounded rivulet-like patterns. He pushed with both hands and rolled over to his knees, paused until the throbbing in his ankle subsided. "How long have I been here? What day is this?" He struggled to his feet.

"Friday." Her eyes became anxious.

"I should be at the synagogue," he mumbled and eased himself down, stretching flat his broad-shouldered body. "Or at least praying."

"Praying? You're not Arab. Maybe Portuguese?"

"Hebrew. My name is Hershlab Ben Yitzhak. Can you pronounce that?"

"You said it too fast."

He smiled. "You can call me Hersh. What happened to my clothes, my talliat?" Instinctively his hands went to his chest to arrange his blue and white striped prayer shawl. He felt no fringe, muttered: "I should be holding the silver pointer in my hand, reading from the Torah."

"I'm Catholic. All your clothes, everything is gone except the shirt you're wearing. I threw away your trousers. They hung in shreds and I had to wash the seaweed and sand from your body."

While Bridget went to check the pit of glowing charcoal behind them, Hersh examined his leg. The ankle wasn't broken, he decided, and when she brought a bowl to him he sat up, held it with both hands and gulped the hot liquid. The taste was strange, spicy but good. Ravenous, he held the bowl to his mouth and drained it.

"Thank you, Bridget. For saving my life."

She leaned over him, whispered in his ear: "I will call you Habib." Close-up her lips looked moist and soft.

By Sunday afternoon, his bruises were still blue-black, but his ankle did not pain and the fresh bandage on his head was dry. He began to feel alive – he had his energy back. Wearing the shirt and pantaloons she had brought him, he leaned back, weight on his arms, and admired her. Today Bridget wore a red skirt and a vest, its front held together loosely with black laces. His head turned to watch her bring him a clay platter of stewed meat then finish chores around the cave, her slim body moving gracefully. When he finished eating, she sat beside him, hands on her knees.

Just as his body warmed to her nearness, several rowdy men, silhouetted in the opening by the sunlight behind, caught his eye. He couldn't see the details of their clothing or faces, but there were no flowing robes. These must be Europeans, he thought.

Bridget followed his gaze. "Portuguese. They're traders. Some nobles from Tangier, too."

One of the men stopped at the entrance, bent and peered in the opening. "Bridget?"

Now Hersh could make out his face – an older man, heavy-set with a neatly trimmed goatee and well-tailored clothes.

When the visitor saw Bridget close beside another man, he waved and hurried on.

Hersh returned the wave. "Who are all these men? I saw one or two yesterday. They don't seem to visit very long."

Bridget was startled. She stared at Hersh in disbelief. Could he be so naïve? Her voice flattened. "All the women here are . . . are for sale."

His mouth fell open. In a hot flash of revulsion, he sputtered, "Whores?"

"Does it matter?" Her chin shot up.

"No-o-o, I guess not." Their eyes locked. Her gaze was steady, without shame.

Wondering how she got here, he patted her thigh as though to say truly it didn't matter. But his hand slid higher, found her breast, squeezed the warm swelling.

Bridget stiffened, then relaxed. And when he reached for her she sighed deeply and pushed him back flat on the pallet. Her hands quickly pulled off his shirt and pantaloons and bent his legs. Kneeling beside him she gently cradled and massaged his heavy sac. She rocked forward and looked with raised eyebrows at his tense face.

"Ahhh. Don't stop." Hersh lifted his head to watch.

Bridget straightened his legs and straddled him. He saw her thick blonde bush slowly slide down and begin a slow movement.

That one time, when he had lain with Miriam, the evening of their betrothal, lovemaking had been nothing like this.

FOUR

The next morning Habib lay wide-eyed on his back, listening to Bridget's regular breathing.

The straw-filled pallet itched. Bridget had stitched two together so they could sleep on one mattress. "Like couples do in the old country," she had said.

When he moved, Bridget stretched and yawned. "Rainy day," she mumbled.

Wide awake, Habib blurted, "Why did you become a harlot?"

Bridget's fair face turned scarlet. Her mouth opened then closed. She twisted on her side to search his face. After a pause, she said quietly, "Did you ever hear of the potato famine?" She didn't expect an answer.

"In Ireland we got them often. At least one in every lifetime. I didn't want to have some tenant farmer's baby every year until I died an early age. Or to keep living just to watch my babies die of starvation. I was relieved – yes happy, when a Portuguese slaver raided our village."

Habib reached out, took her hand. He hadn't realized she could be so brave – and practical.

"Where was this?"

"In Cork where I lived."

"Where is Cork? I don't know much about Ireland."

"On the south coast, the harbor of Baltimore. We had an old watchtower on the hill, but it was a ruin. Never rebuilt. Not since the Vikings sacked the town, or maybe it was the Dutch, I don't know. It was a long time ago."

"Yes, yes, but what happened?"

"Our village had nothing to loot after the church was sacked. We were so poor. My mum had three boys and eight girls before she died. All of us were carried off. I didn't mind."

Habib squeezed her hand again. He could understand that. He'd been happy to get away from the Inquisition in Spain.

"How did you get here?"

Bridget sat up. Her expression changed and she giggled, "In Ireland many girls look like me, I'm not special. Over here Sultans and Pashas, all the Muslims bid high for blond, blue-eyed virgins."

Habib grinned, "I can see why."

"This slaver boat put in at the port of Tangier. For food or something. Signorina bought me right off the wharf. Only me." Bridget looked at him with pride. "None of the others."

Habib hesitated. He wanted to ask her if she enjoyed her work. Not now, he told himself as she chattered on, obviously happy with his interest in her.

"Signorina has been good to me. She gave me that trunk over there. It's filled with clothes and shawls. Embroidered ones. I've met so many rich and famous men. They give, uh, gave me presents too . . . some day a handsome man will fall in love with me and buy me from Signorina." Bridget paused and shyly looked over at him.

He reached for her, gathered her in his arms and silenced her in a flurry of kisses.

The rain became a drizzle that would persist all day. As they breakfasted on fruit and herb tea, he asked: "Tell me about these caves."

"Oh, they're all over. This high cliff, here at the water's edge, it's honeycombed with them. I don't know how many. This one is mine. Two other women have their own caves."

"And the Signorina?"

"She has the largest cavern. Three other women stay there too."

Bridget saw his puzzlement and understood. "Her cavern has many, many places where the walls have openings. They lead to smaller caves. You've seen openings in my cave too. They lead somewhere. But Signorina warned me not to go in them."

Perplexity furrowed his brow.

"The jinn. They live there. That's what Signorina says. She does things, I don't know what, to . . . to . . . ." She groped for the word.

"Appease?"

"Yes, to appease. She has to. Because of all our rich clients here. Jinns are half-human demons; have one eye in their heads. They do Satan's work. Make you sick. Very sick."

Habib snickered, finished his tea and rose. With only a slight limp, he walked to the mouth of the cave, looked in frustration at the rain and returned to her. "I think I'll explore these caves. Maybe I'll see a jinn."

Aghast, Bridget started to protest.

Habib smothered another laugh but asked for her dagger.

He lit a torch from the embers of their brazier and began to follow the wall to the right. The smooth stone floor had several small depressions where once there had been shallow pools. Torch smoke that curled upward became invisible in the vastness; the faint light of the small flame failed to illuminate the wall where it curved upward to become a ceiling high overhead. After twenty or thirty paces, the wall and ceiling surfaces joined, lowered, became one with the floor, leaving only a small hole where water had once gushed in and out with the tides. As his bravado faded, Habib hesitated. But holding the torch before him, peering ahead as far as possible, he crawled through the opening and into a larger cave.

The flame flickered, revealed fragments of bone on the floor. The salt tang of the air changed to a dank mist. Habib listened. It was quiet; but somewhere, far off, he heard the drip of water. Someone or something once lived here, he said to himself. Maybe still does. His fingers sought the dagger handle, touched it lightly. Its smooth hilt in his sash reassured him. His ankle began to ache; he squatted on his haunches, held the torch aloft and listened for the sound of a jinn. Nothing. Squinting, he saw scratching of some sort on a side wall. He rose and limped closer. A sketch had been drawn at random across the wall. It seemed to be a herd of running animals. Curious, then fascinated, he studied the elegance and simplicity of the flowing lines. Some had horns and tusks he had never seen before. He couldn't believe anything like this existed. Who could do these wonderful drawings? Certainly not some jinn. He was humbled, then ashamed. It had been so long since he had made any drawings or done anything creative.

Using the dagger, he chipped out a piece of rock and inspected it. Amazing. Exposed was a complete, small fossil shell, a tightly curled nautilus. He spit on it. The form and color became more vivid. My lucky charm, he murmured, and began to wield the sharp pointed edge of the dagger on the wall. It made a fine stylus for drawing.

After the long day of his absence, supper long since spoiled, Bridget pouted when he returned. She had been well trained not to bother men with questions but had been so worried. Now she needed to know what kept him.

Seeing the nautilus, she asked: "What did you find. The jinn? Is it a spirit? Did it find you?"

"Come, I'll show you."

Bridget backed away.

"Don't be afraid. There's no jinn."

Eyes wide, she stared at him. "I'll go . . . but only if I can put on my blue kerchief and if you light another torch for me. The jinn hates blue. And fire too."

Bridget gave a little cry of delight when she first saw the old drawings. She traced several of the leaping, long-legged animals on the clammy wall with her fingertip. Habib became impatient, and hurried her to his wall. There he saw her mouth droop in disappointment.

"Your scratchings aren't animals or people."

Pleased with himself, Habib ignored her comment. "Just like a wall in the al-Hamra," he said standing arms akimbo.

When Bridget didn't react, Habib explained how he had divided the upper surface of a wall and its sweeping overhead curve into a pattern of several hundred equal squares, and into this rigid grid, drawn diamonds, rosettes and hexagons. He repeated the pattern again and again, covering the entire surface. Below he had filled horizontal bands of rectangular tiles with flowing Arabic lettering.

"Where's that place?" She didn't try to pronounce al-Hamra as they stood close together gazing at the wall.

"Granada. Spain."

"Is Granada as big as Tangier?" She began to move back to the other wall to see the animals again.

He grew more impatient. "Look at the wall and stop squirming." Then, relenting, he turned to face her. "Al-Hamra means 'the red'. It's a huge red pleasure-palace. For Sultans and Kings. I used to work there . . . as the designer." Habib smiled broadly. That seemed to impress her. He fell silent, sighed in memory of his happiness there. Why did I say that, he wondered. No matter. She needn't know I was just an apprentice tile maker, and at that, working only half a day.

Puffed with his new importance, he began again: "I was responsible for the decoration of the Hall of the Ambassadors. That's in the Tower of Comares, facing the fishpond of the Court of Alberca. I was designer to the King of Granada, Abu-Abdullah. Everyone called him Boabdil. He kept redecorating the Hall because he wanted to impress all the Spanish and foreign dignitaries . . ."

Habib stood with his arm around her shoulders. "Don't you see? These drawings are the same as the ones I designed there. The colored enamel wall tiles. And the dadoes, the horizontal bands that run around the room. Its huge tiled ceiling too," he added on impulse.

Bridget seemed more impressed.

"Well, one day," he continued, holding her, "while I worked on the scaffold, Boabdil came by. The King did. He praised my work."

Bridget shivered. "It's so cold in here."

Habib realized she didn't think much of his designs. And no amount of talk would change her mind.

Making drawings that no one would ever see in a hidden, dark chamber soon lost its excitement. Day by day, Habib spent less time drawing and more and more often just climbed the cliff and sat on its edge in the sunshine, watching the waves break on the rocks and roil in the surf below.

The men from Tangier who tethered their horses above the cliff always glanced and waved in recognition before stumbling down the steep slope to the grottos below. And often, even when it rained and the odds and ends of his cast-off clothing stuck to his skin, he walked on the small brown beach where he threw stones at the rows of breaking waves or clambered over the boulders before the cave.

There was little to do except think. He would be forever grateful to Bridget. She not only saved his life, she sacrificed her profession to his comfort, his needs. But the sexual novelty was gone. He was no longer insatiable as before, when he wanted her favors in the morning, sometimes in the afternoon and always at night. Soon he knew by her movement, her moisture and her moans that he too had become adept at giving pleasure. But he was not in love, never had been; didn't know what love was.

The time seemed so long ago when he had labored at the King's palace in the morning. In the afternoon, to please his father, he studied at the Yeshiva and participated in the Friday evening and Saturday morning services. And most evenings, he visited Miriam and supped with her family. Dull, not exciting, but doing something. Here, he lacked purpose. He craved action. He must do something.

FIVE

No, not you again!

Habib eyed the stout woman waiting for him. She stood in his way, both feet anchored in the narrow strip of gritty sand between the cliff and the incoming tide. Her posture, arms folded across her massive chest, belied her practiced smile.

He sauntered forward, a freshly caught fish swinging at his side, suspended by a cord through the gill.

"Un momento, Senhor."

Habib stopped a pace away, nodded acknowledgment of her polite greeting then glanced at his fish whose eyes and scales were already losing their luster in the blazing afternoon sun.

Her glance followed his. She addressed him slowly, pronouncing each word deliberately in the manner of a European court.

"We have spoken before."

"Three times."

". . . Well, what have you decided?"

Habib grinned. He knew she would be pleased with his decision. He knew he had waited too long. A sudden thought flashed through his mind; the grin changed to a slight frown and he pursed his lips. How could he tell the Signorina of his decision before telling Bridget? She would be devastated. In the four months since the shipwreck they had grown very close, although at first he felt embarrassed and humiliated being kept by a harlot. He had even pictured his father's wrath turning to sorrow when he found out. *If* his father was alive to find out. But soon Hersh the Jew accepted Habib the Muslim. Especially after Bridget told him his new name meant, in Arabic, 'lover'.

He reveled in her eagerness to give herself solely to him. Patrons would peer into the cave to see if she was occupied. Some strode boldly in before seeing Hersh back in the dimness of the cave. Bridget's youthful freshness and appearance of virginity appealed to all the men who passed her cave, even though she now went about fully clothed. She turned them all away.

The Signorina shifted her stance. The back of her hands rested on her ample hips. The ingratiating smile was gone.

"I will give you the answer to your request very soon," Habib twirled the fish on its cord.

"*Madonna*! Are you stupid? Request, what request." She stomped closer toward him.

Habib leaned away from her flushed face and flying flecks of spittle.

"What I have told you over and over was you are not welcome here. Me feed you? Hah! No more."

Habib, although long schooled in politeness to his elders, retorted quickly: "You enjoy well enough those silver anchovies and the big fish I bring you. I'm the one who feeds *you*."

"Habib, or whatever you choose to call yourself, you will always be a Jew to me. You belong in a mellah." She made mellah sound like Satan's hell.

A knot formed in his stomach. He thought he'd left this prejudice in Spain. "What you want," he gritted his teeth, "is money. Those escudos you get from Bridget and her clients."

"Yes, money. And I will pay – "

"Help! SIGNORINA COME QUICK."

A short chubby harlot, jumping up and down at the cavern's entrance, waved her arms frantically. Muffled screams sounded from inside.

Habib shot the Signorina a glance. Her expression had not changed. She shrugged and began to waddle toward the noise.

Habib sprinted forward and as he passed her tossed the fish, which she instinctively caught, juggled, then dropped with loathing.

Inside the cavern, Habib paused in the semi-darkness. Straining, he made out some sort of reception lounge: sumptuous furnishings, tapestries on the wall, patterned rugs on the floor. Then at the crack of a whip and another scream he hurried into an adjoining cave, the chubby harlot and Signorina following behind him.

He blinked in horror. A naked, heavy-set man, the one with the goatee who always looked for Bridget, was beating a harlot on the floor while her hands were tied behind her back. Habib could see welts criss-crossing the skin of her belly. The man raised his whip to strike again. She tried to roll away.

Habib leapt at him, grasped his wrist so tightly he felt bones crunch together. The leather whip dropped to the floor like a dead snake.

"Stop!" The Signorina shouted. "Stop, you fool." She reached for Habib's arm. "You are hurting the Count."

The patron winced in pain, glared but said nothing.

Habib remembered they all carried daggers. "Cut her bonds," he ordered the chubby one still huddled against the wall.

The bound woman on the floor lifted her tear-stained face and gave Habib a glint of white teeth behind her large red lips.

Always alert, the Signorina caught the look.

28

"Habib," she said with a sour stare, "you can't have this girl too. Twenty escudos. I'll give you twenty escudos for you to leave."

Signorina Regaldo had been a most sought after courtesan in Tangier. Discreet as well as beautiful, she became mistress to one after another of the most highly placed nobles of the City's occupation forces. Moreover, when age inevitably made her less attractive to men of substance, she did not become bitter or vent rage on younger women. Instead, her vision and the nobles and generals gifts had provided the means with which to buy the Hercules Grottos. She staffed it with the most desirable of young women, promoted it as an exclusive brothel.

If she wished to continue to enjoy the life of the wealthy by selling sex, the Signorina understood the need for discipline with her harlots. The bitter feuds and jealousies of women who lived so close together could destroy a brothel as fast as a harem. Because she herself had been the victim of plots, intrigue and attempted poisonings by others less favored by her current count or general, the Signorina worked her stable of professionals hard, kept them healthy and disease free and watched for the potential of tantrums to erupt into violence. But most of all, she guarded against that rare occasion when one of her harlots fancied herself in love. That would be intolerable.

She treasured the reputation that her brothel made available whatever and whomever, white, black or brown, a man might want. So she observed Bridget with mounting unease, then anger. The most desired of all her girls and her rising star now dared to put passion before work. Violating her own rules, Signorina had let this romance develop too long. Months after the shipwreck cast that Jew without an escudo to his name on her property she had finally confronted him. But he refused to leave. Now she must act.

While Habib wandered along the rocky beach, the Signorina took the gift she'd purchased in Tangier to Bridget.

Smiling in delight, Bridget held the garment to the sunlight. Its silver threads glittered. She removed her plain blouse and slipped the new one over her head. The fit was perfect. She twirled and flashed her small white teeth in glee. "How do I look? Think Habib will like it?"

"Don't fasten the top loops. He will, of course. What man wouldn't, especially on you."

Bridget's fair cheeks flushed with pleasure anticipating Habib's reaction.

The Signorina watched Bridget carefully as she began: "All the women here have been in love, beyond reason, as with you – "

Bridget smiled in agreement.

"But that was when all of us were innocent. Virgins. Before we came

29

here to be admired by all men. Our patrons bring gifts, but not one of them will marry us."

Bridget spun to face her. "Habib is different."

"Has he asked you to marry him?"

Bridget walked to her trunk, sat on the edge and head bent, picked at one of the silver threads. "No." She looked up defiantly. "But he will."

The Signorina's painted eyelids half-closed to conceal her anger. "You brag to the others that your lover is a famous designer from Granada, one who decorated the Sultan's many palaces and will do the same here in North Africa. Do you see yourself with his friends at his palace? Would he introduce you to the nobles and their wives?"

Tears bloomed on Bridget's cheeks. She sniffled as she softly said, once again, "No."

She took off the blouse, folded it, and raising the trunk's lid, placed it with the other gifts.

At dusk, Habib carried a large fish and a palm frond filled with silver anchovies back along the beach. A nice surprise for Bridget, he thought. A fine diversion for today. Tomorrow he would think of something else to do. As he neared the grotto area, he heard voices and the clatter of hooves as several horses departed the cliff above. At the entrance to Bridget's cave Habib heard a man shouting inside. He stopped, puzzled.

"Move . . . move! What's the matter with you." The gruff voice rasped.

Habib dashed into the cave, then froze. Bridget lay on the pallet, flat on her back. The bare, dimpled buttocks of the Count filled the void between her spread legs.

A burst of rage overwhelmed Habib. He swung the fish by the tail and let go. Its scaly body smashed against the flabby buttocks like a slap on the face and left a red imprint where it slid off. As he stood there, teeth clenched, he glimpsed the pleading look in Bridget's eyes. Habib scooped up the Count's clothing, sprinted to the top of the cliff, and turned at the edge to look down.

He raised his arms heavenward and laughed.

Then he was gone.

SIX

In the harem, months went by. Isabel proved helpful, even garrulous. She was the only person Hura could talk to – but Hura always knew where the servant's loyalties lay. One Tuesday afternoon, Isabel arrived at her room with a large basket overflowing with towels, vials and jars. "I've come to take you to the hammam," she announced.

"The hammam? Why today?"

"You must be washed, purified."

"Do I need to be told when to bathe? Look. I've already washed." She waved toward the wet cloth beside the wash bowl.

"It's the custom. Come."

Hura frowned, not knowing whether to be pleased or indignant. Everybody here treats me like a child. Then, as soon as it occurred to her, she smiled. Now she'd get out of the harem.

"Cover yourself," Isabel said. "Come. The bath house is open to women in the afternoon."

Once outside the compound with Isabel, Hura breathed deeply and walked slowly to savor the sights and smells. She passed balconies abloom with pots of colorful flowers; the aroma of midday meals wafted out of open windows. Isabel led down a short lane on the way to the lower market, the Souk el Hots, ducked through a small doorway and descended stone steps to a vaulted series of tiled, steamy rooms. Seven women sat around the central pool, feet immersed in the water, laughing and conversing.

Hura was impressed with the vastness of the underground complex. "We had no hammam in Chaouen." She confided. "This is so . . . so civilized."

"Ah, for us," Isabel nodded agreement, "the bath house is much more than a place to wash. Men can meet and talk at the cafes and the souks, but for us, this is the only place where we women can gossip without men hearing. I often get up before dawn on Thursdays to prepare the ghassoul for Lalla Fatima." She pointed to the black sticky substance in the bowl she was holding. We stay all afternoon so I bring our dinner. But not today." Isabel reached deep in her basket and brought out two pairs of wooden sandals.

Hura took off her soft leather slippers. "Can anyone come here?"

"It's open to anyone who can pay. But not everyone can pay or come at once or come whenever they want. Your husband provides this one hammam for all the people. Everyone is assigned a day. And," she threw Hura a knowing glance, "since we must wash after sex with our husbands, that's a problem for a woman without a bathroom. Because if she comes on a day that isn't her official bath day . . . everyone, including her family, neighbors and the tradesmen, knows what she and her husband have done." Her wrinkled face crinkled in a smile. "We're fortunate. We have water in the house."

Hura followed Isabel to the bathing area to one side where they took off their clothes and squatted on small wooden stools. A stooped attendant appeared and slopped hot, steamy water over their nude bodies.

Hura gasped, held her breath, then relaxed. She wanted to remain there, but followed Isabel who waddled to a second vaulted chamber, where the real washing and scrubbing would take place. Hura was surprised that Isabel's arthritic fingers were so strong as she began to shampoo her thick hair.

"This ghassoul looks awful but smells heavenly. You said you made it?"

"It's everything: soap, liniment and perfume. Each spring, I make it from dried chips of clay and mix it with rosewater, myrtle and other fragrant plants. Then I dry it to a thin crust, add more flowerwater and make a paste of it. I bake it on boards in the sun on the roof. Then when I need it, I just add water." She paused to pour hot water through Hura's hair. "I'll have to make more, now that you're here."

Hura nodded understanding while thinking: so . . . one can walk on the roof.

She peered through the steam at the amorphous shapes around her. The sound of splashing water was magnified by the marble floors and walls. "Who are all these women?" she drew close and whispered. "My neighbors?"

"They're from all over the city . . . some Berbers but mostly *Moriscos*."

"I want to meet them."

"Shall I tell them who you are?"

Hura changed her mind. On second thought, she was not ready to tell her story. It would take time for her to share herself. Maybe the steam would help open her up. She shook her head. "If you do, I'll have no peace. They'll want to know all about me and my wedding gifts."

She turned and drew her knees in closer. "I want new friends, but not today."

The two were quiet for a while until Isabel asked: "Lalla Hura, with all respect, if you didn't have a hammam in your town, where did the women meet and how did you clean yourselves?"

"We bathed in the springs. And at home too. And we women met wherever we wanted to. Berber women don't wear the veil. We went anywhere we wanted . . . well, not to the mosque, of course. We were free just like men."

Isabel clucked, "Tzt, tzt. Well, our hammam isn't just a good place to gossip and wash, it's also good for your health. Especially when you're pregnant. The steam opens the belly. Makes it easy to deliver. And later, you'll come here a week after your baby is born. To relax and let your insides settle. Widows come too. After their official mourning is over. When they leave they can wear their everyday clothes and face powders again."

Hura pursed her lips when she heard the word pregnancy – a gesture lost to Isabel who watched the attendant arrive with more hot water. They rose and entered the third and hottest area: the purifying chamber.

"I've reserved every Tuesday afternoon for our visit."

Hura grimaced. "Yes, I'll be prepared next week. That's when I'll meet the gossips."

Fatima could claim more noble ancestry than Hura and did not hesitate to mention it.

To Hura, she parroted the same phrases: "I am related to King Boabdil, the last ruler of Granada at the al-Hamra. And the niece of Boabdil's powerful Prime Minister, Nazari . . . she too is my relative."

Over and over Fatima described her life as typical of the very rich Muslims in Spain, centering around family, lavish court parties, fashionable clothes and expensive jewelry.

She also informed Hura of her place as a second wife, and what she must do. Hura would never forget her words: "You will honor me in all respects. You will not be forward or challenge my opinions or your husband's. You will not attempt to interfere with my decisions." And she even invoked the *Hadith*: "*There is a special character to every religion and for Islam, it is modesty.*"

A snort of indignant breath from Hura's nostrils accompanied Fatima's last words: "Over time I will instruct and correct you when you err, so that you may learn." Hura clenched her teeth to keep from screaming.

She always knew when Fatima was coming. The jingle-jangle of her gold bracelets, the clicking of necklace beads and the clinking of hair ornaments preceded her arrival. Yes, she was a pompous bore, yet Hura often felt sorry for the older woman. The fire of her Spanish beauty had cooled to graceless hauteur. Hura sensed that only her relationship to King Boabdil had produced the marriage to Mandari. She saw a sadness in

Fatima's eyes, an emptiness. Even the fruit of their marriage – two sons – were gone, both victims of the Muslim-Catholic wars, buried somewhere in the hills of Spain. Hura forced herself to withstand the constant belittling and verbal abuse. She felt pity.

Fatima had her own key to the harem gates and used it judiciously. To her, confinement in the harem was a privilege, she felt safe there.

Here in Tetouan, she had arranged with her husband the privilege of meeting with her peers in the elegant reception room downstairs. She insisted on observing this Spanish tradition and had established an afternoon Salon for the elite women friends who shared her fate of exile. Fatima never tried to hide her bitterness over the loss of her Spanish palace. The humiliation of losing the war to the Christians and moving to this alien land gnawed at her constantly. She made sure that her reception room became well known beyond this rural outback of the North African coast. It would become even more important if the rumor that King Boabdil was coming to Tetouan was true.

Hura never received an invitation to the room. She could have intruded, for she was certainly no secret. To announce his new marriage, Mandari had treated the entire city to a day of celebration shortly after her arrival. But by her absence she became an enigma and excited gossip. Hura didn't attend because, as she said to herself, she didn't wish to go. From the slit in the front wall, she observed the weekly parade of visitors. She snickered as the corpulent clique of women, dressed in ruffles of silk and taffeta, rustled through the courtyard, tittering on their way to the reception room. But secretly she seethed with a prisoner's envy at the freedoms given to Fatima.

If Hura burned, Fatima boiled . . . daily confronted by this lithe, sleek animal with that mane of luxurious hair, with the fair taut skin and the gray eyes of a sorcerer. Resentment stewed inside Fatima. She had a predator in the house. That's what Hura was, a predator who would consume her day by day, take away her position, her dignity. And not just her dignity, but her husband, too. She saw the lust in his eyes. And worst of all, this predator put vigor in the loins that no longer sowed seed in hers. Babies. Her stomach churned at the thought of many babies in the house . . . through their children she, Fatima, would become nobody. Even if Boabdil did arrive.

Fatima did not sulk. Fatima schemed. Well trained in palace intrigue from her years in Spain, she knew what to do even before the young wife arrived. Within days of the wedding announcement, Fatima had prepared to rid herself of the new she-devil. She made contact with a sorcerer in Marrakech, far off to the south, so no one would know. She involved herself with the shour, the ancient magic. It consumed her. She followed

34

its prescribed rituals of astrological manipulation, magic formulas and spell charts. Replete with this complicated array of letters and proper numbers, Fatima became skilled in the sorcery that would eliminate, or at the very least, control this threat to her happiness.

Once a month, for a jewel or pieces of silver, she received by runner fresh instructions to strengthen the rituals. Most important, if this new wife was to stay barren, was the burning of small white candles during each new moon – and of long ones when the moon was full – all the while whispering incantations when *Zahra*, the planet Venus or *Al Mushtari*, the planet Jupiter were in position overhead. Six months had passed since Hura's arrival. Morning sickness would be no secret in this house. Fatima was certain her shour was working.

All this while, Hura was confined to her room where she paced the floor and fingered the mementos of her former life that she kept hidden in her trunk. She became impatient and ashamed that she was not yet pregnant. Although she had no idea what it would feel like to be pregnant, she knew that she would have no monthly blood, that her belly would swell up and she would make her husband happy. She wished she could ask Aunt Henati about these things; the thought of asking Fatima made her cringe.

Hura began to fear that it was her own fault that no child grew inside of her. She must be cursed and barren, and no longer important to her husband because he came to her only once or twice a week now. She knew it must be her fault because often he came to her bed and immediately fell asleep.

July arrived with a blast of heat. Hura longed for the cool mists of Chaouen and her mountains. At first, she continued to wear with pride the heavy red and white skirt of her village, but every day grew more uncomfortable as summer baked the land and the green grasses of the plain below turned to gold. Only high up above the city, near the top of the foothills, was the grass still sweet. At last she shed her heavy costume for the lighter cotton blouses and long, gathered skirts popular among the Moriscos.

That summer as the heat outside mounted, the tempers of the two wives simmered to a boil. Hura had struggled to keep in check her anger at Fatima's attacks until the day the two brushed by each other in the narrow hall.

Fatima's lidded eyes swept Hura's summer garments. "We all know you're an animal, nothing but mountain dirt . . . and now you look like a donkey dressed to pass as a horse."

This latest insult was too much. Tradition and respect vanished. Hura spat back in anger. "Dirt? You treat me like dirt. Fashion? What do you mean about my change of fashion? I don't give a fig for fashion, you sack of fat."

Hura made an attempt to control herself but couldn't hold back her resentment of the months of verbal attacks. In Arabic mixed with Berber, she sputtered, "I'm not like you, I don't spend mornings at my vanity powdering myself; I don't need henna for my hair and the seamstresses to sew until their fingers bleed just to clothe me in fashions from Spain." She slapped her hand to her blouse, "I wear these clothes for comfort. And I have every right to. You want to talk family heritage? My mother, Flora, may she rest in peace, was Spanish nobility too. The blood of my Berber father, who is blood of the Prophet, may His name be blessed, flows through me. I have pride in both."

Stunned, Fatima recoiled speechless against the railing.

Hura struggled for breath. "And you will see. My son will rule this city. More than this city, *Inshallah*, all the Rif. How dare you talk to me as if I'm nothing. When you call me dirt, know that I am the daughter of a holy man, leader of the tribes of the Rif. Dirt? If I am dirt, it is the dirt of nobility. My dirt is noble land!"

Fatima brought her painted lips together and sucked in her cheeks. She must change tactics now. Tradition and polite barriers were gone. The threat of this mountain cat to her power was more serious than just the arrival of a new baby or a change in costume. Her shour was losing power. Her magic was fading. Boabdil must come soon.

The heat of summer passed. By now Hura, who knew every chink in the plastered walls of her room, fantasized about what she would see out the small barred windows. Every day she stationed herself to peer out the narrow slit in the sitting room wall. She watched her husband arrive for the midday meal. Later, after his nap, visitors appeared and disappeared in and out of her line of sight. She began to recognize many of them by their dress: merchants sporting turbans, peaked caps or the maroon Fez; officers strutting in military uniforms; council members shuffling in their official cloaks; soldiers in drab brown; holy men in white jellabas; and, nobles in Spanish pantaloons. She let her imagination soar, guessing where these men had come from and what they wanted from her husband. She despaired ever to see one of her brothers visit. She wondered if they still loved her.

Although Isabel and the servants came to the harem often, it was Miguel's appearance that Hura awaited. Once a week he lugged a long ladder up the stairs to a hatch in the balcony ceiling. He climbed up, pushed the heavy wooden cover aside and later descended with sacks of olives, ghassoul and dried herbs. Once, she began to climb up behind him. He paused half way up and kicked back his leg. He was a man of few words. Understanding him as he spoke with the sunken cheeks and uncontrolled tongue of the toothless was difficult. But she understood his body language.

Miguel evidenced pride in his position with the household. He had been with Mandari for a long time and although too old to fight now, or do heavy manual labor, he was indispensable in helping run the house. He too, had lost a son in the Spanish wars and that strengthened the bond between master and servant.

Always after he left, Hura studied the heavy hatch that prevented access to the roof and wondered if she could move it. I must try, she decided.

In her mind, she had two choices: either climb up to the roof or jump from her balcony to the patio. Not that she wanted to run away. No. All she wanted was the freedom to choose her hudud, her boundaries – to control her freedom in her own house.

She also knew two obstacles must be overcome if she was to cross her hudud: the problem of reaching the wooden hatch and the interference of ever-present Fatima. Reaching the access hole would have to be easy: easy to climb, and the means easy to hide. Surprisingly, when Hura finally figured it out, that part became simple.

Giddy with her proposed adventure, she could barely wait to try it out the next Friday, the day Fatima held her receptions. Awake early that morning, Hura listened to her jingling jewelry disappear down the harem staircase and waited impatiently until Isabel brought the noon meal. At last, when everyone was downstairs, she maneuvered the long bench beneath the hatch, tilted it on end. It rocked precariously. She paused. A blanket. Yes, something to stick under to steady it and cushion the noise on the tiles.

The shimmy up the improvised ladder was easy after years of tree climbing. The hard part was the hatch. She nearly fell trying to lift its heavy cover. Pushing in one direction swung the bench the opposite way. She teetered atop the bench like a child's toy on a stick. Miguel had made it look so easy. Ah! The secret, she found, was to use her head to push the hatch up, then use just her arms, not her whole body, to move it aside. At last she gazed in joy at the open sky, grabbed the roof's edge and pulled herself up. Freedom at last.

Her excitement and the dazzling sun flushed her cheeks. Rising from the cool darkness of the house, she soon began to sweat as she tiptoed around the four sides of the roof. She sought shelter under a thatched canopy that shaded several barrels of olives. She must see everything.

From that side, she could see the back of their compound formed a wall of the city. She stared out on the valley below where rows of tents defined fields of grain and orchards. They looked like orange and mulberry trees. In the distance, a wide muddy-brown river snaked to the sea.

From the front side, the whitewashed roofs of Tetouan sprawled up the foothills. Looking down she saw canopies of large trees that blotted the base of the crenellated citadel walls beside their house and compound. She raised her head to smell a rising breeze, a smile on her face. Freedom smelled good. Later, it wasn't the glare that scorched her joy, but prudence. Afraid of being caught, she quickly retreated, closed the opening and slid down the bench, hardly making a sound.

For her husband, that night, Hura wore a soft white nightgown and drew its ruffles tightly with a light blue ribbon around her neck. Still high in spirit from the adventure, she fluffed her hair then reached for the glass perfume bottle on her bedside table. Using the stopper, she daubed sweet-scented musk behind her ears and in her armpits. Its heady scent filled the room.

She knew he would come tonight; he had settled into a schedule, regular as the call of the muezzin. He didn't disappoint her.

Mandari appeared on time, tired but feigning a good mood. "My dear Hura, tonight you look lovely." He stood in the doorway studying his wife as she lay on her side on the bed. The stretch of her gown accentuated the curve of her small waist and the sudden rise of hip.

"Thank you, my lord." She lowered her lashes.

"I have news of your father," he said the words slowly.

She sat up with a jolt. "Good news? Is he free?"

"No, he is still in prison. But I've just heard from your brother Mohammed." He paused. "Your father's not well."

The words stabbed her heart. Hura bent over, silent. Tears welled up in her eyes and rolled down her cheek, quickly disappeared into the sheets. Suddenly bold, she asked, "Why can't you buy his freedom? That's what others do with prisoners here in Tetouan."

Mandari's jaw tightened in a brief show of emotion. "If it were that simple, your father would have been free long ago." He sat on the edge of the bed. "He's an Emir. Surely you know he's too important. No one else, not even your brother Ibrahim, can unite the tribes. The Portuguese won't be able to control the north, let alone Fes, if he's free to fight them." Mandari's face softened. "I've tried negotiating and every time I think I've succeeded, there's a setback, something happens and all the doors are closed." He lifted her gown and stroked her thigh. "Someone, and I don't mean the Portuguese, someone always prevents it."

"Who? One of his men? One of us?" She tried to ignore his hand and continue their conversation.

Mandari withdrew his hand and shrugged his shoulders. He had no answer. Slowly he began to unbutton his pants.

Hura lay back. Her spirits plummeted. Never again, she thought, would her father take her riding, nor would Mandari. Neither her father nor Mandari would teach her anything. She squinted her eyes as tightly as she could to bring herself back to reality and said: "You often ask if I need anything. Yes, there is something." She raised her head to gaze at him.

His fingers stopped.

"You spoke with compassion about freedom for my father. I want some freedom too. I want to see the city." She sucked in, held her breath. Would he laugh? Would he hit her?

He said nothing, leaned back on the edge of the bed with his back to her and began to pull off his boots, then stepped out of his stiff leather pants. His male body odor overpowered even her strong musk. His face a mask, he reached over and pulled at the ribbon of her gown. It tangled in a knot. Brusquely, he pushed up her gown.

Mandari took a long time to ejaculate while he held her arms down, pinning her to the bed with his full weight. She grimaced from the pain. He won't hurt me like this after he has a son. Peeking through her lashes, she could see him staring down at his flaccid penis, huffing as he tried over and over to stuff it in her. Finally with a heavy thrust his body quivered and his mouth fell open. He rolled over on his back, exhausted.

Thankful he had succeeded, Hura pulled down her gown. She wondered if her arms would be bruised again. She ran her fingers over her left arm and thought: anything for a son. Then she rolled, pressed herself against him and whispered: "Please, I want to see the city. Will you take me with you on your next inspection."

Without moving or opening his eyes, he answered. "No. But I'll show you the city from our roof."

Hura concealed her disappointment. "Tomorrow morning?"

Silence. Could he be asleep already?

"Yes, tomorrow morning."

She pulled her pillow snugly under her neck. Soon he snored loudly. Later when the muezzin began his first call, Hura couldn't remember sleeping at all. She had lain in the darkness thinking of all the questions she would ask about the city and the best way to bring up the subject of her hudud. When Mandari began to dress, she mustered the sweetest tone in her dry throat: "Will you come for me soon or should I breakfast first?"

Mandari hesitated and looked at her as if he didn't understand.

"I hope you haven't forgotten your promise. You said you'd show me your city. This morning. From the roof."

39

"No, I haven't." He resumed dressing. "I'll be back."

True to his word, soon she heard his boots and the banging of the large ladder that Miguel carried up the narrow stairwell. Miguel avoided looking at Hura as he unlocked the iron gate and positioned the ladder securely under the hatch.

Hura suppressed a grin. "Good morning, Miguel," she said sweetly.

The clumping and banging of the ladder also brought Fatima out of her room. When she stepped onto the balcony Hura saw her face sour as she recognized what was going on.

Mandari extended his hand and pulled Hura up the rungs into the soft yellow morning. He led her over to the parapet at the front of the house and waited for her reaction.

Hura leaned over the parapet and glanced down, not daring to give away her familiarity with the scene. The cobblestone courtyard seemed so small below them. A soldier unloaded wood from the back of a donkey into a storeroom. Almost out of sight, three others idly tossed copper coins against the wall in some kind of game.

Mandari's voice warmed with pride. First he pointed to the small domes of the old mosque he was rebuilding, then his forefinger moved to the upper wall of the city and its gate, the Bab Saida.

"I'm expanding that upper part of the city. Those are the old Berber houses that weren't destroyed when the Spanish invaded."

"When was that?"

He ran his fingers through his sparse hair. "Henry III of Castile sacked the city in 1399. Long before I came. Why the rich émigrés want me to build a new city further down the hill I don't understand." He shook his head in disgust. "We have room up here, and spring water."

"If the Spanish sacked the old city, why did you choose to come here instead of . . . of Fes . . . or, some other city?"

Mandari turned to smile at her. "You, more than others, will understand." His hand swept the horizon behind them. "Your mountains remind me of the hills and valleys of my Andalus. Fes is flat, and," his wiry eyebrows shot up, "Fes has a Sultan. Here, I am King."

His words had the sound of finality. Afraid he might end their conversation, Hura turned and pointed down toward the river. "Your ships, how far up do they come?"

"That is the o'Guad-el-Jelu, the Moriscos call it Rio Martil. It flows out of the mountains down to the sea. There's not much trade yet but there will be. I made a deal last month. I gave your brother Mohammed permission to rebuild the port. See it? Just a few buildings way down there by the sea?"

Hura whirled around to search his face. "My brother? Has he been here

40

. . . all this time?"

"Yes, why do you ask?"

She shrugged to mask her disappointment. He would think her unseemly, worse, childish. "Um . . . so many different boats." She pointed. "Do you count them? I'm sure you know who's coming and who's going." She knew he liked being flattered.

Mandari's face creased in a smile. "Some of them hold captives – prisoners we've captured in battle. Many carry refugees. Those who have money or station. They're still coming from the Inquisition. We make it easy for them to live here. My customs agents meet every boat and we register everyone. Of course, they have to pay a tax to disembark. Another tax to live here. But we all know it's a small price for freedom."

Startled, Hura studied his expression. Could it be he really didn't understand the importance of her freedom? She said only: "In the Rif, all the tribes know each other. Here there must be hundreds, thousands of new arrivals. How do you really know who they are? They could be our enemies in disguise."

Mandari gave a self-satisfied snort. "If someone arrives without documents or has no relatives here, they can't build a house or sell in the souk. They need permits. Most are from Spain, and I know the families. We keep records."

Hura nodded. "Where are these markets, these souks?"

Mandari folded his arms across his chest. He seemed to enjoy telling her about his city. He turned around to face the mountain and said, "We have two big ones. The one above us is the Souk el Foki. By the mosque there. Sunday is the big market day. But I am sure that Isabel has told you these things."

Hura shook her head so he would continue.

"Next to us, here to our left behind the citadel, or what some call the al-Cazaba, is the Souk el Hots. It sells more expensive things on Wednesdays."

Happy to be the cause of his unusual animation, on impulse she flung her arms around him, hugged him, ran around him. He responded to his young wife with a little laugh and, as they walked around the parapet, he pointed again. "My city is divided. Not only by peoples but also by trades. Over here is the iron workers area and," he wagged his finger slightly, "the wood district. Over there is the pottery district." He was speaking quickly now, pride in his voice. "And down there, where it smells even worse than the sewers, is the debbaghin, the leather district. By putting the workshops together, I can control the tradesmen. You can't smell it now but when the wind comes off the mountains, it carries the stench of the tanning pits. You'll smell it this winter, here in the house."

41

"I smell it now." She wrinkled her nose. "Tell me, dear husband, why are some parts of the city growing and others have so few houses and tents? Why doesn't everyone live inside the walls?"

"Some immigrants prefer not to. People are different. That's why I build separate areas." He pointed down to his left. "That large area of houses is for refugees from Andalusia. We Muslim Spaniards call them Moriscos because those Muslims converted to Christianity to save their skins. You call them Mudejars." Mandari laughed. "The imam at the mosque keeps busy converting them back again. Most of them will eventually live inside the city walls, *Inshallah*. Over there to the right, that's the temporary place for the Jewish refugees."

Hura rubbed her forehead by habit. "I've never seen a Jew."

"You don't need to. I may let them build their mellah near the mosque in the upper city."

"Why are the Jews set apart?"

"It is the Spanish way. They expect it."

Hura didn't know what that really meant but she had heard they looked different and were very rich. "I've seen some beautiful rugs made by Jews. From a village east of Chaouen," she told him. "I remember because the rugs had people and animals in them, not like ours."

Now below them, in the courtyard, they heard noises. Mandari spotted his construction overseer striding toward the door with his whip coiled around his armpit. He leaned over the parapet. "Ya, Fuad!"

The overseer froze defensively, recognizing the voice but not the direction.

"Up here." Mandari waved his arms. "I'll join you. Stay there."

Hura stared at the man below – even from this height, the hairless giant had bare calves like tree limbs. His skull was larger than it should have been.

All the way back to her room Hura was dizzy with excitement: the vastness of the city, the construction, the smells, the colors, and the energy. How proud she was to be his wife, the wife of the builder of this city. For the first time, she felt happy with her husband. She sensed his responsibility, his pride, and wanted to share it. My sons, she vowed, will rule Tetouan wisely. They will have no enemies.

"My lord," Hura had been preparing and revising her words for days. She caught his arm as he entered her room. "You say you wish my happiness. There is a small favor I wish to ask. I long for the freedom to go on our roof more often to see your great city – to smell the air from the sea and delight in the clouds. Will you tell Miguel to leave the ladder in place so I can go up when I want to? After all," her words rushed out, "Fatima

42

can leave the harem when she wants to."

"Fatima is a royal lady with Spanish ways."

Hura tossed her long hair and pulled away from him. "Am I not royal too?"

Mandari eyed her. "What would you do up there?"

"I would give praise to your strength and wisdom. I would watch the city grow and listen to the birds. I hate being alone and cooped up all the time with no one to talk to."

"No. I won't allow it. You could be seen." His words rang with finality and his foot stomped the floor.

She sighed and came to him again, placed her hands on his chest and looked into his eyes. The brown edges of his iris were cloudy like her father's used to be.

"You could build me a screen of lattice and I could sit behind it. No one would see me then."

He stared at his young wife, so young and spirited, and weighed the possibility. Why should he make her happy? He paused with one boot still on. Romance, love, was for younger men. Besides this was an arranged marriage, one of politics. He exhaled heavily through his nostrils. He guessed he owed that to her father. But he didn't want to be made a fool of. By now, she should have had children to keep her busy.

"I'll think about it." He shook his head. "But if I let you, all the women in Tetouan will want to do the same."

Hura flashed her widest smile.

In less than a week carpenters appeared with Miguel. They carried palm fronds and armloads of wood slats up the ladder and onto the roof. The hammering went on for days. When it was finished, Mandari came to her chamber and announced she could now go up anytime. The roof was hers. She threw her arms around his neck in gratitude. He began to undress before she could utter a word.

Throughout the fall, Hura remained content. The city was hers to experience. She watched as workmen built the city rampart on the southern side and marveled at the number of new tents and houses near the river. She frowned in puzzlement as hundreds of ragged laborers popped up daily out of what looked like a hole in the ground behind the wall of their house. She smiled on market days recognizing the hill farmers in their thick jellabas, and the Rif women in their broad pompom hats. She fought homesickness seeing women from Chaouen in their distinctive red and white striped overskirts, the tassels of their conical straw hats bouncing as they walked. Lying on her back she delighted in the clouds that confronted the mountain tops in the distance, their shapes changing as if putting on a show just for her.

Her favorite time of day was at dusk when the city grew dark. Up there she watched the mauve sky turn purple, then black, alive with the sickle-shaped wings of diving swallows, the yellow lights twinkling in the valley and up the mountainside. It was then that the evening breezes carried the aroma of charcoaled meat, and she could hear the high, sweet sound of the muezzin calling for prayer. Often a lone dog barked from far down in the valley or the music of a flute wafted in and out of earshot. But her reverie always turned to melancholy and she quickly descended.

With the approach of winter, even this show paled. She longed for real freedom, to be a participant in the life of this city, not caged. She ached to be down there in the valley herself or up in the mountains.

She had seen it happen to other women. It was called the 'hem'. When she was a child, Aunt Henati told her that's how she lost her mother. She knew she had the 'hem'– the depression – because it was different from 'mushkila', a problem. She knew because if it was 'mushkila', there would be a reason for it.

Aunt Henati had explained it to her: "If you didn't know why or what was wrong, then you definitely had the 'hem'."

Now she had all the symptoms. She didn't want to eat, she'd send her breakfast back with Isabel and barely touch her dinner. She craved only one thing. Figs.

"But Lalla Hura, figs are out of season." Isabel repeated day after day until it became a joke between them. Hura would sit in her room without moving or speaking, chin in her palm and stare at nothing; her mind emptied of thought. In Chaouen, when a woman was stricken, she might be taken to a sanctuary high on the top of a mountain, like Moulay Abdesslam in the Rif, and left alone. That's where her mother had been taken. The natural beauty and the great peace of nature there were the only recognized medicine for the 'hem'. She longed for the advice of Aunt Henati.

She recalled her husband's reaction when she tried to explain her depression. "Fatima never needs a cure. Rif magic, bah! Women's things," he scoffed. "I'd send traders to Marrakech for a cart load of figs before I'd let you leave and have the whole city mock me."

It was in the depths of this depression that the idea came and shook her free. Why hadn't she dared before? She would explore downstairs. This was her new hudud. Eyeing the ladder, she told herself it wouldn't be too hard to move it to the balcony. There she could slide it down into the patio. Would it reach? Her heart pounded as she imagined her new freedom and how dangerous it might be, for at any time someone, even a male guest, could discover her. I'll sneak down in the afternoon during Fatima's nap, she said to herself . . . when Isabel finishes cleaning up and before any visitors arrive.

The ladder reached. Hura raced around the first floor, rapidly explored each meeting room, the grand reception room, the kitchen and storerooms. No one was there. She even dared to peer into her husband's chambers and the guest bedrooms. Several doors on the front of the house led into the large courtyard, some to adjoining storerooms and others across the open space, to the administration building at the side. The back of the house, she discovered, was a solid, windowless wall. Some rooms baffled her; they couldn't be entered. The doors had massive locks and iron bolts securing them in place. One door in an unused room was more forbidding, more heavily barred than the others and made of iron, not wood. In her village, no one ever locked their doors.

For several weeks, she tasted her newfound freedom like delicious fruit. The house was large and rambling. Their kitchen was twice the size of her bedroom, and its floor and walls gleamed with white tiles, so unlike the tiny, dark kitchen they had in Chaouen. Just inside it, four alcoves with shelves lined with jars, baskets and clay pots of all sizes gave off the heady aroma of coriander and cumin and on one side, there was a wide fireplace cluttered with an array of iron hooks and cauldrons. A thick wooden plank on trestles occupied the center of the floor, its top scarred with the marks of cleavers. Large torches protruded from their iron holders at the doorway, their bound tips blobbed with sap. Oil lamps hung from the high ceiling. Hura imagined they would be used daily; those small windows gave little light. On one wall, seven large iron keys hung from pegs. Fatima keeps a good kitchen, she reluctantly conceded.

Her favorite room was the reception room arranged with velvet-cushioned chairs, soft ottomans and small inlaid tables. She would tiptoe down the four steps to the sunken floor, plush with layers of red and orange kilims. Tiny blue and green tiles decorated the lower parts of the walls where the burgundy cushioned banquettes abutted. Several pierced-brass braziers sat in the middle of the floor ready to heat the room. The reception room smelled of smoke and incense. Sometimes she imagined it filled with her husband's friends, musicians, flowers and trays of food. Frequently, up on her toes, she would twirl a dance of delight to the music in her head.

The long formal dining room was dominated by a claw-footed table running down its center. Massive chairs with tooled leather seats and backs lined its sides. Three round iron candleholders hung from the ceiling on chains and torches stood at attention in their sockets in the walls. The fireplace in the back was large enough for a man to stand in. She imagined this was what a castle in Spain would look like.

Those visits downstairs were quick and timed precisely. At first, she darted in and out of the rooms. But soon she grew bolder, strolled without fear, examining the rooms in detail until they became familiar. Familiar and eventually too familiar. But there were some still locked. Trying the different keys from the kitchen wall, she unlocked each door and checked inside – all but one. It refused to budge. Every time she passed that iron door, she became more obsessed; the bolts and studs and bars began to symbolize her new hudud, a new frontier to be explored.

"I'm meeting your brother Ibrahim next week at Souk el Arba," Mandari confided as he came to her bed one evening. "He's captured sixteen Beni Hassan tribesmen. They're the ones who raided your marriage procession."

Hura's eyes grew large at the memory. She clenched her fists thinking how she wanted justice for the family honor. Yes. Yes, punishment.

"What will happen to them?"

"I'll bring them back and put them to work as laborers. Do you speak their dialect, Tamazight?"

"I have a Beni Hassan cousin, my lord."

"Good," he grunted, undressing boots first. "It's not the Berber they speak here. Nobody on the Council knows it. Ibrahim wants their trial here in Tetouan, to set an example. Do you have any message for him?"

Hura wondered what this meant. Suddenly eager, she asked: "Will my brother return with you?"

"No." Mandari gazed at his gnarled hands. "He's got many problems. There is famine in Marrakech and the Saadian tribes have taken over. They've begun to raid to the north. With your father still in prison, the Rif tribes are doing what they've always done – fight, rob and slaughter each other. Even cousins." He paced around the bed. "They bicker among themselves instead of uniting to fight the Saadians or foreign infidels. Not even respect for Ibrahim will unite them."

Mandari stopped abruptly. He raised her coverlet.

With her husband gone for at least two weeks, and neither Mohammed nor Ibrahim coming to visit, the hem returned again. Fresh flowers, new clothes, sweet oranges, even visits to the hammam brought little joy. With little else to occupy or challenge her, Hura confronted the door – the door of many locks and bolts, the door that went, where? She talked herself into finding out. It was a mountain to be climbed. If I'm ever going to discover its secret, I'll have to do it now. While he's away. I'll do it tomorrow. After all, this was her house and she should be able to do anything she wanted in it.

The next day Hura dropped the ladder and headed straight to the kitchen for the key. Turning the key, she heard a distinct click, took a deep breath, braced herself, grabbed the bottom bolt and yanked it sideways. No movement. Rusted shut. Frustrated, she could imagine herself still puffing and pulling when Isabel came to prepare dinner. Maybe oil would solve the problem. Running like a greyhound back to the kitchen, she grabbed a towel and a cup of oil from the tin on the table then raced back. She slowly dripped the oil on the metal restraints. It made no difference. The bolt would not slide. Patience. I must have patience. Perhaps tomorrow.

Hura returned the following day after lunch. Impatient to see if the seeping oil had done its work overnight, she held her breath and yanked. The bolt slid to the left and the door creaked open revealing a stone-floored, dark corridor. Easing through the opening, she closed the door behind her and gagged. She stood still for a moment, wrinkling her nose at the fetid stink and allowing her eyes to get used to the darkness. She shivered, drew her cape tighter around her shoulders and moved toward a faint light ahead. Wondering what she would find, she tiptoed ahead to another door that was ajar, and pulled it open far enough to peer inside. Under the low ceiling, a wooden shelf to the right held one stub of candle. From its feeble flame, she could see the floor was strewn with fronds. They smelled moldy and sour. A rat scurried about, fixing its black, beady eyes on her as if she were potential food. Racks of wooden bed-pallets were hinged to the slimy walls and beside them chains dangled from bolted iron rings as if it were a prison.

She hesitated. What was all this? Hura's neck prickled in the stillness of the damp stench. Someone, or several, no, many people lived here. She could make out bedrolls of thin blankets, cups, plates and one pair of worn-out boots. A dungeon, she realized, and wondered for whom. Where were they? Just as she turned to leave, she heard a muffled sound from one of the pallets and a bony hand rose in the gloom. The hand became a moving skeleton of a man who struggled to sit up and eye her. He squinted then began a racking cough, chains clanking as his hand went to his mouth. He spat a large clot of bloody phlegm.

Hura's heart hammered.

"Who are you?" he rasped in the thin voice of a man who has been tired for years.

She gulped, spoke in a rush of questions of her own. "Where is this, what are you doing here? Are you a prisoner?"

The man's long stringy hair shook as he attempted to laugh. "You don't know? You're in the pens – the mazmoras. What's a lady doin' in the slave pens?" He sat up higher.

Hura backed away in revulsion. "Why are you here?"

"You loco? We're captives here. We work in the city. Every day we go out. At sunrise. Under the lash. Return at night for some slop called food. It starts all over again next morning." He fell back on the bunk gasping for breath as if his speech had drained the last of his strength.

Losing her fear to curiosity, Hura approached him. "What about you?"

"I can't work, so they just leave me be. The guards here give me scraps of food and water. They still think I'll bring good ransom so they let me live. If that's what this is." He sat up again.

"But my family won't buy me out. I'm forgotten. Three years I've been in this hell hole. Jesus forgot me." He began a long, wet cough that began deep in his chest.

Sickened to think of this wretch living right under her room, Hura backed away further into the long corridor.

His voice followed. "Maybe you are the sign? Señora, come back." He called through the darkness. "My name is Ignacio de Valera-Gottardi. You must save me."

The coughing and mumbling faded and the light increased as Hura ran further into the tunnel. Soon the bright light of midday shone through metal gratings over her head and she heard the sounds of the city. Passing several narrow passageways, each one as odorous, she finally came to an iron gate that was unlatched. It squeaked as she pushed it aside. She stepped over a low stone sill into the glaring sunlight and found herself on a side street outside the outer wall of their compound.

The warmth of the sun cleansed her spirit as well as her body and her trembling ceased as she proceeded to an intersection with the main road. There she flattened herself against the stone wall and scanned the area. Tied to a hitch stood three horses belonging to her husband's soldiers. Flies buzzed around their lowered heads. She could see the saddles had the Mandari crest on their cantles.

Without hesitation, she knew she would go to the port. She would ride to see Mohammed. She chuckled thinking how surprised he'd be to see her. And she'd scold him for never coming to the house. All this time here in the city and not one visit.

No guards appeared or noticed as she untied a roan and led it away. Fifty paces down the road she gathered up her long skirt and mounted, pulling the hood of her cape over her head and kicking the horse into a slow canter toward the river below. She sucked in great gulps of fresh air and laughed aloud with the joy of her new freedom. No one was there to reprove her.

The descent to the River Martil was crisscrossed with worn pathways leading past the tents and makeshift houses of the refugees. Groups of people sat outside, some under trees, the old women preparing food, the old men smoking kif or playing cards. They looked up, startled to see a woman riding a military mount. Ragged children ran to follow her, hoping for copper coins. She paused at a small house where a circle of people crowded around a guitarist fervently strumming for a pretty dancer whose petticoats dipped and swirled as she gyrated. Not smiling, Hura soon moved on. The music of these Moriscos sounded so loud, fast and jarring to her ears. She preferred the hypnotic sounds of the Rif, especially the jajouka. She missed the music of the stringed 'ud, and the darbuka with its head of skin and clay body.

From her roof only a brown ribbon, the Martil river was wider than she thought it would be. On the bank, she headed downstream toward a boat she saw navigating around a large mud bar.

The tide was low, incoming water had not yet covered all the patches of mud littered with debris and partly submerged garbage. It smelled foul. High in the saddle, she watched as the wide-bellied vessel, its deck packed with people, slowly drifted toward her and suddenly veered to the bank. It must be a long walk upstream to the Customs House, she thought. Why is he anchoring here? Twisting in the saddle, she looked around. No one on shore seemed to pay attention; no one came to investigate.

She watched aghast as seventy-five or a hundred passengers crowding the small deck began to throw their belongings overboard then slide down ropes. When they splashed into the chest-high water, they quickly grabbed their belongings, struggled up the bank and ran toward the city. Just as she thought the drama was over, a woman carrying a baby and a sack of belongings hesitated, handed a small boy one of the ropes. Hura saw the boy clamber over the rail, watched in horror as he lost his grip on the rope and fall face down in a muddy pool. He didn't move.

Instantly Hura knew the mother would never be able to save her child in time. She dropped her reins, jumped out of the saddle and ran down the bank. She grabbed the boy by the back of his vest, lifted and shook him, splattering muddy water all over herself. By the time his mother got off the boat, the child was crying. "May the Prophet bless you, whoever you are," the mother said between sobs. "When he is imam, you will be rewarded forever."

Embarrassed, Hura replied brusquely: "I ask no favors." Then added softly, "I am Hura, wife of the Master of Tetouan, al Mandari."

The woman reached for her hand and kissed it.

Watching them disappear up the embankment, Hura wondered where all these new people would find shelter and be fed. How will we do it? For the first time, she thought of the enormity of her husband's responsibilities.

Her concerns were diverted by the loud curses coming from the boat which had listed in the mud. A large man was struggling with the rudder, pulling the huge wooden fin upwards. He was burnt by the sun and had massive shoulders. While he struggled, four men in uniform appeared on the road above her and ran down to the boat, swords drawn.

Waving his sword, an officer shouted, "I have you this time. Surrender or die."

The man, his muscles bulging with the strain, looked up from the rudder. "Ah, I see it's you, Lieutenant." He threw his hands up in mock peril. "Misjudged the tide. My rudder jumped its gudgeon. Carried me upstream, I ran aground."

"You what?"

"My rudder's pintle. Came out of the sternpost socket. Look for yourself."

"You lie, pirate. I know what you were doing. You were bringing in immigrants from Spain, avoiding port taxes. You won't get away with it. This time I caught you. You'll hang."

"Lieutenant, haven't I always paid you baksheesh? I'm a poor fisherman who just wants to make a living. I swear it's my last trip over. The seas are too rough. Sailing season's over."

"You think I'm blind? I see you arrived today with more refugees and not one paid me at the Customs House. This time I'll make an example of you for the others. Get off the boat."

Incredulous, Hura listened as they shouted back and forth. This captain was going to be hanged for helping refugees escape the Spanish Inquisition, and his only crime was taking them to Tetouan and not paying entry tax. She balled hr hands into fists. These desperate people couldn't have money. Some wore rags for clothing, they carried few belongings, their faces looked so gaunt.

Two of the soldiers began to wade toward the boat. The captain had no choice but to disembark. He grabbed a thick halyard, climbed the rail, swung out and jumped to the bank. Raising his arms in frustration, he agreed: "I'll go with you. I'll straighten this out but don't take my boat."

"You're a fool if you think your connections will help you this time. You've gone too far. And even if you paid me double your boat is stuck here and I can't explain it away. Everyone will see it."

Hura had heard enough. She could still picture that poor woman and her son. This was mushkila, a real problem. With the bottom of her mud-splattered cape gathered in her hand and her eyes piercing in the haughty manner of Fatima, she confronted the officer.

"I am Hura, wife of your lord, al-Mandari. I saw what happened here and you, Lieutenant, are wrong. The Captain ran aground on this bank and has done nothing illegal."

The Lieutenant stared in disbelief at the intruder. "You're one of them. Move away or I'll arrest you too."

"I am here for my husband to oversee the operation of his port and customs. You will let him go and return to your post," her voice sounded imperious.

Stunned, the lieutenant looked back and forth between this young woman and the boat captain then up at her horse.

Encouraged with the effect of her manner, Hura flung the cape back from her shoulders revealing the large badge emblazoned with the crest of her husband. "Yes, I am Hura bint Ali Rachid, daughter of the Emir of Chaouen, and wife to al-Mandari."

The officer's troops eyed each other, stumbled back behind him. One began to whisper in his ear.

"Quiet!" he barked, then blustered in an attempt to assert his own rank. "And where do you live?"

"We live in the citadel near the Souk el Hots. Come back with me and bring this sea captain. Tell my husband what you just said to me and see what he does to you!"

The grinning sea captain took off his battered cap, held it in his hands in front of him.

Seeing this, the Lieutenant took a deep breath. "I don't need to bother my lord about this now, I'll make my report. The boat will be here until the next tide." With that, he called his men to order and marched them away.

Hura giggled, thrilled by the success of her royal manner.

"Thank you m'lady. But . . . why did you save me?" The captain scratched his gray-flecked beard in puzzlement.

"I'm not sure," she said, wondering if it was all those refugees she had just seen.

"Well, I gotta get back to my boat, ma'am." He turned to leave.

Hura's mind clicked back to the present. "Just a moment. Tell me what you do. Tell me who you are." The commanding tone was becoming easier to assume.

"I'm Rais Tarek. Captain Tarek. This is my boat. I used to have a sea-going vessel, a caravel. Now I sail cargo across the straits in this felucca."

"Cargo? You mean people, don't you?"

"Uh, yes." The directness of this woman seemed to appeal to him.

Puffed up with her newfound authority, Hura pointed and started walking. "I want to go on the boat."

"No," he growled. "She's dangerous, heeled over, she's filthy."

From the path above the bank a shrill voice shouted: "Father. Father!" Tarek's weathered face lit up. A young girl ran to him, clasped her arms around his waist and hugged him. "I just heard you were here – it's all over the streets, and I heard there was trouble. You are safe, no?"

"I'm safe, thanks to this lady. She's Mandari's wife."

The young girl's mouth opened wide. "Our lord, al-Mandari?"

"This is my daughter, Afaf." Tarek swung his left arm in presentation to Hura. The girl curtsied.

"She's my only child. Her mother died in Spain. She lives here with her cousins, wants to find work in the city."

Caught up in the drama of their meeting, Hura watched the girl. Her imperious manner faded. The girl appeared a year younger than she was, with a small, colorless moon-face punctuated by black bushy eyebrows. Her bright eyes sparkled with energy and her hair was covered by a tightly wrapped white scarf knotted at the nape of her neck. Under her kaftan, she wore multicolor leggings that showed when she moved.

"I'll leave the boat to my crew. Come. You asked what I do? I'll tell you."

"Let me get my horse." Hura scrambled up the bank.

Tarek continued as they walked toward Martil. "You're right, I carry passengers. Refugees from Cadiz. King Ferdinand, wants all Jews and Muslims out of Spain. The smart ones left years ago. But even today some stay. The Moriscos and Conversos don't believe the danger, they think they know their neighbors."

"Do they pay you or the Lieutenant?"

"I don't ask for much. Depends on what they got. Some have nothing but their wedding rings when they get here. They can't pay the Lieutenant no customs tax!"

Hura stopped and faced him. "But Rais Tarek, how do you think we'll build our city? Without this money we won't have walls or soldiers for protection, or fountains with clean water."

"Soldiers? You saw the kind of soldiers we got. The Customs officer takes my money, immigrant money – jewelry, anything he wants, all in the name of protection."

Hura searched Tarek's face. "Are you saying the soldiers here are taking money and keeping it?"

Tarek's weary eyes looked directly at her.

"But these soldiers came with my husband from Andalusia."

"Greed is greed."

"I must tell my husband. Who was that Lieutenant? What was his name?"

"Him? I spit when I say his name. Do you think I'm stupid? My daughter'll be in danger." He changed the subject. "I get all sorts in my boat. One trip last year I had an important rabbi. I remember him 'cause of his fancy robe and skullcap. He had a loud fight with his son at the pier in

Cadiz. Handsome lad."

Curious, she asked, "How do you know he was the son?"

"He wanted to help. The old rabbi hefted one of them double scrolls with blue velvet and something like a silver breastplate on it. It looked big and heavy. Had to be his son 'cause he had those curling hairs too. Looked like sausages hanging down both sides of his head."

"What happened? Are they here, now?"

"The son got pushed onto my other boat when we loaded. Then we had this bad storm. In the Straits of Gibraltar. That'll teach me to sail so late in the year."

Arriving at the makeshift shack where Afaf stayed with relatives, he hesitated, then invited Hura in.

"No, I must return." She scowled. "You know I'll find that officer. Tell me what happened to the rabbi and his son."

"I don't know what happened to the son. I hope my other ship made it to the Jews Beach at Tangier. I heard the rabbi lives here, in the mellah."

Hura smiled at the captain. "I need a maid. If you're interested, send Afaf to my house next Friday. I'll pay her and keep her safe."

Afaf squealed in delight. Tarek squinted and sized up Mandari's wife. "Barakat. The Lieutenant's name is Barakat."

She was going to be late. Hura galloped across the valley and up to the eastern wall. A few children played stickball near the hitching posts. They ignored her as she tethered the horse. Someone would be surprised to find him sweaty. She scurried down the alley toward the gate to the prison pens and tried not to think of the consequences if it was locked. But near the gate, two soldiers seated at a table played cards and laughed. One had his back to her and his large body shielded her approach. She slipped by and entered the cool tunnel. Retracing her steps, she heard voices coming from the cell where she had found the dying prisoner. The door to the cell was closed but she paused long enough to look in through the square of iron bars at the top. She saw a short, plump man and heard him speaking Spanish. He wore a gray tunic with cloth-covered buttons, and leather sandals. But his head, his pink head, was bald on top and so was his face. He was too fat to be a prisoner. She moved on, her heart beating quickly, her breathing fast and shallow. Only when she reached the door to her house did she look back. No one had followed her.

The door wouldn't budge. What if someone had found it unlocked? Cold sweat began to sheen her forehead. What if Fatima found her? The fear of being caught made her lunge into the metal.

The door swung open and she tumbled into the house.

Torn between exhaustion, feelings of guilt, and fear of reprisal, she ran to her room and flustered about. When he returns, shall I tell him what I saw? Then he'll never trust me again. Or should I keep quiet. I could tell him I heard about the bribes from someone at the hammam . . . no, of course not. The Lieutenant saw me. And what about Afaf. I liked her and I promised to bring her here as my maid. Yes, I'll tell him, I have to.

A moment later Isabel called out to her from the balcony. "Ola! I've brought your supper."

"Come in." Hura's voice was sharp. The last thing she wanted was to eat.

"Lalla Hura, what happened?" She pointed to Hura's skirt.

Hura looked down; she had forgotten about the mud. Jumping up she began to take it off. Isabel clucked her tongue, always looking for gossip to bring to Fatima.

"It's from my new garden on the roof," Hura snapped. "Here, take it to the laundry."

Isabel hesitated. "Aren't there some other things you have for washing?"

"What do you mean?"

"Well, it's been six weeks since . . . well, your pants . . . the rag."

"Oh, that. I take care of that myself now." Hura fluttered her hand in dismissal. Could it be?

Maybe that's why I feel so strange, why I have these moods. The thrill of this possibility sent waves of emotion through her: she laughed, she cried in relief and happiness. Of course. It's not the hem. I'm not going mad. *I'm pregnant!* I have to tell my husband, she laughed again thinking of his joyful reaction, then stopped. Should she tell him first, or after she told him about the boat?

SEVEN

That same day, footsore and travel-stained, Hersh bought food and sat eating by the side of the road in the Sebou valley. He had wandered far with many changes of mind and direction. Staring at the tallest minaret shimmering in the distant heat he knew that would be his city. At first, he had walked north toward Tangier. He knew for years it had been a gateway for Moors or Jews fleeing Spain. Then realizing the Portuguese guards at Tangier's gates would be looking for him, he followed other valleys south, then eastward until he finally made up his mind.

His decision was so difficult because it was so easy. All he had to do now was cross the River Fes at the shallow ford where he saw women washing clothes, then find the mellah in the city and go to the nearest synagogue. With so many Jews, Fes would be like home. He could picture well how Hershlab, son of a known and respected rabbi in Spain would be received. The welcome would be joyous, open armed.

The vision sobered him. Somehow, he'd managed to suppress the certainty of his father's death. Now he wondered what his father's reaction would be to seeing his son – without a yarmulke – wearing a sword. And Miriam. What would she think? Would she marry a half Jew, half Gentile? Never. Did he even care?

The Count's boots pinched his toes and the too spacious doublet and pantaloons were ill fitting. He tugged off the boots and massaged his toes. The light rapier, in the new European style, had dangled between his legs and tripped him until he learned to swagger with his hand on the pommel or in the blade's basket. The sword and the raiment of European cloth had gained him entry to roadside hostelries. The escudos he had found in a pocket, now so few to clink, earned the best food and generous drink. It was time to decide: Hebrew or Muslim, Arab or Jew.

Hersh squeezed his blistered, swollen feet into the tooled leather boots, picked up the sword and once more transformed himself into a young Andalusian dandy of proud bearing out to make his fortune. He strode briskly past the monolith of the kasbah that loomed on a chopped-off hill to his right, and approaching Fes from the north, headed toward the open Bab El Guissa gate. Averting his glance from the row of impaled heads, he passed through the gateway and plunged into the maze of narrow lanes jammed with shouting vendors and braying donkeys. Garments for sale hung from ropes strung overhead. With so many passageways arched over to provide second stories, keeping the slab-sided minaret in sight was difficult. But he knew that before a temple to God, whether a Muslim or Christian one, there would be a plaza. Where there was open space would also be bathhouses.

His last coin bought a thorough cleansing of body and clothing. Seated on a heated stone bench in the steam chamber, he covertly studied the wrinkled, hairless man alongside him who rubbed sweat away from his closed eyes.

"I'm from Spain. I'm an architect," Hersh ventured. "Newly arrived."

"*Salaamtuk.*" The other's eyes remained closed. "Most Moriscos came years ago."

Hersh laughed ruefully. "I dallied on the way here."

The elderly man turned his head and squinted his eyes to regard the young man's body in detail. "You've come to the wrong part of Fes. The beautiful girls are in the Andalus quarter."

"I'm looking for something to do, not to play. Or to marry."

The bather's blood-veined eyes closed again and he fell silent. Then as Hersh rose to go to the next chamber for his rub-down, he rasped, "You are in the wrong place. This old city is dying. We old men are dying . . ."

Hersh put one foot on the bench and his elbow on his knee as he leaned closer.

"You know Fes is two cities. Both are walled. Fes Jdid, the New City, that's where all the young people are. That's where the Sultan, Blessed Be His Name, builds his palaces, gardens and broad streets."

Hersh sat down again. "Tell me about your Sultan."

"You're a builder? Muhamad al-Shaykh continues the monument building of the Merenid Sultans." Watery eyes squinted again as he cast a skeptical glance. "Go to the New City. There you'll find whatever it is you seek." He fell silent again.

Again outside, Hersh crossed the large olive grove that separated the two cities then passed through another massive arched gateway. Occupying most of the New City, the looming bulk of the Royal Palace compound was unmistakable. His first impression of the Dar el Makhzen was unfavorable. Big, yes, but not impressive. Our al-Hamra is much more majestic.

Drawing closer, by instinct he headed toward the cloud of dust and the tap-tapping of masons' picks on stone. Surveying the construction site with its horde of busy slaves on scaffolding, he saw a small ascetic-looking man in a blue wool jellaba who held a sheaf of drawings.

Jehovah has made my decision. Thanks be to God for the sign – *drawings.* Hersh did not hesitate or ponder. He approached and placed himself in front of the architect, introducing himself: "I am Habib bin Issa, newly arrived from Granada."

The man's graying brows came together. His lips framed a word but a series of deep rumbling coughs came out instead.

"I was a designer in the service of King Boabdil. Interior ceramic tiles are my specialty. I need work."

"I am Mustafa, architect to the Sultan." His tone became brusque. His quick glance swept Hersh from boots to hat, then down again. His eyes fixed on the sword.

Hersh, feeling bold now that the decision was made and confident to be Habib again, followed his eyes. "I was advised to display a weapon when traveling. But it doesn't fit well to my hand." He held out his small hands and turned them palm up. "See, no calluses. A brush fits me much better." He laughed. "Would these hands be useful here?"

"*Salaam*, Habib. I will need tiles enough to cover hundreds of walls. But I need to see your hands at work." He glanced around, sought a suitable work place. Taking Habib by the arm, he led him to a small cookfire around which several men were clustered eating lamb from skewers.

Pointing, Mustafa said, "Take that burnt sliver of wood and design a tile on . . . that stone block."

"May it please you."

Geometric images of his cave tiles flashed before Habib's eyes as he picked up the short stick with the charred end. Brushing sand off the stone's face, he quickly drew a black square with a circle within.

"Not geometric, not abstract. A design in calligraphy."

Habib stilled the tremble of his hand and swallowed hard. He had never done one. "A phrase of the Prophet?"

"I think not. You have seen all those. Try my name."

Habib moved to another stone; drew a long rectangle, hesitated. He knew what was required was artful weaving of the letters M U S T A F A in a script between and betwixt curlicues and whorls. From watching master designers at work, he also knew that the mark of an amateur was a hesitant, short and choppy stroke. He simulated bravado he didn't feel and boldly drew several long sweeping lines that converged, crossed and curled back. Each letter was partially revealed one at a time in a whorl or interstice so that the rectangle contained a seemingly never-ending line.

Mustafa coughed again. "This cold will be the death of me. You'll have to do another one of my name in ink. Just for me." He clapped Habib on the back. Then his face darkened: "But know you, I'm not the one to please. Only the Grand Wazir Walid speaks for the Sultan. And no one can foretell the Wazir's pleasure."

EIGHT

When Mandari returned from Souk el Arba, Hura spied him from the roof and rushed to meet him, her perfume swirling in the air behind her.

"What's this?" His worn look brightened at her show of affection.

Taking his hand, she led him up to the roof and over to the stools near the parapet. "Come, sit down next to me, I have something important to tell you."

She looked sideways at him. "I went to the river."

His grin vanished.

Her words rushed out in a torrent. "I know you're angry, but listen, please."

"I saw a boat come in that didn't go to the Customs dock. It got stuck in the river. People jumped from it and ran toward Martil. Then one of your officers came and at first wanted the captain of the boat to pay him off, then he was going to arrest him!"

"Slow down! Stop . . . you left the house?" He jumped to his feet and raised his hand to slap her, then hesitated.

She hunched her shoulders, spilled words out even faster: "Your officers are taking money from the immigrants and not giving it to you. I told the Lieutenant who I was and he let the sea captain go."

"What sea captain?"

"Captain Tarek."

"And the officer, what did he do?"

"He said something about his report then left."

Mandari rose and began to pace around the stools, then looked down at her. "How did you get there?"

"I took one of the soldiers horses."

"I'll lash those guards, you – you – what was the name of this officer?"

"Tarek said his name was Lieutenant Barakat."

He looked at her in cold, stony silence. He had put off too long the taming of this mountain girl. He pounded his fist into his hand. "I will deal with the officer tomorrow. And where do I find this boat captain?"

"Please have mercy on Captain Tarek. He agreed to send me his daughter as my maid." She rose to face him.

"He's broken the law."

"He has no money and his boat is aground in the river. Won't his daughter in service to me be enough? I need help with the baby."

Mandari's thick neck pulsed. "*The baby?*"

"Yes, dear husband, I'm going to have your child. I'm pregnant."

His rigid body trembled, he took her hands in his. "Praise be to Allah. We shall have a glorious feast. At last, you've made me happy."

"Then you're no longer mad at me?" She asked sweetly as she reached over to touch his cheek.

"No. But I forbid you to go out again. Or to ride. You could lose the baby. How did you get out of the house?"

She avoided his gaze. "I found the door to the prisoner pens."

His joy was shattered. "What am I going to do with you. Don't you know you could have been killed, murdered for a scrap of your clothing? How could you? And the baby. Have you no sense?" His body grew rigid again.

She lowered her head further. "I won't do it again, I promise. But," she perked up, "You'll let me have the girl?"

He said nothing, eyes turned upward at the cloudless sky. At last, she heard: "Mm-m-m, yes."

"And you won't punish the Captain?"

"I'll think about it. Go to your room before I change my mind."

Mandari remained alone on the roof, puffed up with his good fortune. On reflection, he was more amused than angry at his young wife's venture to the river. Her father was right, she had a mind of her own. He admired that in a man. Why not a woman? He'd have to give her freedom in the house now. But not outside. Never. He shoved his stool against the lattice and leaned back. Sons. Yes. My sons will govern this city. He sighed with pleasure, anticipation. The fatigue of years of hard work left him. My Tetouan will be the most important city in the Maghreb and no power from Europe will conquer it. Our armies will defeat them all. He clenched his fist. This Lieutenant . . . I'll kill him myself. No . . . I'll give him to my overseer. Yes. His lash will be good example in the pens. This thief will have a public trial, of course, so everyone knows he's guilty. No one cheats lord Mandari and gets away with it.

He envisioned the trial, how it would go. Of course, Hura would need to be there, to accuse the officer. And this sea captain, too. Mandari rubbed his eyes. He wondered how long it had been going on. Why didn't he know about it? He sat up abruptly, eyes wide. Tomorrow may be too late. He'd better find this officer tonight. His mind raced. It would be all right if Hura came to court. Yes, she could sit with him in the Hall of Justice, as long as she didn't show her pregnancy, kept her hair covered and said nothing until he told her to. And I could bring that Beni Hassan raider to trial at the same time. He rose and went below, calling for Miguel to bring his Captain of the Guard. They had work to do.

Hura reveled in the new status and freedom motherhood brought her. At the hammam, everyone was curious. If there was one thing all the women of the quarter knew it was when Hura was menstruating. It had been steamy gossip for a long time and as carefully noted as the arrival of new cotton from Egypt.

"She won't be skinny long," said one crone.

"Maybe now she'll speak to us," sniffed a bather.

"I bet she is happy," another sighed.

"I wonder what Fatima thinks," queried a fourth with a knowing look.

The truth was that Hura felt awful. She did not understand her body. One day she would cry at nothing. The next she would argue with everyone. Mornings were the worst. She couldn't eat, or if she did, she couldn't keep it down. The only thing she wanted was yogurt; not even figs. She wished for someone to turn to for comfort and advice. She longed to talk to Aunt Henati.

I'll bet someone from every city in the world is here to see my husband, she thought the next day, impressed with the doings of the court. Why, there had been over fifty people and a long line was waiting. She saw the petitioners for special privilege and the supplicants for mercy come in all sizes, shapes, colors and costumes. Some could barely spit out a word and others could charm a village virgin to bed in a sentence.

This was not the dignified setting she remembered at her father's court. But there was less business and less crime in Chaouen. This place teemed with bleating sheep on their way to the slaughterhouse, the clang of pot-laden donkeys negotiating the narrow streets, the shouts of traders, screams of babies, and the calls of hawkers which often drowned out the words of the scribe and the defendants.

This first day she sat near her husband on an adjacent stone bench in the small domed pedestrian intersection of two streets near their quarter. Their benches were carved out of the whitewashed wall. One arched doorway lead out to the mosque and Souk el Foki, the other, at a right angle, to the Souk el Hots, their compound and the pens. Petitioners, hoping for an audience, lined up outside the court on the street to the mosque; the accused, hoping for mercy, were brought in chains through the other doorway. Both streets bustled like an anthill with the needy, the damned, the sick, the wronged – and entire families, they came too.

She had come with him early, right after breakfast, expecting to hear the Lieutenant's case immediately, then help with the translation in the trial of the Beni Hassan, after which she would leave. But first there was business to conduct: edicts, resolutions and papers to be recorded by the scribes.

And there was also the public: the noisy, demanding, soliciting, needy public. They had their own agendas. They kept intruding. Once a man broke through the line of petitioners and barged into the domed chamber demanding a license. He was quickly thrown out by the soldiers.

"And what did you steal?" she heard her husband ask the next in line.

"My lord, I don't steal. I was going to return the mule, I only wanted to borrow it."

"This is the second time you've been brought before the court for theft," the scribe interjected. "The first time there was no proof."

"You will have the punishment you deserve." Mandari gestured to Captain Abdul, "Cut off his right hand." Soldiers dragged the whimpering man away.

Hura whispered to her husband, "That man expected your sentence."

"Life is unmerciful. Everything is predestined by fate. An Arab can do nothing but look forward to the relief of a trip to paradise."

"No Berber will accept that, husband. We fight for life to the end."

Hura tugged her scarf further down her forehead. She studied the people seeking and meting justice. At first, occupants and onlookers of the court had been curious, even nervous about her presence. More nervous than she. Their questions remained but they soon grew used to her as she listened intently, nodding occasionally at her husbands wisdom, weighing death, retribution, freedom, justice. Just like she used to nod in her father's court. Only this time she took it seriously. She patted her belly. She wasn't a child anymore.

She noticed a beggar in rags who never took his eyes off her. He held a staff of twisted wood in his lap. Did she imagine its head looked like a viper? He squatted immediately outside the arched opening closest to their compound and she knew from there he could see and hear everything as well as she could.

Hura looked out into the busy street. Suddenly she sucked in her breath. Mohammed! Standing by the far wall. Why was he in court, she wondered. She remembered her ride to the port, and how she had set out to see him. She raised her hand to wave then reached over to nudge her husband. Mandari ignored her, annoyed at the distraction.

She gently touched him again.

Mandari growled, "Behave yourself."

Soon another man was brought before them, then another pleaded his case, and shortly after, another. Robbery. Incest. Assault, even murder. Common cases. The last case was the portly Lieutenant. Dragged before

61

them in chains, he stumbled in front of Mandari and fell to his knees. Welts pocked his face, bruises stained his neck and one leg didn't seem to work. Conversation and chatter stilled. Everyone watched in silence.

The scribe read the charge: "The accused, Lieutenant Abed Barakat, admits to taking bribes, extorting money from His Excellency Lord al-Mandari and stealing from City coffers. Further, he has named certain others who worked with him and who have also pleaded guilty. They have already been executed."

"I understand that there are two witnesses. Let them speak," Mandari motioned first to Hura.

"For the record, this witness is Hura bint Emir Ali Rachid, the wife of al Mandari, Governor of Tetouan," the scribe announced.

"Do you recognize this man?" Mandari asked her.

"I do." She stared directly at the kneeling man. "He is the person I saw trying to take a bribe from Captain Tarek at the river."

"Did he receive the money?"

"No, I confronted him and he left."

"And where is this Captain?" Mandari signaled his counselor.

"We couldn't find him. He disappeared with his boat at high tide."

Hura masked a smile.

Mandari's fist balled in his lap. "Prisoner, do you have anything further to say?"

The Lieutenant's head hung low. "No, My Lord."

"Since the witness Captain Tarek is not here, it's fifteen years for you. Fifteen years in prison with hard labor. I'd take your hands, you dung of a camel, but we need them for work in the city."

Relieved he was not to be executed on her account, Hura let out a loud sigh. Mandari paused, again annoyed with her.

Hura's eyes searched the street for her brother, hoping to signal him to join them for lunch. He was no longer there. Disappointed, she sighed, causing still another look of disapproval from her husband.

"We'll wait for those hands when your time is up . . . Scribe, take it down. If he survives, both hands to be cut off."

It was almost time to break for prayers and lunch. Before the proceedings and judgments concluded, Mandari called his councilor over: "When is the Beni Hassan scheduled? I thought it was this morning. What's his name?"

"He's from the family of Aboud. I'll check again, sire. I heard there was a problem."

"Problem? What kind of problem?" Mandari's gray eyebrows shot up.

"I don't know, the guard said there was an accident."

"Find out. It's almost time to break."

A short time later, a soldier approached Mandari and whispered in his ear. They would have to hold his trial in special session tomorrow.

Mandari relayed the message to Hura. "It seems the Beni Hassan tried to kill himself."

"How could that happen?" she gasped.

"They found him in his cell. He had a vine twisted around his neck – must have been too small to hold his weight and snapped. The guards found him. He'll live. At least until tomorrow when we try him."

Hura took advantage of the confusion in the court as the scribe fussed with the schedule. "How did he get the vine?"

"They don't know." He spat out the words. "My guards should have searched him."

"How long has he been in the prison?"

"Several days." Mandari hesitated. He had no choice. "I will need you tomorrow again in court."

Hura nodded. "If you allow it, I'd like to come here every time you hold the court."

He pretended not to hear her.

She repeated, "Can I come to court with you every day? At least until our baby comes . . . I want to know about the city, to learn about your people, and taxes, and new plans and the other things that go on. My father used to let me. You might need me again and I can help you when women come to court."

"Your father indulged you. Besides, women don't come here to trial. Their husbands or brothers speak for them. Most often, the men deal directly with the problem and it never comes to court."

"But I saw Berber women in the crowd," She frowned.

"Yes. Well, they listen but they don't appear before the court."

"Please, let me sit with you." Her frown changed to wide pleading eyes.

"I'll think about it," he shook his head in exasperation.

Suddenly oblivious to everything else around her, she focused on the name she had just heard: Aboud. The prisoner who almost hanged himself. Her fingers pulled at her scarf. "Oh No!" She blurted without thinking.

All heads turned toward her. Negotiation stopped abruptly between Mandari and a land petitioner. For a moment her husband feared she was ill or something had gone wrong.

"It can't be!" she continued, oblivious to the stares around her. She grabbed her husband's arm as if she owned it. "That's Aunt Henati's brother-in-law. You can't harm him. There must be some mistake."

Enraged at her outburst, Mandari grabbed her hand from his arm and flung it back.

"Shut up, woman." The words slid out of the side of his mouth as he continued to face the petitioner in front of him and maintain order.

Trembling from both the shock of his words and the fear of her new discovery, she sat immobile while the rest of the business was concluded.

Immediately after adjournment, Mandari grabbed her by the arm, pulled her off the bench and led her down the street toward their compound. He held her arm so tightly and walked so quickly that she was constantly off balance. Once inside their courtyard, he confronted her.

"You disgraced me. How dare you interrupt the court. How dare you embarrass me. You'll stay with the women from now on. Back to the harem. I'll never let you out again."

NINE

Two weeks after Hura began stomping and storming up and down the harem stairs, shouting and terrorizing Afaf, Isabel and the guards, Mandari threw up his arms in surrender. The Hall of Justice became Hura's second home.

She quickly learned that life and death revolved around three things: dareeba or taxes; sulta or authority; and shari'a the law. In Tetouan, everybody was taxed from birth to cemetery. You couldn't be born, work or die without paying taxes. Then there was authority. Figuring out who had the most power – that was the key that unlocked success, happiness, and wealth. And lastly, there was the law. Happily Hura found it was the same law that her father and Ibrahim practiced in Chaouen – autocratic, but not arbitrary.

Soon her husband relied on her memory of names and faces, bending toward her so she could whisper them in his ear. Her presence gave the Berbers a new voice in city affairs. Throughout the city three languages were heard. Berber as well as Arabic and Spanish. These Berbers had been Mandari's first supporters when he arrived in Tetouan. The mountain tribes, not the newly arriving Moriscos, were the ones who loyally defended and accepted him. But now the Berbers feared the new immigrant money would make them second class citizens. In the souks they grumbled about having to learn Spanish and Arabic and feared that their customs, dress and Rif languages would disappear.

Hura understood the concerns of the mountain people. She took pride in using her new public status to reassure them. At the same time she began to feel possessive of her husband's city, resolving to help him make it grow.

Lord Mandari's attempts to disguise his reliance on his wife eventually fooled no one. She was too assured in her new position. She blossomed in pregnancy. As her jellaba expanded so did her understanding of life in her city. She quickly learned about property rights, inheritance law, licensing and duties, drawing on the experiences and training her father had given her in Chaouen.

However assured and astute, she was not prepared when a grizzled man bowed before their bench in the small court arena and claimed his right of revenge.

Dressed in the Fassi manner with maroon fez, his gnarled fingers punctuated his words. "He killed my youngest, the light of my eyes," he screamed with a contorted face. "I demand '*at wah*, my right to kill him without punishment."

"Order!" Mandari raised his arm for silence. "I demand you show respect for the court. Calm yourself and explain what happened. I don't grant the '*at wah* lightly. Tell me what happened."

The outraged father struggled to compose himself, wiped his brow and began again. "The moon of my eyes, she was. My youngest, and so beautiful." His voice failed while he wailed again. "She was riding on Ahmed Bakr's camel with a load of cedar burl and the camel stumbled. Fell. Fell on top of her. She . . . she was crushed by the load."

Mandari frowned. "Why is this Ahmed Bakr guilty?"

"He knew his camel was sick. It was old. And he wanted my daughter in marriage. He came even last week again, begging. I said no. So he killed her. You see? I must have my three days of '*at wah* for revenge."

Mandari leaned back and crossed his arms in thought. He cleared his throat. "What happened to the camel? Still alive?"

"Yes, Sidi. The mangy creature still lives."

"Why not take the camel?" Is that not fair exchange?"

Hura gasped.

"No. I want my three days to find him and get my revenge. He's hiding. It's not only me, but my whole tribe. They ask you for the three days. We'll find him."

"And what will you do with him if you find him?"

The man drew his right hand across his throat in an exaggerated motion. Then he stood waiting for an answer. His puzzled look indicated the question was dumb.

Mandari looked down on this man, his ragged tunic spoke for the enormity of his loss. "I can't deny your right to '*at wah*. Yes, you have three days to find your own justice."

Hura listened carefully, wondering if she would have faced the same fate that afternoon four years ago if Mohammed had been killed by her horse, and not just maimed.

On the bench, one day late in the afternoon, Hura noticed a foreigner. Far back in the line. Dressed in a dark morning coat, white stockings and a cloth pancake hat stuck jauntily with a thin brown feather, he stood out like a camel on a mountain peak. Finally his turn came and he stood before the bench. With his long gray hair pulled back to a tail, the wisps of gray blond escaping the clasp gave him the aura of a halo.

He removed his hat and bowed with a flourish. "I beg your indulgence, great leader of men. I am Nicholas Kleinatz from Holland, and I request your kind attention to my application for work as a teacher here in Tetouan." He spoke in perfect Spanish oblivious to the buzz of voices around him and the stares of the other petitioners as they pointed to his unusual costume that exposed his gangling limbs and knobby knees. When he finished, he pulled out a white lace-bordered handkerchief and daubed his perspiring brow.

The chief Counselor moved aside to give him more space in the small Council Chamber for his presentation.

Lord Mandari's eyes narrowed in suspicion, then he burst into raucous laughter that stilled only when he felt Hura's hand on his elbow. Mandari's reply was in Arabic. "Tell me about yourself, your training, where you came from, how you got here."

Switching languages with a nervous smile, the stranger answered: "I am a scholar from the Dutch University of Rotterdam who has been traveling in Europe. I make a living as a linguist and teacher of history and mathematics. I was teaching in the University of Salamaca in Spain but left with some Conversos. My friends said life in Tetouan matched that of old Granada."

The Chamberlain snickered.

Hura looked at her husband. His reaction matched hers. Both strained to understand the cadence of his Arabic. He used words – words she had never heard before. She was intrigued.

"Who did you come with?" Mandari asked.

"Professor Issa Asfour, a scholar from the Dar Asfour in Larache."

"Mmm . . . mmm." Mandari nodded. That was a large and well-known family.

"I ask your permission to establish my own school here. I would teach the arts, languages, the humanities and mathematics. I have excellent references."

"The Sultan wants only Arabic taught in our madressa. It's the official language – the language of business, of law and salvation."

The man's blue eyes watered and his pink cheeks darkened. "But Your Honor, may I bring to your attention that Tetouan is international. There are more here who speak Spanish and Berber than Arabic – maybe even Turkish or that guttural tongue of Egypt . . . and I have books."

"Everyone must learn Arabic." Mandari snorted, blowing air through parted lips. "What we don't need here is scholars. What I do need are architects, engineers and doctors, Muslim doctors from Egypt who know the old healing arts, not Christian ones. They should stay in Spain. I won't allow you to start another school."

Hura's baby kicked. She shifted position and her thoughts strayed. So this is what an intellectual looks like. My husband is a very proud, traditional man. Strange, sometimes he has great compassion and wisdom – yes, I see that often – but sometimes he's stubborn like a mule. Oh well, he's a Muslim by birth, not a Berber. He's an Arab with a layer of Spanish attitudes.

Some instinct made her whisper to her husband just as this foreigner was about to be dismissed. "Please, my esteemed husband, I request your consideration. Your city may never rise to greatness unless it allows the people to know the thoughts and books of other civilizations . . . even *you* cursed the burning of the great library at Alexandria."

Carried away, she waved her hands, knowing she was breaking her promise to be silent. "Perhaps he could start a library here. He did say he had books, didn't he? And he could also teach me to read Arabic." She risked his anger, but she hoped he would see the logic of her solution: the city would get a library and she would gain a tutor.

Mandari's chin sunk to his neck and he half turned to glare at her. "Why do you want to read?"

"You just said it was the way to salvation," she demurred, then leaned over closer to his ear: "Please invite him to dinner tomorrow."

Mandari rolled his eyes heavenward and expelled a long breath. He could not think of a way out of this. "Where are you staying Professor?"

"In the Christian quarter at the home of a friend," the perspiring foreigner replied.

"Professor Kleinatz, no – I will call you 'Dutchman'. Come to my home tomorrow, and we'll discuss this further."

"Thank you, I am most honored." He bowed to Mandari then turned to Hura and bowed again; his long skinny legs belied a heavy torso under the parting coat.

News of the dinner invitation and the short notice infuriated Fatima. Throughout the past few months she had suffered in silent humiliation. Not only was Hura the second wife, allowed out of the harem in public with her husband, but outsiders saw her at the Hall of Justice. Sitting at her vanity Fatima patted the sagging skin of her cheeks with another layer of powder and talked to herself. "I heard he even asks her opinion." She winced in bitterness. "He never asks me to go to the Court.

"Now she speaks freely at the table – in her kaftan! See if I join them ever again downstairs for dinner. And she will learn to read. Well, I can read. I've been reading for years. He doesn't need another wife to advise him. I'm the one who knows the right people. It's my friends who came over with him to develop this, this backward mountain outpost. We don't need her Berbers. I'll get rid of her power. And as for that pink-faced

68

infidel, I'll tell my lord that Sultan Mulai Abdl Aziz lost his baraka because he allowed a Christian in his Court. Mandari always used to listen to me. We'll see. When Boabdil comes, I will be the one . . . and things will be put right. It's my city, not hers." Her chin began to tremble.

That evening through the closed door of her husband's study, Hura could hear Fatima arguing. High shrieks of "infidel" and "cursed" sounded the loudest. Later when it was quiet, Hura stood outside her husband's room and saw him peering closely at the accounts of the port in his ledger.

"Thank you for inviting him," she began. The room was lined with maps, weapons and mementos from his castle in al-Andalus.

"Fatima will not be joining us for dinner tomorrow," he said matter-of-factly. "And keep your distance." He splayed the short fingers of his hand in front of her. "Don't use your charms to blind me. I haven't made up my mind about him yet."

Hura quietly closed the door behind her and hurried to the kitchen. Without instructions from Fatima, she could freely plan the dinner. Excited by her very first dinner party, she asked Isabel what to serve. "What do you think foreigners eat?"

"Lamb, everyone likes lamb."

"But we have lamb all the time," Hura shook her head. "What about Christians? What do they eat?" she asked Miguel who banked the coals in the hearth next to her.

Miguel cocked his head. "I've heard terrible things. That they drink blood and even eat pigs. But I, myself, have never seen this."

"We must have lamb," insisted Isabel, "it will show our importance."

"I can have a lamb grilled in the souk and brought to us," offered Miguel.

They both seemed to know all about the invitation, Hura mused.

"All right. Isabel I want you to make couscous and roast chickens, and we should have pigeon pastilla covered with honey."

The idea of having an intellectual in their home, and a European at that, thrilled Hura. And she was going to learn to read! A sudden kick reminded her of the child she was carrying, the child that just weeks ago had been the most important event in her life.

Mandari sat stiffly at the dinner table in pressed military garb. He sported a royal insignia on his chest, a gold triple turreted castle on a blue field and silver crescent overhead. A heavy signet ring on his thumb displayed the same insignia. At the other end of the table Hura sat in her Friday kaftan with its bib of blue embroidery, her hair pulled back and tied with a rope of pearls. When Kleinatz arrived, Miguel announced him and seated him to the right of his master. The Dutchman seemed even taller and paler than she remembered, his huge shoes, decorated with silver buckles, clicked on the tiles as he approached.

"Welcome to our home, Dutchman. We did not greet you in the reception room, as is our custom, because I'm finding it hard to walk on damp days like this." Good breeding required him to say this, it was a small lie that allowed Mandari his position and dignity.

"I am honored at your invitation," Kleinatz responded in his classical Arabic. "I have brought you a gift, a token of my esteem." He pulled a tooled leather book whose cover was emblazoned with gold designs from his jacket pocket. "It is an early Koran. From Cairo, I believe." He handed it to his host with a small bow.

Before Mandari could react, Hura impetuously blurted: "Professor Kleinatz, will you teach me to read from this very book?"

Kleinatz looked to his host for a reaction, and seeing none, replied, "I would be honored."

Hura watched Kleinatz glance at the food on the table. His groomed eyebrows rose and fell several times. She wondered if he was accustomed to such bounty. The table setting before him was splendid. In the center, a young lamb knelt atop a huge platter of couscous, its legs neatly folded under, head lowered to the side as if only resting. The crisp, brown skin glistened with oil and fried almonds. There were steaming bowls of broth and cups of cool yogurt; plates of stacked bread, wedges of crisp, red chicken livers, flaky squares of pastillas, aromatic pickled fish, and a diced salad of cucumbers and tomatoes laced with small green fans of parsley.

"*Bismillah*," intoned Mandari as he broke a piece of bread, then cut off a large chunk of lamb leg with his table knife.

While her husband ate, Hura inquired: "What other languages do you speak?"

The Professor, it became evident, was fluent in more languages than Hura knew existed. And in response to Mandari's query if he knew the writings of Ibn Khaldun, he responded at great length about the *Muqaddimah*.

Mandari looked at Hura and yawned. He hadn't counted on a lecture.

"Actually I enjoy the writings of Ibn Battuta more." The Dutchman continued. "There are others, of course, who wrote good books – take the geographical dictionary of Yaqut, which I find so fascinating."

Hura ladled broth on the tajine in front of her and asked, "Did you read those books at the University, the one in Salamanca?"

"Yes, Madame, I did; and met many scholars. I even conferred with Abraham Zacuto, the great Hebrew astronomer who wrote his *Perpetual Almanach* at Salamanca. He was expelled in 1492 and now lives in

Portugal."

"Do you have other writings? Will these books be part of our library?" asked Mandari.

Kleinatz rubbed his chin and pondered the question.

Hura could feel her husband's growing annoyance with their guest; maybe even with her. She had to liven up their conversation or redirect it. Otherwise, the Professor would never be invited back. Noticing their guest wasn't eating, she spoke up before he could answer: "Please have some lamb, take the sweet eyes."

"Thank you, but I will have your salad and couscous. I am a vegetarian."

Hura saw her husband glance up from his plate to her then back to his food. "A what?" she asked.

"A vegetarian. I don't eat animals." He failed to conceal an air of superiority.

The side of Mandari's mouth twitched. The man was odd, different; this confirmed his decision to deny a work permit.

Hura laid down the strip of fish she was holding between thumb and forefinger. She inquired innocently: "Is this for your health, or the custom of your people?"

"It is neither, honorable lady, I do not believe in killing."

"But in Spain, I hear they eat animals, and they're Catholic . . . and you said you lived in Spain . . . what do you eat?"

"I eat fruits and grains and the products of animals. Holland, the Netherlands where I come from, is famous for its milk and cheese. And, I am a Protester, not Catholic."

"Catholics are barbarians." Mandari snorted. "They live in gloomy castles where light and air never enter and know nothing of literature or mathematics. Even a soldier like me knows more. Is that why you left Spain?" he asked, starting to gnaw on a lamb shank.

"Ya, that is one reason. And I follow the wisdom of that great epic, the *Thousand and One Nights*:

> *We trod the steps appointed for us: and the man whose steps*
> *are appointed must tread them. He whose death is decreed to*
> *take place in one land will not die in any land but that.*

The Dutchman's voice cracked. "I was forced to leave Flanders because Maximilian of Austria's grandson disregarded the rights and privileges of the Netherlands Charter. There is little tolerance for someone like me – but I heard in Tetouan my talents might be appreciated and my needs perhaps tolerated."

"We can use your talents. Tetouan needs a library." Hura understood none of this but encouraged him.

"And what *are* your needs?" Mandari eyed his guest and wondered about his wife's strange behavior. She seemed to welcome this misfit. He mustn't allow another man familiarity with her. He would put a stop to all this.

"My needs are simple: the freedom to say and do what I please and a place of learning where I can educate people."

"Nobody has complete freedom. Not here, not anywhere, to say and do whatever they wish." Mandari said coldly. "What do you have to say and do that's so special," he challenged.

"I have heard that it is not a crime for a man to be unmarried in the Rif and that the kif is plentiful."

Suddenly Mandari laughed and slapped the table with his palm. His fears were groundless. He understood. His honor was safe with a man such as this near his wife. The Professor might even be useful with his knowledge of languages and the courts of Spain and Portugal. He might know about their navies, their tactics. And a library wasn't such a bad idea.

"You, Dutchman, are just what I want. You will teach my wife to read and you may start my library."

With her husband's permission, Hura offered Professor Kleinatz lodging in the compound. The room was comfortable and convenient, and he had chafed at the curfew restrictions in the small Christian Quarter.

"It's worse than living in the mellah," he told Hura.

Spacious, but windowless, the room adjoined the service area near the laundry on the first floor. It smelled of mold, shot and salt. Mandari had used it for storage of gunpowder and munitions until his Captain of the Guard rebuilt the old kasbah. Now sacks of books and manuscripts which the professor had brought from Spain stacked the high walls.

The Professor soon settled into a routine: in the mornings after breakfast, he instructed Hura in Arabic, then gave her lessons to practice in the afternoon. After midday dinner, he taught her to read Spanish. He had never had such a determined student. After his short nap, he sat in on official audiences with Lord Mandari, softly giving advice in those matters that dealt with international affairs. In Spain, Mandari had suffered much from foreign threat and conflict: Castile against Aragon, Spain against Portugal, Christian against Muslim. Of other rivalries he knew little and had patience for none. When Kleinatz reminded him of previous invasions of North Africa and attempted to kindle concern for potential attacks on Tetouan, Mandari always confronted him with: "Don't bother me with ancient history."

The city bustled everywhere with construction. With the constant activity in his compound and the rebuilding of the city walls, he didn't seem to notice that Fatima had retreated to her suite. She seldom joined them downstairs now for meals, certainly never when the infidel was present. But Hura noticed. Once, Hura ordered Isabel to take her a specially prepared dinner. Isabel hastened to obey but soon returned splattered hair to waist with food.

Two weeks later, Fatima brought a strange woman to the house and asked Hura to join them in the sitting room upstairs. "She's a 'holy woman' who has come to talk to you about your condition. As the elder wife it's my responsibility to make sure your birthing is safe."

The old woman, swathed in white cotton from head to toe, had yellow, curled fingernails. Her eyes rolled back when she spoke and lapsed into strange tongues that Fatima translated. Hura had the feeling she was partaking in some strange ritual. The woman bestowed upon her sacks of dried potions, vials of putrid smelling liquids and jars of aromatic oils. Hura listened to the complex instructions, smiled and promised to take the treatments.

Later that evening Afaf brought her supper and pointed to the jars. "What are these?" she asked with the abruptness of a young girl.

"They're for my health. Fatima brought a woman to see me today who said she was trained at the court in Fes."

"Trained in what?" Afaf picked up and sniffed a jar.

"Don't touch those!" Hura yelled.

Afaf put down the jar and sulked.

"They don't smell of life, they smell like death." Hura pointed to a jar. "That powder smells like cherry pits, and this one of elderberry – that one over there must be bloodroot and I'm not sure about the others."

"How do you know these things, from your mother?" Afaf's eyes bulged in wonder.

"No, I never knew my mother, she died when I was very young. My aunt Henati taught me about healing plants and herbs, that's how I recognize some of them. They're all deadly if you take too much."

"Then, mistress, you mustn't take them!"

"Yes, yes, I know. But I must find out for sure."

Afaf clapped her hands. "I know, I'll feed the cats. Isabel keeps cats in the laundry rooms next to the kitchen. To keep the rats away." She giggled. "It'll be funny if all the cats in the neighborhood die."

"Not funny for the cats! You can't do that, I like those cats and I like playing with their kittens every spring. Anyway, what do I do if I'm right!"

"We'll have lots of rats!" Afaf giggled again.

"No, we'll have to find another way."

Late that evening, Afaf sneaked down to the kitchen, took yogurt from the pantry, mixed two of the powders in it then stirred another powder in a cup of olive oil. She called the cats. It wasn't easy to catch them; they were wild and cautious even when hungry. Afaf finally cornered a big calico and shut it in the laundry room. After peeking in to see it hungrily devour the yogurt, she rubbed the smelly oil on the cat's fur.

The next morning the poor calico lay under the wash table, the skin on his side raw. Only strings of hair remained on his once proud coat.

"You were right, mistress." Afaf's large brown eyes stared at the floor. She put Hura's breakfast tray down on her bed and stood motionless.

"Right about what?"

Afaf hesitated. She didn't know which was worse, disobeying her mistress or telling her the bad news.

"Afaf, look at me." Hura's voice sharpened.

Afaf, eyes lowered, confessed her disobedience and the result. Hura, sadness in her voice, thanked Afaf for saving her life and instructed her to bury the cat in the patio near the fountain. At the same time, she pondered what to do next. She waddled around the small room thinking Fatima would never admit her guilt and she wondered if, or when, Fatima would try to kill her again. How could she tell her husband? Would he believe a second wife?

The next morning Afaf ran to Hura in the hammam and bubbled with gossip. "Mistress, I couldn't wait to tell you about Leila. Remember her? She used to come on the same day as you. From a good family . . . remember she wore that amber ring? But now, she's dead." Afaf began to soap her mistress.

Hura feigned interest. Her maid seemed to have big ears like a hare.

"I heard for some time she was meeting a young man, secretly. Now I know the whole story."

Hura perked up. "How did she do that? Was she allowed out alone?"

"Well," Afaf warmed to the gossip, "it started when she saw him from her roof. He lived across the street and had been watching her for a long time from his roof. Soon he stationed himself by the street to the hammam and when she walked by he would lift his eyes to heaven then move his hand to embrace the whole horizon telling her: 'Thou art everything to me. He caressed her with tender words like 'my perfumed couch', 'my golden butter', and for some time they played by making signs. And would you believe she responded by lifting the hem of her kaftan or waving her kerchief. She fell more and more in love. Ah, love," Afaf sighed.

A knot of women gathered around them eager to hear the story and Afaf spoke louder. Hura turned over and closed her eyes.

"Through his sister he found out the names of the women who had access to her house, and those kaouadas who roamed the quarter bringing goods and trinkets to houses to sell. He bribed one of those old women. She took a message to Leila and as the servants admired all those lovely things which they could never own – the veils, cloth, ointments and perfumes – and the mistress of the house fingered the silks, the woman whispered his message."

The women in the bath crowded closer, caught up in the tale.

"Leila sent a message back to him – to come to her house. The following midnight she would be behind the door and he needed only to say his name, and she would open it. So he came and knocked and she let him into her room."

"Into her room?" One of the women cried.

"Did her father find out?" Another voice rose through the steam.

"Yes," Afaf gushed. "Her father told him to make an offer of marriage and to pay the *sadecq,* the bride price."

All the women sighed in relief; Afaf knew how to tell a story, such a happy ending.

"But that's not the end."

A chorus of voices responded. "Tell us."

"The young man refused. He said he wasn't the first and that she cast a spell on him. He didn't even want her for free – without paying the *sadecq.*"

The women gasped, remembering they had seen her just a week before.

Hura sat up. "What happened to her?"

"I heard that her brother ordered her to go with him to the country, up the mountains."

"Did she go?" asked a bather.

"She didn't try to avoid her fate. She must have known."

"She didn't try to escape?" Hura asked.

"No, they found her body in a ditch. Her throat was cut."

The other women clucked their tongues and one by one slipped into the hot mist.

TEN

Through the gray water between ships and shore, two eastbound Portuguese warships plowed foaming furrows.

Garbed in a doublet of Italian blue velvet, young Captain Fernao Dias fingered the basket hilt of his Toledo sword and paced the quarterdeck of his galleon, the 300 ton *Donna Louisa*. He ignored the numerous caravels flying various flags which transported much of the known world's commerce through the Straits of Gibraltar. A larger vision of conquest colored every moment's thought.

He stood wide-legged on his pitching vessel and reviewed his orders to Captain Antonio Gomez, six ship's length behind. It rankled him that Gomez had raised his gray-flecked eyebrows. He thought this a rogue's venture. What else could you expect from someone so close to retirement .. and that one had no uncle, an Admiral favored at Court. His own uncle, an Admiral, had commanded 477 vessels and seized four important pirate ports on the Atlantic in 1471.

After passing Portuguese Tangier, Dias, fretful because he must make do with too few forces, decided to hold one last drill. Alongside the mate on the quarterdeck, he watched the bosun send all hands aloft to get in courses on the square-rigged fore and main masts. Seamen unlaced the two bonnet sails, reefed the top sail, double reefed the mainsails and spritsail hanging low over the bow, and then shook them out again. The simple triangular sail, rigged from an angled yard on the mizzen mast, was furled, unfurled and furled again.

By the third trial the chants of the crewmen at their straining halyards became ragged. They no longer raced hand over hand up the shrouds. Dias knew the seamen thought the drill too hard and useless. He heard cursing. His cheeks colored, his spine stiffened. He said to the mate, "Mr. Barros, order another drill, this time for the topmen only."

The mate's eyes hardened. After three sloppy drills this was not the solution. But their performance reflected badly on him. He shouted: "Topmen . . . Aloft!" The bosun repeated the order.

One seaman, slow to climb the shrouds, was the last to complete the exercise. His end of the furled topsail flapped loosely.

"I'll make an example of that man," Dias snapped thin-lipped to the mate.

"Peres, Captain? How many lashes?"

"Mr. Barros, have the bosun clove-hitch Peres to the main mast. Then pipe all hands to witness his punishment."

With the sullen crew assembled and gazing at the officers and the bosun, whip in hand, the mate repeated, "Sir, how many lashes?"

For answer, Captain Dias raised his hand for silence. When the crew quieted, he said in a crisp voice, "That man was slow to obey an order. That man did not do as ordered. That man is willful or hard of hearing. I, myself, shall provide the remedy."

Rigid in bearing and expression, Dias strode to the bound seaman by the mast. The crew parted, then jostled for position to see. The bosun held the lash and looked at him in confusion. The topman cringed in fear. Captain Dias snapped, "Bosun, give me your sheath knife."

Peres, his eyes following the knife, clenched his teeth to stop their chattering.

Dias said to the seaman in a voice loud enough for all to hear, "I do this not as punishment but to improve your hearing." Then he grasped the seaman's earlobe by its large loop earring.

Peres tried to jerk his head away.

"Be still you fool or you'll lose the whole ear." The knife sliced through above the lobe. The seaman shrieked. Blood gushed and ran down his neck and shoulder, splattering on the deck.

In the hush that followed, Dias, twirling the lobe by its earring, threw it overboard. He casually wiped the bloody blade on the topman's jersey and returned it to the wide-eyed bosun.

And so it went from the stern to the forecastle with Dias timing the alacrity of execution, noting more small irregularities and barking orders to Barros for other severe punishment. But he found little on the condition of his cannon or the military performance of marine Lieutenant Pacheco to criticize. The stern castle mounted a pair of obsolete swivel guns and below it on the gun deck were ten cast iron cannon that never were fired in gunnery practice because they likely would crack or blow apart.

In the waist embrasures were four bronze thirty-two pound cannon whose gunners polished their royal crests sparkling bright. With Pacheco counting in cadence, Dias timed the amidships gun crews that ran out the cannon and coupled the train-tackles. These he ordered fired. He timed the amount of shot per drum beat per man that a broadside of stone or iron balls could produce. He relished the roar and recoil of these monsters that rocked his vessel.

Now at the companionway, Dias knew he had no choice but to go below. Nostrils quivering, he motioned 'follow me' to Barros. At the bottom of the ladder, in the confined space, the stench enveloped Dias like a heavy cloak and the beating drum below deck was deafening. Deep-set eyes bulging, adjusting to the semi-darkness, he studied the scene: ninety criminals and captive Moors chained six to a bench, three to a side, laboring in unison. A burly seaman with a coiled lash turned in surprise, then with hand to cap came to stand before his Captain and First Mate.

"Faster," Dias commanded.

The lash crackled. The drum cadence increased. Grasping heavy oars, with the left foot on the floor and the right leg bent to the bench in front, the oarsmen pressed down on the oars and bent forward toward the stern, their arms stretched high over the backs of the bent rowers in front, then heaved their bodies backward. The blades, with their long sweeps, scooped the water. Over and over the same rhythm: body forward, arms low, leg straightened, arms high, body back. Empty eyed, the men were exhausted.

"Resume pace."

At the top of the ladder, handkerchief to nose, Dias said, "Mr. Barros, you will sweeten the smell from below. Burn Venetian scented oil on the deck afore my cabin." Then he strode aft.

ELEVEN

"Allah-u-Akhbar! God is . . ."

In mid-sentence the muezzin's morning call was muffled by the boom of cannon. A pall of black smoke floated from the two vessels that had entered the harbor.

The port Customs building erupted in smoke, stones, and splinters. Fragments flew in the air from the broadside impact of the heavy iron balls and the explosion echoed up the mountain. Visible sheets of flame erupting from the galleons jarred Tetouan into panic. A volley of grapeshot splattered the blood and flesh of worshipers against the walls of the nearby mosque. A final salvo butchered fleeing guards and merchants. Then the cannon on the warships rolled back from their gun ports. They could not be elevated any higher nor did they have the range capability to reach the walled new city higher up the hill. Shortly after firing, the deep draft vessels tied up at the only jetty near the decimated Customs House. Disciplined Portuguese marines slid down ropes and formed into two attack units.

Mandari had been signing proclamations alone in his office. War-seasoned, he quickly buckled on his battle-worn scimitar, ran to the house and shouted up to the harem.

"Hura! Fatima! Get out. Get out! Run to the kasbah. To the prison."

He waited until he saw Hura appear at the balcony railing then yelled over his shoulder, "You'll be safe there." He raced across the courtyard to the guardhouse where Captain Abdul rousted the troops in ragged order. "To the wall!" Mandari roared, "the river side!"

Afaf, half dressed and still bleary eyed, scurried to her mistress. "What's going on?"

"Get dressed, come with me," Hura ordered. "Fast."

Hura dashed downstairs to the front door, then stopped, turned, ran back up the stairs and along the hall to Fatima's bedchamber. Banging on the door, she shouted: "Fatima, Hurry! We're going to the kasbah. We're not safe here."

When Fatima did not respond, Hura pushed the door open and parted the curtains. Fatima lay propped up on pillows in her bed. Her lips curled with contempt. "In Granada, we had these attacks all the time. This one will go away. Leave me."

Hura stared wide-eyed in disbelief. "You must come. Your husband ordered it. Here, I'll help you."

Fatima hissed, "I said leave me alone!"

Uncertain, Hura hesitated, then hurried downstairs. Just as she got to the outer door she stopped again. The Professor! She ran down the hall to the guest bedchamber and knocked on the door. There was no answer, not even a sound. She pounded it again, paused, swung the door open and saw him. Naked and terrified, he crouched in a corner alongside his bed.

Hastily turning her back, she said: "When you're dressed, run to the kasbah, up on the hill. You'll be safe there. Hurry." Without waiting for an answer, she ran out.

Captain Abdul reported to his Commander, Lord Mandari, who stood on the rubble of the unfinished ramparts that faced the port. Down the hill women carrying their children, and men supporting elderly parents all ran, limped, struggled in panic to escape the attackers and reach the fortress or the safety of the mountains.

"I've stationed all my men on this side," the Captain gestured to the unfinished wall in front of him. "The enemy will see how vulnerable it is."

Mandari absently acknowledged, "Yes, I saw them." He thought to himself: I made a mistake. Why did I complete the mountain sides first? He looked in disgust at the useless piles of cut stone behind him waiting for final construction of the south wall.

Captain Abdul seemed to read his superior's mind. "We expected tribesmen, not Spanish."

"The two galleons fly Portuguese flags, not Spanish. Look at the pennon on the larger vessel. It's a crest. Do you see the sparkle of uniform buttons? Marines. We are honored to receive an important enemy." His tone had no humor in it.

A cloud of white began to rise and mingle with the uphill-drifting pall of black smoke from the vessels. Flames spurted from the houses, roaring roof to roof; blazing tents incinerated their contents.

Mandari's voice rose in anger. "They're coming across the plain burning my city to the ground. Slaughtering anyone in their path. Abdul, get back to the gates. Close them!"

"Sidi, what about all these people?"

"Close the gates, Captain." Mandari's eyes remained focused on the advancing troops. "We're in for a siege. Thanks be to Allah, they're marines and don't have the field artillery to breach these walls. Such as they are," he added with a grimace.

Captain Abdul nodded. He, like most of the other soldiers now defending Tetouan, had been with Sidi Mandari at Piñar in Spain. There they held off Francisco de Bobadilla in a siege no one thought could last all of forty two days. They surrendered only when reinforcements promised by Boabdil, King of the fiefdom of Granada, never arrived. Abdul's loyalty had long ago been forged in the fire of his leader's prowess and courage.

Climbing the ladder to the top of a finished segment of the wall, Mandari studied the plain below. It had become a swarm of marines running uphill – but they were still far off. When Abdul returned he asked, "How many do you think?"

"More than a hundred, almost two hundred. Carrying pikes and cutlasses."

"A few with matchlocks; some with ladders too," Mandari added.

"Do you want the cavalry?"

"Wait. Our archers up here have the advantage and two hundred isn't that many. They must have a battle plan. We'll know soon."

"Look." Abdul pointed to his right. "They're starting to circle."

"Twenty or twenty-five men. They can't do much. Our odds at this wall are better now."

"Shall I post a few men to track them from above?"

"No." Mandari clenched his teeth. "Look where those pig-eaters are heading. Those dogs." He waved his arm. "The pens. They're going to free my Christian prisoners. That's what this invasion is all about."

Mandari chewed his lips in thought. "Forget the prisoners for now. It's the medina we must save. Yes, the odds are better against that other detachment, the main one headed here. Take whatever cavalry you can find. Mount up and charge down the hill."

With Mandari shouting encouragement, Abdul and seventy of his most experienced horsemen galloped through the gate's tall opening, fanned out and dashed headlong down the hill, screaming "*Allah-u-Akbar!*"

The ferocious, unstoppable avalanche of cavalry decimated the first wave of marines. The other ranks halted their advance, stood pikes and cutlasses at the ready. The few marines armed with matchlock rifles fired wildly at the fast moving targets. The well-armed marines on foot faltered before the swift lunge of long lances and slashing scimitars. Passing through the line of marines the turbaned warriors pulled their horses up short then wheeled and just as rapidly burst back again through the ranks, whacking with bloodied weapons. Only a half-dozen horses returned with empty saddles. The bodies of their riders lay on the plain, speared on pikes.

Just as Mandari ordered an aide to close the gate behind his cavalry, an explosion shook the ground. He realized immediately what had happened and his fists clenched in anger. "The tunnel door! They've blown the door to the pens."

81

Over the noise and confusion of milling warriors, Mandari shouted to Abdul, "Stay here. Guard the wall." Then he ordered the ten nearest men: "Follow me!"

Running through the Souk el Hots on his way up to the compound, he heard a jumble of noises including shrieks of joy from stampeding Christian prisoners. Several marines emerged from the open gate of the prison.

Mandari pointed at his men: "You, you . . . and you run to that door. Kill anyone coming out." In mid-stride his scimitar arm swept an arc ending at the midsection of a buttoned uniform. The scream of agony lasted only a moment before the marine fell.

Prodded by curiosity, Hura opened the door of the thick-walled kasbah, peeked out and listened to the tumult of shouts in the courtyard outside. Kleinatz cringed in a corner of the ground floor prison, talking to himself.

"Shush, Professor, I want to listen. Everything will be – "

"Who's here. Show yourself." A tall uniformed soldier holding a naked cutlass approached warily.

Hura's open hand flashed to his face but the marine caught her wrist in a vise-like grip. "Not you. I don't kill women. I mean prisoners, guards." He spun around to face the noise behind him.

"I'm here," Mandari answered and followed the soldier who retreated into the prison.

Both seasoned swordsmen – Mandari who had fought many battles and the soldier, young and fit – the two combatants circled, looking for an opening, assessing the other. Each eyed the other's weapon. The intruder made the first feint followed by a slashing attack. Much taller than Mandari, he had a longer reach.

Mandari parried, then backed off. "Ah, a worthy opponent. Tell me your name before I kill you."

"Pacheco, Lieutenant Pacheco," the young officer grunted and attacked again.

Now the two dueled in earnest, oblivious to the shouting and screaming outside, or to Hura, fists clenched and in the shadows with Afaf behind her, or to the Savant cowering against the far wall.

Mandari drew first blood with a stinging slice to the Lieutenant's left shoulder.

Pacheco gritted his teeth, made no sound. Although his arm hung at his side, the younger man kept coming. His cutlass clashed against the scimitar again and again.

"My troops should be through your gate by now, you haven't a chance," the Lieutenant shouted.

Hura's hand covered her mouth. She saw Mandari slowing down, tiring. The next time he locked swords then pushed apart, he faltered.

With a quick movement, the tip of Pacheco's cutlass sliced Mandari across his right eyebrow and down his cheek. Blood from the gash streamed into his eyes.

"I can't see!" Mandari screamed and began to career around the chamber, swinging his scimitar in the air.

Wary of Mandari's flailing weapon, the lieutenant dodged and circled, seeking the right moment for the kill.

Hura watched horrified then shouted to Kleinatz, "The chains by the wall. The shackles."

The Savant stared at her. In the instant, the fire in her eyes scorched him to action. Kleinatz stooped, hefted one of the chains.

Pacheco raised his cutlass.

Kleinatz ran behind the Lieutenant and crashed the heavy shackle against his head.

Pacheco's weapon dropped. He crumpled to the dirt floor.

"Kill him. Kill him." Hura screamed.

Kleinatz froze. Then his entire body shook and trembled.

"What's happening?" Mandari roared.

Hura bent and ran under Mandari's whirling scimitar, grabbed the Lieutenant's fallen sword from the floor. Leaning over the Lieutenant, who was struggling to get up, she drove it into his stomach.

The lieutenant screamed once before he died.

For a moment, Hura stood aghast. Then she ran to Mandari, now leaning against the wall wiping blood from his eyes.

"Husband, stay still," she said to identify herself as she tore a strip from her skirt and wound it around his head. Over her shoulder she called out, "Professor, cut off his head. Take it to the wall and stick it on a pike."

The Savant's mouth fell open without sound. He bent double and vomited. Hura turned and saw him. Anger turned to determination. She stooped to pick up her husband's scimitar, held it high, then hacked and chopped until the cracking, crushing sounds stopped and the head rolled free of its last shred of flesh. Hura lifted it out of the dirt, dangled the heavy mass by its ponytail and ran out of the kasbah.

At the wall, she called for Captain Abdul.

A wounded warrior answered, "He's dead, My Lady, stabbed defending the pens."

Rushing to a ladder near the gate, she climbed to the top of the high wall and stood there defiantly. In the distance, she made out the prisoners fleeing toward the warships. She jammed the head on a pike for all the marines to see. Somewhere a fife sounded recall. The remaining soldiers fled to the ships.

Now certain the enemy was leaving, Hura began backing down the ladder. Half way, her foot slipped on a rung and she fell, landing face down. A sharp pain curled her in a fetal position. She rose to her knees; the pain held her belly in its tight grip. Then, just as suddenly, the pain stopped. She'd never had cramps like this. She struggled to her feet again. It couldn't be the baby; she was only five months pregnant. Her skirt clung to wet legs and she pulled it free, only to have it stick again.

A fine mess I've made of myself – she looked at her hands, covered with blood. As she slowly started back to the kasbah, the pain came again. This time it was more intense and she fell to her side on the ground, gasping for air. When the pain subsided, she lay still, afraid to get up.

Wave after wave of contractions came and went. She tried to relax and redirect the cramps, but her body was beyond control. Finally she crawled to the wall and propped herself up against it, legs spread in front of her. The contractions grew more painful and more frequent. When the last contraction came she clenched her teeth, pushed her palms flat on the ground and let out a howl as the baby's head emerged.

"*Yummah!* Mama." She lay in the dirt drifting in and out of consciousness. To those who passed by, she was just another victim of the fighting.

"There she is!" Afaf screamed and ran to her mistress. "Oh, Allah, please let her be alive."

Kleinatz came stumbling behind her, tripping over his huge feet. He stopped abruptly when he saw the blood. Hura stirred, turned her head toward the girl, then fainted.

"She's alive. Professor, help me. Take her to the house."

"I can't . . . all that blood." Kleinatz turned toward the wall and began to retch again.

"You have to," Afaf shouted at his back. "I can't lift her." As Afaf gathered up Hura's skirt, she felt the outline of the baby between her legs, lifted her skirt and saw the lifeless form. "May Allah have mercy," she mumbled and wrapped the skirt tightly around Hura's legs again to conceal it.

Miguel ran toward them. Soldiers were already in the courtyard guarding the compound when they arrived. "Take her to the dining room," Miguel ordered. "The second floor is damaged. I'll get Isabel."

Afaf held Hura's skirt tighter as they laid her down on the long table.

Kleinatz asked Miguel in the doorway: "Did Mandari make it back safely?"

"The soldiers have him propped against the kasbah wall."

The Professor found Mandari, led him by his elbow to his chambers and sat him on a chair next to his bed, trying to be helpful but making sure no blood stained his clothes.

Mandari struggled to regain his composure. "Where is everyone? Is everyone safe?"

"Hura was with me. I don't know where Miguel, Isabel and Fatima are, but your soldiers have routed the invaders and the fighting has stopped." Kleinatz backed away in search of a towel for Mandari's face.

"Yes, yes, I sent them to the mosque . . . have they returned?"

Kleinatz saw no towels by the wash stand, pulled his handkerchief from his vest, and offered it. "No, only Hura and I are here."

"Go find out! Don't just stand there. Bring my Captain here! I need to know what's going on. Now!" Mandari barked orders as if the Professor was one of his soldiers.

Already unsteady on his feet from the trauma of the day's events, Kleinatz turned to go, nearly losing his balance.

They heard loud voices coming from the front hallway toward them. "That's Miguel, he is back. Send him to me." Mandari waved the now bloodied handkerchief in front of him.

Miguel rushed to his master's side and seeing the freshly clotted blood on his face, immediately called for his wife: "Isabel, come here! Come here now! Bring cloths, aloe, soap and water."

"Don't fuss over me, I'm fine." Mandari waved the handkerchief again. "Just get this blood out of my eyes so I can see again."

The Professor and Miguel looked at each other; they knew it wasn't the blood that clouded his vision.

Miguel called to the guard at the front door, "Have you seen Isabel?"

"She went to the second floor."

Miguel climbed the stairs and turned in the hallway toward the back of the house. Dust from shattered stone and stucco hung in the air and littered the floor. Isabel's footprints exposed the colored tiles of the hallway. He followed them to the jumble of stone and wood fragments near where Fatima's room had been.

Above him the roof was gone and huge timbers angled downward, blocking his passage. He stood for a moment, eyeing the destruction, then saw his wife on her hands and knees trying to move a large chunk of roofing out of the way.

"Isabel. What are you doing? It's not safe up here. Come back down. You can't get through, it's too dangerous." He pulled her away.

"She's in there, I know it. I have to save her," Isabel wailed, the scraped palms of her hands bleeding.

"I'll get soldiers. They'll clear the way. Come. Sidi Mandari needs you. Go to him."

Numb with fear that her mistress remained trapped in her room under all that rubble, Isabel went through the motions of cleaning herself. Then she filled three large cauldrons with water to boil in the fireplace and gathered bed linens to tear for bandages, hoping they wouldn't be needed for shrouds. All the while, she kept one bleary eye on the sweating soldiers as they carried basket after basket of debris down the stairs and out the door. A layer of fine white dust clung to everything and gave an eerie, ghostly pall to the solemn faces of the soldiers.

Late that evening, Miguel came to her with sadness in his eyes. "They found her. The wall came down on her, she was lying on her bed. The explosion caved in that side of the house."

Isabel began to sob. "Why? Why didn't she leave . . . why didn't you check. You should have made sure she was safe."

Miguel tried to comfort her. She pushed him away.

"It's the will of Allah," he said softly. "But," he raised his voice, "it's the living you have to care for now. I've arranged for the burial. I need sheets to wrap her in. Get them. I'll tell Sidi Mandari."

"Wait." Her weeping eyes sought his. "The baby. The baby's dead. A miscarriage. Afaf is with Hura. She's burning up. Tell him this, too."

"May Allah have mercy! My poor master."

That night, while Mandari mourned his son and wife, he wrestled with the outrage of the invasion. He tried not to think about his eyes.

Hura feverishly tossed and turned in her bed, the dead baby's placenta still attached between her legs.

The sorrow of so many others unleashed long repressed memories for Kleinatz. He tried to stretch out on his pallet and finally took his blanket to the floor. He relived his scandal and disgrace in the small town which had given his father, who served as pastor, so much anguish. He lit a candle and fumbled through his boxes for a book, any book, and grabbed one on armament, the types and sizes of Portuguese cannon.

Isabel relived the discovery of her dead mistress and muffled her sobs through her gnarled, scabbed hands.

Miguel's body ached. He had arranged for a body washer and grave digger and had even helped dig the grave. Lucky to find space in the cemetery, he buried Fatima with only stones marking the site.

Afaf kept wiping her hands over and over on her dress, as if to clean the dead baby off them. She wished her father were here with her. She hadn't heard a word from him in months. He must be dead.

For a day and a half Hura lay on her back, delirious with high fever. Afaf stayed at her side, changing towels soaked with cold henna-water as fast as Hura's brow heated them.

Mandari called in a midwife, then stationed a holy man at the bottom of the stairs to recite appropriate passages of the Koran.

"Afaf, you must rest. Here, let me do that." Isabel reached over and took the towel. "Go get some food from the kitchen and sleep. I'll call you if there's any change."

Afaf hesitated. She didn't know whom to trust. What if Isabel had helped Fatima with that poison? But how could she refuse the order? Quickly she ran to find Kleinatz and pounded on his door.

"Professor, Professor. It's Afaf. I need your help." She heard noises inside the room.

Kleinatz cracked the heavy door open and peered out.

"It's Mistress Hura, I fear for her. She needs you."

"What is happening?" He opened the door wider.

"She's in her room. You're a doctor, no?"

"No . . . but I am trained in the art."

Afaf lied in desperation. "She's calling for you."

"All right. Tell her I will be there. Right away."

Afaf raced back to the hallway, barely avoiding the seated holy man and his candles and jars of smoking incense. She waited at the stairs for Kleinatz and as they arrived at Hura's door they saw Isabel standing beside the bed, a knife in one hand.

"What are you doing!" Afaf cried.

Isabel jerked around to face them. "I want to cut the cord. It's putrid. Its poisons are killing her."

"You want to kill her. That's what you're doing."

"Afaf, move away." Kleinatz pushed past her and into the room. "You say she still keeps the cord?"

"Yes, Professor."

"Afaf, get more towels and hot water," Kleinatz ordered, placed his hands on the chemise covering Hura's belly and began to knead, grabbing and pushing the loose skin. He kept his eyes focused on her face, away from the bloody cord.

Afaf hurried back in time to see Isabel holding a mass of glistening tissue and Kleinatz slumped at the end of the bed, staring at the floor.

"Give me the towels," Isabel demanded.

"What happened? How is she?"

Kleinatz answered in monotone: "The placenta came out. She's losing blood. Now we wait and see."

87

There was silence in the room.

"Why didn't the midwife do anything before?" Kleinatz asked Isabel. "She should have known."

Isabel sighed. "She said it was the will of God."

"Religion," Kleinatz snorted. "When will we be free from the darkness? In the name of religion we kill and maim and enslave, our eyes blind to reason and science." He got up and stomped out of the room in disgust.

Isabel's unsteady voice broke another long silence. "You can sleep now. There's nothing more to do."

This time Afaf trusted her.

The next day everyone said it was a miracle. Hura sipped chicken broth and her fever had abated. Afaf washed and dressed her, fussing over her slightest movement. By the second day Hura ate by herself and walked around her room. But while she ate and gained strength, she didn't speak. She ignored questions and pleadings. Afaf didn't know if she couldn't hear or just wouldn't respond.

Hura's pain was gone. In its wake was an emptiness, a nothingness. Days passed. She saw and heard others around her, watched them come and go, but they said nothing and did nothing of interest to her. Nights were worse. Alone in her room, listless, she sat cross-legged, on her bed and stared at the wall, the furniture, the wardrobe, until her legs were numb and lost their feeling. Then she would stretch. The sudden rush of sensation, like thousands of pins and needles, kept her body feeling alive. But her soul carried the weight of her baby.

She could hear Afaf, and even wanted her there. Afaf, so full of energy and smiles and concern. Afaf, who babbled on about everything. Loyal Afaf.

"Mistress, they've opened up the hammam again. It wasn't damaged, but wood to burn is scarce. You should go today. Isabel says the vapors will be good for you."

Hura found herself nodding.

"We'll come to take you."

After lunch, Hura lay on the tiled bench with steam swirling around her while Afaf massaged her back with her long brown fingers. The ghassoul formed a thick paste on her skin that only hot water could melt.

Afaf bent down close to Hura's ear and whispered, "Mistress, it was a boy. A perfect, tiny boy."

Hura squinched her eyes tight. The familiar rush of sorrow engulfed her again. "I know. What did you do with him?"

"When everyone was asleep Isabel and I washed and wrapped him. We said a prayer and buried him in our courtyard, near the fountain."

"Does my husband know?"

"Yes."

Tears escaped Hura's eyes and fell on the bench mingling with the fragrant soap. Her body tensed. Hotter than steam in the chamber was an inner fire of resolve that consumed her soul. Yes, she would have another child. And yes, she would never again allow invaders to destroy Tetouan. When her husband recovered his eyesight, she would help him gain allies to repel all Europeans.

TWELVE

Hura struggled to comb her wet hair free of tangles. My life is a mess. Like my hair, she thought. When Afaf arrived and tried to help, Hura waved her aside.

"Sit over there, on my bed," she motioned. "What is happening, what have I missed? You hear everything. Tell me. How is my husband? What is he doing – and the city, how much was destroyed – what happened to the invaders, they were Portuguese, right?"

Afaf plunked herself down. "Mistress, you should know that Sidi Mandari moved out. He's in the house next door, right by the entrance to the courtyard. He's in the first room. Miguel said the quarters are small and it's simple. But he can sleep and hold Council all in one room."

Hura lowered her comb.

"And his sight? That's the most important – "

"Isabel bandaged him. He looks like his turban slipped down." Afaf almost giggled then thought the better of it.

"Oh, mistress, there's a new officer here." She looked away shyly. "He's a lieutenant and, and he's so handsome. His name is Hisham and he's helping us with the new roof. And he's not married." This time her lips did part in a broad grin.

"The city, you ninny. Be serious. What about our city? Our people?"

Chastised, for the moment, Afaf answered, "I haven't been outside the wall but Isabel told me the pottery workshop burned down. What will we do now?"

Exasperated, Hura threw the comb down, wheeled to glare at Afaf and snapped, "Buy dishes from Fes, that's what. Enough, I'm going to my husband's apartment."

Still weak, her gait slowed as she crossed the courtyard to her husband's new quarters. After dismissing the guards outside, she took a deep breath, entered and said softly: "This is Hura, your faithful wife. May I speak with you, honored husband?"

Mandari had slept little. Now he sat up straight behind his desk in the folding chair he had kept from his campaign days in Spain. "You needn't be so formal. I have nothing but time." Layers of white cotton bandage encircled his head. Through the gaps, tufts of gray hair stuck out at odd angles like a large scouring brush.

"I don't deserve your kindness," she began. "I've disappointed your hopes for a son. And I haven't properly given you condolences, nor shared your sorrow on the death of Fatima."

"Come closer, my dear. Beside me. You must know by now that death is but a great freedom." His words confused her. She hesitated, then sat down. Freedom, to her, was something entirely different.

Dry-eyed, with tight lips, she told him everything – about Kleinatz, the kasbah, the head of the Portuguese Lieutenant and the baby.

At first, he said nothing. She decided either he knew about everything or he didn't want to talk about their shared sorrow or the fate of Lieutenant Pacheco.

She fidgeted on the chair alongside his desk until he spoke: "You will join us in the mornings for Council meetings."

She rushed to him and kissed his hand.

A day later Mandari roused himself enough to administer the city. He permitted only Hura, his Ministers, the Professor, and Lieutenant Hisham to attend Council in his quarters. As he had on the battlefields in Spain, he demanded reports on casualties and damage.

Hura tried not to stare at his eyes. Yesterday Isabel had told her that her husband insisted his bandages be removed. It seemed he remained silent while Miguel cut the layers away, then afterward he asked to be alone. Miguel didn't know if he could see.

The Lieutenant's handsome, square face sobered to give his report. At least half of Tetouan was in ruins. Soldiers had been stationed at the markets; he had only a few reports of looting there.

Hura ground her teeth but didn't flinch as he reported that his troops still picked up bodies for burial. Earlier there had been extensive looting of houses; homeless children had been brought to the madressa where they could be cared for.

She broke in and addressed her husband: "We need to set up kitchens for the wounded and orphans. I'll supervise the work."

Mandari held up his hand. Everyone paused. "You will do no such thing. You may concern yourself with our women, however."

Angered, Hura slumped down in her chair.

The Lieutenant reacted and turned to Mandari. "Excellency, there's no food for these people. How will we feed them?"

Still upset with her husband, Hura's voice rose in response, "Lieutenant, you said earlier the barracks near the kasbah weren't destroyed. What about their storehouses? Their kitchens? Use the soldiers' food!" This time Hura looked directly into her husband's eyes. Could he see, she wondered? Didn't he want her help?

Mandari raised his hand again for silence. "Lieutenant, continue."

"Sidi, your soldiers still clear the streets of bodies. They had to dig mass graves, there were so many. You said not to collect burial tax, so we're only collecting it from the Jews. The mosque, set up for the wounded, is filled to capacity. The madressa has orphans stacked like firewood. The fires in the city are contained and are slowly burning out. Your troops are loyal and keeping good order, Sire . . . I am proud to be in your service."

"Stay with the problems," Mandari's gravelly voice directed him.

"Yes," Hura echoed, "What do we need to do now?"

Hisham accepted their rebukes and questions with a half-bow. "Sidi, we have real problems outside the walled city, that's the army's concern. Hundreds, maybe thousands of people were killed and everything from the wall to the river was burned or destroyed. Families can't bury their dead, the corpses just lie there, stinking. We can't let survivors in, we have enough problems ourselves. Your soldiers screen everyone at the gate. Only our residents get in."

Hura wondered how long it would be before riots began.

When Mandari began to question Hisham about minor details of the raid and the Portuguese tactics, Hura's attention wandered. Lost in thought, a heavy sadness overcame her. Overwhelmed by her sudden awareness of the extent of damage and suffering, she realized that her husband had not recovered, and might never. She worried if he could govern decisively now. And if she realized it, so did others. She must do something. And she must begin now.

As she left the meeting, Hura took Hisham aside. "I will ask my husband to promote you to Captain of the Guard."

He stood beside her, his tall body fatigued, his eyes sparkling.

Hura tried to become her husband's eyes.

At their dinner every day she reported to Mandari what she saw and heard from the women in the hammam, at the orphanage, and in the markets. She knew Captain Hisham reported on his soldiers, the looting, the lawlessness and the destruction, but she wanted her husband to know about his people, their suffering, their loss – not just the army's activities.

After a week, Mandari announced that he would be taking his meals alone in his new apartment. Crushed, she knew she would see him now only formally, at Council meetings. She couldn't go to his bed yet, for she had almost a month to go before she was no longer 'unclean' from her miscarriage.

It was Hisham who kept her advised of the dangerous currents of unrest among the troops. Guards were often missing at their stations, the rebuilding near the walls was slow . . . and the soldiers resented doing the work that the prisoners used to do.

Concerned for her city and her husband and knowing she could help, Hura resolved to address her husband in his chambers: "My lord," she began, "your people need to see you. They need your leadership and direction and your soldiers need to hear you command them personally. I hear they grumble and wonder if you're still in charge. You need to inspire them."

Mandari banged his fist on his desk. "What do you know! I need to punish them. No, never mind. Leave me alone," he growled. "My men are doing all they can." Hura backed away, frustrated. He would neither say nor hear any more.

As her husband slowly progressed into his cocoon of blindness, only once did he admit his condition. He confided to her that he could see only gray shapes from one eye and nothing, not even a black void, from the other.

Hura worried. If he became blind, who would run the city? How would the city survive? Somehow, she had to help her husband. The perception of his leadership had to be kept up. That's what would save his city.

She came to him again the following morning and spoke more bluntly. "You can't hide in the house or you will lose your people and your city. It is our secret now, but sooner or later everyone will know about your eyes. Let me go with you," she pleaded, her hand on his arm.

"Go? Go where?"

"We could ride through the streets to the mosque, then up to the cemetery and the kasbah, wherever the horses can get through. We can announce your trip at first prayer so people could spread the word and you could even speak. You could thank your people for their bravery, grieve for the dead and inspire your troops . . ." she paused for breath.

Mandari's pride confused him. He placed his fingers over the worst eye, his right one, then rubbed the jagged pink line that divided his face.

Hura stared in revulsion.

His hand lowered to the cup on his desk. He misjudged the distance and knocked it to the floor. A muscle in his cheek twitched. "Darkness of the jinn," he muttered.

The next day Hura insisted on going with her husband on his trip through the city against the advice of his Captain. Hisham told her it would be too dangerous. Hura insisted. She knew better. Her husband would need her help.

Captain Hisham had planned an itinerary that took them from their home in the medina to the mosque, then passed the gates of the Moriscan and Muslim cemeteries, and westward on to the kasbah. From there they would skirt the Souk el Foki to survey the damage, and finally return to the compound.

"Sire, wherever the streets are wide enough, this will be done on horseback," the Captain explained. "But you will need to dismount near the mosque – where it is too narrow, and there will be too many people. After your appearance there you remount. Then before we get to the kasbah you need to dismount again to take a short detour because bodies are still stacked up awaiting burial near the gates and block the way. At the kasbah, I have arranged for you to speak. I've had it announced this morning in all the mosques." The Captain stood at attention, awaiting a response.

"Good." Mandari responded crisply, fingering a row of battle medals on his chest. "I will thank our citizens for their bravery, give my condolences and inspire my troops. I have not forgotten them."

As trumpeters led the way, the entourage proceeded slowly through the city. Mandari sat high and proud in the saddle wearing the heavy black cape with his coat of arms embroidered in gold on the back. A turban sat low on his forehead, covering the raw scar.

Hura thrilled to hear the residents calling from their balconies and shopkeepers shouting from their stalls: "*El Fundador*, Our leader, Our savior!"

He rode stiffly with an air of grave authority; from afar a perfect symbol of strength and renewal. But if anyone else had been close they could have smelled his fear. Hura had never been so proud of him.

At the small plaza before the entrance to the cemetery, the entourage dismounted in front of a large crowd of people. The Captain and two soldiers, in tight formation, led Mandari to the stone steps where he would make his address. Hura followed respectfully, and immediately saw him stumble backwards toward her, but regain his balance, then proceed. Next time, she caught his arm as he tripped again and almost fell. Mandari wrenched it away and cursed: "Why couldn't God have taken my arm instead of my eyes!"

That night Hura had a dream. She found herself in the medina, walking in a black void with her husband and their entourage toward the Grand Mosque. Her husband stumbled and she quickly caught his arm. "God has taken my baraka," he shouted, "taken the light from my eyes." As they stood together his face became her father's and he said to her in Berber: "The light is in your eyes. You must build this city. It is yours now."

In the morning and all day the image of her father's face stayed with her. It wouldn't go away. It haunted her.

The Professor will help me. He will know, she decided. She hurried to his room, hoping he had not retired for the night.

"Professor Kleinatz!" Hura knocked and waited impatiently. "I've had a dream, a vision, and I need your advice. May I come in?"

The reply was not immediate. Then, "Of course, mistress Hura. My door is open to you. I am grateful to you for giving me your husband's old quarters."

Kleinatz sat next to the desk in the far corner. Hura saw at once what was important in his room. His portable writing cabinet sat prominently on its stand alongside. Its open-front, richly decorated with twisted columns, colored panels and gilt inlay supported a large candelabra, the candles half-spent. She could see it was fitted with eight drawers, one deep drawer and a central cupboard. It sat on small bun feet and two iron handles protruded from the sides.

"It's beautiful," she gasped. She had never seen it open.

He said absently, "Ya. I had it made in Spain, I carry all my paper, pens and seals in it – my important letters." He fiddled with one of the pens.

His gaze followed hers to the cot next to his bed. "Your visit here is timely. I have been meaning to ask you."

"Ask what?"

"My good friend, ah, colleague, of whom I spoke before, Professor Issa Asfour, lacks proper shelter. His quarters in the new city are now rubble. I request your permission for him to share my chamber." Kleinatz hesitated, then continued in a rush, "He is more informed on affairs in Fes than I, which could be useful to you."

"Have you discussed this with my husband?"

The Professor twirled the pen between his fingers. "No-o-o."

Hura suppressed a smile. "Of course."

Kleinatz' composure returned. "And now, what can I do for you?"

"Professor, I need your advice. I had a dream. Do you believe in visions?"

He rose and beckoned her to a chair. "Dreams and visions can open doors into a world other than that of the senses. They can bring messages from God or come from the devil. The jinn, I think you call him. The philosopher-historian Ibn Khaldun thought interpretation of dreams a religious science."

"Professor, I have to tell you about my dream. It was so real! Last night my father appeared to me. He told me it was now my responsibility to rebuild the city."

"Remarkable. What did he say? How did he tell you?" Kleinatz watched as she anxiously looked from floor to ceiling then back to him.

"Well, at first I was walking with my husband, and he fell, because he couldn't see. When I tried to help, he turned into my father. I'm confused. I

95

Carol Malt

. . . I don't know what to do. I don't know if I can." She lowered her head, covered her face with her hands.

"If it was a real vision, and you have been chosen, your father will show you the way. Perhaps he has. Haven't you already worked in the orphanage and set up the bread lines?"

"I do what I can. You heard my husband confine me to helping the women. Another hudud, another barrier." She winced, then continued. "I can help him more with the rebuilding. But the overseer curses me for interfering and he doesn't seem to be doing much about our reconstruction. I know he slows the work down when he sees me coming."

"Ya. Always villains make mischief when no strong hand is visible. You want to help? You want to be in charge? Then everyone should know *you* are in command. You need to share this dream you had."

"Oh, I couldn't do that to my husband." Hura shook her head. "Already he hurts from his loss, his blindness makes him bitter and angry. He wouldn't understand. I can't talk to him about this."

Kleinatz stroked his sparse hair and remained silent for a moment. "Then you must make others think he has given you authority."

"How?" She tossed her head, flinging her mane of hair around.

"Perception is everything." He held up his index finger.

Hura's fingers touched her lips; she pondered, then brightened. "Yes, of course. I know. Yes, I have the answer. I'll wear his cape, the one with his coat of arms embroidered in gold on the back. And I'll ride his horse. Yes, they'll see him in me. Thank you, Professor. Oh, thank you."

Before her conviction could waver, Hura hurried to her husband's apartment. Her words were blunt. "There is much to be done to rebuild the city and it must be done soon. I have a plan for the reconstruction and I will work with the Overseer on it."

Mandari slapped his palm on the table before him. "I don't want you out there in the streets with the laborers. You are my wife. I forbid it."

His abruptness startled her and she snapped ramrod straight. "Your people need you more than ever. Just your presence will bring hope to these poor people. But you know you can't go. Let me go for you. Let me ride your horse and wear your cape. I will bring news back to you – news you know you can trust. I'll be your eyes in the city. I am not afraid."

Her words were met with silence.

He lowered his head and pretended interest in the gold seal ring on his finger. Finally he answered. "You seem to fear nothing. Not even my anger. Tell the Dutchman to come see me, I want to speak with him."

The next morning after breakfast Hura sent for her husband's horse and told the Captain to provide her with two police escorts. From that moment, with each observation made during her tour, Hura's excitement and

96

enthusiasm for her venture increased. As planned, she rode through the old and new neighborhoods. She walked with her escort through souks and public places. As she had hoped, her presence, wrapped in the symbols of authority seemed to encourage the populace. Some even cheered her as she nodded to them in passage. But the impact of seeing the damage weighed far more than hearing of it. Hura was devastated.

By mid-afternoon she had had enough. Mandari's cape was caked with the fine dust of debris. She cut short the expedition and returned straight to her room. Self-doubt replaced self-confidence. She was shaken beyond mere sorrow at the enormity of a wounded city. Without food or sleep she debated with herself. What to do now? What to tell her husband. How to build *his* confidence?

As Hura returned to the compound, she saw the Professor waiting in the courtyard. He signaled to her.

"If I may be so personal," he asked, "how did Mohammed hurt his leg?"

"Why? Has he said something to you?" Her retort was quick.

"No, it just might answer some questions I have."

Hura looked down at her scuffed boots. "It's a sad story and I still feel guilty."

"Guilty? Haven't all your readings taught you that guilt is a wasted emotion?"

"Well, it's not that simple. You see, we were playing a game and my horse made his horse stumble. I know he blames me for what happened. Ibrahim told me later how it all started. They were both up in the high meadow above Chaouen, lying in the fields resting when they saw me on my way to the spring above them. I dismounted and joined them. Mohammed said it would be fun to make a small sporting wager . . . and Ibrahim said he never gambled. Then Mohammed said the game would be just for fun. A race.

"I remember it so clearly. Mohammed joked with me and said they were just arguing which one of our horses was the fastest. And who was the best rider. They couldn't decide.

"I said the fastest horse in the Rif was mine, Sacony – and Ibrahim admonished him again about betting.

"Mohammed got up and walked around to my horse and ran his hands over the gray coat. He told Ibrahim not to be so pious and said he would do his chores for a week if he lost.

"Then Ibrahim gave up and agreed to the race.

"As I mounted, I noticed how agitated my horse was. His ears flattened. He made a sudden buck that nearly unseated me.

"Ibrahim said 'Go!' and our horses flew down the trail side by side, kicking up loose stones and dirt. I knew something was wrong. Sacony wasn't responding to me. He was wildly careening past trees and through shallow streams as if he had a mind of his own and I clung atop my demon with my hair streaming around my face."

"How old were you?"

"Oh, I was maybe twelve and Mohammed was fourteen. The contest was over almost as soon as it started. Sacony was galloping next to Mohammed's horse and as we came to a bend in the trail Sacony forced his horse into the rocks by the side. His horse fell and Mohammed was thrown to the ground. I heard his screams over the terror-filled wheezing of his horse. It took all my strength to rein in Sacony. He didn't want to stop. And when I got back to Mohammed, he was lying there, holding his leg in his hands, still screaming. Blood oozed from between his fingers."

"Where was Ibrahim?"

"Right by him. He got there first. I asked him if Mohammed was all right and he said it looked like his leg was shattered."

Hura looked up to see the Professor's reaction.

"Go on," he said.

"Ibrahim untied his sash and began to bind the wound. Mohammed began to cry. I was almost sick just looking at the bone sticking out of his leg. Ibrahim asked if he could ride. When he didn't reply, we both helped him up on his horse. Then as I went back to mount Sacony, he made a sudden hop away from me. Strange, I thought. My horse never acted this way before. Then I saw this line of red running down his light coat. I undid the girth, lifted his blanket and pulled a sharp stone from the underside. I had no idea how it could have gotten there; I saddled him myself that morning. Then I cinched the girth tight again and followed my brothers back home."

"It sounds as if someone played a trick on you . . . and got what he deserved," said Kleinatz. "I see no reason for you to feel guilt."

"But I know he blames me. Ibrahim told me so!"

"Your brother is ugly even without his limp. Don't let your pity blind you."

"There must be something we can do to get his sight back," Afaf said to Isabel as the two sat on a bench and mended towels in the kitchen.

"When I spoke with our neighbor and asked what she did when her son was hurt in the invasion she said she was told by a holy man to kill a chicken above his head and let the blood drip down on his eyes and into his mouth, then to cook the chicken. Feathers and all. Then eat it. She couldn't use any salt or the jinn would want to eat it too."

98

"Was he blind?" Afaf drew her thread tight.

"Yes, his face was crushed by stones from the wall."

"How is he?"

"He's dead now." Isabel sighed as she folded a towel and added it to the pile.

"Well, I guess we don't know if it worked." Afaf tried to hide her smile.

"Be serious for once," Isabel admonished. "Mistress Hura gave me some herbs to boil and make into a paste. We must have hope. I'll put the paste on his eyes. If he'll let me."

Afaf straightened up and busied herself with her mending.

Isabel continued, "Miguel told me our master asked him for a head of garlic and when he brought it to his room he told him to leave – he didn't need help. Miguel thinks he didn't want anyone to see what he was going to do. So my husband put the silver bowl of garlic next to him and pretended to stomp out the door. Our master picked up an ivory tooth, peeled it and began to rub it in the folds of his lids and around the rims of his clouded eyes. So you see, the great Sidi is trying to heal himself."

She was sure that everyone knew about his eyes, but no one admitted out loud that Mandari, the Grandissimo, was now living in the dark and seeking quack cures for what he referred to as his 'problem'.

"I feel so sorry for him," Afaf confessed.

"Some say he's going blind because he's listening to foreigners and women for counsel. I heard that at the hammam." Isabel finished her sewing and got up.

Afaf tugged at the older woman's apron in disbelief. "Don't they know what happened? I mean about the sword fight?"

"They see mistress Hura every day at the hospital, or the madressa or in the streets. And the Professor makes no secret about living here. I heard our mistress even told the overseer he wasn't doing enough, fast enough. Right in front of his men! I think he's spreading rumors about her. That overseer will make trouble. You'll see." She wagged a finger.

THIRTEEN

After an absence of five months, Hura's brothers returned leading two mules laden with their kill. Hanging from each side, like huge feathered saddlebags, were snipe, pigeons, ducks of several colors and sizes, large pheasant and small turtle dove.

Miguel hurried to the courtyard to help them and gasped at the number of fowl: "Isabel could feed two armies with all this, Sidi Ibrahim."

"It's a good season," Ibrahim said. "Especially for duck. On one lake they covered the entire surface of the water."

"And," Mohammed added, "the fishing was good, the rivers are full. We even got a wild boar. I let the dogs have it."

"Yes, the baraka was with us," Ibrahim said. "We heard the beast grunting in some thickets and made a bet. Who would strike him down? Mohammed went to one side and I began to stalk in the other. I had just notched an arrow to my bow when . . . twang! An arrow whizzed past my ear and plunged into a tree."

Ibrahim grinned, turned to his brother. "My arrow made the kill, don't forget our bet." Then he told Miguel to unload the birds from his mule and give them to his men. "All but the pheasants, they are for Hura."

"Have mine taken to my villa," Mohammed ordered. "And have them cleaned."

"What about the feathers?"

"You may have them, Miguel – our gift to you. You agree, Mohammed?"

Mohammed nodded reluctantly, thinking of the money his brother had just given away.

Hura entered the compound as the brothers walked to the main house. Without greeting, she came striding across the courtyard, boots covered with dust, dark half-circles under gray eyes, hair disheveled.

Ibrahim's eyebrows lifted. "Dirty laborer's clothes?"

"And in men's pantaloons!" added Mohammed. "What will you do next?"

"Brothers, I'm tired." She walked past them, said over her shoulder, "I'll greet you properly after my bath."

"Wait. I want an answer." Mohammed shouted at her back. "You are the wife of the Governor of Tetouan, what madness is this – going out into the city like a dirty beggar? Have you no shame? Think how this reflects on us."

Hura whirled, spoke to Ibrahim. "Calm our brother. I'm helping rebuild the city. Without the help of my brothers. There is so much to do. Should I dress like a Spanish queen?"

Visage stern, Ibrahim scolded, "Let the slaves and the soldiers build it. Remember, you are the daughter of an Emir. What would father think?"

"I know what he would think. He's the one who told me to do it." She turned away, left them with eyebrows still raised, responses stuck in their throats, and climbed the harem steps to her room.

Eavesdropping from the balcony, Afaf greeted her with an impish smile. "You told them!"

"That's enough. Contain yourself. I'm exhausted. Bring me a bucket of hot water and tell Isabel our guests will need supper after the hammam."

"Yes, Lalla Hura. I see you have no humor today."

"And get out my turquoise kaftan, the sheer one with pearls. This laborer will dress for her honorable brothers."

"Sidi Ibrahim!" Miguel called as he rapped on the chamber door that evening after supper. "Sidi Ibrahim."

A muffled voice responded from inside.

"Captain Hisham asks you to quick bring your glass and go to the roof. Ships are coming in. Hurry before it gets too dark to see."

Miguel led Ibrahim and the Captain up to the roof. The back wall had been repaired but the parapet was not yet finished. Standing a few steps back from the edge, passing the long tube from one to the other, they watched as several high castled ships slowly sailed up river. In their wake were another forty vessels of various sizes and shapes.

"Our lookouts saw them from the citadel when they first turned in at Martil," the Captain said.

"I can't see the flags clearly," Ibrahim said as he pressed the spyglass to his eye.

The Captain asked: "Are they war ships? I don't see cannon."

"I can almost see the flag. There. Yes, I see it, but I don't recognize it. Here, you look."

He handed the glass to the Captain.

"It's Muslim, must be. I see a crescent moon. But they're merchantmen with a Spanish caravel rig. Someone important what with the size of that flagship. But I don't know his flag either."

"Spanish, you say? I know Spanish boats." Miguel held out his hand for the glass.

After watching the glass aim at several ships, Ibrahim grew impatient.

"Quick man, what do you think?"

"That's someone important, all right. That's the flag of Abu Abdulla." Miguel's voice faltered as he said the name.

"Who?"

"The King of Granada. He's called Boabdil." Miguel slowly lowered the glass.

"Put your coat on and come with me." Afaf didn't wait for a response before holding it at arms length.

"I don't have time to play." Hura buttoned the flap of her pantaloons. "I overslept. It's after dawn. I must get to the wall. We're starting the new gate on the south side."

"You won't work today." Afaf held the coat closer and ruffled it for emphasis. "No one will."

Hura stared up at her maid, so different in background, but close in age. She had grown to trust and rely on Afaf, who was like the sister she never had. She rose, put on the coat and followed her up the narrow back stairway of her home through the covered passageway to the administration building and into the small gallery high above the great reception hall.

The rectangular hall was jammed with men who poured in from the entrance nearest the Souk el Hots and, noisy and impatient, jostled each other to stand facing the dais at the windowless end. Usually decorated simply with a banner showing Mandari's coat of arms, Hura had never seen the hall so festooned with flowers, ribbons, brightly colored banners and pennants. On each side trumpeters waited in full military dress, the brass bells of their instruments resting on their hips; guards stood at attention to the back and sides. Someone had placed two chairs on the ornately carpeted dais. Hura craned her neck to see better from her position. She knew one chair was large and gilded. That one, with arms that terminated in huge lion paws, was her husband's. Positioned alongside was a square ebony chair of simple design. Behind it, a huge red banner with a yellow crescent moon at its center hung ceiling to floor.

Afaf, up early, had already heard this was to be a formal presentation to every dignitary of the city. To ensure a large audience, Mandari's soldiers had hurried through the city to declare a holiday. There would be a free round of bread for all families and a fantasia on the plain beside the river in the late afternoon.

As Hura sat down on a wooden bench, Afaf bent down to her ear and spoke softly. "They say he's very handsome. With blond hair!"

"What is this all about? Who *is* that sitting beside my husband?"

"The King of Granada. He arrived last night. You went to bed early after supper. Remember?"

Hura remembered the night before. It was a night like so many others. For her, time plodded on in a never ending succession of meetings and work. She lived day after day in exhaustion from hard labor, choking on the dust of the stone masons, with the endless hammering of carpenters, the incessant braying of laden donkeys and the clinking of the slaves chains. Yes, she remembered.

Hura pressed her face up against the gallery lattice to watch Captain Hisham lead her husband slowly from a side door to his chair on the stage. With a raised arm Mandari signaled for the trumpeters to begin the program. In the silence following the fanfare, six guards in ceremonial uniform marched out of the opposite side door and took positions beside the black chair, raised their swords, then stood at attention. Another fanfare introduced a vision of dazzling gold so striking that the crowd gasped.

The small man quickly strode to his chair. His head, a thick mass of blond wire; his chin a full yellow bush that covered the upper part of his gold-inlaid armor. More curly yellow hair matted the forearm of his left hand which rested on the golden hilt of his scimitar. The gold inlay of his armor caught the light from the windows. The vision was ethereal, regal, magnificent. When he sat down, a collective buzz rose from the crowd quelled only by another burst of trumpeting.

To Hura, who had never seen royalty, this first image of Boabdil impressed her not because he was a king, or had been a king, but because her husband had been his Captain in Spain.

"I heard the first thing he did was to claim sovereignty over Tetouan," Afaf cast a side glance at Hura. "He says these were his people in Spain and they should be his people wherever they are – "

Hura shifted her gaze to the concerned face of her maid.

"But I also heard Sidi Mandari stood his ground this morning. He would have none of it. Threatened to blast the King's ships out of the harbor right then and there, with the King himself on board, unless the King declared himself a visitor. This reception and the holiday fantasia . . . they're the bargain."

A shiver shot up Hura's spine. She scanned the audience for her brothers. She found them, surrounded by their elite guards in the front row before the dais.

Hura grated. "What else do you know?"

Afaf pressed her forefinger to her lips. "Shhh, look at Sidi Mandari."

Her husband struggled out of his chair and stood facing the crowd. Holding a scroll in front of him, he signaled for Ibrahim to mount the stage, then handed it to him. In his bass voice, Ibrahim slowly read the proclamation: "Noble warriors . . . esteemed countrymen . . . friends. We are honored today to have in our presence . . ."

Hura could only hear snippets of sentences from her perch. She rubbed her nose, irritated from leaning forward against the lattice. Strands of her hair caught on the sharp edges of the wooden screen that hid her. Her stomach began to tighten. How is this going to affect me?

While Ibrahim continued reading, Hura watched the King, sitting radiant in his chair. Then her eyes found her husband. She knew by the droop of his mouth that he was angry and tired.

To Hura, the ceremony seemed short. Suddenly the silence of the crowd erupted into cheers. The trumpets blared as the King and her husband, led by Ibrahim, exited through the side doors. The crowd began pouring out into the souk and down the streets eager for their holiday. Hura whispered to Afaf. "There will be a formal banquet tonight of course . . . I must go." She squeezed Afaf's hand and rushed away.

Slipping into his office, she saw her husband surrounded by his officers and quietly took a seat on the side to listen. The men argued and shouted, it was difficult to hear. She moved to a closer chair.

". . . and send messengers to the Sultan, the governors of all the provinces, even our brethren in Tunis. If they start now and ride at full gallop, the news can reach them all in three days. We will hold the banquet in ten days. Spare no expense. And round up the usual beggars and drunks to make the streets safe."

"Yes, Excellency."

Hisham turned to go, but Mandari continued: "Captain, put the King and his entourage in my guest chambers and the rest of his family and attendants on the second floor of the administration building. We'll put the King's guards and staff temporarily in the east barracks. Your soldiers will have no quarters. They can't stay long."

"Hura, are you here?"

"Yes, I am here." She touched his arm.

"Our guests will stay until the banquet. Boabdil assures me he merely stops here on his way to Fes." His brusqueness made clear his annoyance.

"For this banquet, I want a feast. Like none we've had before. I will show him what hospitality really is. Expect two hundred." He waved his hand in front of him, "and candles, plenty of torches. We need to light the entire building."

Boabdil brought turmoil to the household. The royal guest insisted on special service and food; he wanted his jesters, musicians and taster given quarters in the house. Isabel, Afaf and the other servants worked into the nights cooking, washing, and cleaning.

It was through Afaf that Hura learned about the royal family, their quarrels, and their habits.

"Boabdil's Queen is as dumb as a donkey and the Queen Mother is too clean!" Afaf confided. "She wants to spend every day at the hammam and everyday she has to have clean bedding and," Afaf laughed, "she has no hair. She wears a wig."

"Now, Afaf, how do you know that?" Hura asked, accustomed to the exaggerations of her maid.

"I saw it by her bed when I changed the linens, I swear to Allah. And she's always picking on her son. Pick! Pick! Do this, do that. And, she calls him ugly names. I've heard her."

"Well, they'll soon be gone. The banquet is this Friday. Then they're leaving for Fes."

"No, mistress, Isabel heard her say they were staying."

"Don't tell stories . . . is that what she told Isabel?" Hura put her hands on her hips as if to scold Afaf.

"No. I swear Isabel heard her servants talking."

"I'll see about this. Hospitality is one thing, but taking over our whole house is another. And the barracks too."

During the week the King's family had been in her house, Hura avoided dining with them. During the day, she planned the menus and the activities; in the evenings, she could hear music and laughter coming from the reception hall. Every day she sent her formal regrets and took her meals in her room.

But she was curious about this King. Why did she find him so repulsive? Was it his light hair or something unnerving in the way he had greeted her the day of his arrival? Or the fact that he only came up to her chin? His gaze and open mouth, when they first met, were anything but regal. It was as if he wanted to lick, to eat her up. Yes, that was it. He looked like a hungry animal. The thought made her skin crawl.

She must find out more about this man. She sought Kleinatz and found him, as usual, at his desk writing.

"Professor. I understand you do not join our guests for dinner. Is there something wrong? Are you ill?"

"No, I am well. I take my meals here in my room because I care not for the company of the perfidious."

"Who?" She tilted her head.

"Perfidious means treacherous, disloyal, traitorous."

"Those are strong words, Professor. How do you know? What did he do?"

"You must keep this confidential. It is between us." He studied her face, as though debating whether or not to reveal the truth, then said, "Maybe I am too harsh, after all he is a renowned poet with a honeyed tongue. But when I was in Spain, Boabdil was despised, pitied and laughed at. Some say it was because of his evil father, but regardless, he quarreled with the Moorish rulers of other provinces and didn't support them when the Spanish attacked their lands. He lost battles with the Spanish and was even captured. But here is the worst part. To gain release, that Muslim swore an oath of fealty to Catholic Don Ferdinando."

"What kind of oath? He turned against his people?" Hura sucked in her breath, incredulous.

"He did." Kleinatz kept fingering his pen. "He was imprisoned several times and each time bought his freedom by betraying his friends. And finally, listen to this, when that tyrant fled from the al-Hamra, even his mother turned on him. That is why I don't grace his table with my presence. He is no hero, no leader of men. There are few so perfidious."

"I see. I came to you because I've been troubled by the things I've heard. Here in Tetouan. Little things . . . now I hear he wants to stay."

Kleinatz dropped his pen on the paper leaving a blotch on his journal. "If he stays, I leave."

She grasped his shoulder. "No Professor, no, you mustn't. I promise he won't stay here. I'll think of a way to get him out of Tetouan."

"Mistress Hura, if I could add one more thing. I frankly do not see how your husband can stand him here, either. Remember, he lost his two sons in Spain. They were heroes, they were defending their lands and your husband's castle, the fortress of Pinar. But Boabdil did not help them. I suppose," Kleinatz sighed with resignation, "your husband is honor-bound by those laws of hospitality the Arabs are so famous for."

Hura looked away. With sadness in her voice she said, "It must be hard for my husband. Especially now with his eyes. I wonder what he'll do when he hears the King wants to stay."

The food was plentiful and well prepared, but little levity and long silences prevailed during Friday's banquet. Mohammed, who had managed to seat himself next to Boabdil, began the conversation: "Your Highness, tell us more about the rulers of Spain. I understand you have met King Ferdinando and Queen Isabella."

The King glowered. "Don Ferdinando is ruthless; he is obsessed with the religious purity of his kingdom; he is cunning and not to be trusted."

"There, there, my dear," Boabdil's mother broke in. "He's no worse than that pious zealot of a wife. Isabella sells her soul to the Dominican priests. But let us not dwell on our enemies. We should be talking about our future, here in Tetouan."

106

"Right you are." Mandari punctuated her words by slamming his cup on the table. Silent through most of the meal he now wanted some of his own questions answered. "Tell us, Your Highness, what are your plans next week. Do you need help for your journey to Fes?"

"Comrade Mandari," Boabdil began pleasantly, "I am honored by your hospitality and impressed with the city you have built. You are to be commended. You have made me so welcome I hesitate to leave . . . especially now that I have another five thousand of my people on their way here."

"Five thousand!" Ibrahim repeated. "All at once?"

"Ahh, you see my problem, don't you." The King's hand flipped back and forth in front of him. "I'll have to stay to make sure they get settled. I must. It may be a problem at first, but I realize how good it makes you feel, Comrade, to know my men are here to help defend the city against another attack. Not that I think another one will happen, mind you." He smiled and looked around the table at each of the diners. "But we can discuss my problems later, when I know more."

Another thick silence blanketed the room. Mandari's cloudy eye seemed to grow whiter.

The royal mother purred, "Dear Comrade, where is that charming wife of yours, I've only met her once and was so enchanted."

"Yes, why isn't she here?" Boabdil's wife Catana added in a high falsetto. "We must play together."

Boabdil grimaced at the sound.

"Lalla Hura hasn't been well lately, she sends her regrets," said Mandari in as civil a tone as he could.

"I too am anxious to have her at our table," Boabdil turned to look at Mandari. "Shall I have one of my doctors see her?"

"I'm sure it is nothing." Mandari grunted unable to conceal his annoyance.

Ibrahim shook his head. "Begging your pardon, sir, but that might be a good idea. I also am worried about my sister, she's thin and eats so little."

Mandari conceded, "So be it, send your doctor."

"Lalla Hura," Afaf called at the door of her mistress' room the next morning. "There's a man, a doctor, downstairs. King Boabdil sent him to see you."

"I don't need a doctor. Tell him to go away."

"But mistress, he comes at your husband's orders," Afaf persisted.

Annoyed at their meddling, Hura continued dressing in her work clothes, preparing to go to the work site.

"Oh, all right. Tell him to wait in the reception room. I'll be down soon." Hura's tone was curt.

The doctor brought an assistant, a wrinkled, stooped woman, just in case there were delicate things to talk about, or parts of the body needed to be examined. The doctor blinked his rheumy eyes several times when Hura appeared. She was thin, yes. A wide leather belt cinched her waist and held up her pantaloons. A loose long-sleeved blouse draped from her shoulders. She stood before him and, without touching her, he checked her eyes, inspected her teeth, tongue, and the palms of her hands.

"Mmmmm." He nodded. "Now I will leave and my assistant will ask you a few questions."

When he retreated to the patio, the woman began asking Hura about her monthly periods, whether she had fulfillment with her husband and whether she wanted children.

Hura wondered why all these questions. She replied brusquely: "I am able to bear children, to give my husband a son and heir."

The woman came closer and began to stroke her arm. "Do you not thrill to the sight of His Majesty, King Boabdil?"

Hura frowned at the strange question.

The old woman confided she had heard the King speak her name many times. The woman came closer, both hands moved up to Hura's chest, to feel her breasts.

Hura's left hand pushed her away and the right slapped her face. "Tell your master how healthy my reaction was!"

Mohammed had observed Boabdil closely over the past several days. He soon realized that the King would be a godsend. Exactly what was needed for his own plan. At first, he shared Mandari's and Ibrahim's resentment of this royal intrusion. But the more he thought about it, the more the King's arrival seemed a perfect opportunity. One he should grab. No doubt their interests were the same. Mohammed decided to get Boabdil aside and talk.

His chance came that evening after supper as Boabdil prepared to play chess with his mother in the reception room.

"Your Highness, before you begin your game, perhaps I may treat you to a view of the city and fortifications from the roof. There's a full moon and you can see the river where your boats lie moored."

"Splendid. I'm bored with games. Show me the city."

The breeze was light; it ruffled Boabdil's yellow hair. The starlit canopy overhead was clear, campfires dotted the plain, torches lit the streets of the medina, the moon shone on the flotilla far down on the river. Boabdil breathed deeply as he scanned the vista.

"Your Highness," Mohammed began tentatively, "my family cares

108

deeply about this city . . . as I'm sure you know. For that reason, I have given much thought to its future and the succession of power here. It's no secret that Mandari is ill and will not live much longer. It's deplorable, but also an interesting situation, don't you think?"

"Umm, it's an interesting situation," Boabdil said evasively. "I understand you are a businessman, you trade throughout the entire land. Do you trade along the coast? In the Imperial cities?"

"Everywhere."

Boabdil ventured: "You don't sound very optimistic, or do I misunderstand?"

"I'm a tradesman, a merchant. But were it not for an accident of birth," Mohammed sniffed, "I would be more than that. I would be ruler of Chaouen and the Rif. *I* am the strong one . . . but my brother is the Emir." Mohammed shot a sidelong glance over to catch the King's reaction.

"I see." Boabdil paused to poke his fingers through the end of his thick beard. "Sometimes it is right to take power you deserve."

Eye to eye, they stood in silence for several heartbeats, then the King inquired about the location of the prison, the armory, the kasbah, and the defenses of the battlements. Mohammed pointed to each, pleased with the implication of his words and Boabdil's attention and questions.

Boabdil returned to the subject. "One might need friends, friends in high places, if one were to attempt such a change."

"And one should seek those alliances well in advance." Mohammed fingered the hilt of the jeweled dagger in his sash.

The King continued to look out over the city as he spoke. "You have a fine brother. He seems very learned, very devout."

Mohammed's rejoinder was immediate and to the point. "Of course, he would find it impossible to accept . . . these changes, I mean."

"And your sister?"

"A woman belongs on her back."

They both chuckled.

"So you would not want Tetouan, only Chaouen?"

"And the Rif, and operation of the port here."

"Yes, it is an interesting question about a blind ruler and a wife who has no children. I think we have much to talk about. While I'm still a guest in this house, the roof is a perfect place to meet; we will talk again."

"Thank you, Your Highness, for your kind words. A new kingdom awaits you."

FOURTEEN

"We'll go to the quarry some other time," Mustafa said to Habib as the two walked from the cool of the palace interior into bright sunshine. "It's too far and too hot." Dressed for comfort in a thin jellaba, the architect's large turban of woven cloth made the pale skin of his forehead perspire.

"Then where are we going?" Habib also wore a turban, his concession to Muslim identity. Perched on top of European styled clothes along with a slender rapier, the ensemble made for a dashing figure and attracted many female eyes.

"To Fes-el-Bali, Fes the Old. The head imam there complained. He wants the Sultan to restore the Bou Inania Madressa. I studied there . . . know the college well. It needs more than a stone or two.

"Why does the Sultan want it restored?"

"Because it was built by Sultan Abou Inan' a hundred years ago. At great expense. It does have historic importance. Built over a garbage dump. That explains why the walls are settling and domes cracking."

Habib nodded. In the souk he had learned much about Mustafa, architect of the Abode of Felicity. He was Fassi, a descendent of the highly respected Idrissid tribe of Fes. "If it's that old, a few more years won't hurt."

"Of course the Wazir knows that finishing the Sultan's new palace is most important. The Wazir also knows he has to give some appearance of satisfying this new command. So he made it our task." He cast a glance at Habib's blank expression. "You understand? I look it over, give the Wazir a report, he tells the Sultan, the Sultan then forgets about it and we continue working on the palace . . . which is all he really cares about." Mustafa bent over, hacked and choked on phlegm.

They walked some distance in silence until Habib asked, "How many palaces does the Sultan have?"

"In Fes, the new city? Two, not counting the one we're working on. Why?"

Habib hesitated. Not knowing how to put it, he plunged ahead. "You work too hard and need help. Maybe you should rest and I should do more of the designs."

"Humph. Down this lane. See the minaret? The Madressa is at the end. That is why you're with me today. Time you learned more about our construction here. Unfortunately, you'll have to contend with strong guilds. Like those for Water and Drainage. Ah, there it is." He waved his finely tapered hand.

Habib stood before the large sprawling structure, gazed upward at the exterior shell of a brick dome, steeled himself to enter the entrance chamber to the school's mosque.

The architect noticed his strange expression. Habib knew he should say something. "Needs more than a little repair," he volunteered.

"Of course. I know you know this wouldn't be permitted in Granada. The tiled dome seems intact, but look at the supporting walls. This bulbous dome does sit on a drum but its weight is pushing the structure's walls outward – cracking them." He wiped his perspiring forehead and neck. "While we're here, you might as well learn something about these domes. We may have more of them in Morocco than Granada. Let's get out of this sun."

Habib took a deep breath, removed his shoes and followed into the square-shaped prayer hall. These past many months he had managed to evade Mustafa's suggestions that he join him at the palace mosque for prayers.

"Handsome arches, don't you think?"

Habib craned his neck. Instead of the ordinary honeycomb vault above he pictured the glorious Hall of the two Sisters and Hall of the Ambassadors at the al-Hamra. Their domes sat on pierced drums composed of many small gilded arches that let in soft light. He sighed at the memory of those opulent and intricately spun fantasies.

"Yes," the architect pointed upward, "while the early Christians huddled under their crude post and lintel roofs, we Muslims had mathematics and the curve of the arch."

Habib grabbed his opportunity. "That's what I want to do . . . design handsome buildings."

Mustafa coughed again. "First, you will learn something of restoration. You'll start here."

FIFTEEN

"*El Zogoybi.* Boabdil the Unlucky One," Miguel said as he stoked the hearth and added logs. "That's what we called him in Spain."

Hura nodded absently. "I see we need more wood; I'll have the soldiers bring us some from the mountain. The King and his family depleted everything in the house. It's so peaceful now without all that noise and commotion."

"Yes, mistress," Miguel turned to her. "And the banquet used up most of our supplies. I've ordered oil, flour, candles and salt. We need to restock the warehouse."

Hura noted the drippings of wax hanging from the chandelier. "We'll know soon if they're pleased with the villa Sidi Mandari gave them. It needs work, I hear, and it isn't as grand as his al-Hamra, but it's big."

Isabel, walking into the kitchen added, "His mother won't be pleased. There's no hammam nearby. She'll have to bathe in the river or come up to the city."

"Isabel, take these," Hura said as she pulled on the candle drawer and removed four fat beeswax tapers. "And I want you to keep a fresh supply of yogurt for me. Have it here daily."

"Oh, . . . mistress! Is it? Are you?"

"Didn't Afaf tell you? Yes, I'm pregnant." She smiled and closed the drawer. "But I don't tell anyone yet. Promise me you won't."

"Even Sidi Mandari?"

Hura blushed. "He knows."

"Lalla Hura, I'm so happy for you." The older woman hugged her. "You must take care of yourself this time. And you mustn't work in the city anymore."

Miguel's normally phlegmatic expression broke into both happiness and concern at the same time. He said nothing but nodded agreement.

"Yes, yes. I know. I'm needed more now at Council meetings anyway."

Afaf came bouncing in, smiling. From the looks on their faces, she realized she had intruded on something private. "Oops! Did I interrupt something?"

"No, you lazy girl," Isabel said. "Where have you been? I've been looking all over for you." She put her hands on her hips and waggled her head. "I know you've been talking to that Captain again."

Hura laughed. "Don't be such a scold. Don't you remember when you were young and in love?"

Isabel clicked her tongue.

"If you will excuse, Mistress," Miguel left them to talk about women's things.

"Afaf, I've just told them. I see you really can keep a secret."

Isabel asked, "When are you due, Mistress?"

She took them both by the hand. "In seven months, *Inshallah*. After Ramadan."

Even before the invasion, Mandari had promised to build another hammam in the city. The existing structure had been built when Tetouan was little more than a village. Now too many people crowded into its vaults; the gossiping women often refused to leave and allow the furious men their turn. This serious defiance always brought out the city guards and much female laughter.

Many of the women had petitioned Hura for their own hammam, and now she undertook it as a special project. The new hammam would be built near the Grand mosque. It would be exclusively for men, which meant that the old bathhouse near her home would be available to women at any time of the day.

In gratitude, the day it opened, the women of the city presented Hura with a huge bouquet of mountain flowers gathered by the most honored of them along the high track to Chaouen. Hura's eyes misted, the flowers reminding her of her family home as she lowered her face into the sweet blossoms.

The return to normalcy brought a host of daily vendors to the old hammam. They sat by the entrance selling oils, perfumes, soap, towels, shampoos and even colorful silk robes. Hura began to suspect that the rumors she heard about loose women frequenting the nearby alleys were true. Even *she* noticed the young girls standing in doorways, then disappearing quickly inside, as she approached. They looked Spanish, or foreign. She wondered if she should do something about it.

Hura visited often, certain that the vapors, massage and unguents would strengthen her. Afaf, who found delight in most everything, always accompanied her, and while her Mistress relaxed, would slip away through the steam to gossip with other maids. Through her, Hura became aware of the fights, marriages, divorces and petty jealousies of her people.

One day while Hura lay wrapped in her towel on her bench, Afaf approached with another woman and introduced her.

"Lalla Hura, Selwa here is a servant to the Queen Mother of Boabdil. She wants to talk with you."

Hura raised her head in surprise. What could Boabdil's mother want? The young servant was fully dressed, but held her shoes in her hand.

Selwa made a curtsy in the Spanish Court style, then said: "Lalla Hura, my Mistress would be honored if you would pay her a visit in her new home. She wishes to see you."

"Please thank the Queen Mother." Hura hesitated, seeking a plausible answer. "I will let her know if this is possible."

When the woman left, Afaf whispered: "You've confused her. She thinks you need permission to visit. Will you go?"

"I'll think about it. Keep this between us, but talk to the other women here. Find out everything you can about the Queen Mother. Come back to me when you've finished."

In Afaf's absence Hura dressed and combed her hair. Soon her maid returned, bubbling with excitement, running over the slippery tiles. Hura held her finger to her lips for silence. Not until they were outside and alone did she permit Afaf to repeat a head full of tattletale about the royal family. Afaf always ended a story with a solemn face, saying it all could just be gossip, then would break into a broad grin.

But were the stories just gossip? Hura sought a better reason to decline. I have it, she thought cheerfully. I can't make the journey in my present delicate condition, my husband forbade me to ride when I'm pregnant! And I can't walk, it's too far.

Two days later the messenger again sought Afaf at the hammam and asked to be brought before her mistress. With a face as ingenuous as she could assume, Afaf told her that her mistress was honored by the invitation and would humbly accept if not for the delicate female condition she was in, a condition that did not allow travel. Lalla Hura was sure the Queen Mother would understand and wish her many sons.

"That may be the end of it," Hura laughed with Afaf. "But keep your ears open."

It was not the end of it. Two days later the same young woman appeared and asked Afaf if her mistress would please come to the next cubicle where the Queen Mother herself was waiting to greet her.

Astounded that she had gotten in without being noticed and had come without an entourage, Hura grabbed her towel and followed the servant to a small side alcove where a figure sat in steam, wrapped in cotton gauze from head to toe.

Hura peered through the thick mist, trying to recognize the face. But swathed in white and without makeup, the wrinkled face could have been anyone's. She was sure who it was only when the woman began to speak. That throaty, imperious accent was unmistakable.

"Thank you, my dear, for joining me. I hear congratulations are in order. *Mabruk.*" A jeweled finger pointed at Hura's belly.

"You are most kind," Hura answered, pulling her towel tighter around her as if to protect herself from jinn.

"Since you are not able to travel, I thought I would come to you." Her thin smile exposed long yellow and crowded teeth. "Come sit next to me."

Hura replied in the same perfunctory tone. "Most gracious of Your Highness." She made no effort to move.

"I understand you are the daughter of Emir Rachid, and that your marriage to the *Fundador*, al-Mandari, guarantees him the support of the mountain people. That is important."

Wisps of steam passed by her face then floated away, revealing an eye now, a shriveled mouth, later. "How old are you, my dear?"

"I am a woman of eighteen years." Hura wondered what this woman wanted.

"Indeed you have experienced much." The dowager continued, "Have you done much thinking about what is going to happen here when your husband is no longer able to rule? I'm sure you haven't had to worry about such things and the whole idea disturbs you, but as a mother myself, I want to help you." The teeth became visible again.

Hura scowled and started to speak but the Queen Mother held up her hand.

"Now don't be upset, my dear, I thought you should know that you have a friend in me and . . . if you were to look favorably upon my son, I would not oppose it."

Hura recoiled. So this was the real reason for the meeting, a not so subtle invitation to become Boabdil's mistress! Or maybe his wife? She forced a smile to hide her nervous search for the right response.

"You do me much honor, and I'm pleased that I am favored by your son." Hura shifted from one foot to the other while groping for the right words. "I'm sure you understand when I say I could never marry again while my father sits in a Portuguese prison in Tangier." Hura brightened. "I would look favorably on a future husband who could free my father. And of course that would take a large army, many soldiers and someone with military experience. I'm certain you know of such a person."

The two women assessed one another in silence; the mother recalling her son's lack of valor and Hura proudly savoring her solution to the problem.

"I see you are a loyal daughter. I will discuss this with my son. He is a loyal son."

The Queen Mother rose and Hura bowed as she disappeared through the archway.

115

The next morning Hura listened without comment as Captain Hisham spoke at the Council table and gave his usual crisp report to Mandari. Then he hesitated. "If I may speak freely, Boabdil is a constant irritant. He has refused to move his ships from the city docks, which are now creating jams on the river and tying up trade. My Lord, more of his soldiers and former subjects keep arriving from Spain and he allows them to land without paying an entry tax at the dock he built in front of his villa. The money should be flowing into your offers, Sidi Mandari, but it is never collected."

Mandari clenched his fists and stared in the direction of the Captain's voice.

Hura watched his face become livid. She could only imagine the conflict and resentment growing inside him. A sharp pain arced across her abdomen. Was it morning sickness or reaction to recent disturbing problems? Whichever the cause, what should she do?

Hisham continued, saying Boabdil's soldiers drink wine much of the day, then in the evening they come up to the city looking for women. On Fridays, the soldiers take over the grand mosque, crowding regular worshipers out of the way and not allowing townspeople close to the minbar. Boabdil even plans to steal our imam away. People say he wants him for a new mosque he is building near his villa.

Mandari cupped his hand around his mouth.

Hura clasped her stomach, fought to quell the nausea. She hoped it really was a mosque they were building and not a barracks. Boabdil was trying to divide the city. She shuddered, afraid for her husband. A confrontation was inevitable.

Hisham paced the small meeting chamber while explaining further that ransom money now only trickled into City coffers because King Ferdinando had a new policy concerning prisoners of war. Instead of sending money to free prisoners as the wealthier families used to, the Spanish King now sends priests. Salvation of souls is his new policy. He has convinced the Portuguese to do the same. Our prisons are full.

Hura erupted. "Husband, Boabdil is an open sore that never will heal."

Weeks, months, passed. The feast of Ramadan became a memory and spring flowers began to turn the brown mountains of the Rif into a coverlet of vibrant colors. Snow on the high passes was thawing and soon the roads would be passable again. Already Isabel had aired and stored the household woolen blankets, and the markets were filled with sweet vegetables and tender spring thistle from the southern mountains.

The shrill ululations of Isabel and Afaf pierced the quiet tension of the house. Only one each, not three; that meant it was a girl.

116

Isabel found Miguel sitting at the kitchen table, looking glum. "She's asleep now. Tell Sidi Mandari it's a daughter, and send for a wetnurse." With that, Isabel went to wash and get some sleep herself. It had been two days since the first labor pains and Isabel, too, was exhausted.

The midwife had done what she could despite being unable to turn the baby around – it wanted to come feet first – and none of her pulling or pushing or manipulating could change that. Even so, the delivery proved successful. It was a big baby. She cut the cord, bathed the child, checked its fingers and toes, blew in its mouth, wrapped it and handed it to Afaf. Then she sewed together the torn outer skin between Hura's legs. This time the placenta had come easily. She carefully washed the membrane and bundled it for later ritual.

Four days later Hura regained her strength almost completely.

"It's the chicken soup, I know it," chimed Afaf. She watched Hura rise slowly from the floor, bend and touch her toes.

"Thirteen, fourteen, fifteen." Hura's breath escaped in small bursts. "Soon I'll have my shape back."

Hura turned the sitting room next to her bedroom into a nursery. She marveled how the presence of a baby redefined the entire compound. Her house had welcomed new arrivals and seen visitors before, but none had transformed it like this baby. Daily work revolved around the care, feeding and comfort of the baby, whom Hura had named Suha, after her great grandmother. The baby's slightest pout sent Afaf or Isabel running for the wetnurse or new diapers. A hiccup brought the comfort of protecting arms. Scented oils burned in the hallway and during naptime, the house came to a standstill.

Presents from family, well-wishers, friends, and political allies filled the nursery. Carpets, clothing, and jewelry overflowed the chests and onto the floor. Next to the long bench that had brought Hura her first freedom to the roof was an elaborately carved wooden crib. Large enough for triplets, it stood high off the floor on curved rockers. A small cot backed up to the opposite wall for Afaf, and a large high-backed chair for the wetnurse sat next to it. New carpets softened the tile floor and a wall hanging blocked the slits in the wall. Miguel provided new candles daily for the four candelabra that lit the room.

Hura marveled, adored, inspected, and cradled the infant in her arms, certain and grateful the baby's features favored her and not Mandari. Unable to produce enough milk, Hura reluctantly gave that responsibility to the wetnurse, pleased the baby received so much nourishment and attention. How kind of aunt Henati to offer to come and help, she thought. But as much as she loved her old aunt, she feared Henati would not be well enough to care for herself here, let alone a child.

The arrival of Suha had no pleasurable impact on her husband – no congratulations, no acknowledgment. She heard nothing. The hurt did not dissipate with time. Again and again Hura told herself she was to blame. She must bear him a son.

SIXTEEN

After a doorway had been cut through the stone blocks between Mandari's apartment and adjoining storerooms of the house, Hura moved Mandari into the new space. This freed his former quarters for a new Council meeting room in which some twenty people could now sit. It also gave Mandari more privacy and at the same time, prevented access to him. The Professor repeatedly told Hura: "Public awareness of his weakness and lack of leadership will be Tetouan's downfall. History teaches us that nature abhors a vacuum." For those visiting the Council chamber, it appeared that business was continuing as normal, although Mandari had not presided over meetings in over a year.

Not long afterwards, at the next Council meeting, when Captain Hisham arrived and Mohammed had taken his seat, Ibrahim started the meeting by sharing news he had just received from Fes: "Sultan Muhammad al Shaykh has signed an agreement with the Portuguese throne. In essence, he has agreed to allow Dom Manuel to put his troops on our land."

Astonished, Hura asked: "Does this mean they can attack anywhere? Go anywhere? Trade anywhere?"

"Yes. They have 'normal relations', as the Sultan puts it."

Hura squirmed in her chair. "How could he do that? He must have received our request for support. After that invasion he knows they still threaten us."

Kleinatz gave Hura a wry look. "All is fair in love and commerce. Apparently you did not have whatever it was that the Sultan needed . . . or the Portuguese have more to offer him. Since he hasn't responded to your letter, your only hope of getting his assistance is to arrange a personal meeting."

"Perhaps even pay tribute," Mohammed scooted his chair on the floor, closer to the table.

She pushed her chair away from the table.

"No, my husband would never do that. He has said so. And I won't agree to it."

Mohammed laughed. "He is in no position to say anything, and you are only his wife. A woman."

Ibrahim tried to restore order. "Hura, brother, we don't need this . . .

this . . ."

"This what?" Mohammed challenged. "I think we all know what's going on and I for one don't like it. You know," he lowered his voice conspiratorially, "there is no limit to what a man might become. The slave might become a minister or a general; the scribe a Sultan. But for a woman, never."

Hura shot from her seat. "Tetouan is not yours to tax or rule, dear brother." Standing defiantly before them all, she ordered Mohammed and the others to leave and, with a conciliatory glance at Ibrahim, declared the meeting over.

"Ach. You should not have behaved like that at the meeting." Kleinatz chided when he joined her at the courtyard fountain in the cool of evening. "You are driving a wedge between yourself and Ibrahim. It will end in pain."

"Professor, I couldn't help it. Mohammed is a trouble maker, he always has been."

Kleinatz picked at his gray goatee and stared at Hura. Although still so young, she was mature far beyond her years. She was also a diligent reader with a bright mind and a thoughtful and inquiring side to her nature, all of which he took credit for, as he had done his very best over the past four years. She had progressed to where she could hold her own with the city lawyers on such matters as the Land Tenure Acts and the complicated Water Rights Act that regulated the usage of the waters from the mountains. She had read and absorbed almost all of the Arabic manuscripts in his library, including several which were written by him; astrological scrolls on the names and natures of all the heavenly bodies, and even his manuals on archery and horticulture. She could even argue with him on his own principals of aesthetics. Yes, she was articulate with an enchanting voice. And on top of all that, she was beautiful. He worried about her future, especially with the intrigues in Tetouan, and the very real threat of foreign invasion.

Kleinatz roused himself from reverie, said, "I agree that someone must go to Fes."

"Of course. But who?"

"Your brother Ibrahim. The Emir speaks with much authority. He would cut a splendid figure at court."

"Impossible. The Rif tribes would take advantage of his absence. He might solve one problem and cause another. And don't mention Mohammed!"

Hura ran fingers through her long hair and mused aloud. "Oh, if only my father were here. He would tell us what to do."

120

"That's foolish. He would go. What he would say is: 'You, my daughter, are a Rachid'. He would say: 'You go'."

"I cannot." Hura shook her head. "I promised myself I'd be a good mother."

After a short pause, Kleinatz continued. "Yes, I think you should. Having you go has certain advantages . . . the only drawback is your safety." His head bobbed up and down, confirming his own words.

"But what about Suha?"

"You will be away a month, six weeks at the most. At her age, she won't know the difference."

"Oh, Professor, with all your wisdom, you know nothing about babies."

"Perhaps not. But haven't we forgotten something important?"

"What's that?" His tone of voice startled her.

"Your husband. You cannot go without his permission. The Sultan might see you, but he would never deal with you unless you could prove you represented Mandari, Lord of Tetouan." He reached in his jacket for his pipe and began to tap the bowl into his palm to clear it.

"You're right, of course. I know, I'll wear his cape and his seal ring, too. As soon as the mountain passes are open I'll send a messenger to announce my arrival in Fes. One of Mohammed's traders could do it. I'd pay him well. Then the Sultan will know to expect me."

"You still need to get your husband's permission," Kleinatz insisted.

"I know, I know," she tapped her foot impatiently. "Which do you think will be easier, the permission – or finding someone to go with?"

The next morning Hura personally served Ibrahim breakfast as she had so often done in Chaouen, and confided her plans. Glossing over the issues of womanhood and danger, she asked him for protection in the villages where she would have to stay. Silent support. Secret support. Then she asked for advice about Mohammed and who should go with her.

"I have thought much about the problems here in Tetouan and you know you have my undying loyalty. You, my dear sister, are the legitimate voice of this city. I would trust your safety to no one but myself, but since you wish to travel anonymously, I cannot join you. I am known everywhere, so too are my officers." He fingered the circlet of beads in his right hand as if saying a silent prayer. "Right now, I don't know who should accompany you."

"With all your good troops . . ."

"None are good enough for you. But," he smiled, "I will think hard about it. Perhaps Mohammed has some suggestions."

"Lalla Hura, look at Suha. She's walking on her own. Pretty soon she'll be running all around the compound." Afaf clapped her hands in glee as she sat on a thick pile rug in the middle of the nursery floor playing with Suha. "She's such a happy baby, she's always smiling."

"Yes, I am blessed," Hura said distractedly and closed the book she was reading.

"You seem far away, Mistress." Afaf looked up at her.

"I guess I have much on my mind. I finally received permission from Sidi Mandari to go to Fes, but only if I have an escort, someone to protect me."

"Why not the Captain, or your brothers?" She tickled Suha on her round belly and the child made babbling sounds of delight.

"I want to travel without being known, and they're known by everyone. I'm frustrated."

"Well, why not ask my father?" Afaf's eyes lit up. "He's an experienced traveler. And he'd be loyal. And he's smart too!"

"Your father? Don't be silly." Hura opened her book again.

"You remember, he's a brave sea captain . . . he would protect you."

"Yes, I remember him." The image of a sea-worn and smelly man with hairy, bronze arms and a golden earring came back to her.

"Have you heard from him? Where is he?"

"He's at sea but should return soon. I'll ask him to come here to the house. May I?" Afaf's whole face lit up. "You'll see, he'll do it."

The wait seemed endless. Afaf's seafaring father was last seen leaving for Cadiz to pick up cargo and passengers and was not due back for two weeks. So far, Ibrahim had not been able to provide her with any other escorts and she wondered if he really wanted her to go. Mohammed had taken his time responding to her message. The only good news was that Boabdil would be no threat while she was gone. He and his soldiers were in camp near Tangier. A not so subtle note arrived from the Queen Mother indicating he expected to free Hura's father and claim his reward.

Everyday Hura chafed at the loss of time and imagined the Portuguese enemy growing stronger and bolder. Today both brothers were taking tea in the reception room. She hoped they could solve her problem.

As they sat on large pillows and leaned against the tiled wall, Hura shared her fears about the Portuguese. Ibrahim attempted to calm her. "Your fears are groundless, my sister. Just because foreigners can now trade and travel freely doesn't mean they want to conquer us." The horsehair crunched in his pillow as he moved to face her.

"Besides, the Sultan was wise to sign the pact." Mohammed added. "It's good for business and maybe they'll bring some order to the fighting between the Rif tribes."

Hura stared at one brother then the other. "I can't believe you're saying this. It's everything our father fought to keep from happening. Have you forgotten his dream to unite and free our people? Of his pledge to rid the Rif of foreigners? He's in prison for his beliefs and you dishonor his name with your words!"

"Now, now. I only meant their trade would be good for us. Ibrahim, tell her I'm right." Mohammed looked to his brother for support.

Ibrahim fingered his prayer beads. "Hura, your heart beats true. We must remember our pledge to our father." He sighed. "The easy life of pleasure seems to pull us from our duty."

Mohammed jumped to his feet and lurched out of the room.

Hura's mouth opened but nothing came out.

"Let him go," Ibrahim put his hand on her arm to still her. "What word do you have about your sea captain?"

Hura eased back onto her pillow, and told Ibrahim that the Captain should arrive in the next few days, also that she was uncertain whether he would want to travel with her. When she again asked Ibrahim for an officer she could trust, he replied that he had made inquiries and learned that Captain Tarek was fluent in Arabic, Spanish and Portuguese; that he was from a good family; that years ago he owned several ships until the Spanish took away his license, and that he could serve as well as one of his officers.

Ibrahim moved closer to her. "I've planned your route," and pulled a thick folded packet from his kaftan. He spread it open in his lap. "Of course, it's your decision . . . how and with whom you go. But you asked for my advice."

Hura nodded.

Ibrahim's finger traced the route as he spoke: "You'll go direct, keep away from valleys. Not through the bigger towns but to places where I know you'll be safe. Some of them you've been to before. I've got trusted agents I'll alert to your arrival. The trip should take about nine days." He paused and turned to look at his sister.

"You'll go by way of Chaouen."

Nicholas Kleinatz was waiting for her in the patio, his hands clasped together in deep concern. His head bowed as she approached. "Lady Hura, I have heavy thoughts I must share with you. Can we meet before lunch?"

Hura thought how strangely formal he acted and how sad his voice sounded. She noticed he wore a woolen burnoose instead of his long, cloth jacket. "Of course, Professor. I always have time for you." His manner did not change as he slowly walked away, toward his room.

Unable to contain her curiosity, she went to his room before noon, and finding the door open, entered and stood aghast. Boxes lined the walls and books obstructed her path. Swallowing hard, she raised her voice to get his attention.

"What grave problems make you suffer? Tell me and I'll make them go away."

"Lady Hura," Kleinatz closed the box in front of him and stood up, "I am in your debt, which is why it is so hard for me to talk with you now."

"You can tell me anything. My eyes see what you are doing. I don't know what to say. You're going to leave, aren't you." She knew she sounded like a forlorn child.

He came over to her. "I have watched you grow from a child to a woman, from an illiterate, selfish, pouting girl to a person of ideas, courage and virtue."

Hura made a face. "Was I that bad?"

" – and I have been well rewarded by you and your husband. But now I must go. The time has come to leave. I wanted to tell you before you left for Fes." He sat down and gestured for her to take a chair beside him.

"Leave? Go where?" She shook her head, not wanting to believe what was happening. "You can't . . . I mean you can, but why? Aren't you happy here? You have your books and we need your wisdom at the Council. You're like family."

He expelled a heavy breath.

"There will be changes here soon, I must look after myself; and wisdom is not always admired. But I'm not leaving Tetouan, or not yet. I've found a, umm, friend and I'm going to live with him."

"Oh, Professor, you had me so worried. You'll still be here in the city. Of course you can leave the compound. Where will you stay? In the Christian quarter?"

"No," he cleared his throat, "my friend has a small villa just outside the Sidi Saidi gate, on the road to Martil."

"Do I know him? Is he the Professor who shared your room?"

"No, I doubt you know him. We met long ago in Spain. He lives with his mother. . . there is no reason for you to know him." Kleinatz shuffled his feet.

Hura felt his reticence; saw him become uncomfortable. "Well, any friends you have are always welcome here," she encouraged him with a smile.

Eyes still averted, he answered, "My friend would not be interested in the political discussions of your dinner table. He is a poet."

Hura sought something to say in the awkward silence, then extended her hand, "I will miss you," she said softly. Pushing her sadness aside, she tried to lighten his mood by changing the subject. "And by the way," she motioned toward the dining room, "at lunch will you tell me everything you know about the Sultan's harem? In Fes I understand it's huge. I hear it's a place of beauty and intrigue."

Kleinatz walked with her, appreciating the change of topic, to where a simple lunch awaited them on the table. "I don't know anything about the Sultan or his harem in Fes, but," his finger rose and pointed as it always did when he began to tell a story, "I have heard about the Turkish Sultan."

"Tell me, tell me."

Seating himself after her, he began: "Well, the harem, like most, is run by the Chief Eunuch. He has equal power with the Grand Wazir and reports directly to the Sultan. You know eunuchs were castrated when young, brought to the palace as children from other cities and countries – "

"Why is that?"

"Because uprooted, they would likely be more loyal and not get involved in intrigue and politics." The Professor's brow furrowed. "Turkish succession, which I assume is the same in Fes, goes by age. The eldest succeeds to power. So ambitious mothers of younger sons murder any older claimants who stand between their own sons and the throne." Ignoring his meal, Kleinatz pulled out his pipe and pouch and began his ritual.

"The women, Professor. The harem. I'm not interested in the boys."

"Ya, of course," he nodded. "The harem has a strict code. It is very formal, has its own hierarchy and protocol. The Sultan has 200 or 300 wives, so some never even . . . ah, service him."

"So what do they do all day?" She tasted her soup.

"They spend their time inventing ways to keep busy. They read or make jelly or overeat, or help care for other women's babies, or take female lovers." He sniffed the fresh hashish before he lit it.

Hura listened intently, wondering what life with two hundred other women would be like.

"Once inside the harem, wives and concubines never leave, and those who disobey are executed."

Hura wrinkled her brow. "How did they get to the harem? Do their fathers send them?"

He drew on his pipe. "Sometimes, but mainly they were women from other countries, prisoners of war or kidnapped girls from Africa, Europe, Egypt . . . even the Maghreb. The Sultan couldn't have women from his own city, it was forbidden. There must not be liaison between the Sultan and his own subjects."

"Ya," he drew on his pipe. "And this is interesting," he pulled his chair closer to the table. "There was a school to teach the fine points of love."

"You mean someone teaches that?" Hura laughed; her eyes widened.

125

"Go on."

"Ya, a good lover is to be cherished!" He looked up. "Well, umm, I don't know if it is appropriate for me to be telling you these things."

"Don't stop. Tell me, please."

"Well, I once read about a scene where the Sultan came to choose a woman for the night and they were all lined up in their finery in the prescribed pose: heads thrown back, hands crossed on their breasts. And when they paraded in the throne room they vied for the Sultan's attention with their seductive bodies and eyes. If one appealed to him, he asked her name and she was allowed to approach the dais where he sat. If he chose her she was then taken to separate quarters, given jewels and handmaidens. Then," his voice trailed, "she awaited the summons to the Royal Bed."

"Where did you read all this?" Hura searched the table for some lemon.

"A document written by a French woman who escaped. Of course, she may not have been truthful. But no man has ever been inside that harem and lived to tell about it. I hear the harem in Fes is even larger than the one in Turkey. You must tell me what it looks like, when you return. For my book, you know."

Hura laughed again. "Yes, Professor, for your famous book. And speaking of that," her voice faltered, "you won't stop working for the library, will you? We'll still have our library even if you move?"

"Of course." Indignant, his pale face suddenly flushed. "I plan to make it the envy of the Maghreb. I have not forgotten my promise to Sidi Mandari."

With the mention of her husband's name, Hura got up. "I must get some lemon from the kitchen."

Kleinatz checked her. "What did your husband say? You did get his permission, didn't you?" His blue eyes bore into her.

Hura grasped the back of her chair. "Well, he thought it was a good idea to send an envoy. Yes."

"Yes? That is all he said?"

"Well," Hura shifted on her feet, "At first I didn't tell him I would be going. Later I said I was going with Ibrahim."

"So your husband thinks Ibrahim will entreat the Sultan for him?" A short huff of breath exploded from his nostrils. "You have deceived him."

"It was only a small deceit. After all, Ibrahim is going with me part of the way, and I could tell how upset he was getting . . . in fact I thought for sure my husband wouldn't let me leave. And I have to go. You know that. It's the only way to get help for Tetouan. All I did was some good diplomacy. And, you've taught me all about diplomacy and politics. It's too late to preach to me now." Hura headed for the kitchen.

126

Afaf ran to Hura's room. "He's here. I've brought him. My father's here." She gasped in excitement. "And he says he'll go with you."

"Slow down, catch your breath. You say he agreed to go to Fes?"

"Yes, mistress. He's waiting, ask him yourself."

Hura bit her lip and wondered again if this was really a wise plan. Too late now. "I will. What did you tell him? Did you say why we were going?"

"I didn't say why. I just told him you needed someone for protection and he said yes. He said he owed you."

Hura whisked Afaf away with a hand motion. "Go down and prepare some breakfast for him. We have a lot to talk about. I'll be with him shortly."

As Hura drew closer to the kitchen she was confronted with the malodorous smells of sweat, fish and the sea. She wrinkled her nose. He won't pass unnoticed in the towns or forests, she thought. He stinks of fish. He'll have to spend the entire day scrubbing at the hammam.

Captain Tarek leaned against the doorframe. He straightened when he saw her. "At your service, m' lady."

Hura raised her hands in front of her to stop his advance. "Thank you, Captain. There is much we have to plan. My brother Ibrahim will brief you. Have you been to Fes before?"

"No, ma'am. But I fear nothing!" His muscled shoulders bunched in a show of confidence.

She raised her eyebrows and kept her distance. "You may regret those words before we're through."

"On the life of my only child, Afaf, I'll see you safe."

Hura hid a smile. It was hard to ignore his enthusiasm. "Captain Tarek, you can start your service by washing at the hammam. I want no fisherman on this trip. Let the clear waters of the mountains wash you clean. And, Captain, don't forget your fingernails and your hair!"

The grin disappeared, but the confident stance did not.

"Meet me in the courtyard tomorrow morning at dawn. Oh, and you'll need new travel clothes. Leather. It's still cold in the mountains."

She handed him several coins. "This should be enough."

The Captain's grin returned as he donned his cap and left.

Mohammed heard a tapping on his door and opened it cautiously. This apartment was secret, only a few people knew that he kept it in the city. He peered down the street to the right, then to the left. A few women were heading away from the hammam, otherwise, it was clear.

"What did you hear? Is she going?" He confronted his visitor.

A barefoot man dressed in a long, dirty tunic and ragged turban slipped in and went immediately to the hearth.

"Tell me! I don't pay you for nothing." He shook his fist.

The older man rubbed his grizzled chin, set his cane on the floor beside him and sat cross-legged before the fire.

"Sidi Mohammed, she will go in the spring and maybe with her brother," he said, rubbing his hands for warmth.

"Is that all? Maybe with Ibrahim? Where did you hear this? Did Ibrahim tell you?"

The man picked up his cane and fingered the bulbous snakehead at the top. I hear they're planning it but I don't think he'll go. Maybe you should offer to take her." He looked up and smiled, exposing the stumps of three front teeth.

"Shut up, you donkey. If I wanted your advice I'd ask for it."

"It's the perfect way to get rid of her," the man continued, oblivious to the insult. "She's got Boabdil under control . . . I hear he wants to take her as a wife when Mandari dies."

"What kind of talk is that!" Mohammed made a fist in front of the man's face. "That wasn't part of my agreement. He gets the northern coast including Tetouan. As for my sister, we agreed she has to go . . . maybe he's trying to trick me." His voice trailed off.

"The King's gone. That's right, gone to free Tangier. He'll save your father, then he'll return triumphantly to marry your sister. She can't refuse him if he's successful. And he might be, after a few years, who knows . . . Mandari won't live that long."

"All your fancy madressa education, that's what gives you such an imagination. You're really only a beggar. None of this is true. You lie. I ought to shove your cane down your throat. Boabdil hasn't betrayed me, I don't believe it."

The man sat impassively, betraying no emotion. He looked straight ahead, just as he had hundreds of times before.

Mohammed twitched in agitation. Foamy spittle collected at the sides of his mouth. He limped around the room.

"Who else knows this?"

"No one."

"Who told you?"

"I bribed one of the King's guards."

"Likely story. You don't pay for anything." Mohammed spat.

"Not true, Sidi. Didn't I arrange for Mandari's letter to the Sultan to lose its way? That cost money. Plenty of silver. And what about the poison."

"Enough. Don't remind me of that failure." Mohammed growled. "And now, you want more money, I suppose?"

"If you don't want your sister to get help from the Sultan, or to return from Fes. These things all have a price."

Mohammed walked over to a chest by the side of his bed. He lit the candle next to it, illuminating the four corners of the lid that was decorated with brightly painted serpents. He opened it and pulled out a woven pouch. Standing in front of the man, he dropped it in his lap.

"This should be enough. Make sure no troops are sent, and she never returns. If you fail, I'll see you really do become a blind beggar."

The man grabbed the pouch. It chinked as he stuffed it in the folds of his waistband.

"I will not fail."

SEVENTEEN

"*Bismillah.*" Ibrahim intoned by rote as he grabbed the bridle of his horse.

Hura checked the girth of her saddle. Hot breath plumed from the nostrils of her skittish horse in the crisp air of dawn. He'll do, she thought. At least he's big. The mount for Captain Tarek, small and wide by comparison, seemed sturdy and suitable for someone who didn't know about mountain travel. She walked to the mules and examined their loads: food, clothing, gifts, tents. At last, all was in order.

"Where is that sea captain?" shouted Ibrahim. "Has anyone seen him? It's past dawn."

Impatient hooves tap-danced on the courtyard stones. From the shelter of the courtyard, Afaf held a bundled Suha in her arms and rocked from one foot to the other trying to keep warm. Then she lifted the child's small hand and together they waved good-by.

Tarek came rushing down the narrow alley toward them, breathing hard. He apologized: "I went to pray, then I got caught behind a flock of sheep on their way to the slaughter house, and the street was blocked and then – "

Hura glared but said only: "Never mind. You're here. Grab your horse. Let's go."

The small entourage led their horses under the archway single file and down the alley to the street, Ibrahim leading with his guards and Hura, Tarek and the mules in the rear. Turning the final corner to the main street, tears welled in Hura's eyes as she looked back for a last glimpse of Suha's tiny fingers waving in the air.

Sometimes the smooth dirt track became a stony path between sheer sides of confining rock, other times on the open plains she felt she could reach out and touch the descending feathery-gray fingers of the clouds, they seemed so close. Ibrahim kept a fast pace.

As soon as they passed the village of Beni Kariche, the landscape began to change. Gone were the cactus, the olive and fig trees. The mountains loomed white, high above them. Ibrahim followed a well-worn track that wound around mountainsides, then dipped into small valleys where they were greeted by fields of lacy yellow flowers only to return to the mists of the rocky cliffs again.

At noon on the third day, as Hura turned the final bend in the road, she spurred ahead to Chaouen. Excited to be back home, Hura called back to Tarek: "*Choof iChefchaouen*, that's the real name in Berber. It means 'look at the mountain horns'."

Alerted by lookouts, townspeople, waving and cheering the arrival of their young Emir, lined the main street and small boys ran alongside their horses. They continued riding up the hill and around the city wall, up past the Place El Maghzen. There, on her left, Hura saw the familiar tower of the kasbah and the central square, the Uta el Hammam. Below her now, the town formed a maze of red tiled roofs, crisp whitewashed walls and elegant architectural details. To her right on the square the cafes smelled of grilling meat and spices; the stores and food stalls were jammed with people and goods. While everyone else dismounted, she stood high in her stirrups for just another moment, giddy with the familiar sight. How she had missed her home! Could she change her mind and not go? Stay and let Ibrahim take all responsibility?

Hura sighed, then with a flourish, leapt from the saddle and succumbed to the hugs and kisses of relatives.

That evening the entire town celebrated. Ibrahim had planned everything so well, even the feast. Torches lit the central square; musicians played, acrobats and dancers entertained and the townsfolk ate until past midnight. Exhausted and happy, Hura slept peacefully in her old room in the kasbah. The last drum stopped beating as dawn approached.

In the late morning, Hura chided Tarek for wanting to stay longer: "I agree, one day is hardly enough in this beautiful village. But we must leave. Saddle sores are no excuse."

Tarek spread out his palms, rubbed raw from the reins. "The rest of me is just as red."

"If you didn't hold the reins like a tiller, your hands would be fine." Hura grinned. "Come with me and see the village."

As they walked together around the square, she pointed to the Grand mosque with its octagonal minaret. "This was one of the first buildings my father built," she said proudly.

Tarek grunted in acknowledgement and they continued past fountains down into the city where the smell of fresh bread wafted around them from a nearby bakery. Tarek had seen enough. He headed for a café and sat down stiffly. "My stomach wins over my curiosity."

Hura continued to walk on alone in the peace that only comes from being at home.

After a tearful good-by with Ibrahim, the remainder of their long journey began early the next day in clear weather with a brisk downslope breeze. Thanks to Ibrahim's planning, the two travelers were welcomed each night at their destination. Tarek proved an able traveler once he grew accustomed to his saddle. He even made light of his discomfort, and compared his undulation on his horse to the rolling of his ship.

Even with the careful planning of her brother and her own knowledge of the mountains, Hura stayed in constant alert. She watched Tarek intently . . . he appeared cautious and vigilant for her safety. He also kept a weather-eye cocked on the sky. Only once were they stopped by bad weather when a sudden snow squall enveloped them just outside Et-Tnine, and sent them shivering into the shelter of a shallow cave.

Safely inside, Hura and Tarek sat apart; she, worried and wrapped in a blanket; he, restless and rising often to peer outside at the snow that blew in howling flurries. Hura's thoughts wandered: she worried what would happen if she failed to win the Sultan's support, and most of all, wondered what a young Berber mother was doing there shivering in a cave on the way to Fes? Why had Allah not made her husband well for this journey? She pushed aside that thought. Why couldn't she be like her own mother who, before she died so young, had spent all her time with her children. Shouldn't she be with Suha? She pulled her blanket tighter around her. She missed her daughter. And what did she really know about her escort, Tarek, this taciturn man?

She probed with a statement, not a question. "Afaf loves you very much. I suppose you don't see much of her, or your wife. You're always at sea."

Tarek squatted immobile by the cave's opening and did not turn to face her. His voice was expressionless when he answered. "Afaf has always known the life of a seaman is hard."

No comment about a wife. Hura rubbed her hands to warm them and tried another subject. "You know our port well. Who are all those workers? Where do they come from?"

Tarek turned and sat down facing Hura, large hands crossed over his knees, his back against the rough rock. "Unprotected Christians, all of them. No hope of ransom."

"How did they get to our port?" She persisted.

"Many were galley slaves, some were oarsmen on ships captured by pirates. Pirates bring them to Tetouan."

"Yes, and . . ."

"Your brother Mohammed puts them to work on his docks at Martil. He sells the stronger ones at the slave market in Tangier." Tarek rose, and bending low, resumed his post at the mouth of the cave.

No one kept slaves in the mountains . . . suddenly a vision struck Hura,

132

paling her already chilled face. She saw Mohammed walking freely in Tangier's main square, the famous Grand Socco. Tangier, where her father was imprisoned! She struggled to erase it from her mind.

In an administrative palace adjacent to that of the Sultan of Fes, Grand Wazir Walid sat on a plump silk cushion in the inner chamber of his office suite. The room was impressively appointed with glittering golden objects, a huge colorful rug that had been a tribute from the mountain people, and an ornate ebony and ivory desk, a gift from the Portuguese Ambassador.

The Wazir, aristocratic in his bearing with a long angular face, high forehead and neatly trimmed goatee, had learned to be a ruthless survivor. His eyes, ever watchful, revealed nothing. Of the Merenid tribe, he had seen the last Merenid Sultan executed in 1465, and the one before assassinated. Now the Wattasid tribe was in power and Muhummad al-Shaykh was the first of this new dynasty.

But Walid remained. The new Sultan, indolent and preoccupied with expanding his already enormous harem, appreciated his Grand Wazir's monetary, diplomatic and administrative abilities. He functioned well with the Portuguese, and even had a new ally, the son of an Emir from the belligerent tribes of the Rif.

This morning after prayers, Walid, now seated at his desk, rapidly leafed through the stack of newly delivered messages and reports. His Chamberlain ushered in the first appointment of the day. The man, white-bearded and skull-capped, knew better than to sit in the visitor's chair, or to speak before the Wazir did. He remained motionless, stooped and patient, until the Wazir looked up and acknowledged him.

"You again, Schlomo?"

The man began to speak. He spoke without a flowery introduction. It was not his way and the Wazir did not expect it from him. Each knew the other well after so many years. They both would have been uncomfortable with polite chatter. This was business, and the old man came to the point quickly. "I come before you to explain why we in the mellah cannot pay this year's dareeba. You propose increasing the taxes . . . substantially."

"Two fold. And ordered over the Sultan's seal, not proposed." The Wazir tilted his head back and looked down his long nose as he spoke.

"Two fold. Yes." The old man dry-washed his hands nervously. "You also know that trade in the souks has increased but little over the last year."

"Twenty percent is not a little."

"I see your agents inform you well." The man paused. "The merchants are prepared to pay a tax increase of fifteen percent."

The Grand Wazir did not deign to reply. He sat immobile except for the tapping of his long fingernails on the highly polished desk.

The elder lowered his head. Reflected on the desk he saw the Wazir's narrow, slitted eyes. He sighed audibly. "Forgive me for my persistence in bargaining. It is our custom. We will pay a tax of twenty percent, our profit. Even though last year you raised . . . even though we in the mellah stripped our gold reserves to meet last year's increase. So now we can't pay double. This year, we have no reserves."

"Schlomo, old man, you have lived in Fes as long as I have. But many of your people have not. The mellah is crowded with Conversos whose garments are weighed to the ground with jewels in the hem."

"That is the dowry of our women. It's our businesses that have no gold."

The old man heard the tempo of the tapping fingers increase and hastened to add, "But the merchants think they may be able to pay fifty percent. Fifty percent more than last year's taxes."

"Think? An end to this. Your people need an example. The shopkeepers will be glad to pay double when they see the Sultan's wrath." The tapping stopped and the Wazir leaned forward. "You know the origin of the Arabic word 'mellah'?"

Schlomo answered warily. "Who doesn't . . . comes from *mehl*."

"And what does *mehl* mean?"

"Salt." Perspiration dripped on the beard.

The Grand Wazir grinned as he asked, "And what has the obligation of your people to do with salt?"

Schlomo paled. "We are responsible to drain and salt-pickle the severed heads of criminals and – "

The Wazir turned toward his Chamberlain and ordered, "Have this man's salted head put on a spike over the Dekakène Gate. And use your imagination on his wife and any daughters."

At first Hura saw an occasional hut or garden. Soon traffic on the road increased and they rode through hills of spring flowers, passing people on foot, carts laden with produce and donkeys with their crippling loads. The road widened and as they crested a hill they were surrounded by white marble tombs and engraved and brightly painted grave markers. Cemeteries ringed the hills around and beneath them. At the edge of the last hill they stopped and looked down on the bowl of the white city of Fes el Bali. It was almost sunset, and the red sun turned the city walls to gold. The splendor took her breath away. She had heard much about the magnificence and beauty of Fes. It all seemed true.

Immediately below them Hura could see the flat roofs of the Kairaouine quarter and the two minarets of the Kairaouine mosque, the main one whitewashed and domed, the other square. To the right the tall green-tiled pyramid roof and slender minaret of the Zaouia of Moulay Idriss II stood and far to the left of this trio of minarets was the Andalus quarter.

Tarek broke the magic spell of the scene with two gruff words: "Which way?"

She straightened in the saddle and blurted: "I know what you're thinking. This city is too big, too important for someone like me. It will swallow me up. Well . . . well you'll see."

Grim faced, Hura settled back in her saddle and pointed. "Ibrahim said we pass by the walls of the kasbah, just over there, and go around the area of the leper colony. That's where the gate is, the Bab Guissa."

Once through the gate, they plunged into the busy street on foot, leading their horses and mules, and headed for the Souk El Attarin. Crowds streamed in front, around and behind them. The noise of the shoppers, the mantric prayers of beggars, the bells of water vendors, the shouts of the muleteers ('make way, make way'!) enveloped them. The smell of dung, curing leather, saffron, spices, sandalwood, olive oil, and sour milk assailed them. Dust floated in the air illuminated by the shafts of the setting sun that filtered through the rush roofing. After two false turns in the maze, Tarek wound their way down a street lined with stalls and shops to the bottom of the hill and entered the souk of the spice vendors through an arched gateway. The street widened and they pulled away to the side of a small square.

Hura stood motionless, entranced. She forgot her weariness in the excitement of this big city but remembered the Professor's parting words: "Be careful of the city. She is a siren like in the Greek tales. Her dust will caress your face. Your body will be assaulted. Take care. The city is a flirt, ready to mesmerize and entrap you." She had laughed at his words back then and asked if his new friend, the poet, had penned them.

Tarek brought her back to reality again: "If you don't keep up with me, we'll never get to the palace."

She shook her head to clear it. "Do you really know where we are?"

"I'll ask someone again." He began to lead his horse away. "We need to head into the setting sun, out of the old city to the Fes Jdid, the new city. That's where the Royal Palace is, and this is the only street inside the walls wide enough for our animals with baggage."

Hura looked around her at the labyrinth of alleys leading off the street. It was getting dark and shopkeepers were closing up their stalls, shoppers heading home. To her amazement, she noticed most of the women were veiled. Tarek led on, the street emptied out onto a grassy plain. Soon they saw the double walls of the new city and could make out the triple arches of the massive gate.

She shuddered to see a white-bearded head stuck on a pike that jutted over the entrance. The long beard whipped in the wind. "Barbarians," she gasped.

Tarek responded with a snort. "Seen it in every city."

"Not in Tetouan!" Then, seeing a flicker of a grin on Tarek's face, she rode on, silent for a moment then said defensively: "Yes, I put that Portuguese Lieutenant's head on a pike. I had to. That was war." She spurred her horse on.

Inside the arched main gateway a soldier stood at attention next to the flame of a brilliant torchiere. Above him, outlined in the firelight, three pairs of bulbous shapes were nailed to the wooden door. Hura's stomach turned over. Tarek halted to ask directions to the palace. Hura tried but could not look away. She sickened at the sudden realization that these salted lumps were mutilated breasts – one pair merely buds.

This new city of Fes was completely different from the old city. Even in the twilight she saw order, not chaos. The tops of flowering trees tumbled over high walls into the street and Hura could smell the sweetness of the hidden gardens. By the time the travelers and their pack animals arrived at the Palace the sky was completely dark. Torches lit both sides of the entrance to the massive complex. Hura squinted at the tightly closed doors, the overhanging roof with its green tiles.

Exhausted, Hura lifted the bronze rosette-shaped knocker and let it strike. A guard opened the door, clearly annoyed with the intrusion. He held a long curved scimitar in his right hand.

Hura drew herself up to her full height. "I am Hura bint Ali Rachid al-Mandari of Tetouan." She held up her hand and flashed Mandari's large signet ring. "I am here to see his Excellency the Sultan. I am expected."

The guard peered out at this tall woman dressed as a man, then looked beyond her to Tarek, disheveled in his sweaty leather jacket and behind him to the heavily laden, dust covered mules.

"The palace is closed. No one enters. Come back tomorrow."

"But I am expected. I have an audience with the Sultan."

The guard slammed the door in their faces.

"Your head is filled with dog dung!" Tarek pushed Hura aside and banged on the door with his fist. "I'll teach him not to slam doors in your face!"

Hura glared at Tarek. Tired and disheartened, she realized how they must look and grasped his arm. "We'll go to a fondouk tonight, I saw several inns as we entered. We'll come back tomorrow morning."

Pulling and tugging the now stubborn pack animals, they retraced their steps to the old city, stood outside the tall wooden doors of the fondouk and banged the heavy iron knocker against its plate.

"How do you know it's an inn?" grumbled Tarek.

"It says so on the sign – right there," she pointed. "Can't you read?"

As they waited for the doors to open, Tarek rubbed his stubbled chin. "You're sure not what I expected."

"What do you mean?" She frowned.

Tarek pinched his lip with his finger. "You smile like a woman, ride like a man, and now you can read!"

Before she could respond, the innkeeper pulled the massive doors open and Tarek pushed by him into the courtyard. "We need rooms for the night." While the men negotiated, Hura led the animals inside and stood gaping up at the balconies around the large two-storied courtyard and the open sky above. A small boy emerged from a dark lower room to assist her. When the animals were secure, unloaded and fed, Hura bought bread, boiled eggs and two oil lamps from the innkeepers wife, gave half to Tarek, then retreated to her room on the second floor. It smelled of smoke and lye.

Hura's sleep was interrupted as a large caravan arrived and its forty camels were being unpacked and tethered. In between the shouting, honking and grunting, Hura lay awake staring at the ceiling in the flickering lamplight and tried to focus on her mission. She prayed for wisdom and courage. *"I will get the Sultan to send troops to our defense. I mustn't fail."* She kept repeating these words over and over. The words rose and disappeared with the lamp smoke as it curled toward the ceiling.

The Chamberlain held the door open as the urbane Portuguese Ambassador bowed once more and intoned in Arabic: *"Ma'salame."* Grand Wazir Walid, equally polite, nodded his good-by and replied in kind, in a passable Portuguese accent, *"Adeus."*

The Chamberlain closed the door and looked inquiringly at his superior, who sat, fingers tented and reflective. The Wazir confided, "A worthy diplomat. Always a source of information. Here in Fes he knows more about the Mediterranean and events on the Rif than do all our spies in the villages."

Dubious, the Chamberlain cautioned: "We don't know how reliable his information is."

The Wazir gave him a sharp look. "No, we don't. But Mohammed bin Rachid will arrive in a few days and he will confirm or deny. Who's next?"

The Chamberlain crossed the room to a side door. "The gold caravan arrived last night. Your trader is here."

The Vizier rubbed his hands. "Don't keep him waiting."

Aswad was a short, lean man with a prune-like face burnt black by the glare of the sun and eyes wrinkled from squinting. Slung over his shoulder was a large, leather saddlebag with flapped pockets to either side. After the obligatory obeisance, he dropped the heavy bag on the carpeted floor. "Your share." He grinned, then sat gingerly on the recently vacated chair and launched into a nervous recital of his adventures.

"Later. Later. First to business."

Aswad contorted his lower lip, unfastened the two compartments of the bag, drew out a soft kid-leather pouch from one, and dropped it on the desk. The Wazir opened the largest drawer of his desk and took out an ornate wooden stand and brass hanging scale along with several weights. He quickly unfastened the drawstring of the pouch.

"That one's dust," Aswad motioned with a dark finger.

"I know by the feel." The Wazir retorted and began to load the pans, one with gold, the other with weights. For each load he sought the exact balance then noted the weight in a small leather-bound ledger. He scowled when the tally was finished. Opening the second leather pouch and pouring a handful of nuggets into his other palm did not alter his frown.

"The dust shipment is light," he lifted his eyes to skewer the trader. "So is this nugget pouch."

"I know. I was going to tell Your Excellency." Aswad's speech suddenly became more formal. While the Wazir proceeded to weigh and tally the nuggets, the trader told the woeful account of his trip.

"It's been a year since I left Fes with two hundred camels. I took my usual route down south across the Western Sahara into Mali to the Bure and Babuk regions near the Niger. Well, I spread my goods in the usual place: the colored cloth, blankets, and so on. Made camp, all as usual, a little ways off, and – "

"You mean you left your goods unguarded, you trust savages?" The Wazir straightened, nearly dropping a nugget from the pan.

"It's crazy but that's the way it's done. Next morning, I hurried back to the exchange place. I tell you after five months on a camel, I couldn't wait. But this time everything was different. The natives had been there because they took some of my goods. In their place they left me the small pile of gold dust you've got, plus some ostrich feathers and ivory."

"What kind of business dealing is that? They cheated you." The Wazir leveled his narrowed eyes on the little man.

"No, never. That's the way they do business, it's called 'dumb commerce'. Problem is, seems the Portuguese got there first. A month before, Did you know their ships sail down our coast to the Niger or into the Gulf of Guinea. They barter for red pepper." Aswad began to squirm.

In the sudden silence of the chamber both men heard the muezzin's call to prayer. Neither man moved.

"Your story has the ring of truth." Walid slowly drew the point of his goatee between his fingers. "The Portuguese lust for gold. They are clever. I can see where it profits them to have us do the work. But why leave half the gold?"

"I don't know, Excellency." The trader moved forward in his chair. "But I heard from another trader that the Marrakech Sultan's Grand Wazir wants to take and sell our half to the Portuguese."

Before long, the Wazir had accepted his meager baksheesh of nuggets and had heard more than enough. Portuguese ships brought trade goods and carried away gold. He dismissed this messenger of bad news saying, "You may unload your camels. But remember, my agents will tally your goods. Pray that your percentage is no more than your proper share."

The trader stood up in obvious relief. "Your treaty says nothing about gold, it just says we and the Portuguese are friends."

"Precisely." Walid raised a well-manicured finger. "And our custom says: 'If one admires a possession of another, his friend must give it to him'."

Long before first light, the dirt courtyard of the fondouk was alive and writhing; a maelstrom of motion, noise and smells. Some twenty other travelers were staying there and they all wanted to leave at the same time. The loading and jostling stirred a dust cloud up to the second floor and created a traffic jam of impatient men, horses, camels, mules and donkeys.

Hura asked for directions to the nearest hammam, bathed, dressed in a finely embroidered maroon kaftan, and returned for breakfast with Tarek. Once again, she donned her husband's cape and slipped his heavy ring on her index finger. And once again, she stood before the elaborate gates of the Palace and announced herself to the guard.

"It's a good thing he weren't the same man," Tarek seethed as they entered the Royal compound. "He'd be swallowing his teeth."

"Captain! Behave yourself," Hura admonished, but smiled as she whispered, "watch what you say. Unlike the sea, palaces have ears."

A footman took their horses and a brightly sashed guard led them past a large courtyard filled with men cloaked in white, then through a blue, silk-draped ante room down a long carpeted hallway with archways leading off to corridors and separate courtyards on each side. The hall ended at the entrance to a tree-shaded garden in whose center a tiled stone fountain dripped water into a large flower-shaped marble basin. They were ushered to a bench and she was told to wait for a representative of the Ministry.

When the sun was high, they still waited. Tarek fidgeted. His clean wool pants, loose from the weight he'd lost on the long journey, made his legs itch. Occasionally, a beefy hand shot down to scratch his crotch. Hura sat, hands folded in her lap, staring at the mesmerizing drops of fountain water. A liveried attendant slipped silently in and asked for Hura's petition and her ring.

"It's about time." Tarek growled at his retreating back.

She threw him a sidelong glance that by now he recognized as the prelude to angry words.

The attendant reentered shortly and addressed them: "Allah does not will it today."

"But I am expected!"

"It is not Allah's wish."

Hura stood up to confront him. "We will return tomorrow. Perhaps Allah will favor us with a meeting tomorrow?"

"Perhaps." The attendant bowed and hastened away.

Stunned by the rejection, she suddenly realized he hadn't returned her letter and ring. "My letter! I'll catch him," she said as she ran out into the hallway. "I'll meet you at the entry."

There was no one in sight. Which door did he pass through, she wondered, facing a maze of narrow corridors. She took the first corridor on her right, almost colliding with a young man in Andalusian clothes holding a long roll of papers in his hand.

When she asked, "Has an attendant just passed this way?" The young man broke his stride and turned toward her. His gaze roved her intently from hair to shoes as if he knew but couldn't place her. It stopped on the ornate bib over her breasts.

Their gaze finally met as she was about to repeat her question. His eyes, locked on hers, were dark, large and shameless. They seemed to see behind clothing. The contact prolonged itself. He's different from the other men I've met, she thought – clean shaven, short-cropped hair, but there's a patch of fur under his lower lip going down his chin. As she thought this, he looked at her chin where the dots of her tattoo ran from her lip in the same way, downward. She smiled nervously.

At last he answered with a gesture. "No, not through here."

When he spoke, she noticed his white teeth were not stained with kif, and his accent was that of a Morisco. Their encounter over quickly, he bowed, and after a backward glance, walked briskly away. Frozen to the spot, she began to tremble. Who was he? Why did she feel so attracted to this stranger? Somehow, she found her way back to the entryway.

Tarek saw her empty hands. "What's the matter? Where's the ring? You look like you're shipwrecked."

Hura regained her composure. "I couldn't find him. I'm sure it's safe. We'll try tomorrow."

Returning to the fondouk, Tarek contracted with the jovial owner for a second night and secured their horses. In the full daylight, Hura could now appreciate the size of the inn. There must be fifty rooms. The heavy wooden beams of the balconies were decorated with finely carved cedar rails and balustrades. Off to the right, on the ground, a small fire roasted chickens on a tripod spit. The large courtyard was divided by ropes into corrals for different animals. To her left a sea of camels sat on their haunches in the dirt while a worker raked the ground around them piling up mounds of dung. They were skinny, she noted, as if just returning from a long journey.

By the fourth day, they knew the palace routine well. Upon arriving in the morning, they would be ushered into the garden.

"At least we don't have to wait outside like everyone else." Hura smoothed her hair back. "There must be several hundred people out there."

Tarek grunted in acknowledgment.

"It's not like Tetouan," she continued. "I've noticed the same people at the head of the line. It hasn't moved. Life in the city is so fast, but here in the Palace it seems so slow."

"Too many people. Too much corruption." Tarek spat on the decorative paving.

She walked to the hallway. "If it's like yesterday, we've a long wait. I'm going to see what's in the courtyard next to us."

The tiles in the courtyard echoed the blue of the sky. On the far side she saw a pair of ornate iron gates, partially open, inviting her into another large room. She quietly crept inside. A huge brass chandelier hung from the ceiling and carpets softened her footsteps. An arched doorway opened onto a long tiled arcade from which she could hear hammering and pounding. I'll just peek outside and see what's going on, she convinced herself, and continued exploring.

On the adjoining patio, several workmen were setting tiles in the outer wall; one worker sat with his arms on his knees holding a sharp, double headed hammer. With precise blows he chipped the blue glazed tile before him into small geometric shapes. Other workers chipped at large blocks of marble. Beside them, under an umbrella at a makeshift desk covered with sheaves of paper, sat the handsome Andalusian she had seen on her former visit.

She emerged from the arcade into the sunlit patio and boldly walked over to him.

"Still here?" he rose. "Allow me to introduce myself. I am Habib ibn Issa, from Granada. Architect to the Sultan."

"I am Hura, bint Rachid, wife of al-Mandari, Fundador of Tetouan."

She squinted from the sun and his direct gaze. "I've been trying to see the Sultan . . . but every day I'm told to come back."

He cast her a look of understanding. "I think you want to see the Grand Wazir Walid. He makes all the decisions for the court. The Sultan occupies himself in the harem."

Hura blushed, wondered what to say. His handsome face, the way he moved, made her so aware she was a woman.

"You are here on business, I assume. Not for pleasure?" Habib flashed a provocative smile.

Hura's cheeks colored more deeply: "My business here is of utmost importance," she snapped. "We of Tetouan are in danger, and I've come for the Sultan's help."

"Then you must see the Wazir. I'll take you there." He grasped her forearm.

"Thank you, but . . ." she remembered Tarek, "my guard waits in the garden, I must get him. Please wait for me here."

Wary of this strange young man in elegant clothing, Tarek followed as Habib led them through yet another courtyard and down an arcade toward the adjacent palace of the Grand Wazir.

"The Sultan's Palace is so big! How many rooms does it have?" Hura asked.

"For the Sultan's pleasure," Habib said, "there are baths, aviaries, libraries, dungeons, laundries, hospitals, kitchens, a mosque, eunuch's quarters, slave quarters, a council chamber, dormitories for actors and dwarfs, an execution room, circumcision room, a suite where the pretender to the throne lives, staff quarters for the gardeners, the keeper of the keys, pages, waiting women, grooms, scribes, astronomers and messengers."

"And architects?" Hura inquired with a smile.

"Yes, architects," he laughed. "Well, here you are." Habib paused at the steps and nodded to a guard who disappeared inside. "This building is the Wazir's Palace. Good luck."

She felt a tingle of warmth when he took her hand in his, brought it to his lips and held it there longer than he should have. No Muslim, not even Boabdil's Moriscos from Granada, had done so before.

A Chamberlain appeared. The Wazir had someone with him, he explained, and offered her a seat on a banquette.

I wish we had an architect like Habib in Tetouan, she thought. The Sultan's Palace must be as beautiful as heaven. But someone like him wouldn't want to leave. He's used to the glory here. Besides, we have no money, and he's so handsome he's probably married. At that, she took a sharp breath. What am I thinking! I'm so ashamed. I'm married too!

She looked up to find the Chamberlain approaching.

"Grand Wazir Walid will see you now."
The pit of her stomach rose to her throat.

EIGHTEEN

Grand Wazir Walid looked up as Hura entered, rose, and greeted her in a courtly manner. With utmost respect, he made inquiries about her husband and family. He bowed and offered her a seat in an overstuffed chair beside his desk. Then with a nod to the Chamberlain by his door, he ordered fruit juices and pastries. As he read the letter to the Sultan, Hura scanned the top of his desk, which was piled with maps and what appeared to be decrees and inventory sheets. Mandari's ring sat on top of a small folded paper with the initials MR in elaborate calligraphy. How did he get her ring and her letter, she wondered. And was that Mohammed's monogram on his desk?

"Now tell me more about this problem in Tetouan," he said in a silken voice. "Your illustrious husband has built a fine city and has a reputation for administering it well. Soon, I hear, it will rival Tangier."

"Thank you for your kind words, I will bring them back with me. Neither my husband, nor my brother, the Emir of Chaouen, were able to address you today personally. I have been given that honor. I beg you to listen to me." Hura chose her words carefully. "You have heard about our attack by the Portuguese, and we have heard of your new treaty. Portuguese warships patrol our waters, their merchant ships pay no duties at our port. I am here with a petition to the Sultan for troops and money to help protect us."

Her voice becoming unsteady, she said: "We have reason to fear another invasion from the Portuguese. I need to tell the Sultan our problems. He is great and wise. Surely he will help us."

The Wazir sat immobile behind his desk. Through heavy lidded eyes he scrutinized her intently; his hands formed a tent before him. As she explained the problems of Tetouan further, he nodded occasionally, or smiled, or stroked his short-cropped beard. His encouragement gave her more confidence. She told him about the destruction of the city and even the sword fight between her husband and the Portuguese Lieutenant.

When the refreshments arrived, the Wazir excused himself with a show of great reluctance – saying he had a pressing matter to attend to and would soon return. Out of earshot, in the next room, he called his Chamberlain to his side.

"This Berber woman is trouble. She has the effrontery to come here demanding help for Tetouan."

"Yes, Excellency. You remember our spies told me she was coming. They also said she would never arrive."

"Find out what went wrong. These Berbers! I've had trouble with them before. We've always taken care of it, haven't we? Remember the mountain tribesmen who took Taza and controlled the pass between the Rif and the Middle Atlas? Nothing but trouble, these Berbers."

The Chamberlain nodded agreement and waited for instructions. They came quickly.

"Find a way to keep her from returning to Tetouan. Make it subtle. No witnesses. Use two of your best men."

Inside the Wazir's office, Hura put Mandari's ring on her thumb and twirled it, saying to herself: he's going to help; he seems interested in our problems; he understands.

When the Wazir returned, she gave him more details about the threat to her city and passionately repeated the points the Professor had advised her to relate. Then she spoke of her own vision of unification and peace and of the expulsion of the foreigners in the Rif. While she talked, the Wazir continued to nod understandingly; he consoled her and agreed with her.

Then he admitted conspiratorially that he had problems just like she did: "Our enemies in Marrakech are threatening us with war, and as if that wasn't enough, I am receiving less and less gold from our traders beyond the Sahara. I don't know if we have enough to finish the new addition to the harem." A look of utmost distress appeared on his face.

Flattered by his mention of affairs and problems of state, Hura nodded in understanding.

Finally he smiled and rose, gestured toward his door, handed back her letter and thanked her for coming. In a honey-toned voice he said that Allah would bring her baraka.

"Chamberlain!" the Wazir yelled as soon as she had left. "Imagine!" He flung his manicured hands upward. "Sending a woman to do a man's work. What have we heard from our spies in Tetouan. Find out what's really going on there, and, as I said before, make sure that woman never returns."

"Yes, Excellency. Where do you want the accident? Here in Fes?"

"I don't care. Just get rid of her," the Wazir screamed.

Outside, in the waiting room, Hura stood still in shock. She realized that she had come away empty-handed. He had given nothing but smiles. How could she just let him ease her out the door like that? When Tarek came to her and asked about the meeting, she waved her hand, "Go away." Then, squeezing back tears of humiliation, she stumbled to the palace garden seeking a place to compose herself.

Oblivious to the manicured hedges and neatly planted rows of flowers, Hura wandered deeper into the garden. Consumed by worry, she wondered what to do now. How could she go home . . . rejected, with no good news, her efforts futile. Just as she passed beside a stand of tall bamboo, two massive arms grabbed her and before she knew what was happening, shoved her through an archway. She fell face down onto a grassy lawn, shrieked and jumped to her feet. A giant black slave filled the entire archway, his body barring her escape. Frantic, she looked for help. From the other end of the lawn she heard peals of laughter and stood rooted to see eight women pulling a chaise on tiny wheels. Pink ribbons fluttered from their hair, a short transparent cape covered the elaborate pink harness that girded their loins; they wore nothing else. A man, all in pink and holding the reins urged them on, faster. Hura's eyes grew wide. The chaise tipped over in a tight turn and up scrambled the short, rotund man, his bejeweled turban askew. He roared with laughter, straightened his garments and ambled to his divan on the nearby verandah where he seated himself between two young men.

Hura realized the giant whose huge hand had grabbed her must be a harem eunuch. This is my chance, she realized. The baraka is with me. That must be the Sultan. She ran toward him.

The Sultan looked quizzically at Hura and beckoned with his hands. His fingers glistened with large rings of faceted pink stones. "Come, sit with me. What are you doing over there? Why are you wearing a kaftan? Take it off."

A concubine? He must think I'm one of them! Before Hura could respond, a woman's voice shouted from behind the screen on the verandah: "This woman is not one of us!"

Hura stopped in front of him. She waved her letter in one hand and held high her ring on the other. The eunuch rushed forward and raised his scimitar awaiting the command to strike.

"Wait." A stubby hand stilled the scimitar. "Who are you? What do you want?" The fleshy lips barely moved.

"I have an important petition for you, Great Sultan. I am the wife of your humble servant, al-Mandari of Tetouan. Please read my letter."

"Read it to me," he ordered his elder son, seated to his right. Mohammad straightened his turban, the pinched eyes in his puffy face scanned the document. The other son, Hamad, seated to the Sultan's left, studied Hura while his brother read the letter.

"It asks for money and soldiers for Tetouan. That's all, father."

"Go see the Wazir. He handles these things," the Sultan said and flicked his wrist to dismiss Hura.

146

"Please listen to me," she begged as the eunuch grabbed the back of her neck in an iron grip and started to drag her away.

"Father," Hamad interrupted, "an alliance, even a purchased one, might be profitable. Wait!" he called out to the eunuch. "Don't take her away."

Hura watched as the tall, muscular young man approached and introduced himself as Prince Hamad. He asked to read her letter, then returned to his father. After a brief conversation between them, she heard the Sultan laugh: "Do whatever you wish."

Hamad grinned at Hura, "Come with me, I will see to your problem."

Uncertain and anxious, Hura was escorted back to the Wazir's palace. She followed him as he brushed by the Chamberlain and strode directly into the Wazir's office. Finding Walid alone, he ordered the Wazir to prepare a letter to the Pasha of Rabat for Hura.

"Write that it is the wish of the Sultan that the Pasha send a full detachment of Turkish mercenaries to Tetouan."

The Wazir showed no emotion, his hooded eyes concealed his anger. He nodded understanding. "I will have a scribe prepare one later."

The young prince, hands flat on the desk, leaned over the Wazir. "No, do it now."

The two men stared at one another in a silent battle of power. The Wazir's mouth twisted. His fingernails drummed on his desk. He knew the Sultan's bastard son cared nothing about this woman's problem.

"I am happy to oblige," the Wazir conceded. "In fact, I will write it myself."

Hura and Hamad watched as the Wazir penned the short letter, folded it, then addressed it to the Pasha and stamped his seal on the outside.

"May your problems be solved. I wish you a safe journey," he said in unctuous tones as he handed the letter to her.

Once outside, Hura thanked the Prince for his assistance. She promised she would be forever grateful, and someday repay his kindness. He had saved her people; he was the Protector of the Faith. Giddy with success, she found Tarek in the garden and told him the good news.

"We'll leave tomorrow; tonight I must write to my husband and tell him."

"I'm for leaving this place now. It's crowded and dangerous. Give me the sea. That's what I want."

Somehow the good news made her forget danger. She had won. She had gotten what she came for.

Passing back through the Dekakène gate, Hura smiled at her dour companion: "Soon we'll both have what we want."

As they rode away, they saw a crowd of older women to the right of the road in a barren square baked hard from the sun's heat. They were screaming and throwing stones against the outer wall. Hura stopped to ask a young woman what was happening.

"Stoning. My cousin," she said.

By the time Hura and Tarek circled, the crowd had thinned revealing a young woman, hands tied around a post. Her crumpled torso had slid to the ground, half buried in rocks.

"Must have been adultery. Better the whore is dead," Tarek said angrily. He spurred his horse away in a canter.

Hura wondered why he was so upset. Adultery was a terrible sin, she knew, and she could never be adulterous herself . . . but he seemed to react so strangely. She had never talked with him about his personal life. Surely he wasn't upset about the death of an unknown woman. Death was no stranger to him – he had even pledged to kill in her defense. She took one long, last look at the small bloodied body. It was true. Adultery was the only crime that women were stoned for. A family member probably threw the first stone.

She caught up with Tarek outside the gate to the old city. "Some protector you are," she chided. "I could have been kidnapped."

Tarek scratched his stubbled face.

She added, "After we secure the horses, we'll find a cafe, then back at the fondouk I'll write my letter."

A curt nod signaled Tarek's agreement.

Supper was a skewer of grilled lamb and vegetables, flat bread with honey and yogurt at a cafe in the souk Joutia. They ate in silence. As dusk descended, they walked slowly back to the inn, both deep in their own thoughts. Their peace was shattered by loud voices. Ahead of them two fully laden donkeys, one piled high with firewood, the other sagging under folded carpets, blocked the narrow street. The owners argued and threatened each other at the top of their voices. Suddenly the street around them became empty. Something was wrong. Tarek pulled Hura into a side alley.

"Follow me! Run!" he shouted as two figures clad all in black headed toward them.

She hiked up her kaftan and followed him down a deserted lane until they dodged into a doorway that led to a large walled courtyard. Hura gasped for air against the wall. From the stench lingering in the heavy air she knew they had stumbled into the tanneries. The vast stone patio was pocked with foul-smelling deep, round pools. In the darkness she followed Tarek, as he picked their way over animal carcasses and around the pits looking for escape. There was no exit; they were boxed in.

Out of breath against the back wall, Tarek drew his cutlass. "Move around, left, back to the doorway," he whispered. "Bend down. Stay behind me."

Wide eyed, Hura drew her dagger and scanned the courtyard for movement. She saw the black shadows of tree branches moving in the wind. She wished she had her throwing spear.

From out of nowhere the whoosh of a fast moving scimitar ended with the clank of metal on metal as the assassin's weapon was blocked. This black-clad assailant was no match for the skilled sea captain – he made no sound as he fell dead on the stone walkway.

"One more on our right," she whispered.

"I see him."

The second assassin lunged at Hura, she slipped and fell on a pile of wet skins near one of the open pits. Tarek rushed to engage him: pressing, parrying, retreating, advancing and circling around the dark pit. She struggled to rise from the slippery mass. The assassin's back was to her. Holding the dagger while crawling on hands and knees, she stabbed him in the thigh. He lost his balance, wavered and fell into the pit. Hura watched his black turban disappear into the slime.

Tarek grabbed her hand and pulled her up. "All right?" He didn't wait for the answer. Sword still drawn, he led the way back to the fondouk.

When Hura and Tarek arrived, the high doors to the inn were open and they entered to witness the chaotic arrival of a large caravan. Camels filled two thirds of the courtyard, crowding the horses, donkeys and mules tightly to one side. Dust rose in huge clouds from the dirt floor. Conversation was almost impossible.

From the brightly colored geometric designs of their costumes, she guessed the dark-skinned traders were from Mali or south of the Sahara. They shouted commands at the animals in some strange language as they unloaded and tied them for the night. What an adventure that must be, she thought. I bet it's even more dangerous than traveling in the Rif.

The noise filled the courtyard and rose two stories to the heavens. She turned to Tarek: "We'll leave tonight. Can you ride? I'd rather sleep under the stars than in here. Saddle the horses. I'll write my letter and pack."

She washed her hands and face in the bucket of water at the stairs to the second floor balcony, sniffed her kaftan and wished the hammam was open. Back in her tiny room she lit her oil lamp, unrolled and stretched out a piece of vellum then pulled a vial of ink and a sharp reed from her pack.

She chewed the reed's end while composing, then, with frequent pauses, wrote:

My Honorable Husband:

I trust you are well and your city prospers.

I arrived in Fes safely and have good news. I met with the Grand

Wazir at the Royal Palace. The Sultan has promised us help from the Pasha of Rabat. I carry with me a letter from the Wazir ordering the Pasha to release 10,000 troops to protect Tetouan. I leave tonight for Rabat.
I will return with success and honor to your name.
Your Obedient Wife,
Hura

She packed up her writing box, acknowledging it wasn't the kind of letter the Professor would write. I hope I've spelled everything right and I'll never remember all the formalities. There's so much more I want to say, like how I miss my daughter and how is the new building going, and are there more problems with the refugees and is the river still silting, and have Portuguese ships been seen again. But I mustn't tell him about the attempt on my life. He'd only say he told me so . . . that my mission to Fes was too dangerous for a woman. Dangerous, yes. But I survived. She sighed, sealed the letter and gathered her saddlebags.

Fastening her cape around her shoulders, she called to the innkeeper and gave him her letter with coins for twice the overland posting fee. She was ready. Tarek waited below with the horses and mules. She called down to him from the balcony for help with her heavy saddlebags and he bounded up the stairs.

"What's in these? Stones? Women's stuff? Women don't know how to travel. They take everything. You'd think we were going for a year."

Hura smiled until he picked one up and immediately dropped it on her foot.

"OW!"

"Down!" he yelled. "Over there." He pointed to the right side of the courtyard. "See them?"

Her stare pierced the dust. She sucked in her breath. Three figures, clad all in black were hunched over, slowly making their way among the camels. From her position Hura could see three more creeping toward the porch from the left.

"Quick, go down and cut the ropes." Hura rasped. "I'll get the horses. Watch for me at the outer door."

Tarek stared blankly for a moment, then understood. Crouching low behind the balustrade, he slipped down to the courtyard and began to cut the thick tethering ropes of the camels. In the dim light, he stumbled between the animals trying to avoid being kicked or bitten, fearing the camels would sound an alarm. Occasionally, he looked up to check the location of the black figures.

Hura grabbed a saddlebag and threw it over the rump of her mule, untied it hoping it would follow. In the midst of the camels, she scissored her legs around the sides of her horse in front of the saddle, hung upside down on its neck and pulled Tarek's horse behind her by the reins. Her heart pounded as she threaded her way, unable to see if she was being pursued. If anyone was looking, all they could see would be two riderless horses and a mule moving slowly toward the door.

She waited at the door until she saw Tarek ten camels away, then swung up into the saddle and shouted: "Stampede them!"

Tarek jabbed his knife into the rump of the nearest camel. It bellowed, unfolded its long legs and rose in anger. A chain reaction began. Tarek ran toward her shouting and slapping the camels. Soon the entire courtyard was a thrashing bowl of swirling dust and stampeding animals.

From her saddle, Hura pulled open the double doors while Tarek jumped on his horse. Her heart was still in her throat as they galloped away.

"The mule didn't follow. We've no supplies. I've lost my saddlebag," she said when they finally slowed their horses to a walk.

"Just women's stuff." Tarek winked at her. "That's all we lost."

It wasn't funny but she smiled anyway and looked ahead into the distance. The road to Rabat and success lay open before her.

NINETEEN

Habib laid his brush on the rim of a color pot. This wall design looked best of all. He held the watercolor at arms length, then in the dim light of an oil lamp, brought it closer to his eyes. He had adapted the colorful Italian majolica design to the more subdued cobalt blue and white color palette of Fes. The more restrained geometric effect would emphasize the rhythm of the courtyard arches. It was his best and he knew it. He had learned much from Mustafa.

Until the Chief Architect's illness improved, the responsibility for presenting the designs to Grand Wazir Walid had fallen to him. What he had not learned was how to please the unpredictable Wazir. Sometimes he could be flattering, yet last time, the instant Habib held up his drawing, the Wazir had erupted: "Too Andalusian, too bold. This is not Spain and the Sultan is not a Morisco."

Habib stood, stretched, and rolled up the large watercolor. Since leaving Spain he had discovered a liking for the outdoors. Here, inside all day, his eyes and back ached from bending over a drawing board. His small chamber had no window. Unlike the Fassi craftsmen who lived in the al-Andalus quarter of the Old City, Mustafa was privileged to enjoy quarters in a wing of the Wazir's Administrative Palace. Their rooms abutted each other. The architect's hacking cough carried through the thick wall, reminding Habib the Wazir expected him. He must hurry. He picked up the latest design, hesitated, and then selected an alternate sketch. This one wasn't as good, but then who knew what the Wazir would think.

Habib opened the door next to his and peered in. Mustafa lay fully clothed and immobile on his bed in the sparsely furnished chamber. "Master," Habib said, "I go now to the Wazir." He came closer to unroll and show his designs.

A fit of coughing racked the architect. He waved aside the drawings; did not even look.

It was obvious the illness, whatever it was, had become worse, much worse. "Master, shall I get the physician?"

Mustafa croaked: "Don't keep the Wazir waiting . . . the physician . . . he comes here in his own good time."

Habib silently closed the door and, as he began to walk the many corridors that wended through the palace, he realized that Mustafa would soon die. He could become the senior architect. Then another thought flashed in his mind. Is that what I want?

These past few weeks in the palace he had felt uneasy, unsettled. He didn't know why. Of course the Wazir was difficult to please. King Boabdil in the al-Hamra had been too. Habib knew rulers did not have to be pleasant patrons of the arts. Why should they? Wazir or King, no difference. They could bark orders at cringing slaves and expect platitudes from courtiers. Why tolerate the independence of an artist? Yes, he knew it and he knew himself. He always resented authority. He resented those who wielded it, even his strict father who, both as rabbi and teacher, wrapped him across the knuckles when he misread the Torah. No, this time it wasn't the Wazir.

Was it Fes? The city itself, or the people? He hadn't been able to take time to see much of it. And he was betwixt and between. Here he had neither Hebrew relatives nor Muslim friends. He lived between two cultures: Spanish and Moroccan, between two religions: Muslim and Hebrew. Why couldn't he be satisfied with one or the other?

Still pondering as he crossed the dark marble border of the main interior court, he heard the water splashing in the fountain basin that marked the intersection of the principal corridors. Usually he enjoyed the fountain. Although not as spectacular as the one in the Court of Lions at the al-Hamra, with its twelve lions encircling the basin's pedestal, it had an exotic charm. Today it reminded him of that Berber woman. He had first seen that Queen of Tetouan here. The bulge in his groin hardened. How long had it been since Miriam. Since Bridget? What was her name, that Berber one . . . she was married. Did it matter? Her eyes had been readable. He hungered. For what? Irritating, this indecision, this uncertainty. Everything beyond his control. Especially as a Muslim.

He stopped. Not anymore. With a sudden burst of resolve, he ripped apart the sketches. Good-bye Habib. Shalom, Hersh.

TWENTY

The stillness was eerie.

"This can't be Rabat," Hura pulled on her reins.

Tarek scratched his head, cooler now that he had taken off his knitted cap. "Should be. Look at all the marble."

"But it's all in ruins. Those stones over there, they look like markers. No, they're not. They're royal tombs. So this must be Rabat's necropolis."

"Necwhat?"

Hura ran the back of her hand over her mouth to dislodge the caked dust. "That's a fancy word for graveyard. We better ride on. We can be through the city walls before dusk."

"If our mounts don't collapse."

Out of the corner of her eye, Hura saw Tarek rise in his saddle and rub his backside.

The sun still burned hot as they began to wind through the labyrinth of squatters' shacks on the outskirts of the city, passing two dilapidated mosques and many crumbling palaces of this once Imperial city. Foraging dogs howled in the rubble-strewn dirt lanes.

Hura shivered. "We traveled all the way to this city and look at it. Poorer than Tetouan when I came as a bride."

"Must've been sacked," Tarek grunted. "Long time ago from the looks of it. Seems like an evil omen."

"Nonsense. You sailors . . . always superstitious."

As they spurred their tired mounts up the slope toward the monumental archway between the two towers of the kasbah wall, Hura noticed the facade's unusual decoration of animals. The Professor could have deciphered the archaic lettering over the tall wooden doors. Arriving at the arch, the long spears of four gatekeepers barred their entrance.

The guards scrutinized these two travel-stained strangers arriving without baggage or retinue, and denied them access. While Tarek harangued them that a highborn lady had arrived, Hura marveled at their uniforms. Warriors of the Rif never wore uniforms. There, each acquired his own clothing and weapons. Here they wore identical garb. From gold-colored slippers, to red hose, to voluminous maroon pantaloons, to vests embroidered with gold thread, to clean turbans of tightly wound white strips, these warriors were unlike any Hura had ever seen.

Tarek turned in his saddle, "Turks," he said to Hura. "Royal guards, not gatekeepers."

"You see, a good omen." Hura's face lightened. "The Pasha must be expecting us."

The kasbah wall was three horse-lengths thick. Emerging from the dark gateway onto a parade ground, seeming without end, Hura squinted into the sunlit panorama of color, noise and movement. Close by, a swirling mass of tribesmen on sleek-bodied Arabian horses charged, wheeled, clashed scimitars and jousted. Watching the melee, neither Hura nor Tarek could count their number – the tribesmen occupied more than half the open space.

"Must be thousands," Tarek said.

"More than enough for Tetouan." Hura's eyes shone in delight.

As they circled the inner side of the citadel wall to avoid the mock battles, they came upon several hundred Turks in battle dress and formation. Hura had never seen such pageantry. Each bare-chested soldier wore a conical metal helmet with a spike on top, black chain mail on his neck and sides, black pantaloons and calf-length felt boots. In addition to layers of colored cape, the commanding officer wore a tall, cylindrical helmet from which sprouted an enormous feathered fan, arching high over his face. This looked and performed like a professional army.

Over and over the troops repeated the complicated procedure of loading, priming and fusing their new matchlock muskets. Hura's hopes for success soared. She would save Tetouan with these soldiers.

In the shadow of the palace entry, the Pasha awaited. Swathed in a silk cape and wearing a fez despite the heat, he watched Hura gracefully dismount and approach. "Honored lady," he began, "welcome to my humble abode. Your presence here brings light and joy to this lonely palace. Please enter. My Chamberlain will show you the quarters which await your pleasure, and our hammam, which I hope equals that of your grand city of Tetouan." He swiveled his fleshy neck to the right and left. "Where are your bags? Have you no baggage?"

"Stolen." Tarek grunted and handed the reins of their mounts to a liveryman, then hurried to follow Hura.

The Pasha held up a stubby finger. "Not you. A guard will show you the barracks."

Tarek grinned, continued walking as Hura said sweetly to the Pasha: "My husband, Sidi al-Mandari, Ruler of Tetouan, has charged this man with my safety. Please do not be offended when he sleeps outside my door."

The Pasha cocked his head to one side. He could be deaf when convenient. The expression on his dimpled face did not change. His voluminous chins did not quiver; nor did his large, round eye blink. His left eye stared to infinity in its whiteness. The plump mouth opened: "I will have garments brought to your suite and when it pleases you, dear lady, I will be delighted to properly greet you with refreshment in the Great Hall."

Hura choked back the words that had been simmering during her long journey. She wanted, needed, his reply to the Wazir's letter at once. All this pleading in Fes, all this travel, all this charade – she didn't have time for a courtly reception. But that was what she must do – play the role of a visiting queen at an ally's court. This was no time to antagonize the Pasha. Especially one who had been on the haj to Mecca. The cylindrical cap of red felt wrapped with white cotton gauze indicated he had made the pilgrimage.

He bowed deeply, holding on to his fez so it wouldn't fall, and the taciturn Chamberlain led the way through a series of reception rooms grouped in the al-Andalus manner around a central court, then to the guests' private quarters.

Hura luxuriated in the warm aromatic waters of the hammam, admitting to herself how tired she was and how much she missed the comforts of the city. Later, refreshed and attired in the formal gown the Pasha provided, she walked alone to join him in his Great Hall.

The Pasha motioned for Hura to sit beside him on the pillowed couch. Her nose wrinkled. He had not bathed recently. She forced herself to respond with nods and smiles to those pleasantries he thought a woman, a noble lady, wanted to hear. His familiarity made her squirm. He seemed to know a great deal about her and she wondered how. More importantly, she wondered how to divert their conversation toward her mission. She began by asking about the destruction of Rabat, planning to tie his response to the invasion and destruction of Tetouan.

"I noticed the ruins around the gateway as we entered . . . when did it happen? Was it the Portuguese? The Spanish? What happened?"

The Pasha laughed. He looked almost cherubic with his dimpled cheeks that gave him the appearance of someone younger. "That happened long before I was born." He lifted a finger to signal an attendant.

Hura tried again. "The battle for your city must have been terrible. What does the inscription above the archway say. It's half worn away."

"It is written in Kufic script and says 'Defender of the Faith'. It's a long and interesting story."

Hura tensed. *Now.* This was her cue to talk about a jihad, a holy war. *Now* was the time to ask for troops to repel the invaders. *Now* show him the letter.

But the arrival of food distracted her. His brown eye savored each delicacy; he sampled every dish before continuing. Oblivious to manners, through crunching jaws and bulging cheeks, he began to tell the story.

"You ask about my city. Rabat El Fath, Fortress of Faith, has an ancient history. It had been a Phoenician then Carthaginian then a Roman settlement. My forbears – " here he rambled at length expounding on how long and famous his genealogy was, how he was kinsman to the new Wattasid Sultan and how his title of Pasha was equal to that of her very own brother, Emir Ibrahim.

Humph, thought Hura, Ibrahim's title was centuries older, derived from the holy Idriss tribe. Ibrahim could claim direct descendance from the Prophet. This pompous man's rank was purely political. She fluttered her eyes at the Pasha.

With jowls refilled, he expounded: "The Almohad Sultans launched their conquest of Castile and Leon from the port here, the one across the river. Flush with power and riches, that dynasty rebuilt Rabat . . . I call my city Rabat . . . as an Imperial City with monumental buildings including the mosque of Hassan, of which unfortunately only the tower was ever built. Then Allah, blessed be the Holy One, willed that all, except this kasbah, should become a ruin. Now you know my destiny."

Once again Hura tried to direct the conversation back to her situation, to the letter. But the Pasha kept on talking.

The hairless face creased with mock sadness as he wiped his mouth and right hand of food, and said, "Now it is my lot to deal with invaders. That is why you saw my warriors preparing for battle on your arrival."

Hura seized the opportunity, forced herself to look only at his good eye. "That's why – "

"Yes, esteemed lady, that is why we need so many warriors here. The Portuguese have taken over our coastal and interior trade. They've built a huge fortress at Mazagan, south of here. All their ships dock there. And now a Captain Dias, in a warship with many cannon, patrols my waters." His face flushed with injured pride and impotence.

This time Hura was firm. "Your Excellency, I bear an important, no, an imperative letter for you." She pulled the sealed missive from her sleeve.

"Yes, I know you do. I received a note by runner from the Most High Prince Hamad informing me of your arrival. This note did not divulge the contents of the letter, however. And surely it can wait while we relax. You must be tired from your long journey."

Hura thrust the letter at the Pasha.

He rose and crossed his heart with his hand. "Allah teaches us there is a time for talk and a time for prayer. It is time for prayer. I bid you rest well until we meet again tomorrow."

Seething, and suddenly famished, Hura cast a side glance at the trays of

157

food on her way out. She had eaten nothing.

When she appeared the next morning, the Pasha had just seated himself in his favorite ebony chair. "I hope your slumber has refreshed you."

"Yes, thank you for your hospitality. And now you must read my letter." She held it out to him.

He sat back, smiled and seemed amused by her abrupt lack of protocol and her persistence in thrusting the letter at him. She stood before him as he accepted the missive, broke the seal with his thumb and read it. His lips moved but the rustle of crinkled paper was the only sound in the silent chamber.

"Well?" Hura asked when he looked up.

"Have you actually read this, my dear?"

"No," she frowned. "The Wazir wrote and sealed it. Why?"

The Pasha hesitated, laying the letter in his lap. "Uh . . . it seems to present a request for warriors. Why it is addressed to me, dear lady, I don't know. And . . . the form of it is a bit unusual. I must read it again."

Hura glanced at it before he picked it up again. She could see that it lacked the formal introductory greeting the Professor had always insisted on. "Read it aloud, please."

The Pasha raised the letter close to his good eye:

The Imperial Palace of Fes
Grand Wazir of the Imperial Court
30 May 1509
I am commanded by His Highness, Prince Hamad, son to the
Blessed Sultan Muhammad al-Shaykh, to inform you that he
desires to assist the Ruler of Tetouan, Abu al-Hasan al-Mandari,
in his present difficulties in the defense of that city. As you have
meritously satisfied His Highness in other situations, you are
hereby requested therefore, to inform the Lady al-Mandari as to
whether or not you will have troops . . .

"Whether or not!" Hura interrupted, "I saw thousands here."

The Pasha nodded at the ambiguity of the letter, then read on:

. . . whether or not you will have troops available
for the provision of succor to her husband, who
it appears, is incapacitated.
Your Obedient Servant,
Walid
Grand Wazir

"Is that all it says?" Hura paled then trembled. The Pasha rose, joined her on the couch and took her hand.

Devastated by the discovery that the Wazir's letter was a useless foil, Hura's mood plummeted. Just yesterday she felt elated at the opportunity to save her city. Now the Pasha's words echoed in her ears, half obliterated by the throbbing beat of her own angry blood . . . 'a request . . . why it is addressed to me, dear lady, I don't know'.

Two endless days dragged by and Hura's frustration deepened. At the Pasha's insistence, she agreed to take her meals with him. He remained cordial and solicitous of her comfort. Arguing his courier could bring back clarification from Fes in just four days, she agreed to be his guest while they waited. She agreed because she had no other plan and needed time to make one. She needed to change tactics. If formal diplomatic discussion was not possible, their informal dining would offer the best chance for her to negotiate an agreement. But the Pasha remained elusive just like the foxes she used to hunt with her father. This chase could go on forever. How she wanted to pin him to a promise with her spear.

That evening when the palace was quiet, she opened her chamber door and whispered, "Tarek. Come in." She closed the door behind him. "Sit, have some of these almond pastries. The Pasha feeds me well." Her little laugh sounded bitter. Tarek took a fistful of the small cakes and sat cross-legged on the floor, near her chair. The observance of strict formality between them had loosened on their long journey. Although he never confided details about his personal life, Hura had learned to trust Tarek's common sense, to trust his wisdom and broad experience.

"We have to take matters in our own hands," she said.

"You got a plan?" Tarek continued to chew.

"No, not yet. First, tell me all you know about the Pasha's soldiers. Who they are, why they're here, how much they're paid. Everything."

Tarek picked crumbs off the now empty tray. "Better than the slop they feed me in the barracks. It's hard talkin' to the men - - different languages. And soldiers and sailors don't mix. So far I learned the Arab tribesmen are from the Sahara."

"They're mercenaries?"

"Seems that way. Any more cake? Wish I had wine, too."

"I'll ask for it later. Go on."

"Mercenaries? They volunteer for three years, go wherever that Wazir in Fes sends 'em. That's in exchange for money and no taxes for their families."

"But why are so many here? In Rabat?"

"They don't know why they're here. Saharans were born to fight. They wish they were someplace else. All they do is parade and pretend to fight."

"And the ones with the fancy uniforms? Are they Turks like you said?"

"They say they're Janissaries. Turkish mercenaries. Here's the furthest

159

west they've ever gone. Seems they came 'cause the Pasha pays more than the Egyptian Sultan." He snorted. "They're even dumber than the tribesmen."

"I wish I had the money. I'd hire them all." Hura took a deep breath. "The Pasha . . . where does he get the money to pay them?"

"From the pirates I'm thinkin'. They control the port."

"Pirates?" Hura stood up and paced around the room, repeating "Pirates?"

"Across the river. Tribute. They pay a tenth of the loot. Janissaries here make sure they pay."

Hura stopped pacing and frowned. She tried to hold on to an idea that popped in then vanished out of her head.

Hura's spirits rose with each step outside the city gate. Even the medina appeared less desolate now than when she first saw it. Drawn to the small mellah and souk, she joined the morning shoppers hurrying to buy the day's fresh bread. I'll buy a gift for Suha; she smiled to herself as she entered the maze of narrow lanes. She beat back a wave of homesickness as the aroma of cinnamon and cardamom wafted through the throng, and dodged carcasses of hanging lamb outside butcher stalls. Just like Tetouan.

Passing through a small arch with housing above it, she crossed a lane and walked by a narrow opening in the wall. She paused. Was that a jewelry shop? She turned back again and saw several ordinary necklaces displayed in a small window. Almost hidden amongst them was a brooch designed so its pin would close a cloak. The design, the shape that had caught her eye, was familiar. A nautilus. A spiral in silver exactly like the fossils she often found near Chaouen. Suha would love it.

She entered the workshop, peering into the gloom. A young man wearing a skullcap was bent over a bench littered with a metalsmiths tools. He glanced at her then jumped up with a broad smile. "Lady Hura!"

The voice. *That* deep Andalusian voice. Hura's eyes focused in the darkness. She whispered: "Habib? The architect from Fes?"

He quickly came to where she stood. Softly, he said, "No, not Habib. Hersh."

Hura stared at him and gasped, "Jewish?" She had never before said as much as one word to any Jew.

"Come, sit with me. Please." He guided her to the small shop's other stool, pulling his own near. Leaning close to her, he began to unfold his story.

She sensed he edited as he explained how he had been tossed into a strange country, needed to eat, so he changed his identity to suit the situation. "That's my history," he said. "Back and forth. Hebrew, Muslim,

160

Hebrew again. Here I'm working for my uncle who owns this shop."

Hura smiled awkwardly. What a strange tale; what a strange young man. But he's so handsome.

She roused herself. "Couldn't you have gotten a job as an architect here? Or looked for tile work. This entire city needs to be rebuilt."

He straightened up. "I'm waiting for a big project. Something creative. No more little designs for me."

Hura glanced at the rings and bracelets on the workbench and in the display window, not knowing what to say next.

Hersh laughed. "No, that's not true. What is true is that my work here is temporary. My Hebrew kinsmen in this mellah have a design guild. I would have to join if I stayed. Not me."

He's a rebel, like me, Hura thought to herself.

Hersh leaned closer to her again and recounted the problems he had with the Wazir in Fes. Hura nodded sympathetically and began to relax. She laughed aloud when he told her the story about how he once forgot which role he was playing and spoke in the wrong language. Fortunately it was with the Wazir's Chamberlain, not the Wazir himself. But when Hersh put his warm hand on her knee, Hura froze. Then, without calling him by name, she abruptly stood and pointed: "I came in here to buy that brooch."

"My favorite too." He acted as if he had done nothing, flashed a broad grin of approval and unpinned it from the string that stretched across the shop. He bowed as he handed it to her.

"How much is it?"

"For you, nothing." He reached out, put it in her hand.

Hura glared and slapped the brooch back into his hand. The open pin pierced his palm; he flinched in surprise. As she ran out of the shop she heard him laugh.

That night was sleepless for Hura. She tossed and turned, slipping in and out of several lurid dreams in which a tall young adventurer held her naked body to his, then laughed and disappeared. In between the dreams she lay awake, flooded with guilt for forgetting her husband and abandoning her daughter, steeped in remorse over this rash venture which was coming to naught. She awoke early the following morning, red-eyed from lack of sleep and wished she had Sacony here so she could gallop away from her problems and her emotions on his gray-dappled back.

Now she stood with Tarek on a wallowing raft that a ferryman poled across the shallow Bou Regreg River.

If she had been permitted to climb the parapets of the Pasha's kasbah, she could have seen the large walled city, close by, rising from a bluff on the north side of the wide estuary. Seeing it now from the raft, she

161

wondered what was so special about this port, the one that Tarek said was the haven of the cruelest cutthroats on the coast of Africa. Looking seaward west of the lagoon she saw an outlying reef cut by a narrow pass. The basin's shallow waters washed up to a wide beach before a tall seagate in the city wall. Several small fishing boats furled their sails near the inlet. A larger boat had been hauled out of the water onto the beach and was careened on its side while a sailor caulked its hull. The scene looked peaceful enough to Hura.

"We're looking for Nabil," Tarek called to the ferryman who swept the water with his long oar. Aside he whispered to Hura, "It's not too late to turn back. This Nabil . . . he's the worst pirate in Salé. I hear he don't like women."

"Too early for him at the tavern," the ferryman said. "Nabil won't be far from his boat," and he pointed to a galley beached not far away.

Trudging through sand, Hura saw there was something different about the galley. It had a small cannon mounted on a platform over the bow and a projection below at the waterline. More puzzling was the costume of the short, swarthy man who cursed the crewman beside him who tried to squeeze cord into a seam in the hull. He heard them coming and turned. From the waist up he wore a sweat-stained white shirt with rows of ruffles in front and puffed-up sleeves over buttoned cuffs. Below a crimson sash his gray pantaloons bulged with a purple codpiece. On his feet slippers sported silver buckles now half covered by sand.

"Probably from some captured Dutch fop." Tarek whispered behind his hand.

Hura marched up to the pirate. "Are you Sidi Nabil?"

"Just Nabil, lady." He eyed Tarek's cutlass, loose in its scabbard, and hitched around his own weapon, which was slung from a shoulder strap. Then he smirked at Hura, eyeing her up and down. "And who might you be?"

Tarek stepped forward and introduced Hura with all her proper titles, then himself as captain of a vessel anchored at the port of Martil. As he started to compliment Nabil on the excellent condition of his galley, Hura interrupted: "Are you a pirate? I came here to learn about piracy."

Nabil's laughter stilled her. He glanced around to see if his crewman was laughing too. "Lady, you be with the right man." His expression suddenly changed to suspicion. "Who sent you? Not that fat frog of a Pasha! He don't know his mouth from his ass. I can smell the dung on his breath." He spat on the sand. Seeing that Hura didn't react, his face relaxed. "No matter. They be no secrets here. Everyone knows Nabil. But I'm no pirate. I'm a privateer."

Hura glanced at Tarek, betraying no emotion. She wondered if they had made a mistake in seeking out this arrogant sailor. "Is there a difference?"

Nabil postured, tucked his thumbs in his sash and stuck his chest out. "I'm legal. I got a Commission. A Marque from the Pasha. I got the right to clear our waters of infidel shipping – Portuguese, Spaniard, Dutch, all of 'em."

"So that's why you have the cannon." Hura tilted her head toward the gun.

Nabil looked at Tarek and rolled his eyes skyward. "Yes, lady. But it ain't much good. We sink them slow tubs with this." He tapped the hardwood ram that stuck out of the bow like a fat spear. "Then we boards 'em."

Tarek moved forward and spoke up. "That's what Lady Hura wants to know. How privateers work. She's wantin' to . . . give Letters of Marque to privateers in Martil."

"Where's that?" Nabil arched his eyebrows.

"The port of Tetouan."

Nabil's eyes narrowed as he countered, "If you're meanin' me, I do well enough here. I gets money from loot. But you could be lucky with one of these fishermen. That one-eyed, greedy Pasha takes a tenth of their catch and sells it in his own markets. Makes 'em so angry they're talking bout bein' free, call themselves the Republic of the Bou Regreg."

Behind Tarek, Hura shuddered. The Mayor of a city of cutthroats.

Nabil shouted to his crewman, "Run to the tavern and get them sots here. We're ready to slide her in the water. Got to test the rigging." Turning to Tarek, he asked: "What do you think of her, fine ain't she."

Tarek walked alongside the round bottom, studying it. "My galley's just like her, maybe bigger. I haul cargo. Mostly refugees. But I got the same single mast and lateen sail. Maybe your riggin's better."

"Don't know about that."

"Sure would like to see how she goes when the winds change."

Nabil paused and eyed the stranger again. "I'm not goin' far out. When I get her in the water, Captain, come aboard."

Before long, some thirty men, many the worse for drunkenness, straggled down to the beach, grousing over the sudden call to duty. When they finished pushing the galley into the lagoon, Hura moved to clamber on board with the others but Nabil barred her way.

After much palaver, much pleading and the passing of a shiny coin into Nabil's palm, he finally threw up his hands when Hura agreed, with the sincerity of a virgin, that he could throw her overboard if she became a problem.

The small galley sat low in the water. The oarsmen, twelve to a side, began to row. Hura stood out of the way on the small platform over the bow, clutching the cannon for support as they headed out toward the fishing fleets. Once underway, she looked down through the clear water to the sandy bottom. This isn't scary, she thought. I could walk to shore. She began to enjoy the new experience and the rhythmic splash of oars.

Behind her, Tarek and Nabil walked the raised narrow plank between oarsmen's benches. As they neared, she heard fragments of ship talk. "She's 'clinker' built with cedar from the Mamora forest. That's near Larache."

"So's mine. That little overlap makes 'em sturdy, where hull planks sit atop the other . . . looks like yours is fast."

"Fastest in Salé. Yours as long and narrow?"

"No. More beam. I'd say length to breadth six to one . . ."

Hura heard a scraping noise, then noticed the galley had passed through the reef and was beginning to breast the small, long rollers of the open sea. Watching the water change color from green to blue-green then, as though a line had been drawn, deep blue, she unfastened her hair to let it ruffle in the salty air. Nabil shouted commands and she turned to watch the unfurling of the triangular sail. It dropped from a yard that was almost as long as the mast and tilted so far upward that its lower end almost trailed in the sea. She wondered how the crewmen swiveled the yard around the mast, making the sail billow in the breeze.

She shifted her attention to the men. From the satisfied look on Nabil's face, Hura gathered he was proud to show off the performance of his crew and vessel, and as the two men came closer, she caught Nabil's words: "The sail's canvas is made of the best damn cannabis. Grown in the Rif, it is."

Clinker? Beam? These men were using nautical terms she'd never heard of. The sea was a man's world. What was she doing here? At least she wasn't afraid. If piracy was going to save her city, could she control the pirates?

Nabil snorted with laughter and slapped Tarek on the back. Above the sounds of the rushing waves and wind the pirate shouted: "When I first saw your woman, I thought she'd make a nice piece of padding for my hammock." He guffawed again.

Camaraderie vanished. Tarek grabbed his arm. "So you think she's that kind of woman, huh?"

A cocky stance showed Nabil's answer.

With one quick movement Tarek twisted the pirate's arm behind his back then released it. "You put a hand on her it'll be the last time you see that hand."

"Only joking! Can't you take a joke?" Nabil said rubbing his elbow.

Tarek had been keeping an eye on a vessel half way to the horizon bearing on what looked like an interception course. He motioned to Nabil.

"Saw her hull down on the horizon long ago," Nabil said, and continued ordering small rigging adjustments. Not yet satisfied, he had four sailors climb the shrouds and adjust the sheets that swiveled the long yard. But his casual answer belied a watchful gaze. Suddenly he ordered the men down to the deck then changed course straight for home.

Both men could see the closing vessel was a full-rigged ship whose foremast and mainmast each carried a square sail. The mizzenmast, jutting from the aftercastle, bore a lateen sail. Her altered course was intended to cross theirs.

"She's riding too high for a full laden merchantman," said Tarek.

"We're not chasing merchantmen today."

Tarek pointed. "Three decks, guns on the topmost. She's a carrack, a warship for certain."

"No matter, we're faster. And warships don't attack fishing boats."

"You're a galley with a ram, not a felucca."

By now Hura knew something was wrong. She stood, back to the on-rushing waves, holding on to the cannon and watched this large ship that seemed to have come from nowhere. Why did it look familiar. "I hope it isn't Portuguese," she shouted.

The galley was indeed faster. Instead of plowing the waves it skimmed their tops. But the warship's course brought the two vessels closer, almost within cannon range.

At the reef, Nabil's boat shot through the narrow pass under sail then continued on until it grated to a stop on the lagoon beach. Grinning, Nabil confronted Hura: "Cause me trouble, will you. Overboard with you!"

Before Tarek could react, her chin went up, she stepped on the low side wale and, lifting her skirt, jumped. The warm water wet her to the waist. She waded to shore, her dignity dry.

The crew fastened the sheets with belaying pins and, following Nabil and Tarek, walked to the open doors of the Seagate. There, a crowd from the city had gathered to watch the carrack offshore. Before long, they saw a single puff of black smoke, a shower of sparks, and heard the blast of a cannon with the visible trajectory of a canon ball. It plunked harmlessly into the sandbar, to everyone's amusement. The range was far short of the Salé fortress wall. They all knew that warships' cannon were notoriously inaccurate. The warship's gunner made several more futile attempts then, with a much louder blast, a cannon ball arced over the lagoon and smashed down on Nabil's boat. The mast, yard and sail toppled. The gunner had the exact elevation now and he fired another shot. The explosions reduced the sinking wreckage to splinters. Nabil shook his fists, kicked the sand and cursed.

Fascinated by the spectacle, Hura stood before the seagate. The germ of an idea to make this lagoon safer for these pirates began to grow. She would speak to Nabil about it when he finished his tantrum. Surely he would become more cooperative and help her now.

TWENTY ONE

Dismounting the high, firm bed Hura yawned, stretched and saw the envelope pushed halfway under the door. She scooped it up and recognized at once the cramped hand that addressed it to Hura bint Ali Rachid al-Mandari. No one writes to me unless it is bad news; she sighed, and broke the seal.

Honored Lalla Hura,

Yes, yes Professor, get on with it.

Our Lord Sidi al-Mandari has given me instructions to write you and express to you his great pleasure in your success in securing an audience with the Sultan Muhammad al-Shaykh and the Grand Wazir Walid. In this important endeavor you showed great resource and persistence.

Hura's lip curled. If my husband actually spoke those sweet words, she would kiss Kleinatz on his big nose in front of the whole court.

Your husband speaks thusly:

Your letter was very late in reaching me. Before then, I already knew from your brother, Mohammed, that you were off on some childish chase to Rabat without my permission in search of non-existent warriors who, in any event, would not come to my aid without gold, of which I have not enough. Return to my side at once.

The words swam before her. She brushed away the morning mist in her eyes, climbed up to her bed and read a postscript from the Professor.

Siti Hura, now let me add to your husband's words.

Affairs go not well here.

Your husband's vision has gone completely and his health has worsened. The Council meetings are in such disarray that Boabdil has demanded a seat on the bench. Yes, he has returned to Tetouan without your father. Our Lord ordered him out of the chamber. Now he considers an offer of assistance from your brother Mohammed. Meanwhile, the medina buzzes with gossip mongers' rumors that our Lord may not be fit to rule.

Your daughter, Suha, misses you.

Your Obedient Servant,

Nicholas Kleinatz

The letter dropped from Hura's hand. She slumped against the pillows, motionless, until a servant knocked bearing breakfast and a message. The plain-looking woman curtsied and announced, "Lady Hura, my master would speak with you."

Jolted out of inaction into a frenzy of activity, she pushed aside the tray of food and reached for her pouch of coins. She held out a coin for the servant and told her: "This is for you after you find Captain Tarek and tell him we leave at once. Tell him to meet me at the front gate. Then come back here and pack my things."

This morning she paid special attention to her bath, applying fragrant unguent to her body and rubbing it in. She drew a deep breath. It smelled like the dew of the gods. She tied her luxuriant hair back with a saffron colored ribbon that matched her blouse. Satisfied with her allure, she proceeded to the Great Hall.

The Pasha looked up as she arrived, smiled, and with a familiar motion, patted the couch beside him. Hura sat respectfully but fidgeted as he slowly ate from a painted dish filled with sugared figs. When the dish emptied, he rinsed his hands in a finger bowl of perfumed water and turned to her.

"From your agitation," his lips still smacked, "this morning's letter has brought you no happiness. It was from Fes?"

"No, Tetouan. I must leave. My husband . . . needs me."

"A pity. These days have flown by on the wings of a hummingbird. You have brightened my dark palace with your beauty and spirit. I know waiting for an answer from the Grand Wazir must be difficult, and now this. But I am certain of a favorable reply, perhaps in another week."

Why that overstuffed hypocrite, Hura thought. But he had been hospitable, even lavish in his gifts. I should repay him. She considered several proper gifts for her host; something he would remember her by, then discarded them all. Her idea. That's it. Yes, she would give him her idea. That would be a fitting and memorable gift.

Hura perched on the edge of the couch to face him and spoke while he listened in quizzical silence. "Surely Your Excellency heard what happened yesterday on the Salé beach."

The Pasha nodded and blinked his eye.

"I was there. How humiliating it must be to have the Portuguese threaten you. Yes, I saw the warship's flag – just like the one that attacked Tetouan. How could I forget it? How easy it is for the infidel to control our harbors, to destroy our boats. Your harbor is not a sanctuary, that is your problem. Neither the walls here, nor in Salé protect your fishermen and pirates."

168

The Pasha scoffed, "Those Sallé Rovers are dullards, incompetent. How do you know about them?"

Hura ignored the question. "The big problem is the lagoon. It's not a sanctuary, not a place to hide. The Portuguese have cannon, you don't. What you do have are strong walls. Don't you see?"

"See what? What are you talking about, my dear?"

"The Salé wall. It has a seagate. The archway of that Bab-el-Mrisa is tall. Very tall. Taller than a felucca's mast. All you have to do is dig a channel from the lagoon through the arch and into the city." Hura leaned forward and smiled broadly, proud of her solution. "Don't you see . . . cannon can't destroy the boats, because they're behind the thick wall."

"Ridiculous, impossible!" The Pasha's swinging arm sent the tray, bowls and food in front of him flying. "What do you know about pirates, about politics, about Portuguese! Don't you know both sides are my partners? The pirates can build new boats, they're only brushwood, and they . . . they pay me raiding privileges."

Hura slid back on the couch.

Face and neck purple, the Pasha gasped for breath. In a cold voice, he admonished, "The Portuguese warships protect Portuguese shipping in or out of my city for which privilege their feitor, here in Rabat, pays tribute. Either way I profit – Portuguese or pirate. Get your nose out of man's work, silly woman. Go home. You are becoming a real problem, a *mushkil*."

Knuckles white, Hura rose and stormed out of the room, ran down the hallway and out the palace door, where she found Tarek holding their mounts in the courtyard.

His lips parted to speak –

"Don't ask." Hura shouted. "Don't dare say a word! Just wait here. I'm going to the mellah to buy a gift for Suha. I'll be right back."

His heart was not in the work. Designing a room full of tiles was one thing. That could keep you busy, occupy the mind as well as the hands. But that woman, that Queen or whatever she was, spoke the truth. Making jewelry was just finger work. Cut the metal, file the edges, solder the ten, twenty pieces, polish the surface – all to make a tiny ornament. No, not for him. No big dreams there. He stabbed the air with his metal file.

And this aunt of mine. Just like Mustafa in Fes. Pushing this girl, this nice girl she says is just perfect for me. That buck-tooth comes to the shop every day, eyes downcast, with a bowl of lentil soup from my aunt. I can't evade her. Yes, she would make a good mother. So would Miriam. But who wants to sleep with a frigid mother? Hersh threw the file down on the workbench so hard it gouged the wood.

169

And my uncle. He's in this too. He comes every shabbath to drag me to services. He hints . . . hints, never promises . . . he'll give me a share of the shop profits. He's always saying – Hersh slipped into the bent posture and scratchy voice of his uncle: "Hershlab, my boy, every man needs to feed and clothe his family when he settles down." Nothing subtle about that bribe. Of course the Gentiles and the Muslims do it too, they call it a dowry.

He sniffed the air. What's that . . . perfume? Buck-tooth doesn't wear any. No Hebrew woman in the mellah wears perfume.

Hersh turned to see who it was silhouetted against the pale light that filtered through the narrow door into the shop. He watched the woman enter and take the nautilus from the display string. It had to be. It was that lady from Tetouan!

"Good morning," she said. "I came to buy your nautilus."

Hersh jumped up. "You made a good choice. I'm happy to see you again. Sit over here. I'll put it on for you."

She backed away. "Don't bother. I'm in a hurry."

"Why the rush?" Hersh slid his hand down her arm, drawing her further into the dim shop. "You look disturbed. Is something wrong?" The warmth of his hand and his friendly voice offered comfort.

This time Hura did not resist. Her boiling emotions needed venting to someone. Thinking she would never see him again, she erupted in a gush of words, telling him about the sad events in Tetouan, her frustration with the Wazir, her disappointment with the Pasha, and worst of all, her sense of failure.

Hersh said nothing as they both sat on the small stools, his knees touching hers. Her passion entranced him. He stared at her angry, gray eyes, her heaving bosom. He nodded understanding, but concentrated more on his stirring urge, his rising need, and her rapid breathing.

"You are so easy to talk to. Now I feel better." Hura started to get up. His hand reached for hers.

"Tell me about this idea of yours, the one the Pasha scoffs at."

She hesitated, then sat down again. "The idea is simple, perhaps too simple. Tell me what you think."

He listened with growing interest. He understood that she wanted a big ditch. Now that was a bold idea.

"It would take hundreds of workers to dig it," he said, "just to stabilize the sides, and reinforce the seagate."

She nodded. "The whole city, everyone in Salé would help. I'm sure of it. They're angry with the Pasha."

"It *is* a grand concept. Also a big challenge."

She slipped off the stool. "You've just made me very happy . . . you like the idea? You, an architect from Spain?"

Hersh grinned at her compliment and how ludicrous it seemed here. Ludicrous idea, too. He rubbed a bushy eyebrow with his finger. "Why do you want to build a ditch for those pirates?"

"The Pasha taught me something. Profit. Money is what I need to hire mercenaries. I'll get it from the pirates who use our port. I need to win the confidence of the Sallé Rovers. If they come to Martil, I'll give them a larger share of the booty than the Pasha does."

Her words rushed out. She drew a deep breath. Another idea came.

He read it in her eyes and jumped up. "Oh no you don't."

Hura stood beside him and tentatively touched his shoulder, then squeezed it with intensity. "You know what happened with the Pasha. No one will take my idea seriously – this plan coming from a woman. A woman can't order those pirates to build it."

He shook his head. "Yes, and a Hebrew can't either."

"You could do it . . . as Habib."

He started to laugh but saw her cheeks flushing and felt her warm breath on his face. Grasping her waist and pulling her closer, he kissed her. Slowly he rubbed the smooth fabric over her breast. He felt her nipple rise to his palm.

"Lalla Hura . . . Hura. Where are you?"

Together, their heads turned to the shop front. "That's Tarek, you remember him from Fes," she flustered. "I . . . I have to go."

Reluctant to release her, he said with a self-mocking smile, "Hersh will close up here and Habib will meet you at the seagate. We'll explain your idea to the pirates together."

"Hura, there you are. I see you in there." Tarek stuck his head inside the doorway.

She smiled radiantly at Hersh, freed herself with a gentle push, opened her fingers and showed him the brooch still nestled in her palm.

"Now you'll accept my gift?"

Her eyes answered for her.

Stupid man.

Hura stomped her foot in the sand. Over the buzz of confusion and laughter, she explained her idea again to Captain Nabil and the onlookers.

But as before, Nabil's doubting eyes roved from her to the lagoon, then to the seagate behind them. Tarek stood to one side whistling fragments of a sea chantey. Hura wondered if she was embarrassing him. Maybe he didn't understand either.

"I heard you, I heard you," Nabil barked at Hura. "I understand. We dig a channel from the sea to the city gate. What I don't understand is how you're gunna keep the diggers from drownin' in the ditch and how . . . who is that!" His eyes bulged.

Hura moved aside to follow his gaze, gasped, and put her hand to her mouth to muffle her mirth. Everyone stared at the grandly dressed cavalier who jumped from ferry raft to beach and strode toward them.

By Allah, he *is* handsome, Hura thought. To Nabil she said, "Meet my architect. I consulted with him before coming here. We have the answer."

She watched in admiration as Habib moved closer and began to play his role, as if acting a scene from one of Kleinatz' unfinished operas. With a flourish, he swept the wide curled brim of his plumed hat low to the ground and announced himself: "Señor Habib de Regalado de Corso de Cabrera, recently court architect to Abu-Abdullah Allah, Boabdil the King of Granada, and now in the service of this lady, Hura, Queen of Tetouan."

Nabil looked him up and down, and grunted to Tarek, "A Muslim dandy."

To Habib he said, "Lucky you. If I caught you at sea you'd be with the fishes." He spat in the sand.

Hura started to intervene, but Nabil continued, "So, besides dressing well, you're an expert in ditch digging?"

Habib slapped his thigh with his free hand, "A good jest, Captain." He clapped the hat on his head. "Of course not. But let us leave this hot sun and repair to the magnificent cuisine that I'm sure your fine city offers. When my hunger is satisfied, I will answer your questions."

Nabil had no choice. He led the way along crowded city streets to a tavern. She glanced at Tarek. Clearly, from his clenched jaw and darting eyes, he was worried about her. She had heard that seamen thrived on fresh food, copious wine and compliant women, and they found them all in places like this.

Intent on something besides lentil soup, Habib gorged himself on stewed octopus and fried sardines while everyone else watched.

Nabil hailed a man who entered the tavern and rose to greet him. Hura seized the moment to lean over and whisper to Habib: "Where did you get that hat?"

Still chewing with relish, Habib said, "From a merchant in the souk who deals in used clothing. I bought it with coins from my uncle's cash box. The merchant got it in a bundle of finery that a pirate sold him. Like it?"

Nabil brought a portly, slovenly man to the table and introduced him. "This landlubber arranges ransom for our captives, sells off our spoils, and sees that the Pasha gets his share. Not that we're gettin' much since the Portuguese patrol our shore."

The man pulled the hood of his jellaba over his head so only his long

172

nose was visible. He said nothing.

Hura pursed her lips.

Seeing her disdainful look, Nabil snorted, "You're lookin' at the richest man in Salé. Someday, he'll be the Caid of our new Bou Regreg Republic and he'll tell the townsfolk what to do and what not to." Then Nabil rammed his fist on the table and turned to Habib, "Ain't you through eatin' yet? Let's get to it. You playin' with us for a free meal? How does this lady expect us to dig a channel without nobody drowning."

Hura sucked in her breath. Tarek's hand slid to his cutlass. Habib pushed aside his bowl and wiped his mouth and fingers with a linen handkerchief.

"The big problem," he began, "is getting diggers. You need at least 200, maybe 300 – "

"No problem with that," Nabil interrupted. "My friend here has almost that many slaves and captives in his pens. You need more, he'll get the townsfolk to do it. They know without us pirates, there ain't no town; there'll be no free Bou Regreg Republic."

Habib's grin exuded confidence. "It's true I never dug a ditch, but I've seen it done many times. I saw it in Granada where they brought drinking water from a lake in the mountains, in short, they built an aqueduct."

"I know about the why." Nabil interrupted again. "This lady bent my ear before you got here. It's the how."

Habib spread his hands out on the tabletop. "The only difference between an aqueduct and this channel will be size."

Hura breathed deeply.

Habib bent over the table and pushed his face closer to Nabil. "We plug the channel, then remove the plug."

Hura forced herself to nod confidently. Nabil and his friend looked blankly at each other.

"Give me your dagger," Habib demanded, his face still inches away from the pirate.

Eyes narrowed, Nabil ordered his friend: "Give him yours."

The man produced a dagger from inside his jellaba, laid it on the table point forward, and slid his chair backward beyond an arms-length lunge.

Habib hefted it, then scratched a line on the smoothly worn tabletop. All eyes followed. "That's the edge of the lagoon." Parallel to it he scratched another line a short space away. "This is the Salé wall."

The man in the jellaba hitched his chair closer.

"Where's the seagate?" Hura asked.

"Here." He drew two short lines close together and crossways to the wall. "These are also the channel," and he extended the two lines toward the line of the lagoon, almost touching it but not quite. "That's the ditch to be dug."

"I've got that far," Nabil said, now engrossed in the plan, "But the plug, man. The plug."

"Ah. The plug." With a sweep of his hand, Habib drew a continuous line that formed an oval between the lagoon and channel lines. "This oval," he said rapidly, "is one of your sunken ships, a felucca with no bottom. Put her here. Sink the hull into the ground and fill it with sand. When you're ready, when you've dug the channel, dig out the sand in the hull. Then all that's left is her planking, which divers in the lagoon or the channel can knock apart."

The two men sat expressionless, mouths open, then they roared with laughter. Hura joined them, clapping her hands. Tarek allowed himself to relax.

Nabil jumped up, "Yes, by Allah. We'll do it. My friend'll get the slaves, and . . ."

"Not so fast," interrupted Hura. There's a price for my architect's work. I need to get back to *my* city and the fastest way is by sea. You or one of your captains must take us to the port of Martil. Agreed?"

Nabil frowned. "Why should I agree?"

"Because a pirate leader knows how to reward his friends. Especially if it doesn't cost money."

Nabil laughed louder.

TWENTY TWO

Under a heavy overcast, curious townsfolk and well-wishing pirates gathered along the Salé beach. Channel diggers put down their tools and waited to see what would happen. Captain Nabil stood grinning, hands on hips, as he watched Tarek stow provisions and gear under the small quarterdeck of the felucca *No-Name*. The vessel may have lacked a name, but it had a prominent blue eye painted on its bow to ward off the evil jinn of the sea. Nabil had kept his promise.

Pulling Hura aside out of earshot of the others, Nabil grinned, "Your idea is gunna make me rich. So, I give you this boat. She's got a rusted, useless cannon but she'll get you home. But, if you capture a merchantman with her, you owe a split of the spoils. That's the law of the sea – a share of the gold, the slaves, and even the captured women." He made to slap her shoulder in merriment, changed his mind at her glare. She grimaced at the nearness of the man, but managed to thank him. His gift of the felucca did not include a crew, however. She tried to exchange their two horses for one of his sailors, but had to concede their mounts were part of the price of freedom.

Tarek did not share Hura's optimism. He refused to be responsible for her safety. Although now happy to be back on the sea, Hura wouldn't take his advice. She insisted on taking this boat even though he pointed out the hole in the tub's worn sail, the lack of a cabin, the rusted six-pound carronade, useless on the bow, and the lack of any recent oakum caulk in her seams.

"Load our things," Hura commanded with a stern look. "I have no choice. My husband needs me."

"Aye, but this be a sorry boat to sail in."

Habib stood apart from them, engrossed in his own journey. Much time had passed since the horrors of his shipwreck – his struggle in the sea, the bashing of the rocks. Now, looking from the boat to the placid sea beyond, the painful memories came back. He didn't need to do this. He didn't need to go. Watching Tarek and Hura clamber on board, knowing he would never get over his fear of drowning, he saw Hura turn to look for him. He swallowed hard as his feet moved him toward her.

The pirates pushed the *No-Name* afloat. Hura stood in the stern alongside Tarek who held the tiller. She watched as the people on the far side of the lagoon grew smaller, then she looked down at the sand-bottomed channel as Tarek guessed aloud: "Two fathoms."

Her mind raced ahead to Tetouan. She knew the port at Martil needed more docks, warehouses and equipment, but it could easily become a pirate haven. She had learned much from Nabil. If that donkey could succeed as a pirate, surely she could too. She would learn about sailing from Tarek. Hura's mind shifted to the present. She studied Tarek as he pulled on some sheets and the long, tilted yard holding the triangular sail swiveled around.

"Why did you do that?"

His answer was short as he secured the ropes with his callused hands. "To beat to windward."

Seeing her puzzled expression, he explained: "This here sail, rotten as it is, works in the wind like this rudder works in the water. Our wind's not a following wind. It's not pushin' us. So I tack a zigzag course by moving the sail from one side to the other."

"Oh," Hura said, not completely understanding. She felt the sea breeze catching and ruffling her hair and relaxed to the pitching motion of the boat. It was almost like riding Sacony. She felt an exhilarating sense of freedom: free to speed away from Pashas and Sultans, free to speed home. As Tarek looked over the side studying the changes in the color of the sea he said, "five fathoms," she walked forward and sat beside Habib on the small deck. Would he be part of her freedom?

For a short while, they sat quietly. She waited for him to say something, and even hoped he would touch her or take her hand. But his fist pounded the small cannon between them in agitation. His eyes darted everywhere but at the waves and at her. I hope he isn't seasick, she thought and put her hand on his arm to calm him.

As though reading her mind, Habib suddenly shouted, "I hate the sea!" Then he half-smiled and let go his tight grip on the carronade.

Tarek, several paces away at the tiller, laughed. "Who wouldn't, sailing in a tub like this. Nabil got the best of this bargain."

Habib took a gulp of sea air. "Did I ever tell you I was shipwrecked?" His voice was loud enough for Tarek to hear. "I suppose I should start at the beginning. About three years ago, at Cadiz, the Spanish port, we had to flee. We were in a big boat . . . bigger than this – the Af . . . or Afa . . . or something like that, then a bad storm came up. I was separated from my father, a rabbi, who drowned – "

"By Allah! The *Afafa*! My other ship. I know who you are. Your father's alive. He's in Tetouan. Well, don't you got baraka!"

Habib's jaw dropped and Hura thought for sure that he was going to be sick.

"How wonderful." she said, then added hesitantly, "You'll . . . be reunited."

Habib stood up. The boat rolled with the swelling waves; he grasped the cannon again.

"Sure do remember," Tarek said. "Lost my boat, though some timbers washed up on the shore the next week. Lost everything."

"I don't want to talk anymore about it," Habib turned away and looked out to sea with his jaw set.

"I'll . . . I'll make something to eat," Hura said.

"Can't cook on board," Tarek shouted over to her.

Habib said, "I'm not hungry."

Tarek changed the subject. "I planned us for a north coast course, close to shore. At night we beach this tub, eat and sleep . . . but see them shoals ahead? Over there, at the foot of the bluff. Rocks. We'll have to go further out."

Hura nodded then turned back to Habib, hoping to continue their conversation. "My father was also a holy man, a *marabout*. Do you have any other family?" She asked shyly, "Are you married? Do you have a wife?"

Habib managed a grin. "No wife. Just me: Hershlab ben Yitzhak."

"My name, Hura, means 'The Free Woman'. What does Hershlab mean?"

Habib looked at the roughening sea then sideways at her: "Lion-hearted." He paused, leaned very close to her and whispered, "You *are* free . . . strong, and beautiful."

Hura blushed. No one had ever told her she was beautiful. She tingled from his flattery.

Noting her reaction, he moved even closer, his thigh and shoulder rubbed against hers.

Distracted by his body, her voice faltered, "And 'Habib', why did you choose that name?"

"I didn't." He chuckled. "A friend . . . after I was shipwrecked, called me that. I think she had trouble pronouncing Hershlab."

"Do you know what Habib means?"

"Of course, 'lover'."

"Hey, you two!" Tarek's voice intruded. "Wind's freshened. Looks bad. Hura, come take the tiller. Keep her on this heading. Habib, you and me we'll take to the oars." As Tarek spoke, the small rent at the top of the taut sail split from top to the bottom, ripping with an ear splitting 'crack'.

Hura crouched sideways in the stern, both hands on the tiller, the wind viciously whipping her hair. The pounding of water on the hard wood of the rudder throbbed up her arms. Holding the reins of Sacony was nothing compared to the force she felt. Her ears rang as a fragment of torn sail snapped rigid like a flag in the gusts, echoing the shriek of the sudden gale winds. She watched Habib bend over his oar, struggling to keep up with Tarek's cadenced rhythm. Water sloshed over the floorboards from the high waves and began to collect around their ankles. The wind howled as the felucca breasted the heavy seas; the bow scattering flying foam like the slobber of a madly galloping colt.

Suddenly she screamed, her voice almost carried away by the gale: "A ship. A big one. To the right."

Tarek strained between the stinging sheets of rain to look starboard. "A galleon," he grunted. "She's gettin' larger. She's comin' at us."

Habib gasped in Hebrew: "Praise be to Yahweh!"

"Allah be praised," said Tarek.

"She flies a Portuguese flag." Hura shouted and started to swing the tiller. "Row. Row faster. Away."

Tarek roared at her: "Belay that, you fool. You'll swamp us," and running to the tiller, he wrenched it from her and struggled to swing back on course.

The warship rapidly closed the gap between them, furled the square sails on its foremast and main mast spars, but left lanteens on the two mizzenmasts to control yaw. Soon the ship was positioned on the ocean side, upwind, so her bulk reduced the buffeting of the felucca. The rain abated, but now the waves pushed her closer. A boson's chair swung free. A seaman tossed a line to Tarek who stood on the heaving deck. He caught, and hauled it in. Another seaman shouted, "Look sharp!" and swung a grappling hook. As Tarek watched, it bounced off the side, fell short. Tarek leaned back, strained at the rope and pulled the felucca closer until it banged against the hull that loomed above them while a seaman at the tackle lowered the chair. Habib held Hura by the waist, steadying her until just the right instant when the chair dipped and swung closer. He held it for her and she fell into it.

As soon as the chair was hoisted onboard and Hura stepped on deck, she saw a sailor chop the rope of the life-saving chair with an ax. She screamed: "My friends! What are you doing."

The uniformed mate supervising her rescue shook his head. "Captain said: 'Just take the woman, nobody else'." Hura reached for her dagger. It was gone. She ran to him and pounded his chest with both fists. He warded her off and held her wrists then nodded to two seamen standing by with long pikes. At once they leaned over and thrust down at the felucca. As the waves rolled the boat away, the mate half-carried, half-dragged Hura to a cabin aft.

A strange thump jolted Hura awake from a deep sleep. She was bathed in sweat. In her nightmare, she had been locked up, struggling to escape from a dark, airless wooden box. She looked frantically around the small room in the faint early morning light that filtered through the tiny, salt-encrusted window. She struggled to focus her eyes, switched from dream to reality and recalled the previous two days and nights since her capture. That was what it was, a capture, and not a rescue from the storm-torn felucca. Tears welled in her eyes again as she thought of Habib and Tarek. They must be dead. It was all her fault.

A loud knock and jiggling of the locked door latch brought her upright in the bunk. The gruff voice that she now remembered could carry from one end of the vessel to the other said, "We're here. Come out."

Where was here? Never any explanation. Always that mate. Never the Captain. Why hadn't she met him yet? Hura stooped to pass through the low doorway and blinked in the sudden sunlight.

The mate waited with a length of cord. "Hold out your hands."

Hura glared at him. He shrugged and stuffed the cord in his waistband. She followed him down from the small cabin in the high after castle to the ship's waist. A narrow gangplank with no railing led to a jetty below. She craned her neck to see the tops of two towers on the huge stone fortress that rose from the sea. Each soared higher than the topmast of the galleon. Across the stone jetty was a small seagate.

At the gangplank she stopped. "I demand to speak to the Captain. Where is he?"

The mate pointed. "There's your jailer," he answered and pushed her forward. "Captain's waiting at Porto do Mar."

Chin up, Hura walked the gangplank.

A short, stocky man in an ill fitting, soiled uniform rubbed his hairy hands together as she approached. He had a long knife scar across his cheek that showed white and hairless against his swarthy skin.

"Where is this place?" Hura asked the jailer as he unlocked the iron grille of the portal.

There was no response until they passed through the thick wall and emerged on the other side. He frowned then brightened and said with a proprietary sweep of his arm, "Portuguese fort at Mazagan harbor. Over there, the right bastion, there's where you'll be. That one's called San Sebastin."

Eight or ten kasbahs, each the size of hers at Tetouan, could fit in this fortress, Hura decided. Inside the walls, to her astonishment she saw a complete town with buildings of different sizes, a large cistern and a parade ground as vast as the Pasha's. Her heart sank lower with every step into this impregnable fortress. There was nowhere to run. As she followed her jailer past a casemate in the ramparts, she could see barrels of black powder and large pyramids of stacked shot. Proceeding on into the bastion's ground floor prison, she shrank into herself and gasped at the sight and the stench of chained prisoners.

Her jailer looked back at her with a derisive smile. "That's not for you."

Hura followed in the wake of his sour breath up a winding stone stairway to a landing at the top of the tower. There his booted feet echoed along a short torch-lit corridor that ended at an iron door. He unlocked it with a huge key on a ring, stood aside and said with a twisted grin: "Your guest quarters."

Head high, Hura brushed past him. She swallowed the lump in her throat and fought back her fear until the door clanged shut and locked behind her.

It did not take long to examine the cell. It was better, but not by much, than those of the prisoners below. But at least it was private. She quickly saw it was about five paces square. Its furnishings were few and simple: a wood plank bed, a taboret alongside with one candle, a lidded chest and an iron chamber pot. A small open window criss-crossed with iron bars overlooked the harbor and admitted a sharp ocean breeze. As she watched, a ship's mast disappeared out of sight.

Soon the jailer, puffing from the climb, returned with a tray of food, which he put on the floor. His lip curled with that sickening grin as he said: "This one's free. You want more? You pay." He pointed to the small purse Hura had laid on the taboret. "How much you got?"

Hura stiffened and ignored his question. "Is the Captain leaving on that ship? Who's in charge here?"

"Questions, questions. I'm in charge here."

"And your name is?"

"Everyone calls me . . ." he paused, then scratched his ample belly as if he'd forgotten.

"What's the Captain's name?"

For an answer, he held out his palm.

Hura eyed his broken, dirty fingernails. Anger colored her cheeks but she checked herself. After he accepted her vague promises of payment, she slammed the door behind him then realized he must be slow-witted. She allowed herself an indulgent smile as she thought of Tarek. She could just hear him say: 'By Allah, he's got empty saddlebags'. She picked up the tray and put it on the bed; sat beside it and nibbled on a hard, tasteless biscuit. She pushed the tray aside, lost in thought. The key grated in the lock and startled her again. A nobleman wafted into the room on a cloud of perfume. He was a slender man in a feathered hat, well-tailored britches and a brass-buttoned blue jacket with gold-fringed epaulets. His left hand rested lightly on the hilt of a rapier as he gracefully bowed. "Captain Fernao Dias at your service, Madame al-Mandari."

Hura rose to face him, hoping against hope he had come to rescue her. "You know who I am?" She nearly choked on her words.

"Of course." The Captain's right hand flew to his heart. "Ours was not a chance meeting at sea. I was the one who blew your felucca out of the water at Salé. I had been informed of your silly channel digging and your departure. And this may interest you . . ." his back straightened, "it was my ship that blew up your kasbah in Tetouan. I rescued my countrymen whom you held in your prison."

Dias permitted himself a smug smile. "That was my old ship. The galleon that brought you here is our latest warship, full rigged and a better sailer than the old carrack. With more cannon, too."

Hura wished for her dagger again. Somehow, she found the courage to respond. "So now you are my captor."

"No, dear lady. Not captor. Let us say your 'host'." He surveyed the cell as though seeing it for the first time. "I trust the accommodations are suitable. Much more so than those you afforded our prisoners in Tetouan."

Immediately she feared the worst. He would trade her for Tetouan. "Suitable for what? Ransom? Under that fine clothing, you are just another pirate!"

If her words bothered him, he did not show it. His features remained affable and his manners courtly. "Please sit down, Madame, while I explain." Warily, Hura sat on the edge of the bed. He towered over her. "Comfortable?"

She clenched her fists.

"You and your provincial husband have become a meddlesome nuisance in the larger affairs of nations. Perhaps you were not aware that in 1493 His Holiness the Pope drew a north-south Demarcation line down the Atlantic." He smirked. "Spain had to be content with their newly discovered wasteland of savages west of the line. But that Treaty of Tordesillas granted us Portuguese the colonization and trading rights to all North Africa." He punctuated the word 'colonization' with a pointed finger aimed at her head.

Hura remembered the Professor telling her the Pontiff had hidden in the Castle of Sant' Angelo across the Tiber river. "Pope Alexander's treaty is not valid," she retorted.

"Dear Lady, Pope Julius affirmed it. He made it more specific."

"We agreed to no such thing,"

He flicked his fingers outward. "Calm yourself, Madame. Women of political marriages influence affairs of state not at all. It is men who change our world. Surely, you know that the Sultan is our vassal and the Grand Wazir . . ."

"We Riffians never agreed. We never will."

"Very well, as you wish. But you do agree you are my hostage, do you not?"

"Hostage for what. What do you want, ransom?"

"You and your father in Tangier . . . you're so much alike." He shook his head and sighed in mock admiration. "It's not ransom money we're after. You haven't enough." He went to the door, opened it and peered out at the jailer who leaned against the corridor wall. He looked back at Hura. "I will write to the Crown and seek the King's instructions as to whether you are to remain here or be taken to Lisbon. Meanwhile, you will write your husband so he will ponder your situation and agree to ally Tetouan with the Crown. I will send you writing materials and see to it that your missive is delivered."

"Do I have to pay for pen and paper?" Hura snapped. "You pose as a gentleman and yet charge me for my food."

Captain Dias smiled. "Ah, what can I do? The jailer is not in my employ. I am just a sea captain. I advise you to give him what money you have. You'll have no other use for it."

Hura tensed, furious as a wounded mountain cat. Captain Dias bowed and the door clanged behind him.

Pirate Chieftain Nabil basked in his newfound respect. The digging of the channel progressed with few problems and after two weeks it extended halfway from the seagate to the lagoon. The other pirates and the townsfolk all credited him as the inventor of the idea. He was impatient to be the first sea captain in history to sail directly from the Atlantic into Salé.

Nabil's lofty vision deflated when he spotted Habib and Tarek trudging along the beach at the outer wall of the city. He hurried to intercept them, and through back alleys, led the two gaunt and disheveled men to a remote tavern. Between gulps and swallows of their first meal in three days, Nabil heard first from one then the other, the story of the storm, the Portuguese warship and the abduction of Lady al-Mandari.

"The last we saw," Tarek seethed, "was that galleon disappearin' over the horizon. South bound. Then that damned *No-Name* that you called seaworthy, foundered half-a-league from shore."

Nabil shrugged his shoulders. Under the table, his hand grasped the dagger at his belt. "We pirates have a saying: 'Trust only your own nose'."

The two men stared at each other. The air tensed between them. Still hungry, Habib eyed a joint of lamb, but left it on the plate. "I splashed, dog paddled, kicked my way. Wouldn't have made it if Tarek hadn't helped me."

"So what now?" Nabil said curtly.

Tarek squinted, picked his teeth and decided that a fight in the tavern would be suicide.

Habib's words shot out: "We find Lady al-Mandari. Where do you think the Portuguese took her?"

"That's obvious. To Mazagan. The Portuguese garrison. About forty-five leagues south."

Tarek leaned over the table, teeth bared. "We need money and a boat that'll get us there. This time I'll choose the boat."

Nabil faced him down. "There's been no money since my boat got blown to pieces. What money I got is for food for the channel diggers. Pirates don't give. They take." He rose and tossed some coins on the table for the food. "You'd better start walkin'."

Enraged, Tarek pushed back his stool. Habib grabbed him by the shoulder just in time. "Let him go. You stay here. I'll be back before sunset."

"Where you off to?" Tarek freed himself.

"The hole in my pocket needs a silver lining. Back to my uncle. To Rabat across the river. He has money."

Tarek squinted. "So you're deserting Hura."

Habib grinned and patted him on the back. "You're big and strong. You saved my life and you're stupid. But I like you all the same. My uncle will be overjoyed when his nephew Hersh returns to bring him the good news that his brother is alive and well . . . a rabbi in Tetouan. That's where I'm going. I'll say I want to go to my father to tell him how prosperous his brother in Rabat is. Then I'll tell him the journey to Tetouan takes money."

Tarek shook his head. "You're gunna be Hersh again?"

Habib laughed. "Of course not."

"You Jews. You're shrewd. No wonder you're all rich. I'll stay 'til the sun sets. Then I leave for Mazagan with or without you."

Two months dragged by. Cooped up day after day, each day the same as the one before, and the one to come. Nothing to do. Lying on her bed, in her mind she attempted to reread some of the manuscripts in Kleinatz' library. Nothing to see except the occasional arrival of Captain Dias' ship, then await his oppressive perfume. At first, she had wrinkled her nose, positive he had not been scrubbed in water between his baptism and marriage, or since. More recently, she had stifled her revulsion. She realized she couldn't afford the luxury of hate, of showing her anger. She wanted to converse with someone, even her captor. And he always bought food. She knew she would get more than the twice-daily bowls of bread and yogurt when he was in port. And she realized that she, too, needed a bath. She ached to know what was happening: what news, what message from her husband or from the King. When would she be released?

Besides, she rationalized, his manner was courteous and flattering. His behavior was as she had imagined it would be, that of a European gentleman conversing with a high born lady. No doubt he intended to charm and impress her, and his words probably were just gossip, not fact. Nonetheless, his conversation was entertaining, flavored with fascinating accounts of a world she knew little of.

Often his account of events unsettled her. On his last visit three weeks ago, she had asked him to explain again how a Pope in Rome, whom she knew was very far away, could dictate a treaty which carved up the world – not just the Catholic world – but the whole world.

"It was done with much thought," he said. "After all, His Holiness was the most powerful ruler in the world. So the monarchs of Portugal and Spain agreed to abide by it, and signed it too!"

Hura had argued: "Our tribes in the Rif would never agree to any such division of Northern Africa. No outsider should tell us where our boundaries are!" Her thoughts scattered and she wondered, since Berbers didn't have a written language, what their treaties would be written in. Not all our people read Arabic, and Spanish had all those squiggly letters in it. What would her father or Ibrahim think. Did they know about this Treaty? How she wished she could talk with her father again. She now fully understood what imprisonment must mean to him. How many years had he endured it without weakening his resolve for a free and united Rif? She would do no less. She too would be strong.

Today, she was actually glad to see the mast of the Captain's ship in port. The jailer proceeded him carrying a wooden chair for him to sit in.

After his usual pleasantries, he produced a small box from his jacket and placed it on her bed. "Some spices for you. Our trade in the far east grows. You will find your food more palatable if you use them."

She sniffed the box. "Captain," she answered, "I receive only a small bowl of gruel each day. That is hardly food."

He leaned closer, eyes boring into hers. "If your husband doesn't ally himself with us, either the Spanish or the Turks will massacre your people."

Her anger turned to indignance. "Captain Dias, I am not ignorant. Twelve years ago, the Spaniards took Melilla on our coast, built one of their presidios there. But they never came up to the mountains. *They* never burned our villages to the ground like your people tried to."

His mood changed. "You've forgotten, haven't you, that your Tetouan was sacked and thousands killed about a hundred years ago. Those soldiers weren't Portuguese . . . they were Spanish."

Silently Hura cursed her faulty memory. Was she thinking clearly? Yes, now she remembered her husband had told her that. Perhaps the lack of food . . . she forced herself to focus. "And the Turks? What about them?"

Dias feigned astonishment. "You don't know about Selim the Grim?"

"I know the Ottomans are Muslim. Whoever he is, he's one of us. His janissaries protect the Sultan in Fes and the Pasha in Rabat."

"Dear Lady, have you never heard the *Arabian Night's* story? The one about the camel's head under the tent?"

Mustering as much energy as she could, she demanded: "Captain. Tell me about this Selim."

"Ah, yes. The Sultan of Egypt is now that Ottoman despot's vassal. So are the Pashas in Tunis and Algeria and the entire coastline east of you. You're next. You would do well to heed my wishes and become Christian. As allies, who knows, your city might be saved."

She shook her head. She had rejected conversion many times before. "And how does this Selim propose to conquer our mountains?"

"My dear Lady . . . Hura, I will speak plainly so you will understand. He who controls the sea owns the land. For the first time, those savages out of the East have a navy. It terrorizes the eastern Mediterranean, Already it is the scourge of Cyprus, Sicily, and Venice. And who is the Admiral of that navy? Can you imagine?" He drew closer as if to share a secret. "A pirate. He calls himself Redbeard and he operates openly from Tunis."

Hura was thunderstruck. Kleinatz had warned her – and the entire Council. This was truly a new threat. Her thoughts raced in all directions. As she became aware of his hand on her shoulder, she shivered. "What news have you of my husband?"

Consumed by worry, self-doubt and humiliation, Hura now knew she had been a fool to trust the Wazir and the Pasha. She felt like a simple-minded mountain girl putting herself, innocent as a fawn, into the hands of experienced hunters. What must her husband, her brothers, the Professor . . . everyone, be thinking of her back home. Not only had she failed in her foolhardy quest, she had given the Captain a weapon for their defeat – herself. Was it too much to hope her husband would forgive her? She prayed he would write soon.

Her jailer had made her helpless situation very apparent. From the first moment, he had been churlish, scornful. She had arrived with only the clothes she wore – her husband's cape and his ring, which was carefully sewn into its hem, a few coins in her purse and Habib's nautilus pin. When the jailer's greedy finger pointed at the pin, she refused to take it off.

He swore. "Damned poor pay for climbing these stairs every day." His derision showed in many ways: he let the tallow burn down without replacing it; he refused to bring more blankets or to provide comfort from the damp walls; he neglected to clean the floor around the small, stinking hole where she emptied her chamber pot. And he brought less and less food.

She tracked the weeks as they passed, noting the loud pealing of the bells from the Church of the Assumption every Sunday.

By the eighth week, Hura needed no mirror to tell her she had lost weight. She looked haggard and could do nothing about her matted and stringy hair. Her body had weeks ago developed a constant ache from the cold and the pressure of the bed planks on her bones. She tired easily. But her mind remained alert. At least she hoped it did. By day she stood at the window, counted the vessels moving along the coastline. At night, she made the sleepless hours pass by remembering the stories Scheherezade had told the Sultan in order to stay alive. After eighteen nights, she had to invent others. Usually around dawn, she began reviewing the manuscripts she had read with the Professor.

By the tenth week, Hura was frantic. Five times now the Captain had come to port empty-handed. "No news from Lisbon or Tetouan," he would cheerfully report. On his last visit, he had waxed on about his uncle the Admiral, about experiences at the Portuguese court and the latest gossip. And each time, she recalled, he became more intimate in word and fleeting caress.

At the end of her eleventh week in the tower, as she was leaning against the moist wall, vacantly glancing out the window, she suddenly grasped the bars and pressed her hot face to the cold iron. The Dias pennon was floating from the topmast of a galleon bearing down on the harbor. Despair turned to anticipation. She hoped he brought food. She did not have long to wait before the key turned in the lock; the door swung open and in strode her gallant oppressor. In one hand, he held an opened letter, in the other, a wicker basket with a loaf of bread sticking out.

"A letter from my husband! Thank God."

Captain Dias' voice oozed compassion. "Not your husband, my dear Hura. He is dead. This letter is from Lisbon, from King Manuel's Secretary. Do you want to read it?"

Hura felt a tightening in her chest, gasped for breath, and fell back on the bed. She turned away to hide her tears. "My husband . . . how did it happen?" With great effort, she stood up. "How do you know?"

Dias came close. "I just heard the news myself. I'm afraid there's very little to tell. Apparently, it was just natural causes. You would know his condition better than I."

Hura couldn't control a wrenching sob. Mandari died thinking she had deserted him. Numb, she stared out the window at the darkening sky. She had no sensation of his hands on her shoulders or of his hot breath at her neck until she heard his silken words: "In the letter, the Secretary wrote that His Majesty has no interest in you."

Hura blinked as she thought: *now I'm free to go. Now he'll let me go.*

The Captain's hands slid to her waist then up to nestle under her breasts.

She whirled away, suddenly aware of him. Her hand swung a slap like a pistol shot and turned his cheek dark red.

Eyes slit in anger and teeth bared to curse, his hand caught her wrist. Then just as quickly, his expression changed to a sardonic grin.

"Hura, dear," he began as if speaking to a naughty child, "You know that Muslim men take many wives. That Fes Sultan of yours has far more than the four of your Koran. Alas. I can have but one wife and the church does not permit divorce. My affection for you is more than I can bear. You have just seen how difficult it is for me to restrain myself. Now I won't have to any longer." He backed away and stood arrogantly by the door of her cell.

"My subtle attempts at converting you have failed. Even starving you for your affection has not convinced you. Now I will be blunt. You are mine to do with as I please. If you will not convert, then at least profess like other Moriscos did in Spain. After all, only God will know what is in your heart. In return, I offer you a certain status."

Hura backed up against the far wall.

"Fortunately, Catholic men of means may have mistresses." He smiled broadly. "In two days, after I provision my ship, I sail for Sebta, our Navy's home port. You shall go with me. You will find my new galleon the newest, biggest in our navy, much more comfortable than this cell. In its aftercastle, we'll have spacious quarters and good food. And, you will be happy to know, she has a newly designed bronze cannon . . . we won't have any problems with your Salé pirates." He laughed at his little joke.

"Then, when we arrive in Lisbon you shall have a carriage and servants and jewels beyond the imagination of a mountain queen."

Hura stumbled to the bed and sat with her back bowed, a look of horror on her face. She shook her head no.

"My dear, you must be stunned by these events. You need time to consider."

She lifted her head to face him. "Never, never, NEVER!"

Still smiling, his eyebrows shot up. "Ah, my dear, I see I must speak even more plainly. Very well, you have two choices. Listen carefully." His voice crackled with mock sincerity as he continued, "The first is to assume a lavish life at court. As my only mistress. In time you will learn to love me."

Hura stared up at him defiantly, her jaw set. "And the other?"

He sighed. "You force me to say I will not kill you but you will wish I had. You will subject yourself to degradation." He drew a long breath. "You know the tradition of spoils on the high seas. After we set sail for

Lisbon you will be brought on deck and stripped. You will watch as the two most savage of my crew fight for your possession. After that . . ." he shrugged. "Live or die, the choice is yours."

TWENTY THREE

In the name of Allah, the Beneficent, the Merciful.
Praise be to Allah, Lord of the Worlds:
The Beneficent, the Merciful:
Owner of the Day of Judgment.
Thee (alone) we worship; thee (alone) we ask for help.
Show us the straight path:
The path of those whom Thou hast favored;
*   not (the path) of those who earn Thine anger*
*   nor of those who go astray.*

Bathed in a beam of moonlight, Hura huddled on her bed, arms around her knees. Sleepless, hopeless, she prayed. In a low monotone, she said the First Surah, the opening to the Koran she had memorized as a child. She prayed for forgiveness. She had sinned – had failed in her mission, and had been consumed by pride.

Wild as a young colt she had dashed off to Fes then Rabat, all in the vain notion she could do a man's work. Her husband resisted because he knew better. Her husband must have known the Sultan would never grant her an audience. Her husband knew she thought like a woman from Chaouen. If only she had never left the Rif.

Now her husband was dead; she had abandoned him and her marriage vows to dally with Habib. No. Not Habib, she remembered he changed clothing and names as easily as an endangered chameleon. Yes, she loved a Jew named Hershlab. Her thoughts wandered. It was too late for forgiveness. Now she could face that truth, God forgive her, she had never loved her husband. She loved Hersh passionately. If only she could tell him that. But it was too late now; he would never know. Thoughts of Hersh absorbed her until, head on her bent knees, she fell into a fitful sleep.

Dawn broke and she awoke with a start, energized by a dream. Quickly she leaned over the taboret, picked up the ceramic jar and spit into the dried ink. Balancing a tablet on her knees, she labored with her quill to compose a note to her brother Ibrahim describing her journey's end and confessing her many sins. She wrote that her dying wish was for him to convey to their father her respect and love. As an afterthought, she added she would somehow kill Captain Dias at sea, then jump overboard, herself. Chewing on the tip of the feather, she considered whether to seal the letter with an imprint of her husband's ring. It still weighed secure in the hem of her cloak. No, she decided. She would die in penance to him with it still on her person. She reached up, unpinned Habib's nautilus and waited for the jailer.

Wine-sodden this evening, Tarek slouched at a table near the Mazagan Tavern's door. Each day here, surrounded by prostitutes, card sharks and mercenaries, had been the same. He drank more and more while waiting for Habib to accept the obvious.

"That Hebe's a fortune hunter," he muttered to the empty stool in front of him. "Why won't he listen?" His lips pursed as he bet that even now Habib still loitered at the fortress gate. He's hoping. Hoping for what? Talking to those prison guards. They don't know nothing. That's why they're guards. All these weeks and what's he learned? She's in the tower. What'd he expect? A palace? She'll be there forever . . . or hanged as a pirate queen, Allah forbid. Why won't Habib listen? Weeks ago I shoulda been in Tetouan, shoulda told Sidi al-Mandari and the Emir what happened. They can do something. We can't. Well, I'm ready to face my punishment. I'll tell Habib . . . Hersh, whichever he is tonight. Tomorrow I'll leave.

And Lady Hura, curse me for an old fool. Why did I agree to nursemaid a chit of a girl so . . . headstrong. Naive. But she's got guts. Smart too. He slumped lower, remembering her clever tactic at the fondouk and their escape.

A cold sea breeze blew through the dingy tavern as the door opened. Tarek looked over the rim of his raised cup and saw one of the regulars come in blowing on his hands and nodding a greeting to everyone. These regulars, Tarek thought, bet they think I'll drink up all Habib's money and end up on the beach.

Then he saw it. Instantly he was cold sober.

The clasp! He's wearing Hura's pin. Without thinking what he would say, Tarek waved a welcome to the man. "Sit over here, no fun drinkin' alone. Have one with me."

The man quickly accepted. He shed his shabby jacket and sat down on the stool. "You're in the money now?"

Tarek forced a laugh, "Who me?" and waved two fingers at the barmaid. "Nope. Tonight's my last here. I'm goin' out with the fishermen tomorrow. Would you believe I've sailed up and down this coast as third mate on a galley – even into the Big Sea – and never froze my hands and ass hauling in fisherman's nets? Always a first time, I guess."

"We all got problems." The man said. "I climb stairs – up and down – with never a coin or a thanks from my prisoner."

Tarek eyed the man while the barmaid poured wine from a demijohn.

Looks half-dead, he thought. Empty saddlebags. He jerked his thumb in the direction of the fortress. "So you're a jailer."

"If I was Officer of the Guard would I be wearing these rags?" He burped, and wiped his wine-coated mustache with the back of his hand.

Tarek sipped his wine slowly, thinking how best to proceed. "Mighty fancy clasp you got there," he said tentatively.

"Got it this morning."

"One of your prisoners died, did they?" He tried to keep his voice steady.

"Not this time." The jailer put down his empty cup and rocked back on the stool. "Gota say hello to my friends."

"I'm not your friend? I see you every night here. Come on, it's my last night. Have another with me. You got me curious." Tarek ordered more wine.

The jailer's eyes were blank for a moment. Then he smiled. "When I get prisoners, they never have no money. I got a hard life. My family would starve if I didn't bring in some extra."

"The pin?"

"Yeah." The jailer nodded. "Well, this prisoner's shippin' out tomorrow. Goin' with the Captain. The one with the big ship. She gives me a letter and this here pin. The letter's to her brother. An Emir, she says, from some town in the mountains. And would I please give the letter to some Muslim trader in town for delivery. A huge reward, she said." The jailer pulled Hura's letter from his pocket and jabbed the front of it with a finger. "That says 'Emir', don't it?"

Tarek pretended to read it. "Yeah. Says Emir Ibrahim bin Rachid."

"Means nothing to me." His sleeve brushed the letter off the table as he reached for the pitcher.

Tarek leaned closer: "I know some Muslims here in town who trade in the north. They'd pay plenty for the honor of bringing it to an Emir. You ain't gunna find any good Muslims in this tavern." He reached down and picked up the letter.

"Better yet, I could take it. You'd get half the reward. But you gotta pay me something to do it. How 'bout that pin."

The jailer slapped his hand over the nautilus and eyed Tarek with suspicion. "How do I know I can trust you?"

"You don't."

The jailer's eyes showed his confusion. He didn't know any Muslims, and a Portuguese could get killed in those mountains in the north. He had planned to throw the letter away. Too much trouble to arrange the delivery. He was satisfied with the silver pin. He rubbed the scar on his face. But this new friend says he could get half a big reward for doing nothing. That

191

sounded good.

"Yeah. That'll do." He patted the pin to make sure it was still there. "You get this when I see how its gonna work."

Tarek thought quickly. "I'll make the deal tomorrow; we split the reward fifty-fifty. I get the pin tomorrow."

"Done," said the jailer, gulping the last of his wine.

Dawn arrived cold and cloudy. In the gray light Habib led Tarek and three townsfolk to the fortress gate and nodded a familiar greeting to the yawning guards as they swung the massive door open. The group blended with others entering the compound and hurried to the prison. At the tower entrance, Tarek asked the guard to tell the jailer his visitors had arrived. As the guard disappeared into the dark interior, the group eyed each other uneasily, silent for what seemed an eternity until the surprised jailer lurched into view, bleary-eyed, buttoning his jacket.

Tarek addressed him in Portuguese with a forced grin: "You didn't think I could do it, did you? Well, here we are. This be Ahmed, the old trader who's puttin' up the travel money and his wife, daughter and son. The son here," he pointed to Habib, "will take the letter to Tetouan."

The jailer blinked. It was too early; much too early to think, much less speak. He opened his eyes wider to look at the women. Both were veiled from head to toe.

Tarek noted the jailer's concern. "These women, they insisted on seeing your prisoner. No offense, but they want to know she's not been harmed."

Finally, words came. "Women! Well, I guess so. Just a peek. We're not savages here like the Arabs. Let's get it over with before the Captain comes."

The jailer led the way up the stairway and along the semi-dark corridor. Tarek kept a one-sided conversation going. "The old man, he's a leader in the Muslim community here. He don't say much, but give him respect. We got no deal unless he approves."

"Never mind. Did he bring the money?" The jailer grunted.

At the cell door, Tarek stood alongside him. "He brought enough. What he calls 'earnest money'. You and me get to split that up-front money now . . . if he likes the deal. The big pot o'money comes after the Emir pays up. Oh, and don't forget that papa is paying his son's expenses to get there."

Tarek hoped the grunt he heard in response meant agreement. The jailer unlocked the cell door, swung it ajar and shouted: "Visitors!"

Habib and the trader shouldered past the jailer into the dark cell. Then Tarek, still talking, positioned himself to block the doorway.

Hura leaped from the bed, eyes large and mouth open in fright. Habib put his finger to his lips, and rushed to embrace her. Her arms wrapped

192

around his neck and she slumped against him. They stood locked together only a moment before Habib whispered in Arabic, "The jailer's outside; Tarek's there, too. He got your letter. I'll explain later. Say nothing. There's little time for us to get you out of here. Play the role."

Hura kept hugging him. "What role?" she whispered back.

"You'll see. Yours comes later." Habib motioned to the father to leave and said loudly in Spanish, "Lady Hura will see one of the women now."

As soon as the trader emerged, Tarek drew him over. "Show our friend here the pouch." The man reached through a slit in his outer garment, pulled out the leather money pouch and dangled it by the drawstring. It bulged with coins. As the jailer reached for it, a portly, veiled woman hobbled past him. She gasped in the doorway from the smell, pulled out a handkerchief and put it in front of her face. The trader pulled the pouch away, and put it back inside his clothing.

Tarek laughed. "That'll be all yours. I got my share before I brought 'em here. It'll keep me off the beach and in the tavern from now on. You get yours as soon as the trader is satisfied. I get the pin now." He held out his hand.

The jailer reached inside his jacket and unfastened the pin. Still eyeing the place where the moneybag had disappeared inside the old man's tunic, he handed the pin over.

Now Habib stood in the doorway, back to the interior, blocking the jailer's view. He signaled for the daughter to enter. Still wide-eyed, Hura sat on the bed as the daughter removed her outer garment, her veil and scarf. She had the same exact costume underneath.

The daughter emerged from the cell and stood quietly behind the jailer. Hura hastily donned each of the discarded garments.

Tarek continued his rambling conversation with the jailer, keeping him distracted, ". . . and that pouch is only the beginning. That rich Emir will praise Allah his sister is alive. He'll press a huge gift on this young messenger. We'll split that too . . . should be a lot more than in the pouch."

The portly woman hobbled past him again and stood by her husband.

"And the father, this trader, what does he get?" The jailer rubbed his scar.

"Don't worry 'bout him. The Emir'll will pay him well in future trade."

The jailer's eyes gleamed for an instant then he turned to the doorway, remembering his prisoner. "Hurry up in there," he grated.

From the door Habib said, "We're leaving now." He half-turned and called into the dim room: "Come, Mother."

Hura, veiled and with a handkerchief over her nose, hobbled out of the cell and took his arm.

The jailer saw the daughter rush forward to her mother and take her other arm while Tarek asked the trader if he was satisfied. The old man nodded assent and started to follow the women down the corridor. Habib returned to the cell door, leaned in and shouted in an animated voice, "Don't worry, Lady Hura. I'll carry your letter to Tetouan on the hooves of a stallion." Then he quickly clanged the door shut and said to the jailer: "Give her some time alone. She wants to pray."

The jailer blinked several times. Then he hollered to Tarek who was heading toward the stairs: "Hey. Wait! My money!" He clicked the key in the lock and ran after him.

As Habib led the group back out into the street, he turned. Framed in the doorway of the prison, the jailer was holding one of his new coins to the daylight, carefully turning and inspecting it.

TWENTY FOUR

The soft luffing of the sail and the whisper of water on the bow mesmerized them.

Hura broke their silence. "Those lights on the shore ahead, where are we?"

"Anfa," Tarek replied. "Pirates here give plenty of trouble to the Portuguese, they do. Our friend Dias can't follow us this close to shore. We're safe 'till we pass Larache and get near Tangier. Should be fair sailing. Get some sleep, I'll stay at the tiller. I've strung you a tarp on the foredeck." He scanned the cloudless night sky.

Hura and Habib sat facing him on the rough planks of the afterdeck amidst sacks of provisions, a barrel of water and coiled ropes. She rose and extended her hand down to Habib.

"Come forward with me, tell me about your life in Spain as Hershlab. I'm not sleepy."

Habib followed her past the cover over the hold to the foredeck where canvas hung draped over a mast stay. She pulled the cord fasteners and lifted the flap in the front, crouched and crawled inside. Then she beckoned and moved to one side of the mat beneath.

"Come, don't be shy." The light of a nearly round moon filled the interior with a pale soft light. "It smells like fish." she held her nose impishly. "Help me spread these blankets on top."

Habib had been watching her all evening waiting for a chance for them to be alone, wondering how best to get her away from Tarek. One word from Hura and Tarek's cutlass would make him fish bait. The man seemed bound by loyalty and Habib didn't understand their relationship. Tarek wasn't family, he wasn't a slave or a prisoner . . . yet when they had washed ashore after the shipwreck . . . he spent his last ounce of strength swearing to save her. What hold did she have over him? What bond? Was it love? No . . . she couldn't love a man like that. And besides, she ordered him around. But not all the time, though. On a boat, he was clearly in charge. It was a mystery. He would be careful not to become fish food.

Hura lay back on the blanket, her hair shimmering around her face. "Tell me again about the al-Hamra. You said it was beautiful. Was it like the Palace at Fes?"

Habib stretched out on his side close to her, his head propped up on a palm. The electricity of sex sparked between them. He could smell it . . . her. "You know, you're amazing. Here you are smiling, lying quietly and tempting me as if nothing has happened. As if just a few hours ago you weren't fleeing for your life, running through the streets, splashing through the city fountain, jumping on a boat, and escaping with danger all around you. I can't believe it. What are you made of?"

She rolled to face him, lifted a hand to his face and with her finger, lightly traced the outline of his lips and down the middle of his chin. Her gray eyes smoked. "I have fire inside me."

Habib reached for her, and drew her toward him, kissed her softly, tentatively, waiting to be burned.

Hura's mouth tingled. She pulled away and gasped for breath, then rose on her knees and lowered the flap over the entryway dimming the interior. In the privacy, she felt free to be wanton. She took off her blouse, then her skirt, then all her garments. As he knelt beside her on the mat, her busy fingers found the buttons of his shirt, his belt buckle. She saw the bemused smile on his lips as she struggled to undress him, pulling at his pants and shoes, but did not care.

His reserve made her more excited. Why is he suddenly shy. Is he modest? She threw his pants on the blanket. He was too thin. She would have to do something about that, but she liked his shoulders, and his arms felt right: long with smooth muscles. And his fur – the way his black hair curled on his chest, the way it ran down in a fine line to his navel.

Habib stopped her from pulling the string of his drawers, but he couldn't hide what his body wanted under the thin protruding material.

"Is this my fate? You, too, will fight me?"

In answer, he yanked off his drawers and lay beside her cradling her in one arm.

Her eagerness was awkward. She tried to roll him on top. Somehow they didn't fit together. She was all elbows, knees and angles; his nose got in the way; her fingers grabbed instead of caressed; she poked him in the eye. She wanted his larger body to smother her.

Somehow he seemed aloof. That made her want to cry. And then she was angry with herself. She couldn't even sin properly!

Suddenly they fit. Habib kissed her mouth then her neck, tenderly. He took his time, stroking her lightly from breasts to belly. His lips plucked her nipples erect and his tongue lapped circles around her breasts. He entered her slowly, sliding easily into her wetness. Her eyes closed. Again and again he pressed into her. The slow rhythm increased and she flowed with it, opening her legs wider and arching her back for more of him. The heat from her consumed him. The rhythm quickened, she became rigid then exploded in spasms of ecstasy. Waves of orgasm rippled up and down her body, finally leaving her limp. He kissed her again, quickened his thrusts then groaned.

They lay exhausted together until the sea breeze turned their sweat cold and she covered him. When he slept, she nestled alongside, content in a happiness that dared not disturb him. She wondered if it was Allah or a jinn who allowed this new experience. Her husband, may his soul rest in peace, had always been like a warrior plunging home his spear. But this was love. Why didn't anyone tell her about this before? Could this secret of ecstasy be known to everyone? Was it hers alone? She pressed her fingers hesitantly on her sticky mound and looked at the sleeping Habib, his hair fallen over his brow. My lover, yes, my love, she said to herself. As long as my eyelids are moist, I swear to you my love. And to think, I can have this ecstasy whenever I want it.

She awoke alone and chilly under her blanket. Moonlight had faded but stars glittered in the darkness. Strings of mist rose from the still waters and the boat was barely moving. Her belly growled. Hungry, she remembered the sacks Tarek had brought aboard. She dressed and passing the hold, peered in and saw Tarek's heavy black boots sticking out from beneath a coverlet on the wide planked floor. Habib stood at the tiller, wrapped in a striped cotton blanket. He smiled and opened it to her.

"Why did you leave?" she asked, not knowing what else to say.

"I relieved Tarek. He said to wake him in a little while, but I'll let him sleep. We're in no danger as long as I hold the tiller just like this."

Hura gave him a shy kiss on the cheek. "The first morning of my new happiness." She snuggled next to him and he folded her in his warmth. "Do you think we could talk about Spain and the al-Hamra again tonight?"

"It will be a very, very long story," he held her tighter.

"Good," she blushed. Perhaps you will need some sustenance for the arduous journey. What do we have?"

"I don't know, Tarek got all the supplies."

"And this boat too? I meant to ask him." Hura suddenly became serious. "Where did he get the boat?"

Habib laughed, "I don't know. When I asked him he said he had 'his ways' and wouldn't answer me."

"He couldn't have bought it, he had no money. Maybe he borrowed it . . . you don't think he . . . took it, do you? Is it stolen?"

"Wouldn't put it past him, but let's assume he borrowed it. Otherwise I'd have to start calling you the Pirate Queen."

Satisfied for the moment, she countered: "I like The Free Woman better." She unwound herself from his blanket. "I'll see what's in the sacks."

The first hemp bag was filled with small, dried sardines. She took out a handful and brought them to him.

As they ate, he asked, "Did you really mean all those things you said in your prison letter? Or was it just a ploy to obligate me to save you?"

Before she could respond, Tarek's voice boomed across the afterdeck: "Fine mornin', ain't she." He ambled over to them.

Hura had never noticed he was bowlegged before. Must be the walk of the sea. "Captain, I'll fix you a breakfast fit for an Admiral. Here, start with this fish."

Hura spent the next three days learning about sailing and the sea from Tarek; at night she learned about Spain and Habib.

As a lover, he enraptured her. But she always felt him guarded. He would only tell her so much about himself and there was this layer – no, maybe even a core – that was too private or too personal for him to reveal. She hoped it wasn't his nature. That would mean he couldn't share his soul with her. On her part, she was willing to give her complete being. Not one thought nor past incident in her life would she hide from him, and she knew she wanted to share her future with him. She needed him to love her as she loved him.

She could tell when she got too close to that private place in him. His mood would change abruptly, his brow would knit, and his eyes would wander. Slowly, I'll do it. Slowly, he'll trust me, she promised herself.

Protected by the tent and her baraka, Hura spent her nights in the breathless ecstasy of first love. Habib used his experienced body to teach her about rapture. Soon the nights were not enough. During the day they created a shorthand for their hunger: the smallest signal – a tongue to his lip, a raised finger, a crooked smile – made them run to the tent, fall on the mat and embrace.

Hura marveled that Habib always responded to her. He never tired. He would caress, excite, lick, explore then enter her from different positions. He seemed to have learned an inexhaustible variety of positions, from where she couldn't imagine, and didn't dare ask.

In between their lovemaking, they talked. She told him about silly things, personal things like the foods she liked, her magnificent horse named Sacony, her brothers, her father, Tetouan and the invasion, and of course, the Rif.

"What's so special about the Rif? I've seen mountains before."

"Special?" Her face contorted in mock indignance. "Well, you would see only majestic peaks and valleys, if you looked, but it's more than that. The Rif has many faces, of beauty and of cruelty. The Rif can kill the unwary or the foreigner. But can also shelter the visitor. Sudden ice storms can blow you off a precipice, but mountain brooks can cool your parched throat in summer."

She reached over and ran a finger around his chin and down to his Adam's apple. "And the most beautiful place in all the Rif is my Chaouen."

Suddenly she sat up. "Yes, you'll see. I'll take you there."

Habib grabbed her arm and pulled her back down beside him.

Utterly content, Hura listened to Habib tell her more about Spain and the al-Hamra. Their tales were so completely different, coming from such contrasting lives, that the other's sounded like fairy tales. They were sure their laughter could be heard by Tarek, but she didn't care. She *was* a free woman now.

"You'll be thankful for the calm." Tarek said in answer to her concern about their speed. "Wait 'till Tangier and the Straits, the waters of Hell. The currents pull, tear and spin you 'till you cry for mercy." He spoke lightly but his hand clenched the tiller. "We got maybe one more night before we get to Hell."

Habib's jaw tightened. Tarek's voice sobered, "You be a survivor, you know what it's like. Take the tiller now, I'll get some sleep."

Hura sat down beside him on a coil of thick rope. She tried to make light of Tarek's words: "We must be in heaven, and I have the baraka. I know it. We'll enjoy it until the Straits of Hell."

Habib didn't respond. She tried to change his mood by asking him why he became an artist. "I'm a designer, not an artist," he said. "I used to draw when I was young; my mother encouraged me. Until she died. She even bought me paper. I designed all sorts of things: silverware, carts, houses, belts, even a wine cup for the synagogue, then tiles at the al-Hamra, but you know all that. Of course, when I got shipwrecked at the caves I couldn't make anything, so I drew pictures on the rock walls. We'll pass the caves on the way to Tangier."

He paused and his mind flashed to Bridget with her blond hair and worldly blue eyes and sexual expertise.

"A designer of what?" she drew his attention back.

"Oh, of people, animals, shells . . . nothing great."

"I'd love to see your work," she said eagerly, "maybe we could stop there. Just for a short visit."

He fell silent again.

"You know," she lowered her eyes, "the Hadith tell us not to create paintings and sculpture of people. That's one of the differences between us." As soon as she said it she knew she shouldn't have. It came out all wrong. She was doing this all wrong. She would drive him away, not pull him closer.

Habib remained silent, withdrawn in that place where he always retreated to be alone.

That night in their lovemaking, he said little. She tickled him, trying to get him to laugh. As they lay side by side, she softly addressed him: "Habib, Hersh . . . whoever you are tonight, I want to be your wife. I can give you riches, make you the most famous architect in our land."

From his continued silence, Hura knew that again she had said the wrong thing. Tears flooded her eyes. She added in haste, "I'll give up everything, my rule, my Tetouan, for you. Our different religions aren't a problem to me. We both believe in Allah. You will marry me, won't you?"

When he didn't answer, she sat up. "Tell me, tell me you love me," she begged. Then she grabbed his hand and bit him. Hard. He yanked his hand away, grabbed his pants and crawled out on the deck.

"You silly fool," she said to the empty tent, "now you've ruined everything. Look what you've done. Love has muddled your wits." She quickly dressed and hurried to him at the bow of the boat.

"I'm sorry, I don't know why I said that. You don't have to marry me." She put her hands on his chest and looked into his eyes. "Forget I said anything. Let me love you; let's just enjoy what we have. You'll still be the court architect in Tetouan, but I won't tie you to me. You will have your freedom."

Whether he agreed or not, he didn't say, but put his arms around her and held her for a long time.

Later in the morning, as Tarek slept and he steered the boat, Habib called to her. When she came to him, he began: "I want to say something. I let my past get in the way when I should have been thinking of my future. I want you to know something about me. And I promise I'll only say it once. It's like a huge, heavy hand that tries to squash me . . . tries to control me. What I'm talking about is my religion.

"I grew up thinking, eating, living for Judaism. I told you my father was . . . is . . . a rabbi. For generations, all the men in my family became rabbis. One was a Court Rabbi. Another served the King as comptroller. Then came the Inquisition. Most of my family converted, became Marranos. One of us, Solomon Halevi, converted and became Paulus de Santa Maria, Archbishop of Burgos. Well, my father expected me to become a rabbi too. Only he made me feel I wasn't ever going to be good enough, I mean pious and deserving enough."

Hura sat at his feet and looked up at him. His words poured out in a torrent as if bottled up for years and now uncorked.

"Secretly, I wanted to see the world. I read about far away places and different peoples and I saw that Spaniards could go anywhere, eat and drink what they wanted. They didn't have to live in the mellahs. But I had my loyalty, my tradition, and my tribe. Deep down I know I would have become what my father wanted if we hadn't been forced to leave . . . in a sense, it's like I got a new chance on life. It's terrible to say, but I know that the misfortune of my people was a blessing to me. It's true." He stopped there, lost again in thought.

"Why *did* you have to leave Spain? I know the Muslims had to leave, but Jews too?"

"It wasn't the religion. That's what makes me so angry. It was the money and the politics. For centuries we all lived together and got along. But it was always up and down. Sometimes Jews could live in peace and respect. Our scholars once competed with the Muslims in translating to Arabic the works of Plato, Aristotle, Ptolemy, and the Greek mathematicians and scientists.

"But in bad times we were called obscene, detestable, vile . . . and ostracized from all human contact. Those were the exact words of one of Queen Isabella's most enlightened humanist scholars, Peter Martyr of Anghiera. Isabella is different from her husband, Ferdinand. She had good reason to be grateful to us. A Jew had been an intermediary in her marriage, and one of her father's confessors and two of her ministers were also Jewish. And you'd think Ferdinand would have been more tolerant because Henriquez, from whom the King was descended on his mother's side, was Jewish, a Marrano. So was the uncle of the Grand Inquisitor Torquemada."

"You seem to know so much."

Habib continued, "We lived in a mellah. Only there they were called *alhamas*, then later, *kahale*. All important cities like ours had one and we were independent. I mean, we had our own elected council. All authority was with the rabbis. I would have been more important than you can imagine. For centuries, the mellahs were good sources of income for the King. That's why we were sometimes left alone. Everyday we had to pay an entrance fee to be allowed into Spain. We paid poll taxes, dues for the use of roads, trade duties and we had to accept billeting of soldiers in our homes. And Ferdinand loved gold; we had to pay in gold."

He paused to see if she was still listening, then tightened his hold on the tiller.

"We knew things were getting worse for us and we knew about the Inquisition."

Hura leaned closer to him. "Your family wouldn't convert?"

Habib's laugh erupted. "No. Many Jews did convert, led by that renegade Chief Rabbi, Abraham Seneor. But not my father. We were forced to put our property on the market cheaply."

"Did your father really want to stay?"

"Yes, I suppose. It was his land too. He thought until the end that Ferdinand wanted to get rid of only the Muslims. He and some other rabbis offered to pay 300,000 ducats to stay. The King ordered us all to leave. I can recite from memory the Decree that demanded we leave. My father, he said it was a divine trial of faith. The Christians, they said the suffering of the Jews was divine punishment!"

Habib breathed deeply, saw Hura's eyes brimming with tears. One fat tear ran down the side of her nose and she wiped it with her fingers.

"I'm not sorry we left," he looked up at the cold gray sky. "I have my whole life ahead of me. I can choose what I want to be. No more books, no more prayers, no more guilt. You see, I thought my father was dead . . . and that in some way it was my fault. I'm tired of paying for someone else's sins, of feeling guilty."

He reached down for her and pulled her up. "I'm starting a new life with you in Tetouan. I'll be whatever you want. But no marriage. I'll even convert."

Speechless, she hugged him, backing him into the tiller. Then she raised her head: "I'm so happy! You make me so happy. But," she released him and held him at arms length, "don't you convert. Don't lie to Allah."

TWENTY FIVE

The breeze spanked their felucca smartly as it tacked into the Martil river. Leaving the gray, white-capped sea and entering the muddy waters of the river, they passed landmarks Hura thought she'd never see again: the Customs House, the port mosque, familiar farms. Once just a village, the port area now bustled like a small town. She craned her neck. Way up there, shining white against the mountain face – Tetouan beckoned.

Anxious to see her daughter, Hura grew impatient with the customs agent who had watched their small boat squeeze between slavers and cargo ships alongside the busy dock. She shot him an angry glance, hastily tore open her hem and put Mandari's ring on her finger. Bolstered by this symbol of authority, she ordered the agent to provide three horses and anchor their boat.

The young soldier at the Tetouan gate snapped to attention as Hura approached, a look of amazement on his face. Other soldiers on duty paused to stare as the three rode past their barracks, heading for the administrative compound.

"Not the welcome I thought we'd get," grumbled Tarek in Hura's direction.

"Don't worry, Captain, you'll be a hero, I'll see to that," Hura said.

"Where is everybody? Empty streets. No one's here." Tarek said what the others were thinking.

"Maybe it's a holiday," Habib said. "Is today some feast?"

Hura thought she was riding into a ghost town. The streets in the city were almost deserted and few shops appeared open. What happened? She had left Tetouan bustling, completely recovered from the invasion by the Portuguese. The city was thriving. The number of new homes tripled after the invasion and new settlers arrived every day. The souks had been filled with food, cloth and goods from Europe and the east. Even Kleinatz' library had been completed.

Now everywhere around her shops were empty; the streets had the dank smell of old urine and hadn't been swept in some time. This isn't the city I remember, she said to herself, her excitement ebbing. Of course, after my husband died, there would have been changes, but not like this. What was going on? And how did Martil grow so fast? The market place there was jammed.

Hura led to the stables near the old pens and proceeded on foot to the Mandari compound. At the entrance to the narrow lane, a short, pimpled soldier stopped them and demanded identification.

"Who are you?" Hura bristled.

"No one goes to the Fundador's quarters without permission." Although Hura towered over him, the soldier stood his ground.

"Without whose permission, you donkey!" Tarek elbowed his way in front of Hura. "Who the hell you think you're talkin' to?"

The soldier backed up when Hura raised her hand to show him her ring. He gasped, tried to explain that he had orders to keep everyone but Rachid's officers away.

"Some welcome." Tarek grumbled to Habib out of the side of his mouth.

At the archway before the courtyard to the house, wooden barriers had been erected and sandbags were piled up waist high, closing off access. What is this? Hura confronted the nearest officer.

"Siti al-Mandari? Is that really you?"

"Yes, of course it's me! Hura snapped to Hisham, the Captain of the Guard. "What's going on here? Let us in. Why is everything closed off, barricaded?"

"Here, we'll make way." He shouted orders to soldiers to lift the heavy bags. "We heard . . . Madam, you'd better go inside, I'll tell your brother you're here."

"My brother? Ibrahim is here?"

"No, Mohammed is living here."

Hura's bowels twisted. A prickly sense of danger flushed the back of her neck.

Tarek and Habib had listened to the exchange in silence. As the three walked across the courtyard, Tarek's eyes roved from side to side as if he were back in the souk in Fes, being stalked.

The ironbound door to the house was locked. Hura banged the knocker several times. Tarek kicked it. Slowly it opened, a curious Isabel peering from its frame.

"Isabel, open up, it's me."

Isabel screeched in surprise, "Lalla Hura! It's you."

"Open up. I've got two hungry people with me and I need you to make up the guest room."

"You're back! But I heard you were dead. We all did." No sooner were the words out of her mouth when a shriek came from the harem balcony.

"Mistress Hura! I don't believe it." Afaf rushed down the stairs into the patio to hug her and kiss her cheeks then wipe away tears from her own eyes. Behind her, slowly taking the steep steps, one by one, Suha followed.

The child hid behind the fountain and watched the two women with solemn gray eyes. Afaf spied her, ran over, took her small hand and led her to Hura.

"This is your mother, she's alive. She's really here."

The child's large eyes widened. She backed shyly into the protection of Afaf's long skirt.

"Don't you remember her?" Afaf bent and whispered into her ear.

Suha hung tightly onto Afaf's skirt.

Hura knelt down and kissed her daughter, tears welling up in her own eyes.

"Yes, I'm back and I won't go away again," she picked Suha up and held her close. "Ufftt! Another day away and I wouldn't be able to lift you."

Suha howled.

More tears streamed down Afaf's cheeks, Isabel sobbed and mumbled, "Allah be Praised." Even Tarek turned away from the scene to blow his nose. Habib stood to the side, his face a mask hiding his uneasiness, embarrassed by witnessing such an outpouring of emotion.

The reunion abruptly ended. Mohammed limped across the patio, the uneven gait of his heavy boots clicking on the stones. He wore a yellow Rif jellaba with his monogram embroidered in bright red on its sleeves. He had gained weight since she had last seen him. A stout belly pushed out his garment. Afaf and Isabel froze.

"What's all the noise?" Then he recognized Hura, paused and slowly came toward her. "My dear sister, how good to see you. I had no idea . . . I heard you were killed in Rabat."

"I thought you knew everything!" Hura retorted, putting Suha down. "Meet the men who saved my life. You remember Captain Tarek, and this is Habib, an architect from Fes."

The men bowed their heads in silent acknowledgement.

"Well!" Mohammed smiled and began to turn away. "I'm sure you're tired and need some rest. I'll speak with you later."

"Wait." Hura put up a hand. "I heard you're staying here."

"I'm in Mandari's quarters – just until my new apartment here in the city is finished and," Mohammed added, "he's in the new apartment across the courtyard."

Tarek cleared his throat to get her attention. "Madam, I be off to my house now I know you're safe."

Hura grabbed her brother's arm. "What did you just say?"

"Your husband's taken a new apartment outside, off the courtyard. We had to move him."

"He's alive? My husband's alive?" She staggered. Habib reached to support her.

205

Mohammed fixed his dark eyes on Habib and freed his arm from Hura's grasp.

"I was told he was dead . . ." her mouth opened, closed, opened for a quivering voice: "I don't believe you. He can't be . . . I mean, I was told he died, months ago." She searched Mohammed's face for deceit.

"Well then, we're even," Mohammed tried to jest. "We had news you were killed and now you're both alive." He laughed and limped back across the patio to his room, leaving them all stunned.

Hura struggled to compose herself. "I must go to him. Afaf, take Suha upstairs. Then you can go with your father. Isabel, prepare our guest room for . . ." she paused, "our new architect. And some supper. I'll be back soon." She clasped her head in shaking hands as if to hold herself together. "Habib," her voice wavered, "you must stay. Don't leave, please."

The others stood quietly for a moment after she left, looked one to another. Slowly Afaf and Suha walked toward the stairs and Tarek disappeared through the door, leaving Habib alone by the fountain.

"Did you find the Professor?"

"Yes," Isabel said. "Miguel went to his villa yesterday and invited him. He'll come."

"And my brothers?"

"Only Mohammed is here, mistress; Ibrahim is in Fes on a campaign with the Sultan, but we've sent word of your safe arrival."

"Good. And I want that Catholic, Fernando de Contreras, the one who visits my husband every day, to come too. And we'll invite our imam and ranking officers and the ministers and justices and the tribal chiefs, and of course, our new architect, Habib."

"And Boabdil and his court?"

"It's a celebration!" She hesitated to share with Isabel the real reasons for the reception. It was the only way to find out quickly what was going on in her city; and more than that, she must be the one to sit at the head of the table, not Mohammed.

Isabel skewed her wrinkled face.

Hura sighed. "Well, all right, maybe not the whole court, and not all the officers or judges or tribal chiefs. I'll make a list of twenty. It will be just a small reception."

Isabel's thin lips parted and her head bobbed giving silent thanks.

Preparation took two days. The compound hadn't been so busy since her departure. Afaf scurried cheerfully around the house cleaning, dusting, polishing silver, arranging flowers and sweeping, always with Suha at her side. She had reason to be happy. She was in love. She had confided to Hura that Hisham was going to ask her father for her hand in marriage.

Hura's return had its effect on Isabel, too. Sour demeanor gave way to an occasional smile, and Hura was sure she heard her humming in the kitchen, singing as her gnarled fingers slowly chopped, peeled and stuffed. She told Hura it felt good to cook again. This dinner was a big change from the daily menu of couscous and chicken broth she made for Sidi Mandari and the simple food she prepared for herself, Afaf and Suha.

For the reception, Isabel had the help of two new kitchen maids who now buzzed around her, and Miguel had prepared for the grilling of three whole sheep and twelve chickens. Arrangements had been made at the bakery near the Souk el Hots to start making bread and pastries early in the morning.

Although Mohammed had been staying at the compound for many months, Isabel had never cooked for him. The day after Hura left for Fes, he moved into Mandari's former chambers with his aide and often had his food brought in; but he usually ate in the cafes of the city. Mohammed had announced he would stay until his villa on the hill overlooking the river was finished. Now that Hura was back, he would have to leave.

One thing seemed to bother Isabel. It grew from a small seed of anger and finally made Isabel confront Hura. Every day for months she had seen a priest, shrouded in his hassock like a woman, come to visit Sidi Mandari. Fearful, she wished her master hadn't allowed him in the compound. "How could he forget the wars in Spain and his own sons?" She asked Hura. "Someone had to tell you what the Father is trying to do to your husband. It isn't right. He should leave our poor, blind master alone. He shouldn't try to convert him."

On the day of the feast, Hura spent the morning at the hammam in reflection. She tried to keep him out of her mind. Impossible. He was there, close by in the compound. What should she do about her longing for him and his nearness? Her heart seemed to be tearing apart. Love and honor. She had no room for both. She must find Habib an apartment in the city. He couldn't stay in the guest room at the compound any longer. People would talk. She vacillated between guilt and longing for him; the night before she almost got up and went to his room. She held back because Habib seemed so quiet, so distant, as if nothing had happened between them. She wondered what he was thinking . . . if he still wanted her. They hadn't been alone since their arrival.

For her husband she now felt nothing except pity and respect. Respect for what he was. That first day when she returned and went to him, confused and guilt-ridden, and saw him shrunken, white-haired and lying in his bed, she couldn't touch him, even in greeting. She wanted to ask his forgiveness. She wanted to confess everything. But he didn't seem to care that she had returned. In fact, she wasn't sure he knew she was there! He rambled on about his castle in Spain, the orchards and farms he'd left behind. When she asked the aide who stood guard by his door what he did now, and if he went to Council meetings, she was told that he stayed in his bed and the only people who came to see him were Ibrahim, Miguel and a Catholic priest named Father Fernando de Contreras. But Ibrahim seldom came to the city and Miguel was white-haired and stooped like his master, and spent most of his time in the tiny room off the kitchen that he shared with Isabel, playing cards and talking to himself.

The day of the reception arrived. Now she would watch, and wait and listen. She would find out what was going on in her city.

Nicholas Kleinatz arrived early, dressed as she had first met him, in black and white. He bowed and pressed a small leather-bound book in her hands. "Some poems I composed in your absence," he said.

"Sit on my right." She grasped his book in delight and whispered, "I've missed you so and I need your counsel. You must tell me what you think of our new architect."

"It's been a long time since I enjoyed your company." The Professor smiled and turned to enter the familiar house.

Hura had reserved the chair next to the Professor for Habib; she wanted them to like one another. Habib would be sitting across from Mohammed and next to Boabdil.

"So good of you to come and celebrate my return," Hura said to the couple behind the Professor and again to the couple behind them.

The line of guests pressed forward toward her, and finally Hura spied the Catholic priest, Father Fernando de Contreras. He was alone. In an instant she recognized him as the apparition she had seen long ago in the slave pens . . . that day when she was running back from the port to the safety of her home through the prison. How foolish and naive she had been. The priest was dressed in the same gray, belted cassock, his hair, white now, formed a halo around his bald pink dome. A heavy gold cross on a thick gold chain hung from his neck down to his abdomen. He clutched something in his right hand, shoved it up into his billowing left sleeve. His face was clean-shaven, pink with red spider veins filigreed across his cheeks. His eyes, intense and round, held hers.

Reaching her side, his sonorous voice proclaimed: "It is the honor of my Church to be invited to your home. I humbly accept your invitation and am gratified of your safe return."

Gratified? Hura wondered at his choice of words.

"You must sit on my left," she announced loudly, "I have an honored place set for you. I know how much your company means to my husband."

The guests continued arriving; Hura graciously greeted them. Several were honestly shocked by the news of her return; a few seemed pleased, and others afraid. It was clear she had taken charge. Mohammed stood to her side, accepting the introductions she passed on to him. Everyone appeared nervous. She dared not show it.

The guests included a rich landowner from Martil, who would know about the burgeoning growth there, a ship builder who could tell her about the revenues of the port, and ministers from several important departments of government. She silently questioned their loyalty. She debated whether there was a conspiracy against her and who might have tried to keep her from returning. In her mind, she also went over the details of the menu, the toast, and the seating arrangements. She had agonized over her costume. Fatima had been right. Fashion can speak louder than words. If she was to rule Tetouan as the heir of al-Mandari, she must not look like a mountain girl. She had to look and talk and represent the new Tetouan and hoped her dress, manner and words would be regal enough for a head of state. She had decided not to wear the formal costume of Chaouen. Instead, promoting her new status, she wore a black, floor length silk skirt topped with a ruffled, white high-collared blouse which buttoned up to her chin. She even deliberated about wearing Habib's pin, and in the privacy of her room pressed it against her collar in front of her looking glass. But it didn't look right. It wasn't right. Instead, she decided to wear four ropes of pearls around her neck. Large pearl drop-earrings and a gold filigree ring were her only other jewelry.

The skirts and petticoats she wore now were uncomfortable. They itched. For over a year, on her journey, she had grown accustomed to her snug boots and leather trousers. The new skirt and high stacked-heel shoes changed not only her silhouette but also her posture and walk. Being a lady of fashion was perilous. In the street the day before, she had watched as her skirted shadow moved against the walls of the houses. Up on her high heels she moved like a fawn on its first trip to the stream, all knees and elbows. She practiced walking with swaying hips, like Henati used to advise, and felt more absurd.

Last to arrive, by design she was certain, were King Boabdil and his wife. Their costumes rendered Hura speechless. The King's wife wore a plumed hat of multicolored ostrich feathers that fluttered and swayed a foot out in every direction. Her arms were encircled to her elbows with jeweled bracelets; her full, gathered skirt tinkled with small bells which hung from the hem and rustled so loudly when she moved that conversation with her was impossible. And King Boabdil! His blond hair was teased high on his head. Long gold chains with braided tassels fell from his starched neck-ruff to his waist. His orange brocade pantaloons puffed out his lower body and below them, white stockings led to tiny black silk slippers. Hura chuckled inwardly. The Sultan in Fes would have been envious.

Following the King and his wife inside, Hura saw Habib standing alone beside the fountain. She had wondered where he was and now recalled how taciturn he appeared during their arrival. She hurried to him. "There you are, I wanted to introduce you outside, but I'll do it now in the salon." She gestured toward the door. In a hushed tone she confided: "Tonight I need your help. Please be my eyes and ears. Help me find out what is going on in the city. Tell me what you hear, and listen very closely to whatever King Boabdil says."

Habib nodded and followed her into the salon.

As soon as Hura took her seat at the head of the table, Mohammed rose and tapped his cane on the floor for attention. He lifted his water goblet for a toast. All eyes turned toward him.

"This is truly an important day. I welcome back my sister, wife of the Honorable Sidi al-Mandari. Let us celebrate this happy reunion with our praise to Allah and with our appreciation of this good food."

"Amen." Hura heard Father de Contreras say softly on her left. She rose and made a sweeping gesture with her arm that took in the entire table. "Let me add how my esteemed husband wishes he could be with us, but he is not able to. Both of us look forward to hearing of your own happiness and prosperity." She sat down and turned to the Father: "I hope you will forgive me for not offering you wine with your food, but I do not allow alcohol in this house."

Kleinatz sniffed, "We have not yet convinced our Muslim friends of the medicinal value of the fermented grape."

Father de Contreras took his cue from the lightness of the Professor and added, "Even though they invented the process." Then he queried Hura: "I understand you have been traveling."

"I saw the jewel of our land, Fes, and the ocean on the other side of the mountains." While answering, Hura looked down the long banquet table at the other guests. They were busy in conversation she could not hear. Mohammed was making fast progress through stacks of dried anchovies, leaving flakes of fish skin down the front of his jellaba. She remembered how she had once eaten with her fingers. He caught her disapproving eye.

Tureens of fragrant lentil soup were brought to the table and flat, soft cakes of bread were passed around.

"*Bismillah.*" Boabdil broke his bread.

"*Bismillah,*" many other lips repeated.

Before anyone thought to stop him, Father Contreras intoned his prayer of thanks: "Bless this bread to our use and us to Thy service. In the name of Jesus, Amen."

Guests at the far end of the table looked askance, wondering why this infidel was invited and allowed to speak so freely.

Father Contreras continued unabashed. "Your return seems to be a miracle, Señora. Your husband has told me so." He reached up into his sleeve and retrieved a rectangular object then placed it on the table between them. "This is a gift for your husband and you."

He flipped the cover over and Hura could see Latin writing. My God, she thought. He's brought a copy of the Bible, how rude to take advantage of her hospitality like this.

Instantly Kleinatz recognized what the Father was doing and stretched his ungainly arm across Hura's plate to snatch it up. In an uncharacteristic rush of words he addressed the Father: "I know we could use such an important tome in the City's library. I will make sure it is put there."

Hura's face flushed with gratitude. He had spared her and the other guests a confrontation.

The Father continued as if nothing had happened. "Yes, your safe return is much like a miracle. Perhaps as interesting a story as the saga of Joseph."

"Joseph?" It's a wonderful story." Hura lifted her soupspoon. "But I would rather hear about your life here in Tetouan . . . about your mission. Perhaps we have common goals."

"Ah, patience Señora. Let us share the story of Joseph first. Then you will see the many ways that we are all alike, we Christians and Muslims. And Jews, too," the Father added as an afterthought.

Boabdil narrowed his eyes and studied Habib's face, then dipped his bread in his soup.

The Father accepted a large bowl of carrots, honey and nuts. "Take our literature. Professor, you will concur that we all share many historical sagas, like the story of Joseph. The story has everything of interest for today's society: jealousy, sibling rivalry, sexual temptation, vindication, magic and travel." He paused to taste a glistening carrot. "There's the main theme, of Godliness, but then there are smaller incidents like the fateful encounter of Joseph with Potiphar's wife. In our Bible, it's written in Genesis 39 and in your Koran," he nodded to Boabdil, "it's Sura Twelve."

"Tell your story, please." The high pitched whine of Boabdil's wife floated down the table toward Father Contreras. "Tell me the story, please tell it. I want to hear it." Boabdil shot his leg out under the table; it connected with her ankle. His wife winced.

"Do tell the story, Father." Hura relented, knowing he would anyway. She hoped it related to the situation in Tetouan.

"Shall I tell it? I know it well." Kleinatz interrupted.

Father de Contreras leaned back and pressed his napkin to his lips in deferment.

Habib eyed the two learned men, wondering if he would need to come to the defense of Judaism.

Boabdil watched his wife smile at Habib; rubbed his golden goatee.

Hura studied Habib's hands, remembering their warmth.

In the momentary silence, the Professor adjusted the collar of his shirt as a teacher might do before a lecture. He began: "It is a story of jealous brothers. Jews who lived in Canaan. In the Bible they conspire to kill their brother, the favorite of their father. At first, they put him in a deep well, then they arranged to sell him as a slave for twenty pieces of silver to the Ishmeelite traders who were passing by on their way to Egypt. The brothers killed a goat and put its blood on his coat as evidence of his death and brought it back to their father, who grieved mightily."

"A wolf." Boabdil interrupted. "In the Koran his father was afraid a wolf devoured him."

"Yes, get your facts straight." Mohammed chimed in.

"You'd better let me continue." Father de Contreras smiled at the Professor. "There's much more to the story and I am skilled in apologetics."

"Please do." Hura pointed to an empty basket of bread and motioned to a servant to bring another.

Father Contreras sat up straight and fingered his crucifix. "It was because the Lord was with Joseph that he prospered as the servant of Potiphar when he finally got to Egypt. He became the overseer of his house. But so handsome was he," his glance shot to Habib, "that Potiphar's wife Zoraycha tried to seduce him."

Hura noticed the glance.

"Well, let's see." The Father paused to nibble a chunk of goat cheese. "When he refused, she tricked him into fleeing the room without his clothes. Then she lied to her husband and said he assaulted her. So he was imprisoned. But the Lord was with him and soon he was put in charge of the other prisoners. One prisoner, a baker, dreamed he had three white baskets on his head and birds kept eating out of the top one. Joseph said that he would be hung in three days."

"Crucified," Boabdil broke in. "Not hung. The Koran says crucified." All heads turned in his direction as he raised his chin righteously.

This time Father de Contreras frowned. "So after two years, the Pharaoh himself had a disturbing dream. He dreamed about seven fat and seven thin kine that came out of a river, the lean ones eating the fat ones. In another dream, seven ears of corn grew fat on one stalk, then seven thin ones appeared after them and devoured the fat ones. When none of the Pharaohs magicians or wise men could interpret the dreams, Joseph was brought to the Pharaoh."

"Joseph . . ." the Father emphasized the name with a side glance at Habib, "told the meaning of the dream to the Pharaoh and was handsomely rewarded. Then the story goes on to relate that when Joseph's brothers had to come from Egypt for food – "

Hura's attention wandered. The story, as told in the Koran, was familiar and she concentrated on attempting to read Habib's reaction. Her gaze snapped to Boabdil when she heard him begin a spirited discourse on the guilt of Potiphar's wife. "The women of the city had the audacity to claim her innocent. They actually came to her defense and called her blameless. What do you think of that, architect? You haven't said a thing all evening."

Habib's eyes darted to Hura and he moved his left leg to the side of his chair. His hand caressed the hilt of the knife in the top of his boot. He wondered if this was where Boabdil would expose him. Should he kill the King before he said too much?

"But the story clearly says he was seduced," Kleinatz interjected. "I'm all for the rights of women but as I understand it, they raced one another to the door of the wife's chamber. He was trying to flee – and the wife tore his shirt from behind. When they met her husband at the door she accused Joseph of assault, but a witness testified the shirt was torn from the back."

"Yes, that's what it says in the Koran," Mohammed agreed, frowning that he had sided with a Christian.

Habib's leg shifted, and his hand now lay flat on the table. "I believe that Joseph saw the image of his father. That's why he resisted her advances."

"I think," the Professor said dryly, "that what you're all missing is that both men and women were attracted to Joseph. He was exceptionally handsome. A beautiful man. And a handsome man turns many heads. Habib, you seem to be familiar with this story."

Habib nodded, shifted uncomfortably in his chair.

Hura signaled a servant for another plate of steamed vegetables for the Professor. When it arrived, she positioned it next to his plate. She wanted him to befriend Habib, not confront him. She stole another look at Habib. Strangely, he now appeared calm as he leaned forward to participate in the discussion. She slumped in her chair, feeling exhausted. Was her long journey just now catching up with her? She couldn't afford to be tired now.

"Some Jewish and Muslim sources I've read say Potiphar himself was attracted to Joseph," the Professor added.

"Yes," Father de Contreras confirmed, "Potiphar's attraction to Joseph was mentioned in Jerome's Latin translation of Genesis."

Hura broke into the conversation. "Was Joseph blameless? That's an interesting question. Even though the wife was told that it was her guile that was the sin. The sharing of guilt and innocence is common throughout all the scriptures and the Koran, even in such writings as sura 12:28 of A Thousand and One Nights."

"Young woman, now you impress me," remarked the Father. But let's get back to the real story, shall we? This part is hardly conversation for a celebration like ours today."

"Ah, yes, the story of Joseph's vindication and reunion with his family," said Kleinatz. "Did you know, Father, that the same story exists in the ancient Egyptian tale: "A Story of Two Brothers?" I have a copy in my library."

"And, in the tale of Bellerphon in Book IV of Homer's Iliad," Hura added, to the priest's amazement.

The Professor did not want to be upstaged. "If we're looking for antecedents, in ancient Egypt, Osiris, who is identified with the prophet Idris, brought the first shari'a, the first law, enshrining the same religion of faith in one God and ethics. That is the heart of Islam and Christianity – "

"And Judaism," Habib finished, looking directly at Hura. He noted that Hura's plate had not been touched.

"So we really are alike in many ways, eh, Father? Is that what you mean?" Mohammed's voice had an undertone of sarcasm to it.

Boabdil added, "I'll be going through Egypt on my way to the haj. I'll ponder this togetherness."

Boabdil's wife began to laugh, sure her husband was joking. Her laughter ceased when her husband's foot kicked out again and found her shin.

Hura glanced down the table. Her other guests appeared busy in private conversation. She looked over to Boabdil's wife and caught her fluttering her eyelashes at Habib, then back to Father Contreras who now shoveled his food in quickly while his beady eyes darted around the table from one diner to another. It had occurred to her that the Father was drawing conclusions and making analogies that he shouldn't about her return, her brothers, and Habib's similarity to Joseph. Or was she imagining it? And the Professor was fueling the fire. Why did the Father pick this topic? How could he know about the sibling rivalry in her family, her suspicions about Mohammed's deceit, or her seduction of Habib. She must bring this topic to a satisfactory close, and soon.

Did Hura see what she thought she saw? Boabdil's wife was now winking at Habib. She was staring directly at him. Her eyelids fluttered again and she twirled her shiny hair between her fingers.

Hura quickly glanced at Habib, wondering if he caught the gesture. He seemed engrossed in the conversation.

I must end this, Hura decided. She ordered clean plates to be placed in front of the guests. Perhaps this would be a distraction.

"Father, tell me. Have you ever journeyed to Fes?" She pushed a bowl of olives closer to his plate.

"Señora, my religion and calling have never prevented me from traveling throughout this land, though I've never penetrated Chaouen. I've seen the wonders of Egypt as well as the cliffs of Portugal. My calling takes me to kings and beggars. I, too, have a special place in my heart for Fes. In fact, when I finish my work here, I have souls to save in that city."

"And what is your unfinished work here, Father?" Hura pressed him.

"I'll inform the Sultan of your mission in Fes," Mohammed announced loudly.

"I don't know why we're raising our voices," Kleinatz said, oblivious to the tension. "Is there some vicious circle of complicity or inalterable incompatibility between our religions? We believe in the same God."

Once again, Hura drew the conversation toward her interests. "I will be returning to Fes shortly, Father. I've just learned that my brother, Ibrahim, is marrying the sister of the Sultan and I'll be going for the celebration. Have you met Ibrahim?"

The Father nodded.

"It's in Chaouen, not Fes," Mohammed corrected her.

"Oh," she composed herself. "That's even better."

A large silver bowl of warm lemon-water was passed around for everyone to clean their fingers. Servants removed the plates of chicken bones and four huge trays of mutton and couscous were placed on the table. Conversation stopped as the diners speared chunks of meat with their knives and spooned heaping piles of couscous onto their plates, then poured yogurt on top.

Habib looked askance at the white puddle of yogurt on Boabdil's plate. He had never mixed his meat and milk and wondered if he could actually get it down. He placed a small dollop on his lamb.

From the moment he entered, Boabdil had been eyeing Hura. Did he imagine that she was paying too much attention to that new architect? He watched carefully as she hosted her guests, smiling at one, then the other, listening to the irrelevancies of social chatter but seeming aloof from the philosophical discourse. Good, he didn't like too smart a woman. She let the men talk. He looked over at his wife, who now sat quietly with a frozen smile on her face, her eyes glazed. He was prepared to kick her again under the table if she began one of her tirades about living in Tetouan. He must arrange to get Hura alone.

Conversation about the weather, the crops, and the growth of Tetouan was tossed around and picked at. Hura signaled for the plates to be removed. The feast was over and it was time to adjourn to the salon for fruit, pastries and sugared almonds. She rose from her chair initiating the move to the next room, acknowledging to herself that she could not continue this party as long as she had planned. She was just too tired. She planned to catch Habib in the hallway and ask him to sit with her, but Father de Contreras rushed to him, excusing his abruptness.

"Where are you staying, young man? I was impressed with your words tonight. I'd enjoy talking with you."

Caught off guard, Habib stammered: "I . . . I'm a guest here at the Mandari compound."

"He came with me from Mazagan," Hura caught up to them. "He is our guest."

As soon as the Father had expressed his thanks and left, Hura pulled Habib toward the salon. "Sit over there with the Professor," she nodded to the back of the room. "I want you to get to know him."

A small crowd had gathered around the desert table, picking at the huge pyramid of fruits and nuts. The pointed mound glistened from the sticky dates that held it together. As the three started around the table toward the back of the room, Hura was immediately besieged by other guests curious to know more about her travels. She let go of Habib's arm.

"And the Sultan? Did you see the Sultan?" Asked the Minister of Interior, pushing his way closer as if angry he was separated from her at dinner.

"Yes, twice," She responded. "I had a command performance with the Sultan and his entourage. It was most enlightening." Her feet ached from her tight, fashionable shoes. She longed to remove them.

"Do they plan on a full scale war with Marrakech?" asked the wealthy ship builder as he positioned himself in front of her.

"I have no news of war," Hura answered, looking away to see where the Professor and Habib were heading.

"Will we get our share of gold from the south? Have they put restrictions on the caravans?" The head of the potters cooperative pressed forward to her side.

"I don't . . . Gentlemen, please," she said in exasperation, trying not to offend. She now knew instead of learning from them, they expected to learn from her. "Let's enjoy the party. I promise I will tell you all that I learned. I'll be starting the public meetings again and holding Council in the mornings. Come to those and we'll discuss your questions."

TWENTY SIX

Kleinatz and Habib remained in the salon after the guests had left. Hura's shoes lay on their sides in front of her. She wiggled her toes and slumped down on the banquette. Her eyelids felt heavy.

"So you came from Cadiz?" Kleinatz asked.

"Yes, I went first to Tangier and then to Fes where I thought I'd find good work. That's where I met Hura. I was an architect for the Sultan."

"Where did you work in Spain? I was there myself." Kleinatz returned to his subject.

"That must be an interesting story. Hura has told me a great deal about you and how you've helped her."

"Ya. She is an unusual woman. But back to you. From your knowledge of literature, I see you have many interests besides architecture."

Habib ran his finger down the line of hair on his chin. "I've been fortunate to have many mentors. And speaking of mentors, I understand you taught Hura to read Arabic and Spanish. That's quite an accomplishment."

Kleinatz laughed at this young man's adroitness. He tried another tack. "What did you build in Spain? Will you do the same kind of thing here?"

"I have no assignment yet," he said vaguely as he rose and moved to a chair facing them both.

Thinking he was leaving, Hura revived herself and joined in: "Well, how are you two getting along?"

"I'm being grilled." Habib's expression was wry.

Kleinatz scanned Hura's face. "At dinner you looked so pale, now you seem to be glowing from inside. It must be the good food of Tetouan."

Hura beamed. "Ah, no, it's the company."

"She's such a diplomat," said Habib.

"I don't have to be a diplomat with you, do I Professor? You know me so well. I've got a thousand questions to ask you. But first, tell me if I'm wrong, but wasn't Mohammed being . . . umm, unpleasant . . . at the table? What's he been doing, do you know? I heard he's been living here in the house for months."

"Ya. You observe well, but 'unpleasant' isn't the word I would choose for his behavior." Kleinatz lowered his voice and she drew closer. "While you were gone he tried to take over."

"But Ibrahim and my husband . . . wouldn't allow that!"

"Shush, don't speak so loudly. These walls have many ears."

Hura frowned.

"Ibrahim has been in Fes. His life is there now, what with his marriage coming up and his position as Minister of the Interior for the new Sultan. He hasn't been here in six months. And Sidi Mandari hardly knows what day it is. Only Father de Contreras knows what he's thinking."

Habib listened intently to the conversation, looking from one face to the other. Now he fully understood why Hura wanted him to observe the diners. Affairs here were more political than in Granada.

"So Mohammed has been running things. With whom? I saw the markets were almost empty and the city looks so dirty."

"He's got his own men, some of the Beni Hassan, I think, but also some of your people work for him. I know he's building up Martil. His workers are building storehouses, docks, water works, and roads to make the town as big as Tetouan. Perhaps bigger. From there, he can intercept all trade to Tetouan, except what comes in from the mountains. He's already trading with the Portuguese in Tangier. That's what I hear."

"With the Portuguese? And he's building a new city around the docks at Martil?" She shook her head. "He's taking our money and people and building his own city." She fumed. "He's robbing us and the Beni Hassan are getting rich. And if I hadn't come back, he would have gotten away with it. I bet the souks are busy down there. Well, I'll get it all back!" She set her jaw.

"Slow down. Your brother has men. Spies. Don't underestimate him. They keep order. I wouldn't confront him yet, until you know more." Kleinatz waved his finger at her. "Control your temper. Don't be impetuous."

"Perhaps I can help." Habib interjected.

"How? You don't know anyone yet." Hura frowned.

"Exactly. But I have been introduced as the new senior architect and your brother might want my services."

"Much too dangerous." Hura shook her head. "Professor, tell me about the priest, Father de Contreras. I heard he comes here often to visit my husband. Why is he here? What is he doing?"

"Your husband calls him a friend. He's upset if the Father doesn't come every day. Poor man, no one else seems to care. I understand they talk about Spain – the past. Of course, Spain with an Emperor today is very different from the Spain Mandari knew as a young man. It seems that your husband gave him the right to give the Sacraments to the prisoners. They're called captives now, not slaves, and the priest is buying freedom for many. That has irritated some people here, especially the Overseer. I heard a rumor that the Overseer was told to kill him."

"Fuad's always been trouble," Hura snapped. "One of the first things I will do when we convene the Council is look into prison conditions. We need the captives for ransom. We can't stop piracy, but we can make life in prison more bearable."

"It seems your experience in prison has given you a new perspective."

"I'm serious about this," Hura said. "In fact, I think we need to have a work program for the captives, so they can earn some money. In public works, like a daily wage. Even the women – we can find some work for them to do. They can earn money for their release. Don't you think that's a good idea?" Hura looked at both men for approval.

Kleinatz hesitated. "Some, like your brother, will oppose it."

"I'll make it very plain for him," she said matter of factly. "What else has been going on?"

"There are bad feelings between the Moriscos and the Berbers again. And Mohammed is stirring it all up. There's the water issue. He wants to divert water to Martil from the central fountain up here instead of digging wells down there. There have been fights and even some deaths over this."

"So, we haven't got enough Spanish and Portuguese to fight, we have to fight each other?" Hura shoulders twitched in exasperation. "And, there's a new Sultan to worry about. Now all we need are the Turks!"

"It's very serious, Hura." Kleinatz continued, "speaking of the Portuguese, there's been a lot of activity in Sebta, too. They say the Spanish are going to attack and take that colony from the Portuguese. But we may be attacked here first."

"Who is 'They Say'? We saw many ships when we passed their harbor, but not war ships. Tarek kept us as far out to sea as he dared. I wasn't going to be a Portuguese prisoner again."

Kleinatz cast an admiring glance at his former pupil. "I say. There's a new King of Spain, Charles V. He's also the Holy Roman Emperor, the ruler of Germany, the Netherlands and part of Italy."

"I don't really care about Germany or Italy, and I only care about the Netherlands because of you, Professor. It's the Portuguese who have my father. They threaten us here in Tetouan. I worry about them."

"Care or not, you're a pawn in the game of kings."

"I'm a queen!"

"The other emperor," Kleinatz exhaled loudly, "is Suleiman. He is called The Magnificent."

"What about Selim? Wasn't his name Selim the Grim? What happened to him?"

"He died."

"So get to the point."

Kleinatz sniffed. "I thought you should know about the biggest pirates of all, maybe the biggest threat we have here."

"Who are these pirates?"

"The European kings quake before these terrors of the Mediterranean – the Barbarossa brothers."

Hura bit her lip. "Worse than the Portuguese?"

Habib proposed a second time: "Why not let me talk to Mohammed? I could find out more."

"That's the wrong word to use for an encounter with him." Kleinatz half smiled.

"No. I forbid it!" She knew at once she had offended him, and she knew he was trying to be helpful. But she knew she was right. "You need to learn more about our politics, the family and the city before you can help."

Habib's fist clenched.

"How does Boabdil fit into all of this?" Hura spoke his name slowly, loathing every syllable.

"I hear they're together." Kleinatz responded.

"Together?"

"Ya. Boabdil and your brother Mohammed."

"It figures." Hura sighed. "He wants to rule Tetouan also. They make a good pair. Well, it looks like I've a lot of planning to do. Things have certainly changed. Please forgive my temper, Professor. Everything has hit me so quickly. I'll need your help. I want to start holding Council meetings again. I spoke with two of the Ministers just now. We'll hold the meetings in my husband's apartments, across the courtyard. He won't participate, of course, but he'll be close by, and that won't be lost on the people who come. They still owe him loyalty. Please join me, Professor."

"My dear lady, I have a life of my own now, and my future to watch out for. I have my library and my gardens." He saw the look of desperation in her eyes and quickly conceded: "But I suppose for a while."

"What about your friend here?" Kleinatz nodded to Habib.

Hura turned to Habib. "I'll find you a room, maybe one of those apartments near the hammam; they're new. There are so many projects in the city you can work on, and . . . I want to work closely with you." Her face lit up.

Habib coughed softly in his palm, then rose. "Yes, there is much to be done. But not tonight. "I'll leave you two to your business."

The Professor waited until he was sure Habib had left the room then, face flushed, unable to restrain himself any longer, he spoke out: "Why have you brought that man here? That man has many secrets. I have been observing you both all night. The two of you are lovers."

Hura squirmed in her chair.

220

"But that is your business. As long as you are discreet . . . no, I take that back." His voice rose and cracked. "It is outrageous that you, Hura, wife of the great leader Mandari, would flaunt your affair and bring him to a state dinner. A command performance. Not even the most lascivious ruler in Europe would dare do that!" He shook his head.

"He's my architect."

"Everyone saw who he was in your eyes. Do you deny he is your lover? Don't you think everyone made the comparison between you and Potiphar's wife? Now this gossip will ruin you. You will lose control of your people and the Rif tribes that support Tetouan." Kleinatz put his hands together to keep them from trembling. "I'm sorry," he mumbled, "I had to say this."

Embarrassed, angry, and speechless, Hura stared at her mentor.

The house was quiet now. The guests were gone, the kitchen swept and the compound locked. Hura stripped off her clothes. These elegant layers of clothing were the costume of a queen holding court, not of a woman greeting a frustrated lover.

She sprawled on the bed, gazed out the window at an overcast sky. Silhouetted against the dark blue-gray she saw vivid images of Habib badgered by guests, unhappy in his unwanted role.

TWENTY SEVEN

The morning after Hura's banquet a courier, liveried in Boabdil's royal colors, arrived at Habib's door and presented him with a letter.

Habib recognized the familiar crest, curtly accepted it and closed the door. Stone faced, he unsealed and read:

> *At midday you are to appear at the audience chamber*
> *of Abu-Abdullah Allah, King of Granada in Exile.*

He crushed the parchment and threw the wad across the room. Arrogant bastard. Acting like he rules here. On second thought, Habib realized that Boabdil believed he did. The purpose of the meeting couldn't be to appoint him Court Architect or some such nonsense. So what did Boabdil want? Questions without answers drove him out of his apartment. Today, first of all, he wanted to begin his new role as Hura's architect. He had gotten over his anger from the dinner party. After all, he reasoned, she was under intense pressure and had her reputation to think of. He understood why she ignored him. How different from the hungry eyes of Boabdil's wife at that dinner. He shuddered at the vision.

By midday he had walked up and down steep hills of the city, explored streets in the old Berber areas clustered around the citadel and kasbah, and surveyed the new Morisco town which straggled down the farm fields from the old city gate. He avoided the mellah.

After the imperial cities of Granada, Fes and Rabat, this place was a shabby imitation of a proper fiefdom. Unpaved, irregular streets smelled of slops and had no fountains or plazas. The new town had gaps between houses like missing teeth. The houses themselves were small, and while they borrowed decoration from Andalusia, they lacked style or substance. The exception was the domicile of ex-King Boabdil. He had completely redesigned the villa Mandari had given him. It had substance, if not style.

Habib stood outside the gate to Boabdil's villa, his hands on his hips, his designer's gaze roving side to side over the two-story residence. Though set back on a slight rise with a tree-lined entrance, high walls, gates and stables, he was not impressed. No wonder everyone tells me they're glad I'm here. Hura's city needs a real architect. Hope nobody notices my apprenticeship.

Clapping the dangling brass hand of Fatima on the black iron gate brought a guard who led him across the courtyard to the horseshoe arched entranceway of the main house. He entered an expansive room that had three chairs. Two sat opposite each other against the walls like sentries. Boabdil sat waiting in the third, slumped in a high backed, Spanish style chair, no doubt carried away from the al-Hamra.

"Habib! Welcome to my humble lodgings." His hand made a grand sweep that took in the large carpets that covered the floor. "You may pull a chair closer. So we can talk. I've told my servants to leave us alone so we can speak in private."

Habib knew this European style chamber was designed for courtiers to stand while conversing and awaiting the King's pleasure.

"Thank you. I'll stand." He walked toward Boabdil and stood two paces from his chair.

"What do you think of my tile work?" The King pulled at his yellow beard.

Habib had barely noticed the ribbon of ceramic tile around the lower part of the walls and the entry door. Ordinary. "Yes, typical Andalusian."

He also knew Boabdil hadn't ordered him here to talk about tile work. Any vestige of awe or fear in the presence of this royal personage now vanished. "Not as good as the work I did for you at the al-Hamra."

"Well, well." Boabdil's eyes squinted as his high pitched words thrust home. "Many craftsmen at my palace were Jewish. Of course none were so exalted as to be architects." His hands cupped a sashed belly that rumbled with laughter.

"Is that what you want to tell me? Is that why I'm here?" Habib's face betrayed no emotion.

"Many of my retinue were talented Jews . . . Simon, my financial advisor, for one. Yes, you may be an excellent craftsman. Unfortunately, you know nothing of politics, of power, how to get it, how to use it. I will teach you. And make you my architect, too. I want a capital city, an imperial one with fine buildings. Your country girl knows nothing of such cities and you will never build one for her. But you could for me." He leaned back against the leather insert of the chair and waited.

Mute, Habib shook his head.

Boabdil scratched his beard and seemed puzzled. Finally, he broke the silence. "Maybe your ambition is misdirected? Otherwise you wouldn't be the lackey of a woman who flits from one city to another city, from one man to another."

"I didn't come here to talk about Lady Mandari. And you are not looking for an architect. What is it you want?"

"Later. Later my boy. Perhaps what you do is for the best. Yes, continue as you are. With her you will be more valuable to me."

Deep furrows scored Habib's forehead. "And if I won't do . . . whatever

223

it is?"

"You are expendable. But think what will happen to your patron, a woman who thinks she can be a ruler. What will the people in Tetouan do when they learn that Hura bint Ali Rachid, a direct descendent of the Prophet, is an adulteress. Consorts with a Jew. They'll stone her!" He smiled broadly.

Habib's fingernails cut into his palm. Remembering they were alone, he itched to slap that smirk away. His fingers touched his dagger. Then he paused, beating back the desire to murder. He grated: "At dinner last night you were an expert on the Christian Bible. You must remember that Jesus said:

Let him that is without sin cast the first stone.

Boabdil shifted his thighs in the chair. "Ah, yes, about the adulteress. *I* am not the adulteress."

"An adulteress no, a woman and a sinner, yes. The poets of the Vega and the Sierra sing your pathetic story. What will your six thousand followers do when they hear how you really fled Granada?"

A large bead of sweat formed on Boabdil's forehead, trickled down. "Your interview is over. Go!"

Heedless, Habib moved closer, his eyes a blink away from Boabdil's. "When the Spanish marched on the fortress of al-Hamra you deserted your loyal troops and crept away through a hidden postern. Like a rat running for his hole."

Boabdil jerked his head away. "A ruler retreats to fight another day."

Habib pointed a long finger at him. "But a mother does not heap scorn on her son. When you wept over the loss of your citadel, your mother chided: 'You weep like a woman when you should have stayed and fought like a man'. That's what she said, didn't she!"

Boabdil's glare followed Habib until he disappeared through the archway.

The morning sun brought clarity to Habib's thoughts. Boabdil did speak one truth, he conceded. He was no architect, no designer of monuments. Instead, he was an expert on water and drainage, thanks to Mustafa.

He had hardly slept, awake much of the night, driven to do something but not knowing what. Going to Hura with Boabdil's threat meant giving her another problem she didn't need. Now that they no longer slept together, he couldn't roll over and slip in some casual conversation about Boabdil. But what specific threat did Boabdil have in mind? Why wasn't I smart enough to pretend, to lead him on, to agree, to learn his plans? But suppose I agreed. Then what? Better I should talk to Kleinatz. He seems to be an authority on everything. Why not find Kleinatz and ask his advice?

Yes, he should get to know the Professor better. But then . . . at that dinner the Professor had probed my background in Granada. No, he's an old busybody.

That morning Habib admitted another truth. He had lapsed into the rabbinical habit of his father: worrying a thing to death. Rabbi Eleazer had said this passage of the Talmud means this; other rabbis said it doesn't mean this, it means that. Maybe this, maybe that. Discuss it for generations. For centuries those rabbis did.

Habib jumped out of bed. Today he would begin his new role as an architect. First, he would find Fuad, Overseer of Construction. During Hura's absence, Mohammed had bestowed that title on him. He set out to visit construction sites, but Fuad wasn't to be seen. Near the Souk el Foki, Habib paused to watch several workers stack construction materials. Hura had briefed him on what to expect from the wretches captured by their pirates. Because their ransom for release came so slowly, they worked on city projects. But since her return, she had implemented a new policy. Their labor would earn them daily wages that would bring them more food. He knew she had also found tasks for the women captives, allowing them to help support their children. At Salé, he remembered, piracy was a crude and cruel system; but no worse than the press gangs that brought captives to serve on the galleons in Spanish ports. Here the prisoners were still merchandise, but not slaves to be ill-treated.

Fuad had to be at the port and shouldn't be hard to find. He strode down the hill, still thinking of Hura. He knew she had just given the Franciscan friar three thousand ducats. Strange. Father Contreras then gave Mandari that money to buy freedom for several of the sick prisoners.

Stranger yet, after his blinding by a Christian, Mandari permitted this priest to give sacrament to the Catholics in his prison. There's no understanding these Arabs, Habib thought.

He began to enjoy his long walk outside the city in the countryside; the landscape changed from dwellings to farms. After a time he stopped at a well to drink, later he snatched an orange from a low hanging branch, augured a hole with his dagger and sucked out the sweet juice. He felt refreshed, vigorous and self-satisfied – until he found Fuad at the port.

The half-naked, sunburnt barrel of a man saw him coming, slapped the woven leather grip of his whip against his callused palm and finished growling instructions to a carpenter before acknowledging Habib's greeting. "Heard there was a new architect in town. Been expecting you. Like my addition to the Customs House?" He made it sound like a challenge.

Habib had dreaded this moment. He knew nothing about construction techniques. He made a pretense of inspecting the work. After walking around the three-sided, half-finished work, he returned cloaked in masonry dust. To him the construction looked competent and he said so. The Overseer sniffed, as if to say what did he expect.

"Who ordered the addition?"

"See all that Portuguese cargo stacked up? Mohammed said Martil will become the busiest port this side of the Mediterranean."

Habib turned to look. On his way to find Fuad, he had made up a list of possible public works projects. Anything but buildings. Now he said, "That's right, and Lady Rachid knows it. More and more people are coming here, so she wants to improve the city's facilities . . . meaning streets and water. We'll start with a larger water line to the mosque in the old city. She wants to put a fountain by Mandari's new minaret."

"Not finished here yet." Fuad's tone was belligerent.

Habib stood his ground. "You know as well as I do that the worshippers must wash before prayer. The old pipes are clogged and broken. You know how to build a line to a basin don't you?"

The whip butt imprinted a tattoo on Fuad's palm.

"Then do it."

In two months, Hura had her wish fulfilled, and Habib enjoyed his triumph. By flattery and threats, by working with the Overseer every day, Habib completed the new water system for the mosque in time for its dedication to Fundador al-Mandari on his birthday.

His satisfaction tasted not nearly so sweet as his pleasure with Hura would. He hungered to hold and caress her, to feel her body respond to his. But Hura avoided being alone with him, although she seized any proper occasion to be near him in public. Several times he thought she looked as though she might relent, let him know she wanted him too. Today, together, they walked the length of the two major streets he had straightened and widened. She stood with him when water from pipes alongside the crumbled aqueduct first flowed to serve the old and the new neighborhoods. Although some tongues wagged when they saw the twosome, the Berbers living around the Citadel and the kasbah inside the old city praised Hura for their water; on the other side of the medina gate, the Moriscos living in the new town praised Habib.

The one neighborhood they had not visited together was the mellah. The third time Hura asked him to do something about the water for the Jews, he no longer could avoid her request.

And so, on a Friday afternoon shortly afterward, he was in the mellah and promptly became lost. Many of the lanes ended abruptly against plastered rubble-stone walls. He knew he could speak in Hebrew or Ladino to a passerby and easily get directions to the well. He dared not.

He was uncomfortable in the twisting, turning alleys that became narrow tunnel passageways under the residences. With the sun's rays blocked overhead by buildings or thick vines, the mellah was cool. But the deeper he penetrated the labyrinth, the warmer he became.

Walking in a neighborhood saturated with the aroma of chickens boiling for the Shabbat and the Andalusian-Hebrew slang of children at play, he felt pangs of homesickness. Each time a passerby in a long, black cloak stared at his clean-shaven face, clipped hair and sword, guilt squeezed his heart.

Breathing hard, he blundered through a crooked lane and followed it to its intersection with another. There he saw the cistern – a low wall surrounding a hole chipped through rock. Waiting their turn, three old women gossiped. Habib watched from the corner and listened to them talk. Their conversation was so familiar. "How's your father, he still can't pee? Your son, Schmuel, he hasn't asked her yet? The butcher, again he raised the price of chicken?"

Filling their jars and gossiping took a long time. After the women left, he drew water himself, studied the wooden wheel on its cross-brace as it continued its rotation, and heard the suspended leather bucket make a faint splash. He scrutinized the cistern interior, which was dark without reflection, and wondered how to raise the water level. When he straightened up, he saw another woman in a plain kaftan waiting beside him. As he turned, she gasped. Her dark, lustrous eyes grew large and wet. The dropped water jar shattered.

"Hershlab," she cried and crumpled. He caught Miriam as she fell.

"Thanks be to God," she gasped against his shoulder between sobs and laughter. "I mourned you these many years."

When he gently released her, and held her away from him, she ran the back of her hand across her eyes, looked at his fine clothes and sword. A stream of questions poured from her. "You look so grand. You're different. You're here in Tetouan? You came here looking for me?"

Hersh started to make lame excuses; his eyes darted about, looking to see who was watching. Miriam failed to notice. "My father is well?" He asked.

"No, dear betrothed. He's so frail. You will be his blessing from God before he leaves us. She pressed his hand in hers. He really loves you."

"I know."

Miriam bubbled happily, there was so much to say. "You must come to our house. We live in a big one."

A muscle twitched on Habib's cheek. "First, my father."

Immediately she let go of his hand; her eyes dulled as animation and cheeriness faded. "You're not married are you?"

This he could answer truthfully. He shook his head.

227

Miriam put her arm through his and, chattering and hugging, led him though a small passageway to see his father.

A blank wall punctured by a low rectangular door blocked their path. "His synagogue," Miriam said apologetically, knowing he would remember his father's handsome temple in Granada. "I'll go first to tell him. The shock may be too much."

Hersh waited at the door. He watched her buttocks bulge in the black gown as she walked away. She had no ankles, he noted abstractly. He could leave now. He could disappear. He could run. Miriam didn't know his identity and would never find him. Jews didn't leave the mellah. But no . . . his father . . . after rising from the dead he couldn't vanish again.

Miriam returned, and as was the custom, remained at the rear of the synagogue. Hershlab strode the narrow aisle between benches. The Eternal Flame, suspended from the ceiling by chains, gave off only a dim light. He paused before a slight figure, wrapped in a large prayer shawl that bent over the Sacred Scrolls.

"Papa?"

The rabbi leaned over the scrolls of the Torah on his lectern to peer at the tall, broad shouldered man who approached.

"Can it be you? My son? Come closer." He rasped.

"It's me, Papa." He embraced his father feeling his bones through the tallith as the old man wept.

"What's this?" The gnarled hands clutching Hershlab felt fine cloth then struck metal. "A sword!"

"Papa, it's me. Only my clothes are different."

The rabbi backed away. "It's you who is different."

"It's a long story. We have so much to talk about. I will explain. I'll tell you everything that happened."

"What's to explain?" The quavering voice strengthened in anger. "You come into the holy of holies, before the open Torah, with your head uncovered?"

Automatically Hershlab's hand clasped the back of his head.

"This Gentile I see is not my son. You are a Converso with a sword."

The slap across the face was not well meaning like the raps on his knuckles as a child.

Instantly Habib knew he could never again be Hersh. "Papa," he said, his voice breaking, "I love you."

At the door, he turned for one last look. He heard the lament for the dead: "*Ys'gdal, Ys'gadash – "*

In the evening, Habib stood in the middle of the open-air market, the Souk el Hots. Behind him rose the high stone wall of the Mandari compound and the street to the old hammam. Before him, on the stone paving, lay twenty-some stalls shaded by treetops and canvas slung over ropes. Beyond and to his right were the shops Hura wanted repaired. A babble of bartering voices resonated around the Souk.

As he brooded over recent events, he pushed his way through the congestion of stalls to the far end. There, he scanned the two story buildings housing the more permanent vendors who sold better quality, more expensive goods. Automatically he strode to one where the clay brickwork had cracked and crumbled most severely. Spices of many colors in open, rough-woven sacks were displayed in front. He entered the shop.

While he surveyed the interior walls and ceiling, the shopkeeper attempted to sell him powders of strong shour. The stringy-haired woman in a soiled kaftan must have known he was not interested in cooking spices. She disappeared into the rear of the shop behind a curtain, and returned with two small pots. She removed the lids, waved one under Habib's nose. "Sidi Architect, sniff this." He did not need to. The sweet smell of the potion was pervasive.

"A pinch of this magic powder makes even an eighty-year old man potent as a stallion."

"Wait, she scurried after him and blocked his exit. "I showed that to a virile man like you only so you will want this one – "

"Is for what?"

She held the second odorless, colorless pot against his chest. "Some women do not wish children. A handsome man like you must make many babies."

Habib swept the woman's hand aside. The pot flew across the shop and shattered. Curses followed his stride back to the stalls.

My heart's not in the work.

Where to find a woman. Habib knew the available ones always dallied on the Gold Street. But not for him the harlots. Better now would be the hammam at dusk. He lounged at the stone wall nearby eating roasted seeds, one at a time. Here he boldly observed and assessed each woman leaving the baths.

After his third handful, just as he thought he was becoming too picky, he laughed aloud. His maazul had returned. There was his quarry. What was her name? Ah, yes, he remembered and crossed the narrow lane.

Within earshot as she was about to pass, he called out to the bejeweled woman: "*Buenos Días*, Catana." He bowed with a broad smile as though to a long-time friend.

Boabdil's wife turned in surprise. Her parted lips were painted and she was heavily rouged and scented.

229

Pushing her uniformed guard aside, she said, "Habib! I wanted so much to be with you again. I . . . mean, I didn't expect to see you so soon." Her hands grasped her cloak, parted it to expose deep cleavage.

"I was just going to my apartment. It is nearby," he said. "We can walk together . . . alone . . . and talk."

Her lashes fluttered in the way he remembered. She ordered her guard to remain there.

Habib caressed her ample backside for an instant, then put her hand on his arm and led the way.

TWENTY EIGHT

"I understand why he invited me," Kleinatz pulled off the gloves he wore to protect his rare and fragile books. His warm smile told Hura he had not expected to see her at the library. "But why did Mohammed ask you to bring Habib? Surely your young architect hasn't begun appreciating the other arts."

Hura let out a cluck of mirth. "My, you're pompous today, do you see a problem with everything Mohammed does? He even asked me to bring Suha, but she's in bed with a bad cough and I've told Afaf to stay with her. Couldn't he just want to be friendly."

"I doubt it. What kind of festival is this, I've never heard of this play . . . or whatever you call it."

Hura drew him to the side reading room where they could converse without disturbing others, and chose a chair.

"That's because only we Berbers have it. It's like theater in the street. A street play. Each tribe and each village plays it slightly differently. When I was a child, I was terrified of the *Bilmawn*. He's so ugly. You'll see. I want it to be a surprise. It's a part of a festival after Ramadan between the feast of the Sacrifice, the *'eid el Kabir*, and the festival for the dead, the *'Ashura*."

"Ya. I understand. The two events must mark the passage of time. One brings the old year to a close, and the other opens a new one. Who is this *Bilmawn*?"

"Watch for him. He's the lead character in the play. You'll know him because he's wearing the skins of the animals sacrificed for the feast. "

"Ah! A masquerade. How I loved the theater as a young boy in Holland."

"And you'll want to record all this for your Journal."

"Ya, of course. Who else is in the play? Do they all wear costumes? Do we watch or do I have to participate?"

"Questions, questions." She saw him blush. "It's been so long that I've seen it and I don't want to spoil it for you. I'll just say yes, there are others. Ten I think. They all do funny things. But I've never heard of the festival being put on as a play for a night's entertainment like this."

"Will it matter . . . that I'm Christian?" Kleinatz cocked his head.

Hura stood up, faced him squarely and looked in his eyes. "You're under our protection. Where's your famous insatiable curiosity?"

Kleinatz bent forward then pushed with both hands on his chair seat to rise. She could see him wince as he straightened and wondered if he had the bone sickness that old people get. His question concerned her. How difficult it must be for her friend and mentor to live in this city. She reassured him of his safety and tried to calm any other fears he might have by inviting him to ride with her.

"Come by the compound by noon. Habib will go with us. We'll all go together."

That same morning Habib, too, questioned why Mohammed had invited him to this party and what this special festival was all about. When the invitation came, he fingered the parchment, not believing it real. But the seal was authentic. He considered refusing but the opportunity to see Hura was too powerful. She hadn't smiled at him in a long time. To his surprise, a different woman greeted him. This other Hura had her hair all pushed up into a conical straw hat festooned with red wool pompoms, her gray eyes hidden under the brim, and her body hidden in a billowing linen cape. This was a country girl.

Watching Hura mount up with her guards, Habib queried Kleinatz. "What's this all about? I thought the Ramadan feast was over. God knows I've eaten enough lamb."

"I believe," Kleinatz acknowledged him politely but formally, not knowing the present status of his relationship with Hura, "that Mohammed is presenting a special drama, a masquerade, for King Boabdil. A little diversion. It's the holiday season. It's strictly a Berber custom. The King has never seen it. Neither have I."

Habib confided, "I don't really want to go . . . those two men are trouble. I don't trust them."

Kleinatz nodded. He liked this young man. But he didn't trust him, either.

The ride down the slopes and across the plain invigorated Hura. She sat back in the saddle and admired the construction along the main road. How well Habib is making the city grow, she thought. Feeling the weight of her large hat, she wondered what Habib thought of her costume. She hoped her beauty still enchanted him. Any concern about the real purpose of the festival left her. It would be like old times, a family celebration with Berber food and music. Her mind wandered. She tried to recall the last time she and her brothers had celebrated together.

A trumpet announced their arrival at Mohammed's gate. Servants tethered their horses then escorted them into the courtyard of the villa. Mohammed broke from a small group of men to greet them, his shoulders dipping from his uneven gait. "*Ahlen wa Sahlen*, welcome to my home," he bowed theatrically. Somewhere from within the walled villa musicians were playing, enticing music wafted through the archways.

"This is wonderful, dear brother," Hura offered her cheeks in greeting. "I never get to see you anymore, we're all so busy. Thank you for inviting us. I had no idea you still practiced the masquerade."

Both the Professor and Habib bowed a greeting.

"I don't." He looked behind them as if expecting others. "Your daughter? She isn't with you?"

"How good of you to invite her, but she is ill and in bed."

"Too bad." Mohammed's voice sounded annoyed. "This is special. I've invited a troupe from Ait Mizane to perform. They'll reenact the play, all three days of it in one night. You'll never see a festival quite like this. Some of it will be in Berber," he grinned at Habib and the Professor, "but you'll get the point." With that, he left them and headed for a knot of other guests crowding around the food table.

A flutist and a drummer enticed the guests to move from the outer courtyard through the patio, toward the open doorway into a walled garden. Plots of flowering bushes and colorful mosaic walkways criss-crossed the fragrant, well-manicured space. Tiered benches had been placed against one wall facing a central fountain. Habib muffled a snicker as he appraised the fountain sculpture: a small mountain of painted metal snakes entwined in various positions of strike.

"Follow me." Habib headed toward the makeshift seating. Both men climbed to the top of the lashed sapling scaffold and perched on a narrow plank. A sea of colored turbans bobbed below them on the lower benches.

Panting with exertion, Kleinatz busied himself with a pipeful of kif.

Habib spied Hura. She had let her hair down and it shimmered over her shoulders in the late afternoon light. Her cape was thrown over the back of her chair, framing her body with its crimson lining. She sat on the dais to the left of Boabdil, and next to her brother. Habib could see their mouths move and heads bob in spirited conversation. He wanted that mouth. Sweating, he shifted slightly on the plank as his trousers tightened in the crotch.

Kleinatz also focused on their lips, hoping to catch their words and feel more at ease. Servants scurried up and down the bleachers proffering trays of food, occasionally blocking his view.

"More lamb," Habib grumbled.

"I saw trays of fruit," Kleinatz said.

The crowd hushed and turbans swayed to the vibrant beat of a drum, a drum-tone so low it reverberated in bellies. A troupe of musicians boomed, blew, thumped, whistled and plucked their instruments across the grass stage in front of the audience. Each player took his turn in the spotlight with wild improvisation then blended back into concert. Blaap, honk,

233

plunk, twitter, boom! The colorfully attired musicians at last strutted through an archway and disappeared. A momentary silence preceded the shouts and laughter of the crowd.

A tray of food passed by them and Habib took four fresh eggs; Kleinatz filled his hands with grapes, then in his fussy manner, wiped each one with the handkerchief he always carried in his sleeve.

Bells and gongs announced the next attraction. A group of what looked like masked beggars swarmed into the stage area in front of the guests. Scratching filthy bodies, spitting and farting, they singled out individuals in the front rows, confronting them with ribald jokes. No topic was sacred. Not religion, not law, not love. Certainly not marriage.

"Disgusting." Kleinatz murmured and clamped his knees together.

Guests in the seats below them responded by throwing food, cheering them on. That only encouraged the actors to make their language and movements more obscene.

Habib looked over to the dais down on his right and saw King Boabdil enjoying the spectacle, clapping his hands in glee. Hura's face betrayed a bemused smile. Mohammed could hardly contain himself, waving his arms and doubling over in laughter. Occasionally, Mohammed signaled for the servant behind his chair to throw more food at the troupe. Habib deftly picked the end of an egg with his dagger and sucked out the contents.

"What a waste of good food on bad manners." Kleinatz sniffed. Then he caught Hura's expression. Her smile had disappeared.

Habib didn't know what to think. Now the actors were getting physical with the audience, not content to verbally assault them. This could get out of hand, he thought. He was glad he was seated high in the back row. He brushed away kif smoke then shot a glance of discomfort over to Kleinatz and noticed how rigid the Professor sat. The sweet weed had not yet soothed him.

"There really is some meaning to this," Kleinatz offered uneasily.

"There is?"

"The actors, if I can call them that, all represent a specific character or attribute. There is the old man, his wife, the ass, the Negress, the judge, the – "

"No, don't tell me, let me guess who they are." Habib laughed. "That one, he's actually quite witty." Habib pointed to the figure covered with goatskins that fingered worry beads of strung snails. A goat's skull, its jaws propped open with a stick in grimace, covered his head. The skin's legs draped down his arms and the hooves dangled below his fingers. As the figure talked, Habib's eyes never left the space between the actor's legs where two huge purple eggplants dangled.

"He is greatly feared by women. He's the goat man. He beats women . .

. but my manuscript also said he cures the sick. Another incongruency."

The Professor glanced from the stage to Hura and saw her staring up at Habib. "The ass is easy to recognize by the bleached skull on the actor's head. And the effeminate man with the two gourd-breasts whose head is covered with another large painted gourd has to be the wife of the goat man."

Habib's eyes still followed the dangling eggplants.

"Hura called him the *Bilmawn*. He used to terrify her when she was a child."

"Looks like he still does." Habib could see that Hura, eyes cast down, sat stone faced in her chair. When his gaze returned to the pageant in front of him, a familiar sight made him gasp. A skull cap. Instinctively, his hand went to his head. He looked around. No one noticed him patting his hair.

The Jew was dressed in a ragged burnoose. What looked like two cows tails served as the temporal locks of the 'Children of Israel'. Cowering from the blows of the other actors as well as from the audience, the poor man wept and wailed.

At first mesmerized in memory, Habib now froze in anger. The heat of ardor extinguished, his body tightened and his fists clenched.

Below, on stage, the action quickened. The Jewess tried to protect her husband. The judge intervened, majestic in his enormous turban, staving off the offenders with a slab of blackened cork, which Habib guessed, was meant to be the Koran.

The drama continued. Habib once more sought Hura. She sat passively, staring in her lap.

His angry eyes swiveled to the play. Although protected by his wife, the old Jew now was accused of impotence. Finally, dragging him before the judge and complaining loudly, the Jewess raised her arms to the heavens and said: "His soul is dead." She pointed to his genitals.

More laughter convulsed the crowd.

Habib grit his teeth.

Amidst more whooping and hollering from the audience, the judge pronounced the sentence: "I condemn you to mount her ten times at night, on pain of jail!"

The crowd went wild with laughter.

Habib shot another glance over to Hura and caught her looking at him. She quickly averted her eyes. Outrage began to burn his body. He reached for the eggs next to him on the bench and as the crowd shouted its approval of the judge's sentence, he leaned back and threw the eggs, one after the other, at Mohammed. The first found its mark on Boabdil's leg; the others stained the wooden platform.

Kleinatz watched numbly as Habib grew more belligerent. He hoped the brash young man wouldn't make a scene. All he needed was to be involved with a misguided youth defending his religion.

Habib began to breathe rapidly. How could she do this? Why did she want me to come? She must have known. Below him, the poor wretch of a Jew was being led away by his wife. To their bed, he supposed. Now the outrage rose and overtook him. He reached over to the Professor's pile of fruit, stood up and began to pelt the audience below him.

Kleinatz covered his face with his hands, emitted a terrified gurgle. Fortunately, those who were hit paid little attention. Some turned around and looked up at their attacker but soon laughed as if he were part of the festivities.

"Sit down. What are you doing?" Kleinatz tugged at Habib's pantaloons. "You're going to get me crucified and your head salted and put on a pike."

Hura watched helplessly as her lover began his defiance, not knowing what to do.

"What's the matter, dear sister?" Mohammed leaned close and asked between snorts of laughter. "Not enjoying the show?"

Hura saw Habib stumble over Kleinatz and begin to climb down the bleacher; Kleinatz awkwardly followed him. Where is he going? Out of the corner of her eye, she saw her brother watching the same thing.

"Something wrong with your prize architect? Perhaps it's too hot here on my stage. Is there something he didn't like about the play? He can't leave so soon, it's not over. I'll have my guards find him and bring him back."

"No, I'll find him." She pushed her brother away, stood up and left the dais.

"Your sister's not well?" Boabdil leaned over to see Mohammed fuming.

Hura maintained a dignified pace along the walkway until she reached the archway to the courtyard then ran to the outside gate where she stood panting for breath. The two figures on horseback galloped to a dot in the distance.

Habib and Kleinatz, both deep in thought, rode in silence. For his part, Habib considered himself a new Christian, a Converso. Why then had the play offended him so? Mohammed. Mohammed knew he was a Jew. It was his diabolic jest; this was a way to let Habib know he knew.

Habib still fumed when he entered his large, sparsely furnished apartment . . . and froze.

Someone – the same man who had been with Mohammed – was taking a letter from the small wooden box on his table. Hura's letter. That letter from the prison, never delivered to Ibrahim. The one in which she confessed her forbidden love to a Jew. On the instant, Habib's hand grasped his dagger. One of them must die.

TWENTY NINE

The mountaintop was cloaked in a white mantle. On a lower slope, the main square beside the kasbah of Chaouen was festooned with multi-colored banners and garlands of wild flowers that threaded festively through the trees and across the canvas awnings of the cafes. A steady stream of donkeys and mules swayed under burdens of wedding tribute, and wound their way through the medina to the rocky side entrance of the kasbah where they were unloaded. Inside the fortress, two storerooms bulged with gifts for the bride.

In the late spring warmth, Hura and Suha sat hip-to-hip beside the small fountain in the center of the cobbled courtyard. The aroma of flowers and spices perfumed the breeze. Hura basked in the comfort of old memories; her eyes captured the familiar walls and buildings of her family home. Suha dipped her hand in the water and drew lazy circles with her fingers. This was Suha's first visit to Chaouen and Hura felt like a proud travel guide, telling her daughter about its history.

"Tetouan is your home, but don't ever forget Chaouen."

"Do you? I mean sometimes?" The girl's soft voice questioned.

"No. Never. I find my comfort and strength here."

"Please mother, tell me again about grandfather. He built this village, didn't he."

Hura glanced at her daughter. Strange. Why hadn't she noticed how her voice had matured. "Yes, your grandfather, Idrissid Prince Sherif Moulay Ali Ibn Rachid founded it, some forty years ago . . . as a Berber fortress in the mountains. These high mountains hide and protect us. It's hard to attack us and so easy to defend. No surprises here, not like in Tetouan."

"What about these Moriscos I see here. I thought they only came to Tetouan."

Hura frowned thinking about Suha's question. She smoothed the folds of the heavy wool skirt that covered her knees.

"Some of the people who fled Spain came here also. They're the ones who built all the elegant new houses you see. Now I hardly know my town. Our old houses were plain and now you can't walk down the streets without seeing bright tile work, ornate iron grills and window decorations. Even the public wells are tiled."

"Nicky would like it here, I smell kif everywhere." Suha grinned impishly.

Hura's eyebrows shot up and she recoiled in mock horror. "Does the Professor know you call him that?"

Suha's laugh was infectious but Hura quickly became serious. "Our Christian friends are not welcome here, he wouldn't be allowed here."

A servant brought a tray of juice and honey cakes and put it between them. Decoratively perforated tin cones covered their glasses and the sweets, protecting them from the persistent bees. Suha waved her hand back and forth to scatter them but their number only grew. Soon the lid on top of the honey cakes was studded with buzzing insects.

Hura pushed the cakes closer to her daughter. The idea of food, even honey cakes, made her stomach lurch.

She gazed over the walls to the octagonal minaret of the Grand mosque, one of the first buildings her father had built. It made a fitting memorial to him. His death two months before made this homecoming and celebration bittersweet. She stretched to look behind her at the stone Tower of Homage in the kasbah wall. These were her childhood landmarks; they were filled with secrets of the past. They had defined her world. How much bigger her world was now. And her new secret . . . it would be hard to keep from others much longer.

Suha chattered on, talking to the bees and playing with the water. She looks more like me every day, Hura mused. She'll never be as tall, but her sweet smile and happy laughter will make her life easy. She's not a tomboy, either. How time has slipped by; I see the small buds of breasts through her kaftan . . . time to think about a suitable husband some day soon. Hura's eyes misted. Weddings. Husbands. Love. It will be different . . . happier, for my daughter.

"Mother, can I have a tattoo like yours?"

Taken aback, Hura hesitated while admiring her daughter's fair face. "I didn't let them tattoo you when you were younger because I want you to belong to everybody – I mean I don't want anyone to identify you just as a Berber. The world should be yours. You have Arab and Spanish blood in you too."

"But I'm proud to be a Berber and I want to be as beautiful as you. Please, mother."

"My dear," Hura patted Suha's knee, "your world is different from the one I knew as a child. I never thought I would leave my hometown. But now I've seen how people in other places treat women and especially Berbers. Sometimes they look down on us."

"What do you mean?"

"Well, when I was in Fes, the Arabs had a law that all Berbers had to be out of the city by the last prayers of the day. And, if I hadn't had your fathers ring and cloak to give me importance, I never would have been able to see the Sultan or the Wazir, or even the chief of the Pirates in Salé! I can't do anything about my being a woman, but things would have been easier if I didn't have my Berber tattoo. Foreigners don't know that only the noble born and free women here can be tattooed."

Suha stroked her smooth skin in puzzlement.

"People treat you by the way you look. If you're not from the right class or sex or color you don't get what you want. Do you understand?"

"I guess so. But everyone here has tattoos."

"Of course. That's the Berber way. Up here people who don't have them are outsiders."

Suha covered her chin with her hand.

"If you want, we'll get a henna design painted on you. Then you'll look like everyone else."

Suha nodded enthusiastically.

They turned and walked hand in hand to the main house. The east side of the second floor had been reserved for the bride, her half brother and their entourage. Dozens of candles flickered throughout the house: lighting, scenting, warming the stone fortress.

"I can't wait to meet the bride." Suha gushed as they stood by the steep stairs to the bride's quarters. "She's so lucky to marry uncle Ibrahim. When I grow up I want a husband like him."

The look of happy innocence on Suha's face brought a pang of loneliness to Hura. She thought of her own marriage and looked away.

When they returned to the courtyard, a servant came running toward them, calling above the clatter of construction: "Lalla Hura, Lalla Hura. He's here! I saw him. He's come back!"

"Who? Who's back?"

"You must come. It's Sacony."

Hura ran to the side gate and looked outside into the thrall of gift bearers and animals. There he was: Sacony! A young boy held him by a rope halter. Her heart sank. The once proud stallion now slumped feet apart, neck lowered, ears to the side, his coat unkempt. There were scars on his knees and flank and a dull glaze clouded his eyes.

"Where did he come from? Who brought him?" Hura shouted at the young boy in front of her. An old man in a dark burnoose rushed away.

"I am Yusuf, from the Beni Zait. My family won this horse in battle with the Beni Bouzra tribe near Targa. We're giving it in tribute to the new bride."

He seemed totally without guile. Hura couldn't believe her good luck. Her baraka had returned. She thought of nothing else, grabbed the rope and called to her horse: "Sacony! Sacony!"

The long gray neck slowly lifted. "He's been broken!" She rushed to hug him and felt his bones through the uncurried coat. "I'll take him," she told the workers. "And you, young man, here's a coin for your good deed."

Leading him to the stables, she spoke softly to him: "Where have you been! I'll take care of you. I'll fatten you up. You'll have that gleam back in your eyes soon, don't worry."

Suha skipped over the cobbled walkways in the courtyard, scattering flower petals in all directions. The striped canopies and torches were still up and the pits where meats had been charcoaled still smoldered with white ash. It would take another week to untangle the ribbons from the trees and sweep the confetti from the grounds. The wedding had been the grandest celebration the town had ever seen. Ibrahim and his new wife had inspired romantic dreams in many young hearts.

Suha had gasped when the bride appeared. "The gown!" It must have had two thousand pearls sewn on it. "And the tiara, mother. Look at that!"

The bride wore the Sultan's gift of golden olive branches entwining a host of 'olives' made of emeralds, pearls, rubies and sapphires embellished by a band of coral and greenstone leaves. Noticing her mother's somber expression, Suha asked, "Something wrong?"

Hura stroked her daughter's long hair and studied her flushed, excited face. How could she speak of her flash of envy . . . yes, envy of Ibrahim's bride and her radiant happiness. Hura sighed and shut that window to her soul. She touched Habib's simple, beautiful nautilus pin while forcing a smile. "For a moment, dear, I thought it might rain."

After the wedding ceremonies, Hura sought Ibrahim alone. She should have known better than to bother him with all that was on his mind but she feared she would have no other chance to talk with him. As always, Ibrahim welcomed her, listened carefully and tried to give her advice. This time, however, his words brought no comfort.

"I understand the very real threat to Tetouan. You're right about the possibility of another invasion from foreign powers," he said, "but I'm appalled by your foolish idea of going to the Turkish pirates to get their help."

Hura bit her lip to keep silent.

"Bring the Turks here? Janissaries in Fes are one thing, but giving the Emperor's Admiral a chance to openly take over Tetouan is madness. Where did you get such a wild idea? Leave such matters to me. Of course I'll help if you are attacked, without a strong Tetouan the whole Rif is in danger. As part of the wedding agreement, the Sultan has committed 40,000 troops for the defense of the Rif. You have my pledge that I will come to your defense. But I can't spare my warriors while I'm fighting for the Sultan. When you need me, I'll be there."

Hura pleaded, told him more about her recent problems at the port, and described the man she saw when Sacony was returned. "I'm certain he was the same blind beggar in Tetouan who always sat outside when we held court. Now I don't believe he was blind."

But the more Hura became adamant that someone around her was a traitor, that someone always seemed to be a step ahead of her to put her in danger, or a step behind her to unravel her plans, the more Ibrahim insisted that her problems were just a part of the life she had chosen – the price she paid for daring to be a leader – a price no less than her father had paid, and no less than he was paying.

Hura was surprised to learn about the worsening problems that Ibrahim faced. Grudgingly she realized he couldn't commit troops to help her city. But didn't he know that the fall of Tetouan was the first step to conquering the Rif? If their enemies captured Tetouan, they could amass the provisions and troops for an assault on all the northern lands. She smiled at the irony. To think she had helped to build Tetouan and now it had become important for the safety of Chaouen.

On this seventh and last day of the celebration, Hura sat under the canopy attempting to enjoy the festivities. Tetouan was still on her mind. She applauded as a team of acrobats performed on ropes above them. She looked over at Ibrahim – she had never seen him look so handsome, so regal. His white, silk brocade turban accentuated his swarthy face and black goatee. Hard days in the saddle had kept him fit and muscular. She was happy for her brother, and he seemed genuinely pleased with his new wife and his alliance with the Sultan.

Ibrahim caught her gaze, leaned over to her and confided: "As soon as my wife bears me a son I will go on the haj to Mecca."

"*Inshallah*," she said, "If God wills." Then despite herself, she asked, "How can you afford to leave affairs of state at such a crucial time and go off to be pious?"

Calmly Ibrahim replied, "Peace with one's self and one's God should not be based on convenience. And you, my dear sister, should understand that when one is called, one has an obligation. It is the will of Allah. And in my absence, Mohammed will be ruling."

"How could you entrust our homeland to him?"

"Mohammed has had bad luck. As the second son, his fortunes aren't going that well and he is, after all, family."

This was not the place or time to argue. And she knew any argument would be based on feelings and unproved allegations. Disliking Mohammed wasn't grounds for accusations.

She stared ahead without seeing the elaborately transformed courtyard and all the important visitors. It was a magnificent and important wedding . . . . a union of two peoples, two cities; a wise political marriage, a brilliant alliance. Why then did she feel so alone. Why did she feel so isolated and endangered. Her family, with all its power, was not unified. Was she the only one who still remembered her father's words . . . who lived for her father's goal of unity? Brother Ibrahim sought fatherhood and the respected life of a pious nobleman; brother Mohammed found satisfaction in his fattening waistline and expanding change purse, spreading manure on carefully nurtured friendships along the way. He didn't seem to care what family ties he cut for the sake of his business.

And Hura? Who was she to criticize? Good deeds and loyal service to her husband and his city had all been betrayed when she took Habib as a lover. It didn't matter that she thought herself a free woman when it happened. She had betrayed her dream. She had forgotten her father.

Suha came to her from behind, covered her eyes, and then with a merry giggle kissed her. Her daughter slid into a seat next to her behind Hamad, the bastard son of the former Sultan of Fes. This same Hamad had been so helpful to her by making the Wazir write the letter to the Pasha in Rabat. Not that the letter had gotten anything, but now he was the official escort of the bride and had risen to an important post in the new regime. Hamad leaned back in his chair and complimented Hura on having such a pretty daughter.

Two weeks had passed and living in Chaouen had brought Hura a clear understanding of what she must do. She calculated: I didn't wear the cloth last month, but that could have been because of all the travel, the shock of seeing my husband, or maybe the concentration on my duties. I'm bloated and I'm short tempered, but maybe that's because of all the pressure. And now, I can't eat. But maybe that's because of all this rich food.

Or maybe I could stop lying to myself.

The pleasures of a new life as the bride of Habib were folly. They were childish. How could she have believed they could be happy together? How could she be blinded to her duty? How could she forget her heritage? She was as blind as Mandari.

During the day, her heart was filled with the comfort of family and tradition, but at night, her dreams confused her with memories of Habib and images of the child she was carrying. Soon everyone would know. Morning sickness and an expanding belly were hard to keep secret. In her confusion, a wild thought came and played in her mind. What if I say the baby is my husband's? There's a chance that people will believe it . . . and why shouldn't Habib's son be heir to Tetouan? Why not? She looked down at her tightly balled fists, then relaxed them. She knew why.

Slowly Sacony regained his strength. Every afternoon Hura walked him; stable hands curried, massaged and fed him; the farrier fit him with new shoes. She found his old saddle and bridle in the stable. The saddle was too big for his skinny body but tight for her new womanly figure. The rapport between the old friends was slow to return. She needed him. He would save her life by destroying another. Not today. Not this morning. Not on this beautiful morning. But perhaps tomorrow. Certainly soon.

The memory of their first meeting flooded back. That first time, when she bounded onto his back, he had twisted that long, gray neck around to look at her. His stare, without frenzied eyes or flared nostrils, was inquisitive. Then he bucked once and bolted. Two hours later the twosome returned content with each other. That was long ago.

The morning horse and rider left the kasbah, soft warm breezes from the south caressed Hura's face and ruffled Sacony's mane. She proceeded on carpets of flowers, higher and higher up the mountain under a deep blue sky, accompanied by a potpourri of fragrance, the chirping of birds and veils of undulating yellow butterflies. She rode on to her mission.

Finally, she arrived at her destination, a long pass that spread for miles on rolling land just under the steep rise of the rocky cliffs. Ages ago this pass had been blessed with protection from the raging winds by the cliffs. Not only trees but lush flowers and grasses grew in its confined space. At the far end, a stone cairn and hut had been built for travelers.

In her youth, she had often come here with Sacony in training for the Fantasia. The ground was level in places, and littered with fallen trees in others. It made a good obstacle course, good for jumping. There was little sound. It was as if God had plugged up the ears of the universe. Even the noise of Sacony's hooves was muffled in the soft earth. She heard only her own breathing and the powerful snorting of Sacony as he expelled the thin air. The leather saddle squeaked, its high pommel jutted menacingly in front of her belly.

Hura adjusted the saddlebags behind her legs. They contained a change of clothes, a blanket, food for two days, a vial of emetic and a kidskin of water. She had told everyone that she was meeting with emissaries in the nearby village of Ichtal, a day's ride away, and would be back by the end of the week. Everyone knew that Hura would go and do whatever she wanted.

Suha had pleaded, "Mother, can't I go with you? I love these mountains now."

"This, my dear, is a mission only I can do, one I must do alone."

Now cloud fluffs dappled the trees and flowers with shadow. She drew quick, fragrant gulps of air as Sacony picked his way even higher and shut her eyes to the beauty around her. I must do this, she told herself . . . for the sake of my people, for our future, for my father and for my dignity.

At the entrance to the long pass she reigned in, pulled out the vial she was carrying in her bag, and drank it. Then she surveyed the land again; the land and sky of her forefathers. She reined in tightly, arching Sacony's neck in preparation, holding back on the signal that would launch him. Taut with anticipation, Sacony bolted when she released her grip and squeezed her legs in command. They flew over the hills, across the uneven ground, vaulting logs and fallen trees, jumping bushes, galloping up the inclines then plunging down into stream beds toward the far end. She shouted him on until she could no longer keep in the saddle and Sacony slowed in exhaustion. She pulled him to rest and slid off near a small stream by the stone hut. As she lay on her back, looking up at the blue sky, her pulse pounded in her head so loudly that nothing else intruded. Before long, she felt the sharp cramps in her belly. The pain was joy, just for a moment, as she realized she would abort. She moaned in the vast silence as the cramps continued.

As they grew longer and sharper, she called his name: *Habib*!

THIRTY

"Oh, mistress, I'm so glad you're back," Afaf sobbed. "I didn't know who to turn to. Miguel found him when he brought breakfast that morning."

Hura put her arm around the girl and sent Suha up to her room with her saddlebags. For years, she had known this would happen . . . but that didn't make it any easier. "Who else knows?"

"Only the Professor and Miguel . . . and us." Afaf's sobs became hiccups.

"You did the right thing." Hura held her close. "There, stop your crying, it will be all right."

Afaf straightened and wiped her nose. "Oh mistress, it was awful, and you'd been gone just a week. The Professor said he and Miguel would bury him secretly."

"You did the right thing. Now dry your eyes." Her own were tearless.

"And the Professor wants to talk with you as soon as you're back. He said he's leaving. He's going to leave Tetouan."

Hura tightened her grip on Afaf's shoulder. "Leave? For where? Did he say?"

"No. He just said to fetch him when you got back. And he told Miguel to bring food to your husband's apartment every day, like nothing had happened."

Hura frowned in thought for a moment. "I'll send Miguel for him now. And, in the meantime, say nothing."

Afaf stood there, looking down at her feet, not wanting to move, as if she had something else she should say, but couldn't.

Hura knew that stance. "What's wrong?"

"Lalla Hura, I have to tell you." Afaf swayed from foot to foot.

"Well?" Hura reached out and with a finger, tilted Afaf's head upward.

"I told someone else . . ." she looked up, her eyes ringed with red. "I shouldn't have, I know . . . but he swore to secrecy."

"Who did you tell?"

"I told my fiancée, Hisham."

Hura sighed in relief, she knew the Captain could be trusted.

"That's all right. Go now. See that Suha has what she needs, then ask Hisham to join us when the Professor arrives."

"You're not angry?" Afaf looked relieved.

"No."

Hura climbed the stairs slowly to her room and sat on her bed. Guilt. A huge wave of guilt swept over her. She remembered the Professor saying that guilt was a wasted emotion. Her eyes focused on the large trunk at the foot of her bed. In it, she had folded her husband's cape. She retrieved and spread it out on the bed. The hem was torn lose in several places and the front clasp was bent but the colors of the embroidered coat of arms were still brilliant. It had survived the trip to Fes and her imprisonment well. It had cloaked her in his family's honor and helped her assert her power. I'll wear it at the cemetery, she said to herself. Not only will I insist on being at his burial, I'll wear his cape. There'll be no question that this is now my city.

She refolded the cape and carefully placed it in the trunk, then went to find Afaf. "Ready yet?" She found Afaf giggling with Suha over her daughter's presents from Chaouen.

"Such beautiful things!" Afaf gushed, apparently forgetting her recent sadness.

"Put them away, Suha. Wash yourself and meet me downstairs by the door. Afaf, come with me. Where is Isabel?"

Afaf's face fell. "Mistress, she grieves in her room. She won't come out."

Hura understood her grief. As they descended the stairs Hura hesitated, then whispered: "What have you heard about our new architect, Habib? Where is he working now? Has he inquired about me?"

"No, Lalla Hura, I haven't seen him since you left. Do you want me to . . . find out?" She broke off as Suha caught up with them.

"No. No. That's not necessary. It doesn't matter." She hated herself for asking.

Later that afternoon Kleinatz and the Captain arrived and the two met with Hura in Mandari's old office.

Hura embraced her old friend. "Tell me what happened, Professor. I see I owe you again for saving me."

Kleinatz flushed and began while filling his pipe with a plug of kif, lighting it and slowly inhaling: "Miguel was the one who found him, early in the morning. He came rushing out of the apartment and ran headlong into Afaf. When he explained what he'd seen, she had the common sense to ask him to go get me and keep silent. Fortunately I was in my lodgings and so came back with him."

Hura swiveled in her chair. "How did it happen. I mean, was there an accident?"

"No," he drew again on his pipe. "It seems he died in his sleep. When I

246

saw him he was lying in bed, peaceful, his eyes closed."

Hura sighed. "Afaf said you and Miguel buried him."

"Yes. According to your customs. That night we took his body away in a cart. Hisham helped. He dug the grave, in the cemetery, in a place not far from the city wall. It's by a big tree and there's a square marker on it with the name 'Abu Hassan' painted on it."

Hisham nodded. "It's painted white, on a small hill overlooking the city. There's plenty of room for a kubba to be built around it."

They were silent for a while, each engrossed in private thoughts. "Thank you both for keeping this a secret," she said finally. "I must plan the right moment to announce his death. We'll have official mourning in the city, and of course the family ceremonies. Do you have any other suggestions?"

Kleinatz offered, "You could have an empty casket paraded and buried nearby, then switch them later."

"Yes, that's what I'll do." Hura nodded.

"I'm concerned about Father Contreras. At the time, the Captain and I agreed the best way to keep him from finding out was to tell him that Mandari had the fevers and couldn't see anyone."

"And," Hisham said, "I placed extra guards outside. But every day he'd come, and every day he'd be told he couldn't go in. I think he's suspicious."

"He would be," Hura agreed. "I can see we have to act soon. We'll announce it in three days. Anything else I should know?"

Kleinatz tapped his white ash into a bowl and said, "Did you know that King Boabdil is here? He returned from his campaign in Tangier."

"And Mohammed?"

The Captain answered. "Haven't seen or heard from him since he left for the wedding. He's not been in the compound."

Kleinatz cleared his throat. "You have a very dangerous situation here. The talk is that the Turks are coming. They are very close and raiding villages all along the coast. It's likely they want Tetouan."

Hura's hand plowed through her tangled hair. "You sure?"

His head bobbed. "Ya."

"Tell me, how did the Turks get so powerful so fast? I thought the Spanish controlled them in the Mediterranean."

"They tried, but can't," Kleinatz said. "The whole world balance of power has changed over the last year. While the Portuguese easily established presidios on your Atlantic coast, they were checked by the Spanish. And King Fernando tried to protect Christian shipping by conquering the Barbary pirate bases of Oran and Bougie. But the Turkish cavalry of Suleiman keeps sweeping westward toward us. He vowed to make Spain Muslim again, and Tetouan, um, Martil, is the best launching port. He gave those pirates – the Barbarossa brothers – Letters of Marque.

Aruj Barbarossa tried to retake Bougie; the youngest brother, Khair, now commands the Turkish fleet at Algiers."

Hura thought for a moment. It was obvious she could not call for a jihad like her father had, nor could she summon six thousand tribesmen to Tetouan's defense.

Kleinatz and Hisham waited.

"I'm not going to sit here like a dove. I'm going to the hunter, to Barbarossa in Algiers. I'll join with this Khair."

Kleinatz looked aghast at the Captain. They both protested at once. "These men are cutthroats," Hisham said. "They don't respect women. They'd just as soon slit your throat," said Kleinatz. "That's madness!"

Hura brushed aside their protests. "I'll send Suha to Fes for safety. Professor, you always wanted to go to the Imperial City. Please grant me this favor. Be my emissary. Take Suha there. I'll give you a letter for Ibrahim, he'll take care of her."

The Professor stared at her, amazed that she really meant what she said. "I don't agree with your plan."

Hura gave him a hard look. "Tell me, Professor, I heard that you were thinking of leaving. Where were you going? Perhaps to Fes?"

He put his pipe down. "I decided things were getting too . . . ah . . . complicated here in Tetouan and we planned to move to a place on the coast near Al Hoceima. I miss the sea. I guess it's my Dutch ancestry. My friend has family with a villa there."

"But you can't! It's right in the path of the Barbarossa. Go to Fes, take Suha, and you'll be safe."

"Mistress Hura," the Captain intervened, "I'll take Suha to Fes."

"No, Captain. I need you here to keep order in Tetouan when I'm gone."

Hura and the Captain watched Kleinatz light another plug of kif.

Hura tried again: "Nicholas Kleinatz, I'm begging you. Please take my daughter to Fes. You'll have a full escort and I'll pay all expenses. You can go with your friend and then do whatever you want."

"I'll think about it."

Late at night when the house was still, Hura crept down the stairs and silently crossed the patio to the fountain. She gazed down at the ceramic tile that marked the tiny grave of her son, drew a deep breath that failed to quell the pang in her heart, and continued to the door. She slipped by the guard station and noticed the soldier was asleep. Some security, she said to herself.

She drew her dark burnoose tightly around her and headed straight to the cemetery above the city. A half-moon lit the area; the trees and markers cast grotesque shadows on the ground. Her shadow wound its way to the eastern edge where a large tree stood. There, ahead of her, she saw the square marker. As she fell to her knees beside it, she could barely make out the name painted on it: 'Abu Hassan'.

Where do I start? She sighed. She wanted her father and the wisdom of the Professor, but one was dead and the other on his way to Fes. She wanted Habib. In the semi-darkness, she began to pray.

Footsteps startled her. They approached, came closer, from behind. She grasped the handle of her dagger, strained to see the figure walking toward her. She unsheathed her knife, holding it close under her cloak. It was a tall man. She sprang to her feet to face him.

"Who's there!"

"Sshh. Not so loud," a familiar voice answered.

"Habib! It's you!"

"Sshh. I followed you. As soon as I knew you were back, I waited at night hoping you'd come to me. And when you didn't, I decided to go to the compound myself. I saw you leave. You have a night guard who sleeps all the time. What are you doing here?"

Hura dropped the dagger and rushed into his arms.

"Habib, how I've missed you. Everything is going so wrong."

He held her trembling body. For an instant he thought how fitting, here in the cemetery, to tell her about the play, her letter and the dead burglar.

Instead, he said: "Sshh. Come back with me, to my place."

She opened her mouth to respond but he placed a finger on her lips. "Later." He put his arm around her and drew her away from the grave. They walked through the dark, deserted cemetery.

Hura wanted so much to go to his quarters, to be comforted by him, to be loved by him. But near the entrance, she stopped. "No."

"Now tell me what's wrong."

Tears welled in her eyes. "I don't know where to start . . . my husband . . . Mandari's dead. That was his grave . . . where you found me."

Habib pulled her close again and held her tight.

Her voice muffled, she continued. "It will be announced tomorrow at the mosque. He died three weeks ago but they kept it secret until I returned. I've sent Suha to Fes. I'm confused . . . I'm free, but I feel like I'm in chains . . . I should be happy but I'm frightened. And the Turks are coming . . . and your baby. I . . . I lost your baby."

Habib's sucked in his breath.

"Yes. You didn't know, did you. I couldn't have your child. Do you understand?"

Habib held her shoulders, looked into her eyes. "How could I know? *My* child?"

She stood only a foot away from him, her hands clasped tightly together in front of her. The silence between them was vast.

Habib took another deep breath. "I want to marry you. You once asked *me,* do you remember? I couldn't then. Will you marry me now?"

Tears blurred Hura's eyesight. "Habib . . . my love. I want to; I will."

Habib grabbed Hura around the waist, lifted and swung her in a circle. Then he kissed her. Her lips responded, then they hardened. She broke away and whispered against his shoulder, "First, I must leave Tetouan and go to the pirate, Barbarossa."

THIRTY ONE

By the fifth day of her return, Hura had slapped Afaf for spilling a pot of tea, had driven Captain Hisham into hiding from her wrath, and as for Habib . . . his face continued to darken. Tense and uncertain, she put on a brave, strong face in Council meetings. Mandari's advisors seemed to respect her sovereignty, but would that last after his official mourning period was over?

Enough. Let her personal problems wait. She would face her challenge head on.

Early the next day, the crisp air reddened Hura's cheeks. She raised her head to the sky, delighted to be riding Sacony through the lower reaches of the mountains. Tarek led, and behind her galloped Habib; each more dour looking than the other: Tarek angry he couldn't talk her out of this insane quest, Habib determined she shouldn't go alone.

Habib was costumed in an ill-fitting Andalusian Captain's robe and sword that he had purchased from a widow in the lower city. Tarek was . . . Tarek. A middle aged seaman with a huge seldom-used cutlass. Hura wore her late husband's clothing, cape and scimitar.

"The baraka is with me," she responded to their protests when they mounted up outside the compound. Dark auburn hair peeked out from under Mandari's large turban. His cloak and shirt fit. The too-short pantaloons ended in high boots. The heavy scimitar made her lean to the left. Her half-spear was at hand, slung from the saddle. She worried about her disguise. She had stained her pale face with boiled bark, covering her tattoo as best she could, and bound her mature breasts. She did everything she could think of to pass as a young lord.

The Professor, Hisham, and Tarek had plotted the route with care: not so far up into the low hills as to encroach on tribal holdings or bandit turf, not so close to cliffs and beaches as to be challenged by Spanish forts. They traveled light. No tent. No servants. Only saddlebags with bread, fruit and salted fish. Water would be plentiful from the many streams along the way.

Midday, still traveling in silence, the trio penetrated a wilderness of sparse vegetation amidst rocky outcrops, where Sacony's hooves startled a herd of wild goats. Hura surprised her companions and whooped after the animals with the thrill of the chase. She leaned over Sacony's neck, urging him in pursuit. With the reins in the left hand, she drew her half-spear. As she cocked her arm, the wily goats leaped over the rock-strewn ground. Sacony slipped and stumbled. Hura jumped out of the saddle and ran after the last animal shouting: "You'll be dinner tonight!" The range was long, and though the goat swerved erratically, her arm whipped the iron-tipped spear in a whistling arc that pierced the animal between its ribs.

That evening, they sat on saddle blankets around a small fire crackling with fat under a star pocked sky, sated with grilled goat. Even so, Habib remained bitter and sullen, like a rebuffed lover. He now understood her consuming passion was Tetouan; she could spare little for him.

For her part, the conspiracy of the port disturbed her. "I know Boabdil was involved, but can't prove it," she said to Habib. "The court of Granada may have thought him a pompous braggart, but Boabdil was a King. Somehow he maintained his power."

Habib shrugged. "In the end, he didn't. That King of Granada was Ferdinand's dupe and he had little loyalty from the court or family."

"How do you know?" asked Tarek.

Habib stretched out on his back with his hands behind his head. "Boabdil is cruel and treacherous. He falsely accused his queen, his first wife. He said she was unfaithful. He locked her up in a tower with one small grated window."

Remembering her own small prison window, Hura began to breathe rapidly.

Habib sat up and faced her, only to lie back again. He decided against telling her about his meeting with Boabdil. Instead, he added: "This King is dangerous. He kills even those he loves. Be careful of him."

"What do you mean?"

Habib shifted on his blanket. "I wasn't there of course, but one morning shortly after, I did see the blood. It was on the tile floor of the Court of Lions. In the al-Hamra. That's where he murdered his sister and her two children . . . in full view of the Court. First, he stabbed her two young ones. As they sat at his feet. Then Boabdil grabbed his sister, held her bent over the fountain and watched the blood spurt as she was beheaded."

Two uneventful days later, after skirting the coastal cities of Spanish Melilla and Turkish Oran, Hura rode to a ridge and looked down on the city of Algiers. The Professor's map was accurate. She had expected it to be. Habib, acting peculiar again, began to sing an Andalusian battle song he had learned in the tavern at Salé. He stopped only when Tarek rode alongside him and, with a surly look, kicked his foot out of the stirrup.

On closer inspection, wall-encircled Algiers appeared more like a village than a city. No more than three or four hundred souls could live inside. As Hura proceeded toward the crude gate, Tarek convinced her to change course and go first to the harbor.

Approaching the port from the west, Tarek drew his horse up sharply. "So this is the famous harbor of Algiers."

Hura saw disappointment in his face. The site belied its reputed importance. Although small fishing craft plied the bay, she saw no large vessels – certainly not any pirate ships. Worse, on the island of Peñon offshore, a high-walled fort bristled with cannon. Hura turned away. With a heart heavier than Mandari's scimitar she said, "Let's see if there really are pirates in this village. Tarek, find us a tavern."

Once inside the gate, the clamor coming from a nearby shack identified a tavern. Tarek pushed open the door. Hura followed, eyes stinging from the dense smoke. She gasped from the assault of rancid meat and the fumes of sour wine. Tarek swaggered past tables of seamen; some of the men were playing cards, others were slumped down, faces flat on their tables. He threaded his way to a table in the far corner where six men sat, their backs to the wall. Tarek eyed them. "Anyone Khair Barbarossa?"

From the doorway, Hura heard the loud guffaws. A small man with a white scar showing through his black beard scowled and said, "I'm Sinan the Jew. Only Christians call him Barbarossa. To Muslims he's Khair ed-Din."

The thickset man next to Sinan growled, "Who wants to know?"

Tarek jerked his head toward his companions at the door. "We come from Tetouan. We have a letter from the Emir for Khair ed-Din."

The pirate's hand slapped the table. "See? Our fame spreads. Some Emir wrote me from Tetouan. I'll take it." He stuck out his hand for the letter.

At Tarek's wave, Hura and Habib joined him at the table and stood waiting. Tarek cleared his throat loudly. One of the pirates grabbed stools from a nearby table. While they waited, Hura studied the man who appeared to be the leader. Sturdy and big in stature, he had an impressive bearing. She had never seen anyone so hairy. Hispid brows and eyelashes jutted from a sunblackened face; his beard a bush, and every hair a bright orange-red.

Seated, Habib introduced himself and Tarek then pointed to Hura, "He's Ibrahim, eldest son of Emir bin Rachid of Tetouan."

The redheaded one remained expressionless. Either he was deaf or he had no idea who this foreign Emir was.

Without a word, Hura pulled the folded kidskin from her shirt and laid it on the table. She hoped Mandari's seal looked enough like her father's for this deception.

She watched this redbeard's thick fingers break the seal and stare at the script. Neither his eyes nor his lips moved.

253

Hura stilled her body's tremor, leaned back, hands on the table.

Habib smoothly removed the letter from the pirate's hands. "The Emir's scribe does tend to overdo things. The script is more artistic than readable. I've seen this already, so it will be easier for me." Then he read it aloud.

The other pirates bent closer to better hear the proposal. When Habib finished, Khair grabbed the letter, stuffed it in his sash alongside his three-pointed dagger and leaned against the wall. He eyed the two young strangers.

Hura covered her chin with her hand and pretended to cough. He looked like he was sizing them up for a fight. Instead, he looked straight at Hura and asked, "What's your father Emir of?"

There was no way to avoid an answer. Hura spoke in as deep a voice as she could muster. "All the lands and Berbers of the Maghrib. From the Pillars of Hercules to the Rif, including the cities of Chaouen and Tetouan, both much larger than this place." She sniffed, pretending disdain. "What should interest you is our deep water port at the Martil River. It would make a better base than this for fighting infidel warships."

Khair's lips curled in a sneer over his mug as he rocked back and forth on his stool. "Why do I need you?"

Hura said nothing.

"I'm almost an Admiral now. The new Sultan in Stambul, Suleiman the Magnificent, he made me his privateer, wants to make the eastern Mediterranean an Ottoman sea. Now you say your father wants me to do the western sea too?" He winked at his companions. "So now I could rule this whole Mediterranean and its seacoast?"

There was a long pause. "Berbers, you say. That must be why it's called the Barbary Coast. His guffaw became a slash of white in a red flame.

His men snickered with him. Even Sinan.

Just as quickly he sobered, slammed down his mug. "We're privateers, not saviors. We want booty. And more boats to do the job. Am I right your father's got none?"

Hura still made no reply.

"So I'm to commit my men and galliots on credit?" He thundered. "You take me for a fool?"

That same question had been raised by the Professor when he wrote the letter for Hura. She knew that Ibrahim would forgive her the use of his name on this pact, because Tetouan needed these pirates. But her father would never have forgiven her using his name as guarantor of payment. She spoke slowly and carefully. "It is I who give you the Marque of Privateer to the Berbers. I also promise that you will have a tenth of all the Spanish and Portuguese booty you capture. From Algiers west to the Pillars of Hercules."

Redbeard's laugh was more derisive than before. "I'm Privateer to a Sultan. The Ottoman Sultan. He gives me many more honors." He drained his mug and looked at his men. They all knew that Suleiman had not made him Admiral yet, nor given money for even one galliot. "Half," he demanded.

"A fifth." Before he could say no, Hura added, "I will use my share to pay for your fleet, and my customs duties to pay Turkish Janissaries to protect the port itself."

Redbeard glanced around the table. The gleam in five pairs of eyes met his. "We'll go to this port of the Emir," he declared. "I'll see if it suits me. Tomorrow afternoon come to my boat. East on the bay."

The pirate anchorage was easy to find. Hura and her companions walked alongside a noisy stream of porters and donkeys who pulled small carts laden with barrels of fresh water and cured lamb, casks of wine and stoneware jars of small black olives – enough provisions for 400 or more men. In front of them, near the gangplank, two carts packed with shot and heavy sacks of gunpowder moved not at all. Their donkeys sat with hindquarters on the ground, and beatings and curses only made the animals bray louder without movement. Ahead, ships crews separated the stores and transferred provisions to three vessels.

Hura worried with each step she took.

Was her bold venture in vain? Did she leave her city in its precarious state for this? Would Barbarossa really go to Tetouan with her? She had come to him fearing assault, humiliation, or even death. What of all those stories she heard: Barbarossa did this, Barbarossa did that. And now? This was no grand fleet in front of her. And he looked like a jester with all that red, wiry hair and his gold-embroidered blue vest, bulbous turban and baggy crimson pantaloons. Had she given away her Marque to a braggart, one with a false reputation? Where were the dreaded ocean-going ships whose pirate flags struck terror in the Mediterranean? All she saw were four single masted vessels careened on their sides and, floating in the bay, one two masted vessel whose white-crescented red flag flapped from the taller mast.

But Tarek seemed to think differently. The more enthusiastic he became the more her anger mounted. She watched him hurry ahead, walk the length of one of the boats whose crew still scrubbed and scraped its smooth hull. "No barnacles," he told her when she joined him. "Not even slime. And count the oars, seventeen each side. These corsairs are skimmers. They'll do seven, eight knots, easy." The galley offshore was just as sleek looking to Tarek. He guessed her length was three times his felucca with low freeboard and twenty-four oars to a side. From her waist hung a five-rung rope ladder.

When the borrowed skiff bumped the two masted galley's planking, Habib made to climb first. Hura gave him an elbow in the ribs and, hand over hand, climbed aboard ahead of him. Sinan half nodded to the arrivals but continued shouting orders at several crewmen stowing stores below. When Hura asked about quarters, he acknowledged her with a grunt and jerked his thumb toward the aft half-deck. Hura entered the Captain's cabin where Khair and four men from the tavern crowded around a table covered by a sheaf of charts. Habib, close behind, ducked his head and stayed under the low doorway while Tarek, behind him, breathed on his neck.

Khair's flash of anger at the intrusion changed to a grunt of tolerance for his new found patron. "Welcome aboard the *Scorpion*. My spies checked you out. Looks like we'll be headin' to Martil."

Hura took a step forward, and Habib squeezed into the room behind her.

"Meet my captains. There's none you'll find better. This here is the Turk, Rais Saleh. He can pick a captured vessel clean as a plucked chicken in less time than it takes to pray. That Rais rollin' up the charts is Mahjoub. He thinks his men row faster than mine. We'll see, next battle. I've bet him a cask of the best Spanish brandy." The two exchanged mock glares.

"That one-eyed'un is Rais Dragut. We're both Greek, but he's born Muslim. Me? I was born Kheyr ibn Yakub but baptized Khair, a Christian. He's a born raider who can spot Spanish warships further away than anyone. Over here is Rais Aydin, another converted Christian. Know why the Spanish call him 'Drub-devil'? I'll tell ya."

Redbeard put his pipe on the now bare planks that served as his utility table and, using his hands to illustrate the position of opposing vessels for his new audience, boasted of his first naval victory. "Last year that jackass Admiral Don Hugo de Moncada came at me with fifty square rigged ships. Had a huge army of mercenaries too. Can you believe he was gunna steal Algiers from me? Well, the Sultan in Stambul had just made me Beglerbeg of Algiers. Governor-general."

The men around him stamped their feet in approval.

"That was after the Spanish killed my brother Aruj. See? After that, this Admiral would only get Algiers over my dead body. Well, these pig-eaters came at me lined abreast." The spread fingers of his right hand slapped the plank in front of him. "Like all them Europeans, the misbegotten bastards thought they was fightin' a land war. So I rowed west, windward around their flank." His forefinger shot to the left. "Aydin took his galliots east and around." The little finger pointed right. "Well," he tugged at his beard, "you know their cannon only fire forward. So not one broadside hit us. We boarded and cut that fleet to pieces. I had to stop Drub-devil from killing all them Spaniards. He wasn't leavin' any to ransom!"

Laughter erupted in the small cabin.

Hura felt an appreciative comment was necessary. "I'm glad he's going to escort us to Tetouan."

"Him? He's not goin'," Khair scowled. "He and Saleh, they'll stay here. In case a merchantmen comes along."

Hura refrained from mentioning the Spanish flag still flew over Penôn, a short distance away, and wondered if Tarek was thinking the same thing. Here in this tight cabin, the atmosphere had become jovial. Hura wondered again if she had trusted her welfare to a bunch of useless braggarts.

"Now we drink to our success before Dragut and Mahjoub return to their vessels." Redbeard bent to the cupboard below his bunk, pulled out a jug of brandy and several mugs with gold crests. He held one up to Hura's face, "Gift of Pope Julius II," then he filled the mugs. "My brother and me, we captured two of his war galleys. Bound from Genoa to Civita they was. Captain Paolo Victor didn't expect no trouble from our small galliot. We boarded before he fired a shot!" He roared with laughter while the men around him gulped their brandy.

Khair slapped his thigh and quaffed a refill. "Then we changed clothes with the crew, took our galliot in tow. When the second war galley came alongside to ask *us* what happened, we boarded her too!" Khair's glance saw he had his passengers impressed. "Soon we had both crews at the oars and rowin' back to Tunis."

Redbeard and his Captains must have laughed over this story a hundred times before but they seemed to enjoy it now as much as the first time. Impressed, Hura began to hope her decision to come here was a wise one. She leaned against Habib's shoulder, breathed in his ear above the din: "Did you hear all that? These are real pirates, not like that Nabil and his Salé crew."

Khair gulped down the last of the fiery liquid in his mug, wiped his dripping beard and charged his men: "All right, back to your boats. We sail with the morning tide for the glory of the Sultan and the booty of the sea."

"Aye, Khair." By their knowing grins, Hura knew he said that every sailing.

As she moved aside to let them by, she said, "Captain, will you show me your ship?"

"Tomorrow." He said curtly while buckling on his cutlass. "When we're under way. And don't go wanderin' round. I never had no passengers before. And you ain't no paying passengers."

Hura retreated with Habib and Tarek to the deck overlooking the wharf. She held tight to the railing, then grabbed both men's arms. "I will go alone. You two ride back. I'll see you in Tetouan."

Immediately Habib thought of Bridget, of leaving Bridget to that Count.

He couldn't let Hura be alone with Barbarossa. He had to go with her. Even if it meant going to sea again. She was mad to think she would be safe with that pirate. Even in disguise, she wasn't safe.

Outraged, Tarek faced her, put his hand on her shoulder. "I'm a sailor, not cavalry. Besides, you might need me shipboard. You know nothin' about the sea."

Hura tried to back away. "Nothing can go wrong. I'm safe as the Emir's son. Go soon. And don't stop at every tavern."

"You can't go alone, Tarek insisted.

Habib pried Tarek's hand from her shoulder. "I can't let you go alone. Don't ask me to."

She looked back and forth between the two men's faces.

"All right." Hura decided. "Tarek, you return with the horses.

I'll be safe with Habib."

THIRTY TWO

Habib, hammock in hand, followed Hura into the poorly lit, windowless cabin. He stood, head alongside the hanging lantern and watched her sit on the hard, narrow bunk then pull off her boots. They looked at each other. Neither said a word. He threw the hammock in a corner, saw Sinan's spare trousers hanging from a hook on the wall. Two large cutlasses hung from nails nearby. Habib studied the weapons. On the trail, Tarek had motioned to Habib's dress sword then pointed to his own cutlass.

"Know how to use this?"

"No," he had admitted.

Now, he took both weapons off the wall. One in each hand, Habib tried experimental chops. He examined them. Both blades were sharp and wiped clean; one had dark stains at the hilt. He shook his head – too heavy, not for him. It took brute strength to slash, hack or chop. He'd rather parry and thrust. He hung them back in their place and leaned his dress sword against the wall. Maybe he wouldn't need it.

Hura, bent over beneath the overhead beam, had watched all this in silence. That's the way he had been: moody, strange, unpredictable since their last embrace in Tetouan. She thought God was punishing her for killing his baby. But what could I have done? What choice did I have? Does he think my baby meant nothing to me? It was either that or humiliate and dishonor my husband. I would have been stoned. Just like that woman outside Fes. Habib said he wanted to marry me, and now he can, but I can't. His religion allows it; but mine doesn't. No, I know that's not really the reason. I can't until I know that Tetouan is safe. He doesn't understand that. I prayed we would be together again. But why always in boats?

Hura swung her legs onto the bunk and lay on her back. She stared at a small roach scuttling across the beamed ceiling. That's the way it is, but why does he say so little. Why can't he come to me, kiss me? The lamplight created a shadow of her body on the planked hull as she contorted herself under the coverlet. She struggled to remove her pantaloons and shirt, and threw them on the floor. When she leaned forward to unfasten her chest bindings, a breast popped out. She pulled the thin coverlet to her chin and lay still but aware of the scent of male body.

Habib squirmed on the stool beside the wall and watched Hura. Showing her breast isn't going to make me change my mind. No, by God.

There'll be no more crazy ideas like this that could get us killed . . . get me killed . . . get a Yeshiva Bohar killed by a bunch of Muslim pirates. Play acting, wearing swords, all that is going too far, Habib looked at the pile of clothing on the floor. Let her be the brave one. Redbeard's going to find out about her. Then what. Throw her overboard is what. Yes, that's the way this affair will end.

Hura's arm dangled over the edge of the bunk. Her small hand was clenched, the knuckles shone white. Habib moved to sit on the floor with his back to the bunk and took her fist in his hand. In silence he pried her fist open and intertwined his fingers with hers.

Hura's other hand slid up his neck and into his thick hair. Her lips curled in a grin as she grasped a handful and yanked.

"OW!" Habib whirled around, expelled a heavy breath, and began pulling off his boots. Hura sat up to help unfasten his shirt.

"Ouch!" Her head bashed the beam above. She reached for him as he threw off the coverlet and, with one foot still on the floor, slid into her.

At first, their movements were slow and the sounds were soft: her murmurs, his kisses and the sucking of nipples. Soon her hands pressed his buttocks downward, urged him faster. She wrapped her legs around his back and arched her body to meet his, oblivious when her knee scraped the rough hull planking. With his last thrust, her body collapsed in joy. A loud snort and a drawn-out gurgling snore from the next cabin made her giggle. In the future, she must remember how thin the walls were.

The rolling of the vessel jostled Habib awake and onto the floor. He grimaced at the ache in each joint and twisted his head to look up at Hura. Rubbing his stiff neck, he saw her watching him with a bemused grin. He began to rise. "OW!" He rubbed his head. "That's the third time."

She was still laughing when he tumbled on her, flattened her on the hard bunk until she cried for mercy.

Later on deck, both surveyed the scene. Under a half-covered sky the late autumn breeze behind had freshened and bellied the sails. The two smaller vessels astern followed several ship's length apart.

Rais Sinan and Khair had their heads together. I bet they're talking about me, Hura thought and approached them.

"Captain, I remind you of your promise."

For only a moment, his hard eyes remained inscrutable. After a quick look at course and sails to ensure all was in order, he grunted, "Admiral Khair always keeps his promises. Not much to see here at the stern. That's a twelve-pounder pointed aft. So's the one you see at the bow. Both bronze. Taken from a galleon out of Venice. Let's go fore'ad."

Hura and Habib followed on the narrow latticed wood grating that ran the length of the galleon from the half-deck to the forecastle. Athwartships, crewmen, their oars shipped out of holes in the wales, gazed curiously at the passengers. Then, at a bosun's shout, resumed sharpening scimitars. Hura noticed the rowers at each bench wore no chains. She wondered if these men were slaves.

As if reading her mind, Redbeard bellowed: "Turks, every blessed cutthroat. No slaves on my ships. Why would a slave fight for me? Sit on their oars, they would. Besides, I'd have to carry and feed marines."

Hura admired his logic.

Habib noticed the Turks were fully clothed in turban and pantaloons; he had never seen more villainous looking seamen. After counting 144 at the benches, he wondered how so few seamen could capture so many large sailing ships. Or were the stories of Khair's exploits just that – stories.

On the low short-decked forecastle, the bow-chaser was set high along the center line for a clear field of fire. "How do you use this cannon?" Hura asked looking at its carriage and ropes to the hull that held it in place.

"Pack'em with ball and chain. Tears away rigging. Takes the fight out of a pig-eating captain." He spat on the deck as if to cleanse his mouth of the infidel.

Habib asked: "What is this platform over the cannon for?"

Khair answered, "Main deck's too low. This high one's our boarding platform. Climb up. I'll show you the beakhead."

Hura and Habib cautiously peered downward over the bow to see the long battering ram at the waterline. Where it emerged from the hull the hardwood was as thick around as Redbeard's chest.

"Fastened to the keel," Redbeard joined them. "This one's holed many a hull."

Habib eyed the endless swells uneasily as the ship cut through the water. He would never feel comfortable on the sea. He could see no land in sight. "You're not hugging the shore. The Salé pirates never went far from their shoals and reefs."

"How do you think I raided Mallorca, Italy, Sicily, all the Greek islands? And sailed at night too. Khair spat over the side. Well, since we're partners now, I'll show you." He disappeared, leaving them at the rail. Hura noticed he was even more bowlegged than Tarek, then congratulated herself on her instincts – and on her orders to send him back. She could see she would be safe with this pirate.

Soon Redbeard emerged from his cabin and strode toward them, beaming with pride and holding a thick brass disk. "Bet you a hundred dinars there ain't but two or three of these 'star-takers' on all the seas. Got her off a Mallorcan pilot. He didn't have no further need. Ha hahahah."

"Can I see it?" Hura asked.

"Drop it an' I'll have your head." He held out the disk but it remained attached to his thumb by a ring at the top.

The astrolabe had a long pointer, pivoted in the center and with upright tabs at each end. She noticed the upper rim of the disc was marked off in numbers from zero to ninety at each side of the swivel point.

Habib was fascinated. The engraved number of degrees, signs and notations made it look like a large, ornate piece of jewelry. "How does it work?"

Like a child with a favorite toy, Redbeard explained: "You shoot the sun or the North Star. You hold it straight up like this – keep it from rolling too much with the ship. Turn the pointer to the sky until the beam of light passes through the pinhole in the upper tab into the hole in the lower one. Then you reads the angle above the horizon on the scale. Simple.

"But how does it actually tell you where you are?" Hura asked.

"Pilot's table converts it to degree of latitude."

Habib leaned to Hura and whispered, "Poor pilot. Probably was tortured to teach him that."

A light shower began. Rais Khair had ordered there would be no cooking on his ships. No fires. Hura and Habib ate a meager, salty lunch of pressed goats milk cakes and olive oil in their cabin.

Habib had been reserved all morning and Hura wondered if the memory of his shipwreck haunted him again. Determined to change his attitude, she shot a seductive glance at him. The look that sparked between them was enough. Clothes were hastily tossed in a heap on the floor; Hura's hair tumbled down. Each took from the other until all hunger was satiated.

Later, back on deck, the rain had stopped. The lovers approached Redbeard and Sinan at the wheel. As Redbeard casually glanced at Hura, his jaw dropped, his face colored to match his beard. He roared: "A woman! A damned woman on my ship!"

Hura froze. Habib's eyebrows rose. Redbeard was staring at the front of her shirt. He leaned over and whispered: "You forgot to bind your breasts." She looked down, saw her nipples outlined through the thin cloth.

Khair rushed across the deck at her, fist upraised. Habib stepped between them. Redbeard's arm suddenly dropped. He clutched his belly and rocked with laughter. Gasping for breath he said, "A woman who wants to be a Pirate Queen! By Allah, you had me fooled." Then just as suddenly he checked himself. "So who are you . . . and . . . what about our agreement?"

Hura collected her wits. Her voice changed but was no less imperious. "I'm Lady Hura bin Rachid. Ibrahim's sister. *I* rule. *I* wrote the letter. *I* will keep my promises. If *you* keep yours."

Khair had survived by his ability to make quick decisions. And his nature was never to look back or retreat. He turned to Sinan at the wheel, whose contorted face blazed hatred. "Not a word of this to the crew. And you don't need to tell me a woman on board is bad luck. I'm not superstitious and you damned well better not be. As for you," he snapped at Hura, "get to the cabin and strap yourself together."

That black night a gale tossed the *Scorpion* further out to sea. Tarek had warned that it was the end of the summer sailing season and to expect bad weather. Habib rose from the bed struggling to keep steady and dress. Sweat filmed his body and remembering the Pillars of Hercules, he swallowed frequently. By the light of the swinging lantern, he saw that Hura lay with her eyes closed, her hands clutching the bunk. Her lips moved but he heard only the shriek of wind in the rigging above and the pounding of waves on the hull alongside. He wondered what she was saying.

He lurched on deck. Instantly a sheet of salt spray stung his body. The tilt of the deck heeled before the wind carried him to the waist-high wale. He grasped its edge. With every roll of the narrow beamed galley, water poured through the scuppers and swirled around his legs. He leaned over the wale. The howling wind blew vomit back over his face. Blinded, he clung to the shrouds and stood there until the rain washed him clean. Hersh prayed to Yehuda to save him once more – to save him from the sea.

By morning, the sky had cleared. Hura appeared fresh-faced and, as Habib sourly noted, with a bright smile for everyone. She glanced at the oarsmen and the two galliots parallel in the distance before approaching Khair who was still at the wheel with Sinan and the helmsman.

Oblivious to his haggard look and salt-encrusted red beard, she asked, "Where are we?"

Sinan ignored her and shouted to the crew, "Stand by to go about."

Hura backed out of the way as the helmsman spun the wheel. With several pirates pulling at the rigging, the long yards overhead swiveled around the fore and main masts and the sails swept across the deck. The galley leaned to port, turned to a new tack.

Hura approached Khair again and in a louder voice asked, "Admiral, where are we?"

He rubbed his eyes. "Course was northwest but the gale was from the northeast. Damn gusts came from every quarter. Now we got a headwind. We're north of Sebta."

"Can't you use your brass disk?"

"Can't use the astrolabe. Too much roll for an accurate sighting and it don't tell longitude."

Habib leaned against the wale. With his arms crossed, he listened with increased apprehension to the conversation. It would be some time before they found land.

"Sail Ho!" A voice blared from above.

Khair cupped his hands to his mouth, shouted against the wind to the lookout atop the mainmast, "Where away?"

"Starboard . . . two more!"

Khair squinted against the glare of the sun on the water. "Merchantmen? Convoy?"

The wind gave an eerie pitch to the response. Habib cupped his hand to his ear.

"Can't tell . . . square rigged."

Khair shouted to Sinan, "Order formation flags run up."

Hura joined Habib at the starboard wale. Both tried to make out the vessels approaching on parallel but opposing courses. When Hura looked back to see what Khair was doing, she saw him emerge from his cabin wearing a blood red turban and a coat of mail. On a thick woven fabric were sewn horizontal rows of iron rings; it looked odd over his pantaloons. A cutlass dangled at his side.

High above, the lookout hung on with one hand, leaned toward the deck and shouted, "Warships! Two galleys and a galleon. The galleon's got a high castle over the sternpost."

"Hah! Cross-kissing Christians." Redbeard's face lit up in anticipation.

"How can you tell?" asked Hura.

"I can tell, that's how!"

Habib mustered a grin for Hura, went to their cabin and soon returned holding his sword by the pommel. He jabbed the deck with the weapon like it was a walking stick, oblivious to the line of holes that appeared in his wake. Confident, he said to Hura, "Don't worry. Redbeard will make a run for it. He knows how lightly armed his galliots are."

Hura's eyes shone in concern. "Not this Madman. Suleiman's pirate won't run away while a woman is watching."

"A queen could order him to turn away. He won't dare risk your life."

Hura snapped, "A queen doesn't run, either." Leaving Habib at the rail, she returned to Redbeard.

Khair had figured the relative position of the other ships, had estimated the speed and that of the wind. He jabbed Sinan in the ribs. "See that? That commander moved his three ships into close formation. A straight line. Some dung-head thinks he's leading a cavalry charge."

Sinan nodded, "Must be Spanish or Portuguese. Allah keeps them stupid."

By now, Hura could see the long peñon streaming from the largest ship's mast and the huge red Maltese cross on her mainsail.

"Order halyard flags up for Dragut and Mahjoub to alter course. Flank

264

attack. Tell the helmsman to steer for that galleon." He turned away, saw Hura behind him. "As for you, go below. And stay there."

Hura's chin jutted. "I can take care of – "

Boom! Out of the puff of black smoke from the galleon she saw the huge cannon ball soar in a high arc and splash down three ship-lengths off the starboard bow.

"Twenty-four pounder," Khair muttered to himself, judging the range. He jumped to the main deck, strode the grating and, gauging the long paddles of the oars as they dipped in unison, ordered the oarmaster: "Speed the drumbeat. We'll ram her."

The pirates bent to their oars and cheered him as he walked past. Each rower had battle gear close at hand; each eager for his share of captured booty.

She did not see the incoming ball but heard it whoosh through the rigging and raise a fountain of water harmlessly behind. All the ships were moving so fast now and everything was happening at once. She saw Dragut's and Mahjoub's galleys circle to windward behind their opponent galleys. Like pincers they came together, bow facing bow, large triangular sails blanketing square ones caught windless a-lee, sails flapping from yards. Without amidships cannon with which to retaliate, the Portuguese became unmoving close-range targets for Redbeard's Turkish bowmen. Horrified, Hura watched their volleys of 'Greek Fire'. Flights of arrows flaming with resin, pitch and oil of naphtha blackened the galley's sails then burst into a raging blaze. Across the water she heard the agonized shrieks of seamen and saw them, clothing afire, jump overboard.

By now both formations had dissolved. The large 400 ton galleon's aft cannon fired and in an instant Mahjoub's mainmast shattered and his sleek galley became a wreck. Without pause, the Portuguese galleon ploughed onward. Hura saw the distance was closing.

The galleon's heavy-bore forward firing cannon ran out until their long muzzles projected through gaps in the gunwales. Flame erupted though a billow of smoke and a moment later came the roar of thunder. At the same time archers, high up the swooping forecastle, loosed bolts from their crossbows. But the command to fire came too late. The wind-blown galleon plunged downward on a wave crest. The shot fell short, raising a spray that soaked Hura. Only four of the archers' bolts studded the half deck but another whizzed by, nicking blood from her ear before embedding itself in the mainmast. Hura looked indignantly at the blood splatter on her shirt.

Sinan laughed; she glared at him, yanked the bolt free and showed it to Habib. It looked like a long dart with a pointed iron nose. The butt end had no notch.

Habib pointed with his sword and said, "I'm going to join Redbeard."

Hura held his arm, "Stay here Habib. Stay with me, please." A wild look enlarged her eyes.

Habib shook his arm free. "You'll be all right here in the back of the galley with Sinan."

"That's not what I meant."

"I know." His lips brushed her cheek.

Hura watched that lean body she knew so well and loved so fiercely swagger forward. He knows I'm watching, she thought. He's doing this for me. He thinks I want him to be a hero.

On the pirate's jammed foredeck, Barbarossa bellowed orders. Habib jostled for a small space. Now that he was here, he cursed himself. What was he, a scholar of the Talmud, thinking of? He was no fighter. In spite of himself, he was intrigued by the professional expertise and the almost casual way that Khair and his gunners performed. He admired craftsmanship in any trade.

Hustling as a team, three gunners at the bronze twelve-pounder tore open sacks, poured powder in the muzzle, rammed it home with a wad of felt or held ready the ball and chain. At the four culverins, gunners rammed down small iron balls while others stood ready to swivel the guns, aim and fire.

Habib watched, spellbound. The most dangerous task of all was performed by Khair himself. First Redbeard coolly gauged the wind, then he estimated the distance to the target and its closing speed. Next, he cut the slow-burning felt fuses to proper length and inserted them in the cannon vent holes that had already been filled with primer powder. He picked up a burning brand from the fire pot – touched the wick on the first culverin. The cord singed but failed to burn. "Damn! Wet from the rains." Khair yanked them out.

"Better pray to Allah," the cannoneer at the twelve-pounder jeered in Habib's direction as Khair inserted dry wicks. "Those iron culverin can explode. Kill us all."

Flame and screams swept both vessels. The flailing shrapnel of Khair's four culverins shredded the opposing archers who, moments ago had stood with one foot in the stirrup of their crossbows, holding them erect for reloading. A flash, a puff of smoke and Khair's bow-chaser recoiled, pulling the truck restraining ropes taut as its cast-iron cannonball tore away the galleon's sprit sail and fore-angled mast.

Habib heard the shuffling feet of the impatient bowmen stamping on the fighting platform overhead.

Khair shouted: "Fire." They launched their first flight of arrows too late. Other archers on the enemy galleon had reloaded their crossbows. A bolt struck the cannoneer in the neck. He slumped against Habib, drenching him in spurting blood. Habib stood transfixed, remembering the time he had helped his father kill a chicken for the Shabbath feast. Holding the squawking bird while the knife slit its gullet, blood had spattered his hands and a glob flew into his open mouth.

Still transfixed by the image of his father, Habib pictured the old rabbi quoting a proverb: *Never try to straighten a dog's tail. In vain you do.* His reverie snapped, he shouted, "Yes, I'm Hersh. Hersh, not Habib!" He rushed out of the smoke-filled cage and scrambled atop the forecastle platform just as the galley's armored beakhead raced to meet the galleon that was sluggishly beginning to turn aside. Whump! The long ram pierced the galleon at the cannon deck. Wood splintered. Riddled gunners screamed. The impact knocked Hersh off the platform to the main deck. He rolled aside before the *Scorpion's* oarsmen, led by the blazing red turban, ran forward with scimitars flashing. Screaming "Allahhhhh," they swarmed over the galleon like a roiling sea. Hersh wanted to lie there sheltered in the lee of the wale, out of sight of the galleon, but he heard the ring of steel on steel, the whooshing of arrows, and the curses shouted in a jumble of languages. When a one-armed body plummeted atop him, he dashed to greater safety at the stern.

Hura had retrieved her spear from her cabin and stood shaking it at the galleon. She ran to Hersh and sobbed on his shoulder: "Habib, Habib. When the attack started I thought I'd lost you."

He held her for a moment, then pushed her away. "Habib is no more. God saved me as Hersh. I am Hersh the Jew." Over Hura's shoulder he saw Sinan staring at him with new interest.

Hersh smiled at her confusion, gently touched the tattoo on her chin, then surveyed the situation. The pirate at the wheel had kept his station, holding the helm hard to starboard. That, and the beakhead and grappling irons held the two vessels together. Hersh shouted over the din: "This is no place for you. Come with me to the cabin."

"No, wait." Hura called out to Sinan, "What's happening? We've won, haven't we?"

Sinan answered, with a glance at Hersh, "Khair controls the forecastle. Their archers with crossbows didn't last long – but amidships not looking good. Too many marines, maybe two hundred."

"Lady Rachid."

Startled, Hura looked up. All eyes on the halfdeck searched for the source. Hura shivered. "I'd know that voice anywhere."

Six decks above the waterline, on the poop deck of the *Gaspar Fereirra*, stood Fernao Dias, wearing a breastplate more ornate than Khair's tunic. He leaned over the taffrail and cordially waved as though greeting a long lost friend. "Jesus has been kind to me." His right hand held a firearm.

267

On the *Scorpion* below, no one moved. Sinan swore. "He's got an arquebus. I've seen one other. Makes a big hole."

Hersh saw the sardonic smile above them harden into a grimace as the weapon swung to Hura.

"Lady Hura," Dias' voiced boomed, "my marines have control. Call off your lackey Barbarossa. I will be merciful in victory."

Hersh pushed Hura aside, ran to the shroud and began rapidly climbing hand over hand. Hura grabbed his foot. He shook her loose. She began to follow him up the shrouds.

When he reached the swivel intersection of lanteen yard and mast, he grasped the mast, straddled the upward tilted yard and twisted to see Dias. Across three arm-lengths of open water he was standing spread-legged, his aim wavering from Hura, halfway up the shrouds, back to him then to Hura again.

Hersh swayed, recovered his balance. The creaking yard began to swivel. He looked down. Sinan had pulled a belaying pin and now ran across the deck, hauling the rope attached to the yard's low end. The high end came swinging around toward the galleon. Hersh crawled higher and shouted to Sinan, "Let go."

The yard began to swing back but Hersh jumped over the open water. He heard the trigger slam the hammer down on the priming powder of Dias' gun. The arquebus misfired. Hersh sprawled on the deck a few yards away from Dias.

Hura reached the intersection of mast and yard. She held on with one hand, in the other, she grasped her spear. She saw Hersh struggle to his feet. "No. No, no," she cried. "Surrender!"

He was making a gallant but useless gesture to fight.

Dias coolly prepared to fire again. He uncovered the pan of priming powder, and trying to make it burn more brightly, blew on the serpentine hammer which held the smoldering match of lint.

Now on his feet and limping, Hersh drew his sword. With a sardonic grin, Dias tossed his gun aside and drew his heavy saber.

Hersh circled warily, attempted a feint, followed by a quick thrust.

Dias parried and laughed. With an upward stroke he knocked the light rapier from Hersh's hand, and looking at him defenseless, smirked.

Hura threw her spear.

Dias chopped sideways severing Hersh's spine above the collarbone.

As if in slow motion, Hura saw her lover's head roll around, held to his torso by a shred of tissue. His sightless eyes fixed on her for the last time.

Hura blinked, then saw Dias flat on his back, her spear pinning his body to his deck.

THIRTY THREE

Mandari's minaret jutted against the azure sky; the stone walls of Tetouan rose intact. Hura almost wished city was gone, in ruins again. Then she would have nothing left to care about.

Why did everything seem so normal? She was surprised to see it just the way she had left it. Shoppers and traders still bought and sold in the markets; the flowers bloomed; the trees were still green. The smell of roasting chickens, garlic and cumin still pervaded the souks; people still jammed the streets on their way to shop, pray and visit. How deceptive. Well-fed people have no cares. Didn't everyone know their world was different now? Too soon, they would know that she had failed, that they were in danger. The Turkish threat remained. Barbarossa had returned to Algiers cursing . . . never again would he allow a woman aboard his ship.

For now, people stopped, waved, bowed, and threw kisses as she passed by. Hura acknowledged them with a quick nod of her head, a slight flutter of her fingers. Her heart was empty. Only family dignity kept her proud on her horse. What am I going to do, she wondered. She could think of nothing else to save her city and nothing else to live for.

She remembered Tetouan as she had known it in the past: first as a stranger, delighting in its exploration, in its diversity . . . then as a student, learning its cultures, its needs; later as a participant in its rebuilding . . . finally as a leader planning its future. Now she had no future. She was alone. Gone was her husband, the respected Fundador mourned by her city; gone was Habib, the man she loved. Even her daughter and the Professor . . . gone. She closed her eyes and clenched her teeth thinking again of so many losses.

Arriving at last at the compound, it too, looked the same as before.

"I will see no one. I want no visitors," she informed the guards in the courtyard.

Afaf greeted her, the wide smile fading, the outstretched arms dropping. Hura tried to soften her face, failed, and pushed past.

"From now on, I want to be alone. Tomorrow, make up my husband's chambers downstairs for me. Move my things there. Put his furniture in storage and give his clothes to the poor. Ask Father Contreras if he wants anything – mementos, whatever. And tell Isabel I want my meals alone in my new chambers. I want no visitors. If someone comes, tell them to leave a message or come back. I don't want to see anyone."

Afaf nodded. "Yes, Lalla Hura," and trailed behind her mistress.

Alone in her chamber Hura washed herself, then fell on the bed. Sleep would not come. Her body twitched; her heart ached; cries of Habib's baby filled her ears; oaths of commitment filled her head; moans of remorse moved on her lips; images of Habib and her husband flashed behind her eyes. Dias' death brought no comfort.

The next day walking with Afaf to the hammam, Hura passed Habib's old apartment. Someone had freshly painted the door a light blue. A new tenant already? So soon? Must life go on? She saw no comfort in the future.

Even the hot steam of the baths failed to warm her heart; the chatter of the other women dispirited her even more.

Weeks passed and she began to see angry notices and petitions piling up on the spikes of the madressa door. Her people were becoming restless. Although she still met with her ministers for Council meetings, she had not held any court sessions or trials since her departure for Algiers. Merchants and clergy sensed that no one was in charge. Prisoners sat neglected in their cells, their families angry and appealing to the imam for resolution of their cases.

She pulled one of the notices from its spike and read:
Has the city shut down? Do we have a leader?

Each time Hura came by she saw more complaints. She yanked another small parchment from its nail. Shame burned her face as she read it:
Let the King, our King Boabdil, rule the city.
We need a leader now that Mandari is dead
- the Rachid's aren't from our people. We
aren't Berbers! Declare him ruler of Tetouan now!

No signature. None were signed. Sadness overcame her as she remembered that just last month her people had cheered her return. Now she wondered how long she could count on the loyalty of the army . . . or the imam. While the city prospered, her rule could continue. But as soon as Tetouan was in danger, her leadership would be challenged. She wished Ibrahim was there. Perhaps . . . perhaps she should ask Mohammed for help. Even if she didn't trust him, he had troops. She immediately dismissed the thought. No. I'll find a way. I just need time.

"Lalla Hura, you have a letter! Lalla Hura, please open up." Afaf banged on the door.

Hura stood before her maid and eyed the thick parcel with the bright seals and ribbons of royal office covering it. "What is this?"

"Look! It's from Fes. The messenger told me so."

Hura grabbed the packet. "I have eyes. Now leave me alone."

What could be coming from the court of Fes but bad news. Maybe Suha is ill, or there's been a palace coup, or the Professor is in trouble, or Ibrahim has . . . her hands shook as she broke the seals and unstrapped the missive. The stiff vellum unfolded to a large square that took both hands to hold.

"It's from Hamad," she breathed deeply. "Ah!" He wants to marry my daughter and requests my approval for the engagement. "Oh, my!" She gasped. "And he humbly submits to my consent and the will of Allah."

Hura turned the velum over to check the official seals again. "Oh, heavens." She repeated each word aloud as she reread: "He wants the engagement to be in two months . . . when Suha is thirteen . . . and the marriage to take place when she is fourteen."

As she read further her smile grew broader. She clasped the letter to her chest. It's happened. I know it. I have the baraka. My luck has changed. Tetouan will be safe!

She called out to Afaf who was lurking in the hallway hoping to hear what was in the letter. Afaf returned, expecting more bad news. But saw Hura, flushed with a smile, eyes twinkling.

"Afaf, I could hug you. You've brought the answer to all our prayers. The letter you brought asks for the hand of Suha from the son of a Sultan. What do you think of that?" She danced around the room waving the letter like a flag.

Afaf, often ecstatic from less exciting news, broke into a confused giggle. "You mean your daughter? Suha is going to marry a Sultan?"

"No, silly girl, the son of the former Sultan. They met last year in Chaouen at Ibrahim's wedding. The engagement will be in Fes in two months. If I approve, of course. She tossed her head and ran fingers through her hair, then began to fold the vellum.

"That's wonderful, Mistress. I'm so happy for you." But her expression flitted from grin to frown.

"It's the answer. Don't you see?" She looked into Afaf's questioning face. "Of course not, how could you. That's all right." She hugged Afaf.

"I've been waiting for this sign. Now I know how I'm going to save Tetouan."

Afaf nodded slowly as if still wondering how a daughter's wedding in far away Fes could save Tetouan.

Hura whirled around to her desk, lifted the lid to examine her supply of ink and paper. "Have Isabel prepare a big dinner tomorrow at noon. I'm going to invite the Council. Then ask your father to come here. Late this afternoon. I have good news for him."

"Good news for my father, too?" Caught up in the excitement, Afaf ran to tell Isabel, her slippers clapping staccato down the hallway.

Time was precious now. This was the City's last chance. The plan was a simple one that she hastily shared with the Council and the imam, one that depended on timing and their loyalty: once the engagement was formal, Hamad would move to Tetouan and help govern the city. She counted on a powerful ally in her new son-in-law. This new alliance would control the invaders better than Mohammed or Boabdil could. The might of the Sultan would protect them all. With the full approval of the Council, she hurried to make preparations.

The household spurred into frantic, sudden activity. This time Hura was going to Fes not as a supplicant, but as a ruler, as a leader of an important city. She filled two large wooden trunks with jewels and spices and two leather cases with the fanciest clothing in her closets. She ordered the ceremonial carts repainted, and re-shoed the horses and mules. Even if I have to empty the coffers of Tetouan, it's a bargain she thought, watching Miguel lock the heavy trunks and slide them across the patio. This time I will ride into Fes in style.

When Tarek heard the news, he asked to accompany her. "After all, I know the way, and haven't I proved my loyalty? And no one is a better fighter."

She stopped him by using the one thing that he desired most. "My dear Captain Tarek, you've served me well. How I wish I'd never ordered you to leave me in Algiers. But this is different. You must stay here."

Tarek began to shake his head. His golden earring flopped back and forth against his thick neck.

"I am appointing you the Admiral of Tetouan. I have prepared a letter of Marque for you as my privateer. I want you to build up our port as the most prosperous in the Mediterranean. Our ships and men will be the most feared of all pirates, even those of Barbarossa. I have gold for you to build your boat and I will tell the Sultan that our ships are now allies of the Turks. You see, I need you here."

He followed his stupefied expression by kissing her hand. Then they both laughed. "And besides," Hura added, "you have to make plans for Afaf's wedding! We should return in four months."

Afaf danced around her father on one foot then the other, overjoyed with her marriage and her trip to Fes.

Captain Hisham was much harder to convince. He saw it as his duty to escort Hura on the long journey. She would need troops for protection. But Hura trusted him to keep order in Tetouan in her absence. He had proven himself a loyal and capable leader. Now she would reward him with a house in the city as a wedding present.

The sudden activity around the compound did not go unnoticed.

In the morning, before leaving for Fes, Hura dressed for one last visit to her husband's grave. After breakfast she dodged the trunks and boxes lining her patio, and hurried into the courtyard. She stopped, then abruptly retreated into a doorway when she heard shouting and saw access to the street blocked by a line of soldiers crouched down behind a makeshift barrier of barrels and carts. Quickly skirting the far wall of the courtyard where she could not be seen, she approached the barrier.

"What is this?"

Captain Hisham shouted as she approached: "Get down! These are Boabdil's men. They've surrounded the compound. No one can get out. He's got the streets around us blocked off."

Hura flushed in hot anger.

An arrow thunked into the barrel beside them. Around its shaft was a curl of parchment. The Captain broke off the shaft and read the message.

"It says that Father Contreras will bring a letter to Madame Mandari." He handed it to Hura.

"Father Contreras, how does he fit into this?" She suddenly realized she had underestimated him. His friendship with her husband was only a ruse. Boabdil is the one behind this. That stupid King had been the willing dupe of the Spanish before, back in Granada. He doesn't know the Spanish will trick him again. The Father has been free to operate in the city under my husband's protection. Of course, she reasoned, the Spanish want control of Tetouan. And he is their agent. She turned on her heel and returned to the house, summoned Afaf, Isabel, Miguel and the staff and warned them all.

Soon the Father passed through both lines of soldiers and appeared in the courtyard. He handed Hura an official document. On the outside, the seal of the King of Granada shone in red and gold.

"I assume you require an answer," she said as she accepted it. Before he could answer, she added, "Come back tomorrow morning before first prayers. You'll allow me to pray about this, won't you?"

Hura retreated to the safety of her house. Afaf stood beside her as she ripped open the letter. It proclaimed Boabdil the new leader of Tetouan, the savior of the City, the Governor of the Province. As the new leader, he invited Hura to participate with him in the governance of the city and promised her an honorable role and recognition.

Hura snorted an indignant breath. "A role? Recognition? That swine."

She reread the letter. His last paragraph contained not so subtle inferences to her good treatment, her 'favor in his eyes' if she gave herself up and called off her troops.

Hura spat on the letter. Glaring at Afaf, she said with sarcasm, "What happened to his proposal of marriage? At one time, I was worth marrying. Now I'm just a 'participant'. I'll show him. He'll find Tetouan too big to

273

conquer . . . and tougher than Spain." She ran to her writing box and penned a response.

Afaf trembled watching the quill scratch loudly on the vellum like a talon scraping the body of its prey.

Hura thrust the note at Afaf. "Go to Hisham. Have him bring three of his men here. Right now. Tell him to nail this note to the front door."

Very soon the soldiers stood at attention before her in the patio alongside the boxes and trunks. "Captain, can you get our horses from the stable?"

Hisham hesitated. He knew there was no way to get horses in or out of the compound without being seen, or even a message to his troops at the kasbah. He shook his head.

Frustrated, she rephrased her question. "Can the horses and carts be taken from the stable and brought near here without being stopped?"

"Well, yes, we can get them out of the stable but they will be seen and captured as soon as we bring them close to the compound. The streets in this quarter are blockaded."

Exasperated, she said, "I know, I know. All I want is for you to get them on the far side of the Souk el Hots, the south side. There's an alley there by the wall. Could you do that?"

"Yes, I'll find a way. Somehow I'll get word to my troops."

"Good. Listen. That's where the old entrance to the slave pens is. It's covered up and overgrown with weeds. I was in the tunnels once."

He did not seem to understand.

"You remember, we used to keep prisoners and captives there for ransom until Captain Dias blew up the entrance. So years ago we built bigger prisons in the northern part of the city and boarded these up. A door to the old pens is here. In the house. We can escape through the tunnel. It comes out just behind the wall of the Souk el Hots."

The Captain saluted and readied to return to the barricade. But Hura had not finished.

"Captain, tell one of your soldiers to go to our roof. From the back, he can look down on the streets around our quarter. He's to find out where Boabdil's troops are and let me know if there are any near the souk. If I'm right, they're only stationed here by the front of the compound. Bring two other soldiers with you, we're going into the tunnel."

Still on its peg on the kitchen wall, Hura found the rusted key that had offered her the first taste of freedom. Heavy beams had been bolted across the prison door. It took hours for the soldiers to dismantle the hinges, braces and frame. Darkness and a damp, moldy stench overwhelmed them as they entered the passageway. The stone floor, once polished from hundreds of shuffling feet, was now littered with rubble. Hura cautiously climbed over the fallen timbers that blocked her way. She felt rats scrambling at her feet, but led on, vaguely remembering the right direction, past the openings to countless cells until she saw tiny pinpoints of light ahead. Relieved, she knew that must be the entrance. Dust stifled her breathing; she bent over, coughed until her head began to ache. A pile of stone and brick blocked the opening. The soldiers began removing the debris, throwing rusted metal and stones away from it and finally cleared a hole just large enough to crawl through. Then she ordered brush gathered and placed by the outside wall to hide their escape. Boabdil's soldiers were nowhere to be seen.

"Tell your men to go to the stables and prepare my horse along with seven others, two mules, and one of the carts. All must be brought here when the muezzin begins his evening call to prayer. Don't let your soldiers tell anyone about this. Swear them to secrecy. It's best if you go to the front and be seen. There'll be less suspicion if you're there."

"Captain." the soldier who had been on the roof walked briskly to him. "Boabdil's troops are at the front of the compound. Nowhere else."

"You were right." The Captain said. "He must think he has you in a box." To the soldier, he ordered, "Keep watch up on the roof. Let me know of changes."

Hura finished supervising the soldiers who moved the trunks and provisions out of the house and down the tunnel. She wondered where Isabel and Miguel were, and headed for their room. "Isabel, you and Miguel get your personal things, just those things you can carry through the tunnel. Go to Tarek's house as soon as I've left. Don't wait long. Too soon they'll know they've been tricked." She hugged Isabel and saw tears welling in her eyes.

Before her own eyes could mist, she turned and sought Hisham in the tunnel. "Hisham, I'll need nine of your best soldiers to accompany me. Pull the rest of your men away from the barricade in small groups. Time it so that no one is left at dawn. Retreat through the tunnel. Leave the house open." A sly smile grew on her face. "Boabdil will not destroy it. He's going to be very surprised."

The last thing Isabel saw as she peered out the tunnel exit was the silvery tail of Hura's horse as Sacony disappeared into the dark night.

275

THIRTY FOUR

A day's ride outside of Fes, Hura sent one of her soldiers galloping ahead to announce her arrival. In the darkness before dawn, with the walls of the city before her, Hura arranged her procession: five uniformed soldiers preceded her, the first two carrying banners with the seal of Tetouan; directly behind her rode Afaf followed by the cart that carried the trunks, provisions and gifts. Two more soldiers brought up the rear, each holding pennants emblazoned with the coat of arms of Mandari. The lead soldier held his bugle, ready to announce the procession.

She impatiently waited in front of the Bab Dekakene which, she remembered, opened at first light. The route to her brother's home would take them directly to Fes el Jdid, bypassing the old medina. Ibrahim had taken a villa near the Sultan's Palace so that his wife could be near her family.

When the gates opened and her herald blared a path down the main street, Hura suddenly recalled the sickening sight that greeted her years ago – an old Jew's head stuck on a pike and women's breasts tacked on the door. This time there were no such gory displays, no such evil omens, but inside, far to the right, her eyes caught what looked like the statue of a man, a European by the clothing, set atop a low platform.

Greeting her inside the gate, Ibrahim's Lieutenant swung his horse in line to escort her to the villa. Familiar landmarks appeared to welcome her. The blast of the herald's bugle echoed off high villa walls and ornate doors of the wealthy. Tradesmen, on their morning rounds, hastily pushed their carts to the side to make room.

Ibrahim's villa occupied half a block just off the main street before the tall crenellated gate of the Bab Smarine. Hura dismounted in front of a simple wooden door whose dark blue paint contrasted with the whitewashed walls. It opened to reveal a lush garden of trees and flowering bushes that surrounded two large, shallow pools of water. A figure came splashing through a fountain by the door of the main house shouting: "Mother, Mother."

"Mother, you're here! I've missed you so much. Oh look, I've gotten you all wet! Oh, mother, I'm so happy you're here. You're going to love it. It's so beautiful, and Uncle has everything . . . we have marble baths and fountains, and food from all over the world, and our very own musicians . .

. and I have my own servant!"

"Slow down, slow down." Hura kissed, then held her daughter at arms length to admire her. Gone was the baby fat on Suha's face. She was taller. Dark hair pinned high on her head allowed ringlets to escape down her back. A few short tendrils curled around her forehead. Her tight bodice, emphasizing her small breasts, was attached to a full skirt whose hem was appliquéd with brightly colored sequins. High fashion, Fassi style.

"My, what a beautiful young lady you've become." she hugged, squeezed her daughter again.

Afaf bounded into the garden to greet Suha. The two chattered as old friends while Hura proceeded to the house. At the threshold, Rema, Ibrahim's wife, waited to greet her formally.

"Welcome to my home, Lalla Hura. My house is your house."

Exchanging kisses, Hura looked beyond her. "And Ibrahim, is he here?"

Rema smiled, "I'm sure he regrets not welcoming you, but he left for the haj over a month ago." She rubbed her large belly. "When the doctor said it was twins, he was certain that God wanted him to go on the pilgrimage to Mecca. He's sure it will be boys."

"*Inshallah*." Hura intoned.

"And I'll be here to help her," Suha said. "It will be such fun to have babies around. Don't you think, mother?"

Hura's lips parted in a faint smile. She asked, "How far is the hammam?"

"It's here. Here in the house!" Suha couldn't restrain herself. "I told you they have everything. Just like the Sultan's palace. There's a cistern under the house and we use it for the baths. It's beautiful, it's built of marble. We don't have to go outside."

Rema excused herself and Afaf and Suha began to unpack the boxes.

Hura couldn't contain her curiosity any longer. "I want to hear all about your fiancée . . . when did Hamad ask for you?"

"Well," Suha plopped down on a huge cushion by the bed, "I saw him when Ibrahim and Rema took me to a feast at a cousin's house. He was there and he just kept staring at me. It was so embarrassing. I didn't know what to do. It was right after I arrived and I didn't know anybody. Anyway, I guess he asked Uncle Ibrahim who I was. Then two weeks later I saw him on our way to a picnic and he smiled at me! I can't tell you how it made me feel. Like I couldn't breathe and my heart began to pound in my chest and I turned red."

Hura chuckled, "yes, that's how some men affect us."

"Do they feel it too? Do we do the same to them?" Suha's eyes grew round with innocence.

"Yes, dear, we do the same thing to them, you just can't see it. They

277

hide it better than we do. Now, come with me, I'm ready for this famous bath. We can talk there."

A servant led them down rock steps to the subterranean hammam. As the steam engulfed them, mother and daughter propped themselves up on the edge of the pool. Afaf sat on a stool nearby mixing up ghassoul. The mist to the side of the room suddenly turned orange and Hura quickly slid into the water.

"What? Who?"

"It's all right, mother, it's only Najib." Suha didn't move. "He's a eunuch. He's Senegalese. Rema told me he came to Fes as a child from somewhere around the Niger. His leader sold him and fourteen others for one Berber horse. He doesn't say a lot but he'll do anything for me. Uncle Ibrahim said he's the tallest man in Fes. Ibrahim gave him to me as a present. I call him 'stork'."

Unaccustomed to being naked in front of men, even eunuchs, Hura slowly rose out of the water to sit on the pool's edge next to her daughter. In this eerie, steamy light, he was the blackest man Hura had ever seen. Even the whites of his eyes were yellow and his fingernails a dark sienna brown. Najib placed a silver tray between the two women then left.

"What's this?" Hura stared at the milky looking drinks, then sniffed hers.

"It's special in Fes. It's made from dried melon seeds. You crush them and mix them with milk, orange-flower water and cinnamon. It's called zeri'a and they like to serve it in the hammam. Try it, it's good."

Hura sipped the cool liquid, "Mmmm," and licked her lips.

Afaf began to shampoo Hura's hair.

"Mother, did you come through the Dekakene gate?"

"Yes, why?"

"Did you see it? Everybody's talking about it."

"See what?"

"The prince."

"I saw no prince." Hura thought for a moment. "That statue on the platform? A real prince?"

"Yes," Suha giggled. "*The* prince. The Dom Ferdinand of Portugal. It's his body. It's been there a while. Soldiers hung him by his heels for four days at the gate then took him down and stuffed his body with straw. The Wazir says he'll keep it there forever."

"How gruesome. The people of Fes have strange customs. Why did they kill him?"

"Mother, I thought you knew everything! He and his army fought the Sultan and lost. I heard he gave himself up as a hostage so his army could escape. The Sultan demanded the Portuguese give up Sebta in exchange for his life but the prince's brothers wouldn't do it. So the Wazir killed him. Can you imagine brothers who wouldn't help each other?"

Hura shuddered. Suha was so innocent. Thoughts of Mohammed shriveled her heart. "Let's talk about happier things. Tell me more about your fiancée."

Suha's face became radiant. Afaf moved closer to listen and began to massage Hura's back. "He's so handsome. And Uncle Ibrahim said he's smart too. Smarter than the Sultan, his half brother . . . but he also has a temper."

"Be careful, dear. Watch what you say. You must learn to be discrete."

Suha made a face. "Like you, mother?"

They both laughed.

"Hamad isn't like the Sultan. The Sultan has a hundred seventy three wives. That's what my eunuch says. And I heard that Khadijeh, she's the Queen Mother of the Sultan, she still lives in the harem and she's evil and she spies on Hamad for that old Wazir, Walid."

Hura shivered and mumbled. "So Walid is still in power."

Suha nodded then squeezed her mother's hand. "Now that you're here, I can go out in public. Maybe we can go by Hamad's quarters in the palace tonight. Uncle Ibrahim took me to see the mosque once, with Uncle Nicky."

"The Professor? Still here? Where is he? I must see him. I have to thank him again for bringing you safely."

Suha knit her brows. "I don't know. Uncle Ibrahim said he had a vision. A strange vision. He said something about giving up his earthly life and locking himself up forever in the Kairouan library."

Concerned for her friend and mentor, Hura had been listening intently. Suddenly she began to chuckle. "He's found his heaven. He's found the most important library in the world. I knew he would love Fes – the library here is rivaled only by Baghdad. He'll never leave. I'm so glad he's found happiness. And that reminds me. How are your lessons coming?"

"Oh, mother! I'm going to be married."

"That's no excuse to stop studying."

Suha made another face. "All during our trip the Professor tried to get me to study. He brought boxes of manuscripts and every night we would read by the fire. But my heart wasn't in it. So the next day, I couldn't recite for him. He must have thought I was you. I must have disappointed him. But mother, I'm not interested in politics or books or history, I just want to be a wife and have children. Is that wrong?"

Hura melted. She arched her back and asked Afaf to knead her neck. A pounding headache arrived from nowhere. Her daughter wanted the simple things: a family, love, and children. Somehow, Suha believed there could be happiness ever after. She believed in fairy tales.

Late this cloudy morning Najib carried a large basket of breads and the coffee tray into Hura's room. As Afaf poured the dark brew into a cup, Najib came over to the bed and, bowing low, handed Hura a letter. The raised waxy seal of the Sultan glistened. She opened it quickly, read it, then sent Afaf for Suha.

"A banquet in your honor?" Suha squealed. "I'll get to see Hamad, too! When is it?"

"The invitation is for this evening. I wish the Sultan had given us more time, we have hardly enough time to prepare ourselves."

Afaf brought the coffeepot to refill Hura's cup and bent toward Hura's ear, "I heard the Sultan does things all of a sudden. Gossip in the harem is that he's quick to change his mind, too. He marries in a sneeze and then some of his wives disappear. Nobody knows where they went."

Hura turned to her daughter. "You believe that?"

Suha nodded.

"Remember my advice . . . about being discrete and how ears live in walls. Afaf, we haven't much time. Tell Najib to fill the marble pool with perfumed water, and get out my silk gown with the black pearl bodice. I call it my diplomatic gown. And Suha, my dear, you wear the special one I brought. You will look lovely in the white gown of a virgin."

"Oooh, let me see yours first," Suha said. Afaf drew it out of the wardrobe and brought it over. "It's beautiful!" Suha ran her fingers over the bands of large, round pearls. "It must be so heavy, and it's cut so low. Mother, isn't it a bit too fancy. I mean, you're a widow and all that."

"Don't you think I want to look beautiful? I know, I know . . . I'm just a mother, an old mother."

"No, no, I didn't mean," Suha blushed.

"It's really quite proper. It's widows black, or at least the bodice is. And I'll wear a lavender cape. The same color as the skirt."

"Afaf, somewhere in that small red box over there is my black pearl choker and bracelets. Suha, you can wear any of the jewels in my trunks. Only remember, at this banquet, you're wearing only white."

At dusk, the Sultan's guards, dressed in white brocade kaftans and maroon vests, escorted Hura and her daughter into the palace grounds. As they entered the front door, Hura recognized Munzer, the Chief eunuch of the former Sultan. He was older now and his hair was graying. His expression had become more sour, more menacing. She wasn't sure if he remembered her. She hoped not.

Mother and daughter followed Munzer down a hallway toward a large reception room. They proceeded slowly past colonnades and alcoves lined with cushioned banquettes and taborets topped by trays of cakes and pyramids of marzipan. The hallway opened into a large banquet room. Several male guests peered through the smoke of their water pipes as the two passed by. Hura heard the low rumble of their voices behind her. Skirting the side of the room, avoiding the musicians and dancers in the center, they passed the screens that hid tittering palace wives. Finally, they came to the raised platform where the Sultan was seated.

She did not recognize him. On the previous occasion, that brother had said little and Hamad was the one who spoke to her cause. And now, the new Sultan had grown a more than full-size beard. Black bristles had bloomed into whiskers that seemed to cover his entire face. As Hura took her seat her eyes locked on the Wazir sitting stone-faced on the other side of the Sultan, next to Hamad.

The Sultan made no sign of recognition, his eyes were transfixed on the woman gyrating before him. Her semi-nude body, decorated with the tribal scars of the Saharan, quivered to the tempo of the musicians. Her monstrous breasts shook in one direction while low-belted hips undulated in the other. Only when the dancer finished and the musicians retreated to a rug by the side of the room did the Sultan cast a quick glance at Hura. His eyes went directly to the white mounds pushed up by her tight bodice. He said nothing.

Hura smiled inside, pleased at her choice of costume.

The Sultan clapped his hands twice. Immediately five servants rushed to his side; others began rolling up the carpets on the marble floor and carrying them away.

As she sat admiring the scene, Hura heard the sound of squeaking winches and pulleys from high in the center of the dome. She looked up to see a large metal-ribbed gazebo with sides of golden fabric being lowered to the floor. As it descended, Hura could see through the open front that the gazebo was carpeted and six plump cushions surrounded a low golden table.

Long tables were carried into the banquet room and lined up on the sides. No sooner were the tables in place than waiters topped them with trays of breads, vegetables, fruits and couscous. To her right, four servants carried in a large ox on a metal spit. Smaller platters of wild fowl and game followed. A huge copper cauldron wheeled past her, pungent white steam curling from its wide mouth. If the Sultan meant to impress her with this pageantry, he had done it well.

The Sultan raised one manicured hand and two attendants appeared instantaneously. One opened his shereefian umbrella and held it above his head as if to protect him from some indoor sun. Soundlessly, they escorted him to his gazebo.

Another contingent of attendants came for Hura and the four other guests, leading them one by one to the cushioned cage. Again, Hura was seated next to the Sultan. Her plan was going well, so far. He was childish in his obvious pride, love of extravagance. She hoped he wasn't boorish, like his father. Out of the corner of her eye, she studied him. A shiver of revulsion passed through her at the sight of so much hair.

The golden table was covered with plates, jars, platters and bowls of food. Brochettes of lamb lined the small charcoal grill in the center. With another wave of his hand, the Sultan gave the command to raise the gazebo. Slowly they swayed upward until suspended high above the heads of the other guests. Through holes in the fabric on the sides, Hura could see other members of the court surround the tables below and begin to eat. How insignificant they looked, buzzing like bees in a hive. Their costumes reflected many different cultures. There were kaftans, breechcloths, pantaloons, capes and robes. The heads that bobbed below her were covered with scarves, puffed silk caps from Venice, brightly colored turbans, stiffly curled powdered wigs, the fur of the leopard, the diadem of princes, and the cotton kerchiefs of Egyptians held firmly by round black braids.

The Sultan grinned at Hura and fussed with his clothes. He was obviously pleased with this cage, his latest toy. Hura and the others waited for him to begin eating first, but he dallied before saying to Hura: "The Ambassador of Portugal informs me that he has seen no other such gazebo as this. And he has seen much of the world. My engineers designed this marvel so that with the twitch of this golden rope," he patted the braid, "I can order it lowered or raised at any time. The world will know and respect our genius. Don't you agree?"

Hura noted the elaborate pulley system above her. She remembered the Professor saying how the Egyptians, before the Ptolemys, used such a system to draw water and how one man could lift impossible weights with one hand. She nodded.

Tiring of his presentation, the Sultan rubbed his hands together and gazed at the platter in front of him. He leaned forward to spoon a stuffed sheep's stomach to his plate and ladled creamy, fennel-dotted sauce over it. The pouch made a popping sound as his knife pierced it; he scooped out the rice inside. "Ah," he joked, "the same sweet sound my sword makes when I interrogate prisoners." With his mouth full, he addressed Hura. "So you're here for your daughter's wedding. My half-brother made a good choice." His gaze shifted to Suha.

"Yes, Your Highness, we will announce the engagement this week."

Still chewing, he said, "I remember you, you know. Yes, I was there

282

when you intruded on my father's little party in the garden. You were lucky Hamad saved you. I don't suppose he knew you had a daughter then, did he?"

"Your Highness, it was a mistake, I never should have intruded. I needed help for my husband, for Tetouan."

"He sent a woman to do a man's work." The Sultan arched an eyebrow expecting a reaction.

"My husband, may he rest in peace, was ill at the time and we feared another attack from the Portuguese."

"Still. Sending a woman! What could a woman do? Women know their place in Fes."

Hura's expression didn't change, didn't betray her feelings. "Surely, you honor women highly in Fes. I heard that your great Karawiyyin Mosque was founded some seven hundred years ago by Fatima, bint Mohammed ibn Feheri, a wealthy woman from Tunisia. All Fes must be proud of her."

"That was a long time ago, doesn't count." The Sultan sniffed. The Wazir made a sound that passed for mirth.

"And her sister, Meriem, founded the Mosque of the Andalous, isn't that so?"

The Sultan shrugged and resumed eating.

Suha nibbled on a triangle of bread, shyly glancing at her fiancée between bites. The Wazir and Hamad wisely kept silent.

Into their busy silence, the Sultan suddenly interjected: "Yes, I've heard of you and your exploits. You're the Pirate Queen. Your city does a good business in piracy. Getting rich, no doubt. My Wazir here keeps me informed." He reached out and tapped Walid's tunic with his greasy hand. The fastidious Wazir didn't flinch. For such reactions, his Merenid predecessors had been murdered.

Hura puzzled over his comment. She wasn't rich. And not much money came in from piracy. At least not to her. The city was always in need of money for roads and services. Where did the Wazir get this information? If there was so much money, where was it going?

"Piracy. Hummm. I've always wanted to sail," the Sultan raised his arms and fluttered them in a breezy simulation of waves. "The sea fascinates me. How sad, I'll just have to dream about it." His eyes rolled upward and he sighed. "They say a Sultan will lose his baraka if he goes to sea. There aren't many things I can't do in this life – but that's one." Abruptly he leaned forward across the large table stretching for a skewer of meat. The shifting weight swayed the gazebo.

Hura began to respond, but the Sultan spoke again. "Tell me, how do your sailors feel about a woman on board?"

Hura watched him slice off a chunk of lamb with his knife and shove it

283

in his mouth.

"Don't they jump overboard? Everyone knows a woman is bad luck." He laughed and turned to the Wazir for confirmation. In silence, Walid silently tapped his fingers on the table.

"The only place a woman belongs is in the harem." The Sultan nodded at his own wisdom.

"If you think that, Your Highness, why did you invite me to publicly dine with you?" Hura didn't try to control the quiver of anger in her voice.

The Sultan raised his hands as if in surrender. "I've heard how you cut off the head of one Portuguese officer, escaped from prison, and then killed that Portuguese Captain, Dias. How did you escape from the prison? Was the jailer blind? How did you get Barbarossa and his men to fight for you? Have you some special power over men?"

Hura drilled him with a stare. He seemed to know a lot about her. What else did he know?

The Sultan grinned. "I invited you because you interest me. There are no other women like you. The only women I see are those procured for my harem." He saw Hura lower her spoon to her plate.

"You are not eating. Are you not pleased with my hospitality?"

Hura tried to direct the conversation. She looked across the table at Hamad and the Wazir then back at the Sultan. "If I have any talents, they are dedicated to the service of Tetouan and to my family," she said, then continued in a stronger tone, "Your Highness, you say you know me. If so, I will come right to the point. I cannot keep silent any longer. As we speak, I fear for my city. I need soldiers for defense, and I need support to keep Tetouan controlled by my family. If you help me, I will forever be in your debt."

"I see." The Sultan rubbed his nose and thought for a few moments. Twice he looked up as if ready to say something then shook his head and resumed his exaggerated pensiveness. At last, he commanded: "You will marry me. And of course, your gift to me is Tetouan."

Feigning fury, Hura jumped to her feet, the cage tilted violently. The other diners held their plates and the slaves below hastily began lowering the cage to the ground. Food spilled from platters, flowing onto the carpets.

"I am a free woman, I will not be ordered to marry."

The Sultan grasped the Wazir's arm to keep from falling over and held it tightly. With the cage securely on the floor, he let go, straightened and yelled: "Woman, sit down! I will send thirty thousand Janissaries and the money to pay them . . . I will save your city, isn't that what you want? Neither the Portuguese, the Spanish nor the Ottomans will attack. They will know that the Arabs of Fes and the Berbers of the Rif are one. And, I'll give Tetouan to Mohammed to administer. That will keep it in your family. How

284

can you refuse?"

Hura winced. Oh no! Not to Mohammed. Wild-eyed, Hura looked at Hamad who responded with a quick sideways shake of his head. What did that mean? She glanced at the Wazir whose bloodless lips had formed a humorless smile. Ever so slowly she sat down and lowered her eyes. Somehow, she would deal with Mohammed.

The words "I accept" were barely audible.

Later, after the banquet, an aide entered the Wazir's office and announced: "The Queen Mother is here."

"Show her to my salon and leave us."

"Welcome, Most Honored of Women," Walid bowed and greeted her as she shuffled toward him from the secret passageway he had built to the harem.

Although Khadijeh had never been called attractive in her youth, no one ever doubted her intelligence. Now the years had taken their toll on whatever beauty there had been. Her body was bent, her skin wrinkled and spotted with dark moles. She raised an arthritic finger and jabbed it without preliminaries: "This is dangerous, this double wedding. The palace chatters about nothing else. I don't like it – this Berber woman is nothing but trouble. I don't care whether Hamad or Mohammed get Tetouan, it's just a backwater town. But my son . . ." she huffed through her long, curved nose, "my son . . . why does he marry that Pirate Queen? You must kill her."

Walid stood quietly listening, thinking while she ranted. So many times he had helped this woman in the past – and handsomely been paid for it. He had helped her keep control of the harem and keep her sons in line for power. With the palace's Chief Eunuch as an ally, it was Walid's agenda that sent a steady stream of wives and concubines to the Sultan's bed; on his authority abortions or assassinations were performed and Khadijeh's line kept safe. Never before had he seen the Queen Mother so upset.

"That woman has shour, magic. That's why. She and the jinn. She got him to ask her to marry him so she and her children could rule Fes. She'll kill off my family, all the male children. There won't be a Sultan from my womb left. She wants to rule Fes. Did you hear what he called her? Pirate Queen! He's fascinated with her. Queen of the jinn! That's what she is."

"Perhaps you should think of some reason why this woman won't marry your son." The Wazir said.

"I can think of many ways to prevent it," she stepped closer to him and whispered hoarsely. "I need your help."

He nodded. "I, too, have a plan. The wedding won't take place until Mohammed comes. We have time. I want to meet with you and the Chief Eunuch as soon as he arrives."

THIRTY FIVE

Hura sucked in a deep breath of concern. Seated before the imam while her marriage was officially recorded, she worried if she was doing the right thing. Will I really save Tetouan by marrying the Sultan? If I give up my freedom, will I fulfill my father's dream? Her forehead wrinkled in a deep frown. What about Mohammed ruling Tetouan? Is that better than giving the city up to Boabdil? She closed her eyes, blinked upon hearing her name.

"Hura, bint Ali Rachid," the imam said much louder a second time. "Answer me. Do you agree to this marriage?"

Quivering lips formed the words. "As God is my witness, I do."

The imam wrote on the large document in front of him, turned the vellum around to face her and handed her the quill. "Your name. Sign at the bottom."

Now it was legal. She could never turn back.

Again deep in thought, she walked down the stone pathway to the harem where she and Suha had moved into special apartments. The Sultan had ordered a double celebration to honor his marriage to Hura and his half-brother's engagement to Suha. He invited not only members of both families, the ministers and nobles of his court, but also all ambassadors and visiting dignitaries. An alliance as important as this would draw thousands. Hura had requested a smaller private party for the two brides to be given by women of the court in one week. With the urging of Queen Mother Khadijeh, the Sultan agreed. Hura allowed ample time for announcements and preparations but not enough time for her to change her mind. The interval also provided time to enjoy her daughter. She worried about Suha's innocence. Had she protected her too much, not prepared her for the world?

On the seventh day, at the women's private party, Suha had to shout to be heard above the din. "Have you ever seen so many beautiful gowns and costumes?"

In the outer reception room, Mother and daughter were seated side by side next to husband and fiancée. One by one, to the accompaniment of an orchestra of 'uds, cymbals and drums, the women of the court walked down the narrow isle, bowed to the Sultan and his brother and offered their gifts, then retreated to their seats in the audience.

Hura saw the Sultan yawn. His eyelids drooped. She could tell his interest was fading even as the carpet in front of him filled with gifts. In the jumble of the two large mounds of gifts, she could make out bolts of fabric, inlaid jewelry boxes, caged animals, bound books, art objects, manuscripts, rolled rugs, jars of cosmetics, hoops of lace, boxes of spices and dazzling jewelry. A sudden commotion from the rear revived the Sultan's interest. Women's voices buzzed as Mohammed slowly proceeded from the entryway down the center isle and took a seat in the front row. He cradled a small yellow sack in his lap. When his turn came to offer a present, Hura could see the sack move – as if something inside was violently trying to escape. Threading through the collection of gifts on the floor, Mohammed limped to her.

He placed the squirming sack in her lap. "A special gift for my illustrious sister. I wish you much happiness, and I apologize for my past behavior. You are indeed fit to be a Queen."

Hura's smile faded as she looked at the sack, felt it moving on her knees. A sudden thought repulsed her and she stiffened. The only thing special to her brother in the past was money – and snakes.

Mohammed saw her reaction and laughed. "Open it. There is no danger, you will be pleased."

With all eyes upon her, she untied the knot and pulled at the drawstring. Out popped a tiny brown monkey. Hura gasped with relief as the delicate creature scampered up her bodice and sat on her shoulder. She laughed: "Thank you, dear brother."

Watching Mohammed return to his seat, Hura felt a rush of happiness that she and her brother might be reconciled. Surely, their new alliance would bring them closer.

At last, the most important woman of the court brought her gift. Queen Mother Khadijeh rose unsteadily from the front row. She hobbled directly to Hura and offered her a small glass flask, elegantly striped with a red velvet ribbon.

"I present you with a gift of rare importance. It is for the pleasure of your union, in respect of your eminence and your beauty. May drops from this exquisite flask bring fulfillment to your life now and ever after."

Her eloquent presentation left Hura speechless. The Queen Mother extended a frail arm and placed the flask in Hura's hand. The monkey jumped from her shoulder and sniffed it curiously.

Just as Hura lifted it, the Sultan reached over and grabbed it. He raised it to his nose, and smelling nothing, pulled out the stopper. He sniffed, kissed, and sipped it. Khadijeh's face twisted. She stretched to grab the bottle back and lost her balance, falling to one knee.

"Mother, I knew you would give the most important gift of all, an aphrodisiac."

Too late, she shouted to her son: "It's not for you! No, it's hers!"

"Mother, what is hers is now mine."

It was well past midnight. Hura, alone in her chamber awaited the Sultan and played with her new pet. The silken monkey chattered and somersaulted at her command. The bed linens were turned down; her supper grew cold on the table by the door; her hair hung freely. She wished she hadn't sent Afaf back to Tetouan, but she had many servants now and Afaf was eager to marry Captain Hisham. She straightened the folds of her nightgown one more time and continued to wait on her bed. Maybe he doesn't desire me. Maybe he won't come. No, she decided, he will come. He has to consummate this marriage.

Then she heard the curses of soldiers. Suddenly the Chief Eunuch threw open her door and stood inside glaring at her. Face livid, he screamed: "The Sultan is dead. You killed him! You will die." He wheeled, left as quickly as he had arrived. Hura ran after him, pulled on the door, but it was locked from the outside. Heart pounding wildly, she ran to her dressing room, threw on a jellaba, and waited. Waited for what? She didn't know.

All night the sounds of heavy boots, men shouting, and the clash of swords reverberated near her chamber. Early the next morning, Hura heard a key rattle in the door lock. In the faint morning light, she barely recognized her new son-in-law. He rushed in, sword bloody in his hand.

"It's all because of you." He lunged toward her.

Hura stood to face him, defenseless. She could see dark blood stains on his clothes. He stopped in front of her. An angry torrent of words poured from his mouth. Some made no sense: "They're all dead! You've brought death, nothing but death."

Hura thrust her hand against his chest in protest.

"She and the Wazir planned it. And Mohammed, too. May Allah forgive me. They're all dead."

Hura stood motionless, hands clasped in terror, eyeing his red blade. Somehow, she found the courage to speak. "Last night I was told the Sultan had died, and I had killed him. Then I was locked in here. I did not kill him. You must believe me."

Face purple with blood lust, Hamad raised his sword.

"What really happened? Please tell me." She asked in as calm a voice as she could muster.

Hamad spat: "Poisoned! From that gift to you. His servants heard him scream in pain and fall on the floor of his chamber. Dead. In his hand, he held the flask, the one from the Queen Mother. The one meant for you."

"But why, why would she – "

"It was for you. You were supposed to die. It should have been you!"

"I've done no wrong." Her hand went out to touch him again.

Hamad stiffened, then backed away. "I know, I know. But you're responsible. You can't deny it. One of his other wives said she saw your brother Mohammed give the flask to the Chief Eunuch when he arrived from Tetouan. That's how the Queen Mother got it. Torture makes any man talk. Before Munzer died he confessed it was the Wazir's plan. I just came from the Wazir's chambers. He denied everything. Insisted it was you who planned the murder, then before I killed him he blamed it on Mohammed. The palace guards and I found Mohammed trying to flee, running toward Ibrahim's house. He didn't get past the first sentry."

"Suha! Where's my daughter? Is she all right?"

"She is safe. Last night the Queen Mother tried to enter her apartment, probably to kill her. But her eunuch, Nagib, saved her. That evil woman no longer breathes."

Hura took a step away. "I must see Suha, where is she?"

"You will see no one. Not even your daughter." The sword swirled in small circles of indecision.

They stood staring at each other, both breathing heavily.

Regaining her wits, Hura raised her head. "I am at your mercy. Now I know what you're doing and why. A bastard son can't be Sultan so you want Tetouan. You've always wanted Tetouan. I curse myself that I made it so easy for you."

Hamad glared at her for another tense moment. The sword wavered, then he jammed it into its sheath. "Yes, Tetouan will be my kingdom. And I will spare you. I will send you into exile. Be thankful that I banish you and do nothing else. You will return to Chaouen and never leave. Pack up and go!"

For a long time Hura stood gazing at the marriage bed, reliving the events, reliving the conversation with her son-in-law – how the Wazir, the Queen Mother, and her own brother had conspired against her. Now her daughter would begin a new life in Tetouan without her. She was alone, utterly alone. With the emptiness of that realization, her shoulders began to sag. Then she took a deep breath. She was free of the harem and her beloved Chaouen beckoned.

She straightened and walked to the wardrobe by the wall. Searching through her clothing, she pulled out her cape and put it on. She bent over her jewelry box, poking with one finger until she found what she wanted.

With trembling hands, she pinned Hersh's nautilus brooch over her heart.

289

LIST OF CHARACTERS

Afaf: Hura's maid

Moulay Ali bin Rachid: Emir of Chaouen, father of Hura

Ali Abed Allah Muhamad al-Mandari, a.k.a. **Abu Hasan, al-Manjari, al-Manziri, Al-Mandari al Garnati, El Granadino, El Fundador**: husband of Hura

Khair Barbarossa: a.k.a. **Kheyr ed-Din, Redbeard**: pirate

Boabdil, Abu-Abdullah Allah: King of Granada

Bridget: prostitute

Fatima: first wife of al-Mandari

Father Fernando de Contreras: Spanish priest

Fernao Diaz: Portuguese sea captain

Hamad: Sultan ech Cheik's bastard son, husband of Suha

Hershlab ben Yitzhak, a.k.a. **Hersh, Habib**: architect, lover

Hura bint Ali bin Rachid: the Free Woman

Moulay Ibrahim Ali bin Rachid: older brother of Hura

Isabel: maid of Fatima

Miguel: al-Mandari's servant

Mohammed Ali bin Rachid: younger half-brother of Hura

Muhammad al-Shaykh, a.k.a. **Muhammad ech Cheik**, Sultan of Fes

Muhummad al-Burtughali: Sultan ech Cheik's eldest son: husband of Hura

Nabil: pirate captain in Salé

Nicholas Kleinatz: émigré, Dutch savant, teacher of Hura

Suha: daughter of Hura

Tarek: sea captain, father of Afaf

Walid: Wazir to sultans in Fes

GLOSSARY

Acha	(eshe), evening prayer, the fifth prayer
Ait-el-Kebir	(Eid el Kebir), festival, 7 weeks after Ramadan
Al-Andalusia	Southern Spain, especially Granada
Al-Hamra	(al-Hambra), the red; palace in Granada, Spain
Allah	God
Arousa	bride
Bab	gate, doorway
Baraka	luck; blessing; good fortune
Ben	(bin, ibn), son, son of
Bint	daughter, daughter of
Bismillah	a blessing, in God's name
Burnous	man's woolen hooded cloak
Cadi	judge
Caid	governor of a district; military leader
Carrack	Portuguese warship
Dooh	prayer at noon
Ducat	Spanish money
Eid	feast, festival or holy day
Escudos	Portuguese money
Fantasia	festival, display of horsemanship
Fassi	natives of Fes (Fez)
Feitor	Portuguese agent and consul
Fondouk	(funduk) inn, hotel for people and animals
Fundador	founder
Ghassoul	mud and herb cleanser
G'nafa	match maker
Haj	(hadj), pilgrimage to Mecca
Haik	woman's black outer covering
Hammam	public bath
Harira	thick soup
Harkas	light cavalry; armed expedition
Henna	vegetable powder for coloring; medicine
Hudud	frontier; threshold; barrier
Imam	leader of mosque prayer
Imazigen	Berber
Inshallah	(Insha' Allah), God willing
Janissary	Turkish mercenary
Jellaba	(djellaba), woman's tunic with hood
Jihad	holy war
Jinn	(jenn, djinn), genie, evil spirit, devil

Kadish	Hebrew prayer
Kaftan	(caftan), long cotton garment
Kaouadas	women peddlers
Kasbah	fortress, citadel
Kif	hemp, marijuana, hashish
Kohl	sulfur of antimony, eye cosmetic
Koran	(Qur'an), holy book of Islam
Koubba	(kubba), domed shrines for the holy
Lalla	woman's title of respect
Mabrouk	congratulations
Madressa	(medersa) school, place of study
Maghreb	NW Africa: Morocco, Algeria, Tunisia
Makhzen	palace of the Sultan
Marabout	holy warrior or ascetic
Marranos	Jews converted to Christianity, (Conversos)
Ma'salame	goodbye
Medina	downtown, the city
Mellah	living quarters of the Jews
Minbar	pulpit in a mosque
Moghreb	prayer, four minutes after sunset
Moharran	feast for the New Year
Moriscos	Muslims from Spain living in Morocco
Moulay	my lord, man's title of distinction
Muezzin	announcer of prayer
Nao	type of Portuguese ship
Ramadan	Islamic holy month of fasting; 9th month
Rif	northern Moroccan mountains
Sadecq	dowry
Salaam	peace, greetings
Shalom	peace, greetings
Shabbath	Jewish Friday services
Shari'a	law
Sherif	(Cherif) noble, descendant of the Prophet
Shour	magic
Sidi	(sayyidi), my lord, my master
Soobh Fegr	first prayer of the day, at dawn
Souk	marketplace
Sura	chapter or section
Tajine	(tagine), stew
Wazir	(Wazar, Vizier), political official, chief minister

Carol Malt in the Jordanian desert tent of Sheikh Mohammed Abu Tayeh, son of the Sheikh who fought the Turks with Lawrence of Arabia.

ABOUT THE AUTHOR

Carol Malt, Ph.D., has been the Executive Director of three art museums and curator of numerous exhibitions. She has a great love for travel, exploration, and writing about the Middle East. She has received several awards and Fellowships including a Fulbright Senior Scholar award for the study of women and museums in the Middle East. She participated with Sir Edmund Hillary in an Explorers Club camel trek in northern India, and is a private pilot.